"Mercy . . . I beg you!"

Before the man could turn and flee, the Shining One whispered in the air and flashed in a deadly downward arc. Bright Zhaligkeer filled his horror-stricken eyes with its unearthly light, and he threw his hands over his face. The stroke caught him at the base of the neck, cutting short his last cry of remorse. The man pitched forward into the road, dead when he met the ground.

The rage which had burned so hot in Quentin's veins left him as suddenly as it had flared. The King stared at the misshapen heap in the dust, then at the sword in his hand, and his heart froze in his chest. Zhaligkeer's fiery blade now appeared as any ordinary metal, glimmering darkly in the fading light of late afternoon.

The bright white flame of the Shining One had gone out.

Avon Books are available at special quantity discounts for bulk purchases for sales promotions, premiums, fund raising or educational use. Special books, or book excerpts, can also be created to fit specific needs.

For details write or telephone the office of the Director of Special Markets, Avon Books, Dept. FP, 1350 Avenue of the Americas, New York, New York 10019, 1-800-238-0658.

STEPHEN R. LAWHEAD

THE SWORD AND THE FLAME

BOOK THREE
OF
THE DRAGON KING TRILOGY

AVON BOOKS • NEW YORK

AVON BOOKS
A division of
The Hearst Corporation
1350 Avenue of the Americas
New York, New York 10019

Copyright © 1984 by Stephen R. Lawhead
Cover illustration by Tim Jacobus
Published by arrangement with Crossway Books
Library of Congress Catalog Card Number: 83-73341
ISBN: 0-380-71631-3

First AvoNova Printing: August 1992

AVONOVA TRADEMARK REG. U.S. PAT. OFF. AND IN OTHER COUNTRIES, MARCA REGISTRADA, HECHO EN U.S.A.

Printed in the U.S.A.

RA   10   9   8   7   6   5   4   3   2   1

For the cousins:
Tiffany, Robbie,
Erin, Annie, Jeffrey
With much love

This is the third book of the DRAGON KING TRILOGY.

The first book, *In the Hall of the Dragon King*, tells the tale of Quentin, a young temple acolyte, who leaves his place of service to the god Ariel to join the loyal few who would rescue the good King Eskevar. It tells of the evil loosed by the wicked Nimrood the Necromancer, and young Quentin's growing awareness of the Most High, the One True God, who has called him to a new faith. Book One details Quentin's perilous quest to vanquish evil, restore the King, and establish justice once more in the realm of Mensandor.

The second book, *The Warlords of Nin*, is the story of the invasion of peaceful Mensandor by the merciless armies of the dreadful Nin the Destroyer. It tells of Quentin's growing wisdom in the ways of the Most High, and of the prophetic quest for the mighty sword, Zhaligkeer, the Shining One, symbol of the Most High God's presence. Forged deep in the lost mines of the Ariga of the mysterious healing metal, lanthanil, the Shining One becomes an instrument of judgment in the hand of a triumphant deliverer, the long-awaited Priest King. Book Two closes with the death of Eskevar and the ascension of Quentin to the throne of the Dragon King.

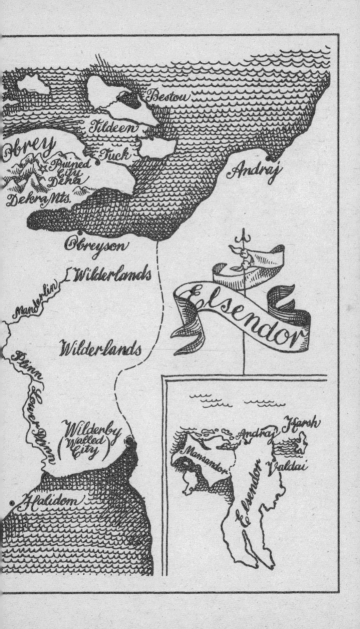

1

THE HUNCHED FIGURE TOILED UP THE WINDING TRAIL leaning heavily upon his long crooked staff, stopping frequently to rest and to look down upon the placid lowlands, gazing toward the west in the direction of Askelon. He was an old man of years beyond counting, dressed in the robes and cowl of a priest. The hood threw a dark shadow across his features, and though the day was hot and the sun bright, he did not uncover his head but went on his way wrapped head to toe. Seen from a distance he might have been a black beetle scrabbling up a hillock bearing the weight of his burdensome shell.

When he reached the summit of the plateau he sat down on a rock beneath an ancient wind-worn tree that threw its sparse, gnarled branches over the road. Many a pilgrim had sat there upon that rock to offer up a prayer to the gods for a fortuitous oracle.

But this traveler was no pilgrim and offered no prayers.

Instead, he sat and with narrowed eyes gazed out over the countryside. The air sang with bird-song and shimmered as the heat rose in waves from the land. In the misty blue distance his sharp eagle's vision could see the dark green line of Pelgrin Forest, lying like a vast green sea away to the west. In the valley below,

1

peasants labored in the fields among their new crops. Their shouts to their lazy oxen drifted up the side of the hill like petitions to an unhearing god.

The old man turned his face away from the peaceful landscape shining green and golden beneath clear, untroubled blue skies. He looked toward the temple rising white and silent as a tomb above him. Then he lifted himself heavily to his legs once more, took up his staff, and continued on.

When he reached the temple yard he stopped and leaned long on his staff, as if waiting for a sign, or as if, having come this far, he was unable to decide whether to finish what he came to do. After some time he turned his face to the east, toward the mountains whose mighty heads could be seen rising above their heavy shoulders. There, above the far peaks, he saw dark clouds assembling and moving westward on the wind.

The old priest nodded to himself and then went across the stone-paved yard to the temple steps. He climbed the stairs, raised the iron ring on the great wooden door, and knocked several times.

After a few moments the door opened and a man in a red cloak poked his head out. "The temple is not open at this hour." The man looked at the old priest unkindly. "Come back at the seventh hour if you want prayers or an omen."

"Do you not see that I am a priest?" asked the old one. "I have come to see the High Priest of Ariel."

"He sees no one," the temple guard said. "He is in retreat."

"Is he, indeed? But this is a matter of greatest urgency. He must see me."

The guard glared at the wrinkled old priest, and his features proclaimed that the old man and his crooked staff were a great nuisance.

But before he could reply, the old priest spoke again. "It is not for you to decide. Bring someone in authority.

If not the High Priest, then the under-High Priest, or the Day Priest."

The temple guard glared a silent curse on the old man and closed the door. The elderly priest stood for a few moments and waited, head bent down. Just as he was about to raise the ring once again he heard steps on the other side of the door. A gray-cloaked priest, a young man with a pocked face, thrust his head through the opening. Behind him the guard stood frowning.

"Well," the young priest said, "what do you want?"

"I wish to speak with the High Priest. That is allowed, surely. It is a matter of some importance."

"He sees no one unannounced," snapped the priest.

"Then I wish to be announced at once," said the old man softly. His faded eyes hardened to stone.

"High Priest Pluell is in retreat; he cannot be disturbed. I am the Day Priest; I am empowered to help you."

The old man smiled slyly. "That I doubt most heartily. Still, you will do. Announce me to him. I can readily see that you are a man of some resource—you will find a way."

The young man's face convulsed in a mighty frown. He drew breath to shout the old man away. But before he could speak, the elderly priest raised his hand and said, "Do what I say." This was spoken simply, but with utmost authority. The younger priest felt it like a slap. His mouth snapped shut instantly.

"Wait over there," the Day Priest muttered. He pointed to a stone bench under a tree away across the temple yard by the wall.

"I will abide," said the old man. He turned and began slowly descending the temple steps.

"What name shall I give him?" shouted the young priest after him.

The old man paused, leaned on his staff, and seemed to ponder the question carefully. "Well?" called the Day Priest.

"Tell him," the old man began at length, "that a friend from the east has come." One gnarled hand disappeared beneath the folds of his robes. "And give him this." He withdrew his hand and held out a darkly glittering object.

The young man came out of the temple and took the talisman from the outstretched hand. He held it in his palm and examined it closely.

The object was a flat round medal made of black stone, and was inscribed with strange symbols which he did not recognize. It was cold in his hand, and a strange feeling came over him as he held the talisman— a feeling of deep foreboding, of doom gathering around him like the high dark clouds overhead.

Without another word he turned and went back into the temple. The old man continued down the steps and made his way slowly to the bench under the tree. He settled himself to wait in the shade.

THE DAY PROGRESSED LEISURELY. AT MIDDAY A STRAG-gling few pilgrims came to the temple. The Day Priest met them and took their offerings. The pilgrims waited and then were admitted into the temple for their oracle. They came out and went away chattering happily, full of the good fortune which had been assured them by the priests. None noticed the old man sitting quiet as an idol beneath the tree by the wall.

Evening came on, and with it a cool breeze out of the east, scented with the sweet musty smell of rain. As a crimson sun set in fiery brilliance away beyond the golden fields of the valley below the temple, a priest came out of the temple with a brand and lit the torch that stood in a stone pylon in the center of the temple yard.

The priest stood with his back turned to the old man, raised the brand and lit the torch, then turned slowly— feeling unseen eyes on him—and peered into the shadows at the old man still seated on the bench. From out of the darkness two bright eyes glittered back at him in the torchlight. The priest jumped back, almost dropping the torch. Then he turned and fled into the temple. The great wooden door slammed shut behind him, and the sound of its closing echoed through the empty yard.

The old man did not move; he merely closed his eyes once more and waited.

High clouds, flying swiftly on the upper winds like tattered sails, obscured the moon rising over the valley. The breeze came in gusts now, and in the distance could be heard the muted rumblings of thunder far away. A few dry leaves flittered across the stone flagging of the temple yard, their tumbling shapes like skittering mice. The torch in the pylon sputtered as the wind played with it.

The old man sat with his head down; he drew his robes more closely around him and waited.

At midnight the courtyard was dark and silent. Clouds covered the sky, and the distant mumbling of thunder sounded ever closer. The wind was fresh and steady out of the east, guttering the flame of the torch, making shadows leap and dance around the pylon.

Then, from the far side of the temple, came the faint glimmer of another light. The winking light approached, swinging in the hand that held it, accompanied by the muffled slap of sandals on the stones. The old man raised his head and smiled in the dark.

In a moment the stranger had come to stand before the seated figure. He raised the shuttered lantern and opened one of the small doors to let out more light. In the yellow glow of the lantern the priest studied his visitor.

"Who are you?" asked the priest.

"So, Pluell, you have come at last."

"How do you know me?"

"You are the High Priest, are you not? Does not the High Priest have a name?"

"I have and you know it. I would know yours."

"I think you do, sir."

The High Priest squinted at the old face and held the lantern closer. "I have never seen you before, never." Then he added slowly, "Have I?"

The old man shook his head. "No, perhaps not. It has been a long time since I have been in these parts."

"You are no priest," Pluell asserted, "though you wear the priestly garb. If you have not been here for many years, how is it that I should know your name?"

"You received my talisman, did you not?"

"I did." He stuck out his hand and held out the black stone. The old man took it and held it up. "It is a most curious piece."

"Yes, most curious." The old man concealed it in his robe.

Just then the sky above was torn by lightning, illuminating the two figures in stark, unnatural light.

"The storm is upon us," said the old man.

"Who are you?" asked the High Priest.

"I tell you that you know."

"Bah! You're wasting my time. I'll have nothing more to do with you. You are keeping me from my bed." He glared at the old man. "It was foolish for me to come."

"And yet you came. Why, I wonder?"

The High Priest opened his mouth to speak, thought better, and closed it again.

"I will tell you why," intoned the old man softly. "You came because you had to come. You had no other choice but to come and see for yourself if what you thought was true."

The High Priest said nothing. The wind gusted and the torch flared. The tree branches above them creaked and groaned in the wind.

"You came because I summoned you."

"You lying old fool!" said Pluell. "I will not listen to this."

"You came because you know trouble approaches, and you know I can help."

"You are insane. I have finished with you. Be gone!" he shouted.

"Very well," said the old man evenly. He stood slowly as if he would leave at once. As he rose his hood fell back from his head, revealing long wispy locks of white hair framing a face as creased and lined as a furrowed field. Sharp black eyes shined out of the ravaged face. "I will go, but once there was a time when the name of Nimrood commanded a measure of respect."

The High Priest stepped back involuntarily at the sound of the name. "Nimrood!" he gasped. "It cannot be!"

"There, you see? You do know me."

"But—you are dead! Years ago . . . I was but a boy . . . I heard . . . you were killed in the battle with the Dragon King . . ."

"As you see, I was not," replied the old man.

"Nimrood! I dare not believe my eyes!"

"Believe them, sir! It is Nimrood and none other."

Lightning streaked the sky, loosing thunder to march out in booming steps across the valley. Heavy drops of rain began thudding to earth, splashing against the stones in the temple yard.

"You spoke of trouble," said High Priest Pluell. "How can you help?"

Nimrood turned his face to the sky. "The storm is come in force. Would you not rather invite me into your private chambers? I think we might have much to discuss."

High Priest Pluell stood in momentary indecision. He glanced at Nimrood sharply, weighing the matter. Rain spattered down into his face. The torch on the pylon guttered out, hissing like a serpent in the dark.

"Very well," Pluell said. "Follow me." He led them to the little-used side entrance, leaving the temple yard to the rain and the night.

2

BRIA LAY FOR A MOMENT LISTENING TO THE DRIP OF the rain onto the bartizan outside their chamber. The doors were thrown open wide and the gentle summer breeze blew in, bringing with it the fresh clean scent of rain-washed air. Tiny blue birds twittered on the balustrade, making joyful music to the morning.

The Queen rolled over and flung an encircling arm to her side. Her hand patted the empty bedclothes where her husband would have been. He was gone. She opened her eyes lazily and murmured, "Oh, Quentin, do you never rest?"

She rose and threw on a robe. At once a maidservant came scurrying with a fresh summer gown of sky-blue samite with a belt of finely wrought gold.

"My Lady slept well?" asked the young woman.

"Well, thank you, Glenna. Isn't it a beautiful day?"

"Yes, my Lady. Beautiful." She smiled, and light shone in her eyes. "Almost as beautiful as my Lady."

"Your flattery is as easily given as the bird's song." Bria laughed and the room was brighter. "Have you seen the King?"

"No, my Lady. Shall I send for the chamberlain?"

The Queen shrugged. "There is no need. I know where he has gone."

The servant helped her Queen dress and then set about

tidying the room. Bria went out from the royal apartments and made her way to the kitchens.

She passed lightly through a corridor and down a flight of steps to a banqueting hall. No sooner had she set foot in the hall when there was a squeal and a sudden flurry of motion toward her.

"Mother! Did you hear? Oh, did you hear the news?" Two young girls rushed up to her on prancing feet and grabbed her hands, pulling her toward the breakfast table.

"And what news have you heard, my darlings?" She smiled and stroked their golden heads.

The younger of the two children, Princess Elena, her hair in long braids woven with golden thread so that they shined and shimmered as she danced on her tiny slippered feet, smiled happily up at her mother, her green eyes twinkling with the merriment of her secret. Her sister, Princess Brianna, slender as a new spring shoot and dressed in bright blue like her mother, pressed the Queen's hand and said, "Come and sit with us, Mother. We have so much to tell you!"

Princess Elena shook her head vigorously. "Yes, oh yes. So much to tell you!"

"Very well," said Queen Bria, settling herself lightly on the bench at the table. "What is your news? I cannot wait another instant!"

The older girl glanced at her sister, and both burst into laughter. The sound was pure delight. Several kitchen servants stopped to look on and smile, arrested by the little Princesses' happiness.

"Will you keep your poor mother in suspense? I confess I must know at once!" Bria took their hands and squeezed them both.

Still laughing, the words tumbled out. "Esme is coming! Esme! Isn't that wonderful?" they shouted. "Esme will be here tonight!"

"That is indeed wonderful news!" cried Bria, hugging her daughters.

"Oh, but please don't tell Father," said Brianna. "We want to tell him. Please?"

"Yes, you shall tell him. It will be your surprise."

"Oh, let's go find him!" cried Elena.

The two would have darted off at once, but the Queen called them back.

"The King is not here, my doves. He rode out this morning early to the temple."

"May we go, too? Please, Mother?" they asked excitedly.

"Come and eat a bite of breakfast first, and we shall see." Bria glanced around the room quickly. "And where is your brother? Still abed? The day is fleeing!"

"Oh, no. He grabbed a seedcake and ran off a long time ago. He is meeting Toli in the stable yard. They are going riding."

"Riding again! Always riding. It is a wonder the boy does not grow hoofs and a mane."

The girls giggled at the thought. The Queen sighed. She did not relish the idea of one so young riding such big horses. Still, she thought, as long as he is with Toli no harm can come to him.

"Now then, eat your breakfast. We have much to do this day to make ready for Lady Esme's visit!"

They sat down to eat, but the girls were in such high spirits that they could only peck at their food. At last their mother dismissed them, and they ran laughing from the hall. Bria smiled, watching their braids flouncing as they went.

So Esme is coming. That is good news, she thought. How did the girls find out, I wonder. Well, however it is, she will be greatly welcome. It has been too long since she was in Askelon. Too long. I have missed her.

QUENTIN STOOD AT A LARGE, ROUGH-HEWN TABLE IN the center of a great rectangle of stone. His head was bent in concentration over a huge parchment roll which was weighted down at either end with a stone.

"See here," he said, pointing to a place on the plan. "If we raise this wall within the week, we can begin laying in the beams. What do you say to that, Bertram?"

Bertram, the grizzled old master mason, squinted at the place where the King's finger pointed, then raised his head and scratched his scruffy jaw, nodding at the wall before them across the way. "Aye, it is possible, Sire," he replied diplomatically. "But the corbels must be set first and they are not ready yet. Nor the trusses, neither."

"Hmm," said the King, frowning.

"But we'll see her raised soon enough, m' lord. Indeed we will. Count on it. Up she'll go soon enough." He nodded his head and then called over to one of his masons. "Excuse me, Sire. I must attend—"

"Yes, of course. Go on. I am returning to the castle soon."

"Good day to you, m'lord." Bertram bowed and hurried away.

Quentin stood for a moment with his hands on his hips and gazed at the work going on around him. The morning was clear and bright, the long grass still wet from the rain through the night. The masons and their many workmen toiled away with vigor. Quarrymen with sledges loaded with stone added their loads to the rockpiles at either end of the rectangle, while laborers selected rock from these mounds and tumbled them into wheelbarrows, ferrying them to the walls. Mortar makers and their carriers stirred the mud pits and loaded fresh mortar onto pallets, supplying the masons who continually clamored for more.

In the midst of this ordered confusion, the walls of the new temple, the temple of the Most High, rose slowly and almost imperceptibly. The work was in its sixth year, and it sometimes seemed to Quentin that it would never end.

He was impatient for the temple to be finished, for its completion would inaugurate the new era; and in this temple he would lead in the worship of Mensandor's new god. The temple would be a symbol to all the realm that the new age had dawned at last.

The old gods are dead, he would proclaim. Worship the new god, the Most High, Creator and Ruler of all!

Word of the new temple had quickly spread throughout the land since construction had begun. There was not a house in all the realm that did not know of the King's Temple, as it was called. But six years had passed, and four more at least were needed before it could be completed. Until then . . . well, there was much work to do until then.

Quentin heard the jingle of bells behind him and turned to see Blazer tossing his head impatiently. The great horse had cropped all the sweet grass within reach and was ready to move on. He tossed his head restlessly, setting the little bells braided into his mane and along his silver bridle ringing, as if to say, "Away! The sun is up; the day is good. Let us run!"

Quentin smiled and walked to the animal, placing his hand on the horse's broad nose. "You are impatient and so am I, old friend. Very well," said the King, raising his foot to the stirrup, "we will go. I have bothered these good men enough for one day."

He swung himself easily up into the saddle and jerked the reins. Blazer lifted his forelegs off the ground and spun around. Quentin lifted his hand to Bertram, who waved back, and then Blazer leapt away. They raced along the road leading down the broad slope of the hill, dodging the ox-drawn wains bearing food and supplies to the workmen. Then, feeling the sun on his face and the beauty of the day springing up inside him, the King spurred Blazer off the road and let him run down the side of the hill and out onto the plain below Askelon.

The castle rose up on its crown of rock, shining like a jewel in the morning light. Red and blue pennons fluttered and snapped from a thousand spires. The high battlements soared above, topped with turrets and barbicans—strong, safe, forever secure.

Quentin enjoyed the strength of the animal beneath him; his heart raced as they thundered over the still-damp ground. Blazer's hoofs struck up muddy turf and flung it skyward as they galloped on.

Presently they came to a great stone cenotaph standing alone in the center of the plain. Quentin reined Blazer to a trot as they approached. They stopped in front of the cenotaph, and Quentin dismounted. He walked to the monument and knelt at its base.

Inscribed in stone on both sides of the slab were the words Quentin knew by heart. Yet he read them once again. They said:

Here upon this field did the warriors on Mensandor meet and defeat in battle the barbarian host of Nin, called The Destroyer.

Here Eskevar, Dragon King, Lord of the Realm, fell, and many brave men with him, nevermore to rise. Peace was purchased with their blood and freedom with their swords.

After reading the words he had read so often, Quentin stood and remounted and rode off once more toward Askelon.

3

AWAY EAST OF THE CITY, IN A MEADOW RINGED WITH ancient oaks, secluded from prying eyes, Toli and Prince Gerin rode together. "Try it again, young Prince," called Toli, turning the cantering Riv toward a well-worn path where the great trunk of a fallen tree lay.

The Prince, a hardy young boy of nine with a touseled mane of dark brown hair, studied the obstacle before him, his quick green eyes narrowed in utmost concentration, his mouth pulled into a pucker. Flushed with excitement, color rising red to his cheeks, Gerin thrust out his jaw earnestly. The act was such an exact parody of the King that Toli chuckled behind his fist in order to keep from laughing aloud.

Then, with a flick of the reins, the Prince kicked his heels into his pony's flanks and away they flew, back down the path toward the fallen trunk.

At the last second the little Prince threw the reins ahead and leaned forward against the horse's neck. The pony lifted its legs and soared over the obstacle with ease, landing with a bump on the other side. The young rider rocked forward in the saddle and bounced to one side, but retained his seat on his mount.

"Very good!" cried Toli. "Excellent! That is the way! Come here now and rest a little." He beamed at his charge, nodding well-earned approval.

"Just once more, Toli. Please? I want to remember what it feels like." He turned the horse again and started for the log.

Toli reined up and dismounted, watching the Prince carefully. This time as the boy's horse approached the obstacle, the animal hesitated, unsure of his rider's command. He jumped awkwardly and late, throwing himself over. Prince Gerin slipped sideways in the saddle and hung on, trying desperately to stop the horse. But he could not; his grip failed, and he fell to the ground with a thud. The brown pony jogged on riderless.

"Ooof!" The Prince rolled heels over head on the soft turf.

Toli rushed to him. "Are you hurt?" He picked up the boy and brushed him off. There was mud on his chin and elbows.

"No—it is not the first time I have fallen. That, at least, I seem to have the knack of."

"I am sorry it will not be the last time, either," laughed Toli. "But I must keep you in one piece, or your father will have my head!"

The Prince looked up at his instructor, frowning, his smooth brow knitting in consternation. "Will I ever get it right?"

"Of course, in time—"

"But the hunt is less than a fortnight away!"

"Do not worry, young master. You are making good progress. You shall ride with the hunt, I promise. And your father will have his surprise. All in good time. But first you must learn not to hesitate when you approach a jump. It confuses your mount, and he will jump badly."

"May I try it again?"

"We should be getting back. I've duties to attend to."

"Please, Toli. Just once more. I would not like to end the day's practice with a fall."

"Well said. One more jump, and then we race for home."

The Prince dashed to his mount, Tarky, who had stopped to nibble the grass at the end of the path. Toli went back to Riv and remounted. "Think about what you are doing, young sir!" called Toli. "Concentrate!"

The boy climbed into his saddle, a look of dire determination on his face. He eyed the obstacle ahead, gauging the distance, then snapped the reins and spurred the horse ahead.

Away they galloped down the path. In a twinkling they were hurtling toward the log. Prince Gerin leaned low in the saddle, lifted his hands, and the horse flew up and over the log as graceful and light as a deer. The Prince pulled the reins and with a whoop of triumph wheeled the pony around and broke for the far trees across the meadow.

"Well done, Prince Gerin!" shouted Toli. "Well done!" Then he, too, spurred his mount for the trees and beyond them to the road leading back to Askelon.

The two reached the road side by side and raced laughing all the way to the castle. The sun was high in the clear blue sky, and both felt the joy of life running strong in them.

DURWIN'S WORKTABLE WAS STACKED HIGH WITH DUSTY scrolls and hide-bound volumes. He sat hunched over the table on a high stool, chin in hand, mumbling to himself as he read. His hair was long and almost completely white now, but his eyes were quick as ever and his limbs sound. He appeared a man half his natural age.

Abruptly he raised his head and sniffed the air. "Ah!" he cried, jumping up. He dashed at once to a small brazier where a black iron pot was bubbling away on the hot coals. It had boiled over, and black smoke rolled toward the rafters. He picked up a long wooden spoon nearby and was stirring the pot when a voice called out from the doorway.

"Phew! Good hermit, what is that prodigious stench? It is most foul!"

Durwin glanced up to see the Queen Dowager standing in his wide doorway watching him, her nose crinkled in frank disgust.

"Alinea! What!—you do not care for my poultice? 'Tis a powerful curative for aches of the joints."

"It is to be wondered whether the aches would not be more enjoyable."

"My patients, I assure you, do not mind its aromatic qualities."

"Your patients?"

"I call them patients, my Lady. This is for Toli."

"Certainly Toli has no need of this."

"His horses, madam. I am making it for his horses, although it would not hurt the rider in any case, if need were great."

"And nose were strong!" she said, laughing. "But mine is not. Come away from your labors a little, hermit. I would have someone to walk with in the garden."

Durwin smiled and bowed. "I would be delighted. Just the thing. I have been too long among these vapors, or I would have thought of it myself."

They went out together, through the castle, past the Dragon King's Great Hall, and out onto the garden steps. "See how brightly the sun shines," said Alinea, "and how fragrant the flowers."

They walked down the steps and into the garden amidst the fragrant offerings of roses of all kinds. The spring flowers were gone, but the blooms of summer were just opening and everywhere one looked the eye was filled with color.

"Ah! It is peace itself to be here," sighed Durwin. He turned to regard his companion. The years had been kind to her. Her hair was long—braided, gathered, and bound in a snood. There was much silver now among the auburn tresses, and lines had formed around her eyes and lovely lips. But her eyes were still as green as forest pools, and her voice held the timbre of laughing water.

Yes, thought Durwin, the years have been good to us all. I would not trade them for any others. The God Most High is good; he has poured out a blessing on the land. We have much to be thankful for.

"What are you thinking, my friend?" Alinea asked softly.

"That these have been happy years, my Queen, and full. I am content." He paused, and his voice struck a faraway note. "Though I lay down to die tomorrow, I would have no regrets. None at all."

"And I might say the same," replied Alinea. "But come, let us not speak further of dying. That will take care of itself."

"So it is! Aye, so it is." Durwin nodded slowly. Brightening he said, "Then tell me, what news have you? I heard that a messenger arrived early this morning. He brought good tidings?"

"Yes! Yes, I was going to tell you. He brought word from Hinsenby—"

"Hinsenby? From Theido?"

"From Lady Esme. She is on her way here even now. She will arrive before dusk this evening. The day is good for traveling."

"Ah, Lady Esme. Her I have not seen for many years, it seems."

"She has been missed within these walls. And, sad to tell, no one felt her absence as keenly as Lady Esme herself."

"Yes, an awful business. Very sad. It bears remembering that there are some among us whose lives may not be as free of regret as our own. I am certain she would have chosen differently if she had known."

Alinea was silent for some time. They paced the garden paths, each feeling the warmth of the day and of companionship from the other. "I wonder if any of us would choose as we do, if we knew the future."

"Perhaps not. But it is a blessing nonetheless. The burdens of the day weigh heavy enough; we could not bear tomorrow's as well."

"Of course. How wise you are, hermit. Yes, it will be good to see Esme once more. Perhaps we may help heal old wounds."

Just then they heard the happy twitter of childish voices and looked up to see Princess Brianna and Princess Elena running toward them as fast as their spindly little legs would carry them. Behind them Bria walked at a more leisurely pace.

"Grandmother! Oh, Grandmother!" called the little girls. "We have a secret! A very great secret!"

"A secret? Whatever could it be?"

"You must guess it, Grandmother!" shouted Brianna.

"Yes, guess! Guess!" shouted Elena.

Alinea placed her hands together and raised them to her lips. "Let me see," she said, her eyes shining at the sight of her beautiful grandchildren. "Are you going on a trip?"

Both little heads wagged from side to side, their braids flying.

"No?" continued their grandmother. "Then you have learned a new game and have come to show us!"

"That's not it!" they cried, and burst into giggles. "Lady Esme is coming! She'll be here tonight!" Both girls began hopping up and down.

"That *is* good news!" said Alinea.

"Did you hear, Durwin?" they shouted. "She'll be here tonight." Then they looked at each other as a new and better thought occurred to them. "Maybe she'll bring us presents!" said Brianna.

"Yes, presents!"

They clapped their hands and then darted away among the rose bushes toward the fountain.

"Very like hummingbirds," mused Durwin.

"There you are, Mother," said Bria as she came to stand with them. "I see they have told you their secret."

"Yes, dear. How happy you must be."

"I am almost as excited as they are—if that were possible!" she replied and laughed, her eyes following the girls as they ran. "Good day, Durwin. I am glad to see Mother has dragged you from your noisome den. I was beginning to wonder whether you would ever come out."

"Oh, in time, in time. But once this old head gets hold of an idea, it will not let it go." He smiled broadly. "That is why I have you two to look after me. I know you will not allow me to remain too long alone. I thank you for that."

"There is another who I wish were as easily persuaded," said Bria.

"Quentin?"

Bria smiled a little sadly and nodded. "Oh, I know he is very busy now. He is preoccupied with his temple. But he is gone from morning until night nearly every day, closeted with his builders and architects. He never stops. I rarely see him anymore."

Alinea looked longingly at her daughter. "With a King it is ever so. You must remember, my love, that he does not belong to himself, or even his family. He belongs to the kingdom, to the people. Quentin carries a very great burden in this temple. Old ways die hard, and he seeks to fulfill the god's leading."

Bria hung her head. "I know I should be more patient. But he has become a stranger in his own house."

"Quentin is called to high deeds. Through him great things will be accomplished."

"So it is," said Durwin. "But my Lady Bria speaks truth. He also must look to the nurturing of his home. King or no, that is a man's first responsibility. The Most High is happy in small deeds, as well as large. I often think he must care less for temples than for the simple strength of a family." He paused and looked at Bria. "I will speak to him if you wish."

"Thank you, but no. I will wait. The temple is important—I know that. Perhaps when it is finished we will once again find time for ourselves. Until then I shall wait." She smiled prettily and glanced at her mother. "The women in our family have had long experience with waiting. We are very good at it."

4

UNLIKE THE PRIESTS HE LED, HIGH PRIEST PLUELL LIVED in sumptuous splendor, with the richest appointments. While the lower priests' cells were spare, devoid of all objects and ornamentation, except those few articles necessary to a minimum of comfort—a bed with straw-filled mattress, a stool, a rough table, a wooden bowl, a tallow candle—the High Priest's apartment was hung with heavy tapestries, and carven chairs stood around a great table spread with expensive cloth and laid with fine silver. From golden candle holders burned candles made with perfumed beeswax. His bed was high and curtained, the mattress stuffed with eider down.

This, he told himself, was no more than his due—the perquisites of his position, the rewards of his rank.

High Priest Pluell and his visitor had been holding conference for many hours. The High Priest stared ahead dully, his eyes red-rimmed from lack of sleep, a deep frown cast over his arrogant features.

Old Nimrood watched him carefully from his seat, with gnarled hands folded beneath his sharp chin. He seemed the picture of a shrewd merchant who has just struck an extremely fortuitous bargain. The faint wisp of a smile curled his thin, bloodless lips.

"Then it is agreed?" asked Nimrood, breaking the silence at last.

Pluell raised his head slowly, a sneer twisting his mouth. "What other choice do I have? Yes! It is agreed. I will do as you say."

"See that you do and all will be well. You will save the temple; and what is more, you will hold the power of the kingdom. The realm will be yours and the King your servant. Think of it!"

"It is risky. I am not fond of taking chances."

"Without risk there is no gain, my friend. And as you yourself have said, you have no choice. I tell you, this upstart King means to pull down the High Temple and drive out the priests. With every passing day the King's Temple grows; when it is done, yours will be destroyed."

"Still, would he dare? It would inflame the people against him. I would see to that."

"He dares all things in the name of this god of his. He must be dealt with at once. Too long have you hidden beneath your robes of office. Wait any longer and it will be too late."

"Yes, yes. So you say." Pluell looked at his guest sharply. "I do not like this King at all, and I do not fear him. The sanctity and authority of the High Temple must be preserved. When and where do we begin?"

Nimrood smiled expansively. "I will choose the time and the place. Leave all to me. But I will need six of your temple guard—six who know how to obey and to keep secrets concealed."

"You shall have them. What else?"

"Nothing, for now." Nimrood stood slowly. "Only a place to rest and a morsel to eat. Then I will be on my way."

"Very well. Tell the priest waiting outside what you require. He will arrange everything for you. I will go and choose the men who are to accompany you."

Nimrood dipped his head and then went out. The High Priest sat for a moment in his chair, still staring blankly into the shadows. Then he drew his robes close around as a chill shivered through him, for the room had grown quite cold.

THE AFTERNOON SUN SHONE A HAZY GOLD AS IT SANK below the green, tree-lined hills. The road bent down into low valleys, sinking into cool shadow. On the crest of the hill the small traveling party stopped.

"Yonder lies Askelon, my Lady," said Wilkins, one of Lady Esme's traveling companions, "and a fair sight it is."

Esme filled her pale blue eyes with the glittering scene before her. Askelon Castle, its towers and turrets fired by the golden rays of the setting sun, sparkled like a jewel. The great walls stood strong, impenetrable, glowing red in the fading light.

She shivered, remembering another time when she sat astride a horse in exactly this spot and gazed upon the castle standing just so in another sunset long ago. *Nothing has changed,* she thought. *Oh, what folly!* Everything *has changed, me most of all.*

"I may have been wrong to leave," she said finally, speaking softly to herself. "But I have returned. Perhaps I can make a new beginning."

Without another word Esme gathered the reins and started down the hill into the valley. Sensing food and water and a warm stall at hand, her horse began to trot and then to gallop along the road. The others behind her joined in the race and soon they were all flying toward Askelon, their jubilant voices ringing through the dells.

They reached the village below the walls and clattered through the streets, hardly slowing at all. Then they were over the drawbridge, through the gatehouse, and jogging to a halt in the ward yard, where squires scampered to take the horses and lead them to the stables.

"Esme! You are here!" There was a shout behind her, and she turned to see Bria emerging from a doorway across the yard. Two little faces peeked out from either side of their mother's skirts, their eyes shining.

Esme knelt down and held out her arms. "Come here, my darlings!" she called, and was instantly smothered in giggles and kisses. "And how big you have grown!" she said in amazement. "Oh, I have missed you so!" She kissed both girls and hugged them tight. Then she stood and embraced their mother. "Bria, it is wonderful to see you."

The two women clung for a long moment and then stepped back to view each other at arm's length. "Esme, you are more beautiful than ever. You are! It is . . ." A tear formed in Bria's eye. "I have missed you so much!"

"And I you. You have no idea how good it feels to be here at last. I have wanted to come many times, but—"

Bria caught up her hands and pulled her away, saying, "Come! There is much to talk about. Leave your things for now; I will have them brought up to your rooms." She turned to address the others in Esme's traveling party. "Please, you are our welcome guests. Rest; take your ease from your long journey. If you like, you may dine with us in the banquet hall this evening. Or if you would prefer, food will be sent to your rooms."

Wilkins bowed low. "Your Highness, my Lady has told us so much about you and about this place, we are all eager to see it. We will join you as soon as we have washed the dust of the road from ourselves. I, for one, wish to meet the Dragon King. His name is renowned in the land." The others nodded their agreement.

"I am sure my husband will welcome the news you bring. I will send the chamberlain directly to lead you to your rooms."

Esme said, "Chloe, you may remain with me." A slim brown-haired young woman dressed in riding clothes like Esme's stepped shyly forward. She curtsied to the Queen, then held out two bundles to her mistress.

"Ah, yes. I almost forgot!" said Esme, taking the packages. "I have brought something for my little friends."

The Princesses squealed in delight. "Presents!" they cried. Esme handed them each a bundle tied in bright silk. "Oh, thank you! Thank you!" Both girls kissed her and then ran off to open their gifts.

"They are treasures, Bria. Treasures."

"That they are. But come, you must be exhausted. Your rooms are ready and waiting for you." She led Esme away and smiled at Chloe who fell silently in behind them. "Both of you can rest a little before dinner."

The Queen led them from the ward yard into the corridor of the inner curtain and into the castle itself. Along the way they talked about the journey and all that the travelers had seen. When finally they reached the Queen's apartments, Bria announced, "You will be staying here, Esme. I want you close. Rest now and refresh yourselves. Water has been prepared for you. I will come back in a little while and bring you to dinner."

"You are so kind, Bria. Thank you. But now that I am here, fatigue seems to have vanished. I want only to sit with you and have a long talk."

"Oh, we shall, Esme. We must have many long talks before I am satisfied." She paused and added on a more somber note, "You have often been in my thoughts."

"Thank you. And you have often been in mine. Yes, we have much to talk about."

QUENTIN AND TOLI WERE STANDING WITH WILKINS JUST inside the wide open doors to the banqueting hall. Others stood a little way off talking among themselves, awed to be in the presence of the King himself. Wilkins enthusiastically recounted the journey to Askelon and related the news he had heard along the way.

Quentin, happy to entertain guests—for it had been some time since the castle had held foreign visitors—pumped the willing man for information which was happily supplied.

He found the Jher, head to head with Wilkins, sitting at the far end of the high table. They were deep in conversation, oblivious to all that was going on around them.

Quentin looked to the lower table; all eyes were on him, waiting for him to begin. He reached out and took a piece of bread, broke it, and put it on his silver trencher, nodding to his guests. At once they began to eat; platters were passed, cups filled, and glad conversation bubbled forth.

While they ate, the bard approached the high table. He bowed to the King and said, "Your majesty, is there a ballad you wish told? You have but to name it and Larksong is at your service."

"Something befitting the lively mood of this summer's eve," declared Quentin. "Let brave knights and their bold deeds wait until another time. Tonight I would hear a lighter tale, one to make the heart rejoice."

"If it is good cheer you wish, sire, I know just the thing!" He bowed again, saying, "Excuse me now. I must retire to compose the lyric."

How great an honor to be a King, thought Quentin. Truly a very great honor. Indeed I am blessed.

He looked down upon his guests and shared their amusement and high spirits. Life is good in Mensandor; all is well in the realm. He felt his heart fill with happiness and swell almost to bursting, so deep was his joy.

5

THE PALE MOON HAD RISEN FAIR IN THE SKY, THROWING down a silvery radiance upon all below. Toli stood alone on the bartizan outside the banquet hall, overlooking a portion of the garden. Laughter drifted out of the hall through the open doors, and flickering torchlight from the hall splashed the stones and turned them to gold.

The bard Larksong sang his ballads to the high acclaim of all gathered inside. Toli could hear his strong voice lifted up in song, but could not catch the words which were drowned now and again in waves of laughter. At the end of a song or story there came clamorous applause and cries for more.

But Toli did not attend to what was taking place inside. He had grown uncomfortable and slipped away quietly to be alone. No one, he thought, had seen him go. He breathed the soft night air and wondered what he would do when he met her once again.

He did not have long to wonder. He heard the sound of a soft brushing tread, turned, and she was there, standing in the doorway, the light framing her, shining all around her. A sharp pang arrowed through him. He turned away.

Then she was beside him. He smelled her delicate

scent, warm and pleasing. Her nearness burned him with a glowing heat.

"Ah," she sighed, "how peaceful and cool here. The hall, for all its light and laughter, grows stale." She spoke softly. He did not reply. Then she touched his arm, and he felt a flame leap through him. "Hello, Toli," she whispered. "I saw you leave the hall."

He turned toward her. "Esme . . ." He could think of nothing to say. She, with the moonlight in her eyes and shining on her long dark tresses, was even more lovely than he remembered. And she had come back.

Esme laid her fingertips to his lips. Her touch was cool. "Shh. You do not need to speak. This is awkward for me, too."

Toli stared at the woman he had loved. Why? he wanted to scream. Why did you leave me? What made you go? And now, after so many years, why have you returned?

But he said nothing, only turned away again. Esme felt the distance between them as a physical presence: a risen wall of bristling emotion which she could not breach. Suddenly all that she had kept locked away in her heart for so long came rushing forth. Her throat tightened. Her hands quivered. She bent her head, and tears began to fall.

There was a movement beside her. "Toli, I—" she began, then glanced up. He was gone.

INSIDE THE HALL LARKSONG HELD HIS LISTENERS IN thrall. He was in high form, bowing to cascades of applause, his broad, good-natured face beaming from beneath his wide, low-crowned hat with its long green plume. He allowed the acclamation to wash over him and then, as it started to die away, held up his hands for silence and began to sing.

> "In fair Mensandor,
> On a summer's eve,

When all the hills are wearing green,
Give an ear, my lords and ladies,
To the tale I'll weave—
Of bold Quentin and his Queen!"

This was greeted with shouts of laughter and ringing cheers, for now the King would be celebrated for their amusement. Larksong bowed low and began, his voice rising in clear tones to tell his tale. It was a song about a King who sought the hand of the most beautiful woman in the realm and found her in the daughter of his enemy.

The song was an old one, of course, known to all who heard it. But Larksong sang it well, inventing new verses which played upon Quentin's and Bria's names and the well-known events of their lives. The listeners sat captivated—enraptured from start to finish.

When at last the Quentin of the story won his bride's hand and made peace with his enemy, a resounding cheer went up throughout the hall.

"Well done!" they cried. "More! More! Sing it again!" Everyone shouted their praise and cried for more, though the evening was growing late. But Larksong took off his hat and made a sweeping bow to all assembled.

"Thank you! Thank you! Thank you, one and all!" He bowed to the King. "My songs are finished this night. Perhaps I may come again."

"Yes, come again!" they cried. "Come tomorrow!"

Larksong looked inquiringly at the King. Quentin nodded his approval, and all his guests added theirs. And then reluctantly—for it had been a wonderful night—the people began to leave.

Quentin rose. "Oh, my sides are sore for laughing! What a night! What a night." He peered around. "Now where has Toli gone? I would speak with him."

"I think he is occupied at present," replied Bria. "Come along. Speak with him tomorrow."

"Esme?"

"Who did you think? Come along." Bria tugged on his

arm and led him away. They left the hall and the servants began dousing the torches, giving the great room over to the night.

No sooner had they reached their chambers when a knock sounded upon the door. "Who can that be?" asked Quentin. He opened the door to see Esme's companion, Chloe, wringing her hands and tugging at her apron.

"Sire, I—" She stared past him to Bria. "My Lady, I do not know what to do."

Bria stepped forward. "What is it, Chloe? What is wrong?"

"My Lady," she curtsied. "I . . . could you come?"

"What is it?" demanded Quentin.

"My Lord," said Bria, "go and see to the children. Tell them good night. I will look in a little later. Go on now. I will take care of this." She eased past Quentin and closed the door behind her.

"Where is she?"

"In her rooms. She returned some time ago and has been weeping ever since. I can do nothing for her. Oh, my Lady! I have never seen her this way. Even when my lord—Lord Rathnor—was angry with her, she did not carry on so. I am afraid—"

"Calm yourself, my dear. All will be well. Have no fear."

When they entered Esme's apartments, Bria could hear someone sobbing in the chamber beyond. "Stay here, Chloe. I will go in to her," she said softly, and moved to the door. She knocked gently. There was no answer. She opened the door and went in.

Esme lay facedown on the bed, her shoulders heaving, the sobs welling up from deep inside her. Bria sat down on the huge high bed beside her. She placed her hand on her friend's shoulder, feeling instinctually the depths of her misery.

"Esme, I am here. I am with you. Tell me what has happened."

It was a time before Esme could talk. But at last Bria

got her to sit up, dry her eyes, and tell her what had taken place.

"Oh, Bria!" she sniffed, her eyes wet from crying. She twisted a damp handkerchief in her hands. "He hates me! Despises me! And I do not blame him. I should not have come hoping to . . . Oh, I should never have come."

"There, now. Toli does not hate you." Bria said his name; she had guessed what had happened. "I am certain of it. You know how he is."

"He ran from me. I went out to him, and he left without a word!" Her lips trembled and she seemed on the verge of another torrent of tears, but took a deep breath and kept them down. "Oh, Bria, how I must have hurt him. I thought—I thought . . . Oh, I do not know what I thought. I was wrong to come here. I was never born for happiness."

"Nonsense. Do not talk so!" chided Bria. "You are welcome here; it can never be wrong to come where you are loved and cared for. As for Toli, perhaps it was a mistake to approach him so openly. Obviously, we will need to plan very carefully how best to win him back. But unless I am far wrong, he does not hate you. Never say it! If we could see inside his heart, we would see his love for you has never waned."

Esme sniffed miserably. Bria put her arms around her and drew her close. "You have suffered much, Esme. And yet in all your pain you never allowed yourself to cry out." To Esme's questioning glance she replied, "Chloe told me. But why? I would rather hear it from you."

Esme gazed at her hands folded on her knees. "I have made such a ruin of my life, Bria. How can you still call me friend?" She placed her hand on Bria's. "But you always were so much more kind than I."

"Nonsense!"

"No, it is true."

Bria pulled Esme more tightly to her, and both women fell silent. When she turned to her friend once more, she found Esme sound asleep. The Queen drew a comforter over her and left the room quietly. At the door she paused and looked back. "There is healing here, Esme. Stay with us and let it begin."

QUENTIN WAS SITTING AT HIS GREAT TABLE FROWNING over sketches of his temple's design. The table bore the full weight of a score of drawings, dozens of work-men's plans, countless lists and inventories of building materials, several clay and stone models of the finished structure, a large plumb bob and line, three mason's levels, a leather parchment case, and a stone from the site which acted as a paperweight.

"You are tired, my lord," said Bria, coming up behind him. She rested her hands on his shoulders and lightly rubbed his neck. "You stare witless at the scratchings before you."

The King raised his face from the page before him and pressed his fists against his eyes. "You are right, my love. Yes, I am tired. There is much to do—"

"Nothing that will not wait until tomorrow. Come to bed."

Quentin put his hands flat on the table and pushed the sketches from him as he stood. He gazed at his wife and smiled gently, then asked, "Is all well with our guest?"

"Her travels have worn her down, as may be expected. But I think she suffers still from the memory of a love-less marriage, and that is the pain she bears."

"He has been dead two years."

Bria nodded. "Yes, but deep wounds heal slowly. We do not know how cruelly treated she was."

"She will not talk to you?"

"She speaks of it to no one. But it is plain to see that all is not well. There are many who do not share the joy we know, and Esme is one of those who have traveled a most difficult road."

"We will hear of it in time, I imagine. When she is ready, she will tell us." Quentin yawned and stretched,

and together the King and Queen went in to their bedchamber.

Quentin lay for a long time staring into the blackness
of the darkened room, thinking about the events of the
day past and those of the day to come. He fell asleep with
a vision of the completed temple filling his eyes, and
dreamed of the day when he would lead his countrymen
into the temple to worship the Most High on its day of
consecration.

6

THE DAY OF THE KING'S HUNT DAWNED WITH MELANcholy reluctance; low dreary clouds spread over the Plain of Askelon and gray mists draped the treetops. Those camped abroad and those boarded in the town and in the castle feared rain would spoil the day. But as a wan yellow sun climbed higher into the great vault of the heavens, it gathered strength, flared brighter; its white-hot rays burned away the clouds and warmed the air. Travelers and townspeople streamed into the streets and began the trek to the field. Those still abed in Castle Askelon awakened and rushed to ready themselves for the day's festivities. Lords and their ladies—from as far away as Endonny and Woodsend, and all places in between— dressed in their finest. Knights donned riding clothes of leather and saw to the grooming of their horses, plaiting tail and mane with ribbons of gold and silver entwined with bells, or dressing their steeds in brightly colored caparisons: red and blue, gold and green, violet and yellow.

And everywhere, from the chamber of the King to the tents on Askelon Plain, excitement simmered beneath the surface, breaking out in laughter and song and impromptu games. Wagons and hand carts emerged from the castle keeps loaded down with foodstuffs and supplies for the makeshift kitchens arranged on the field under bright yellow canopies.

Everywhere around the sporting field colorful pavilions of red and silver, bearing the royal device—the red writhing dragon—began filling. Smoke from cooking fires drifted lazily into the windless sky in silken threads. It appeared to anyone observing from the battlements of Askelon Castle that a bold, colorful army had encamped round about, an army whose numbers swelled by degrees ever greater as more and more people made their way to the field.

"Father! Father, come quickly! Look! Oh, look!" cried the children. They ran and seized Quentin's hands and pulled him out onto the bartizan outside their rooms. "See! The hunt is almost ready! Look at all the people! Oh, I have never seen so many!" they cried.

"Can we play in the games, Father?" asked Princess Brianna.

"Of course," said Quentin. "There will be games for you." He reached out and patted her head.

"And watch the circus?" added Princess Elena.

"Yes! Yes!" laughed Quentin.

Young Prince Gerin did not ask a favor, considering himself too big for such childish pleasures. He looked out on the scene below and beamed, his face flushed with excitement.

"And what about you, my son? What will you do today?"

Prince Gerin turned and smiled mysteriously. "I will show you—but not now. It is a secret! A surprise!"

"Very well," said Quentin. "If I must wait, I must. But tell me soon, for I do not think I can endure the suspense for long!" He laughed again and pulled the youngster to him, rubbing his slim shoulders affectionately.

"There you are!" said Bria, stepping out onto the bartizan. "The sooner we have our breakfast, the sooner we will join the others and the festival can begin!"

The Princesses frowned disapprovingly. Prince Gerin whirled away and dashed for the door. "I cannot eat now!" he called. "I must find Toli!" He was gone before his mother could protest.

"Breakfast is an unwanted intrusion today," said Quentin. "Besides, there will be time enough and food enough for eating at the field. If any go away hungry this day, it is their own fault and no one else's."

Bria sighed and herded the girls before her, and they went down to eat a hasty meal before departing for the hunt.

FOR MANY DAYS THE CASTLE HAD BEEN BUSTLING WITH activity. There was food and drink to organize, folded pavilions to haul from storage, and the field to prepare. Minstrels and circus performers, some with trained dogs and bears, had begun arriving in the town. Merchants readied wares which they would offer to the crowds; food vendors prepared their special delicacies.

Toli and Prince Gerin had arranged their surprise in their own way, practicing the more difficult jumps time and again. The Prince had, after many painful tumbles, learned to jump with ease, handling his horse with an expert hand at last.

"Very good! Excellent!" called Toli that final day. "You are ready for the hunt, young master. I have taught you all I can."

"Do you really think so, Toli?"

Toli nodded solemnly. "A finer rider in this realm would be difficult to find. You are ready. Just remember everything we have practiced and you will ride with the best."

"Truly?"

"Truly."

"Father will be so surprised!" the Prince shouted. "You will not tell him—"

"Never fear—I want him to be surprised, too."

Those last days had been hard ones for the Prince,

trying desperately to keep his secret. It burned inside him, threatening to leap to his tongue each time he opened his mouth. But somehow he had managed; the secret was safe.

Now, as he dashed to the stables to find Toli and to see to his horse, he ran with the speed of his own racing heart. He found Toli saddling his mount for him, examining each tack item as he placed it on the horse. The Prince slowed as he came up; Tarky nickered softly as the boy reached out and patted the sleek jaw.

"You will ride beside me, won't you, Toli?"

"Certainly. I shall be right beside you all the way. How else am I to keep up?"

"Do you think we might find a trophy?"

"We have as good a chance as any, I'll warrant. And better than some. We just might find a trophy."

The hunters were allowed to hunt for game, but as an added reward there were prizes hidden throughout the forest: trophies of gold and silver, cups and bowls, and other objects of value. This heightened the competition and gave extra delight to the sport. Many of the hunters did not even carry weapons, preferring instead to concentrate solely on finding the valuable trinkets. This was what Prince Gerin had in mind as well; he wanted to find a trophy for his father. That would complete the surprise.

When all was ready the Prince hoisted himself into his saddle, heart thumping in his chest. Together Toli and Gerin rode to join the others at the gates.

"VERY WELL," SPAT NIMROOD FROM THE SHADOWS. "You know what to do. You have had a good look at him. There must be no mistakes."

The six men gathered around him nodded silently. There would be no mistakes because they had come to fear Nimrood greatly and would not risk his disappointment, though none of them had much stomach for what was about to take place.

"Then disperse carefully. I will await you here. Remember the signal, and look sharp! Yes, my lads, look sharp! I do not need to remind you that this is a most dangerous game we are playing. Most dangerous," he hissed, his eyes darting from one man to the next. "Now go. And be ready!"

The six men, the best chosen from among the order of temple guards, faded silently away, their dark clothing melding with the green leaves and deep shadows of Pelgrin Forest.

Nimrood's cruel features creased into a malicious grin. "Now it begins. At long last, it begins," he whispered throatily to himself. "At long last I will have my revenge."

7

THE INNER WARD YARD BUSTLED WITH ACTIVITY AS
THE King assembled his family and friends. Bria and
the Princesses would ride to the field in a gaily fes-
tooned coach. Quentin and his son would lead the procession on horseback, followed by Durwin and Toli
and as many of the noble visitors as had not already
left for the field. Esme, however, would not be among
them.

When all was ready, the armorer came hurrying up
with two squires at either elbow. One lad carried the
King's shield, burnished bright as a mirror; the other carried, on a long satin pillow, the King's sword,
Zhaligkeer, the Shining One.

The armorer knelt and offered the King his weapons.
Quentin nodded, and the squires helped their master
fasten the great sword in place and then handed up the
shield, which the King slung over his shoulder.

Word of the shining sword had long ago spread far
and wide throughout the land. There was not a peasant
anywhere who had not heard of its forging in the lost
mountain mines of the Ariga out of the fabled glowing
ore, lanthanil. Far beyond the borders of Mensandor tales
of the Shining One were told, and of the mighty Priest
King who had come to the throne by a strange and

wonderful enchantment. Those who looked upon him now believed those stories more fervently than ever, because he appeared so strong and fearless.

Quentin mounted Blazer and the milk-white stallion danced sideways, anxious to be off. He raised a gloved hand, the inner ward gates were opened wide, and the parade began. They passed into the outer ward and then through the gatehouse, over the huge drawbridge and down the ramp into the city. And though many towns-people had already left for the festival site, there were still enough to line the streets to wave and cheer and welcome their King. The happy people fell into place behind the procession as it passed, and all made their way to the field.

Young Gerin, his heart fluttering within him like a captive bird, gawked openly at all around him, feeling proud and important. This day the hunt wore a different look; nothing appeared the same as he remembered it. All had changed, becoming more colorful, more excit-ing, more thrilling than ever before. For this day *he* would ride with the hunt!

He swiveled in his saddle and threw a conspiratorial glance back at Toli, who rode behind him. Toli was talking to Durwin, but saw the look and answered it with a wink.

Gerin turned his eyes to the sights around him. Jug-glers tossed knives and hoops high into the air and caught them deftly; a man with a trained bear on a chain made it stand on its head; acrobats tumbled and threw one another spinning into the air; some boys had made a pair of stilts from the limbs of trees and were trying to master the art of walking on them; vendors cried over the shouts and laughter, hawking their trinkets: fancy ribbons, jewelry, and tiny lacquered boxes.

The world was alive with sound and color. Here and there music swelled as minstrels gathered small audi-ences to hear their newest songs; horses cantered and neighed, tossing their heads and setting their bells ringing; children ran laughing, their bare feet skipping over the grass.

The parade entered the field itself, and Gerin turned his eyes to the competition. Ranged around the long rectangle of the field were tents and small pavilions, each with a standard before the entrance bearing the banner of the lord or knight within. Some of the riders were outside their tents, seeing to the last-minute details of tick or weapons. Hunting hounds lay on the grass waiting for the chase to begin, or strained at their leashes, yapping eagerly at one another as they sensed the moment of their release drawing near.

Gerin gazed among the pavilions, reading the devices and looking for those that he knew. There was the green oak on a barred field of azure and gold—that was Sir Grenfell. The boar and spear on scarlet belonged to Lord Bossit; and the silver lance and shield on checkered black and white was the blazon of Sir Hedric of Bellavee. There were also Benniot's silver and blue double eagle, Rudd's red ox on sable, and Fincher's gauntlet clutching white thunderbolts.

There were more that he did not know—harts and hounds, mailed fists and morions, poniards and preying birds—but he did not see the two he hoped most to see: the black hawk on crimson, and the gray gauntlet clutching crossed mace and flail.

"Where is Theido, Father? And Ronsard? I do not see them," the Prince said, craning his neck around the perimeter of the field.

"They will be here before the hunt is through. Theido sent word that he will arrive tomorrow, and Ronsard likewise. They will not miss the hunt. Do not worry; your friends will come."

They arrived at the King's pavilion and dismounted. The ascending rows of banks were already filled to overflowing, and more people were crowding in. In the very front row, however, were chairs set up behind a banister for the royal family and their entourage. The Queen took her place, and the Princesses beside her, smiling and waving to all who greeted her. The King, instantly surrounded by well-wishers, slowly made his way to his chair where he remained standing and signaled the herald.

A long clear blast of the trumpet summoned the riders, who began filing onto the field, arranging themselves in ranks before the King's pavilion. When all were ready, the King nodded to a man with a wide leather baldric from which dangled a hunting horn.

The man was the Marshal of the Hunt; he led his bay horse to the front of the assembled ranks and in a loud voice began reciting the rules of conduct. When he was finished, Quentin looked over the crowd and shouted, "Do you one and all pledge your oath to abide the laws of the King's Hunt?"

"We so pledge!" the riders shouted as one.

"Well said!" cried Quentin. "Let the hunt begin!"

A great hurrah went up from the hunters, and all the spectators gathered around the field. The marshal raised the horn to his lips, but before he could sound the note someone called out, "We would have our King lead us!"

"The King!" someone else shouted. "Yes! The King!" the rest joined in. "We want King Quentin. The King must lead the hunt!"

Quentin smiled and glanced at his Queen. "Oh, you must go, Father! You must!" cried Princess Brianna and Princess Elena.

"Yes," agreed Bria. "Lead them, my lord."

"Very well," said Quentin. "I will ride!" He made to leave the pavilion and mount Blazer. Another hurrah went up from the throng.

"The King will ride!" they shouted. Actually Quentin rode every year, but it was always custom that the contestants ask him to ride and offer him the lead. Usually he rode only for a short while and then returned to officiate over the other games.

"Are you coming, Durwin?" Quentin asked as he descended from the pavilion.

"I am getting too old for breaking my neck on horseback. Leave it to the younger men. I shall wait here for your return."

"Durwin!" the crowd called. "Let Durwin ride with us! Durwin! Durwin!" The call became a chant.

"You see, they want you, Durwin. You would disappoint them?"

"Very well, I will ride. Lead on." He followed Quentin down to the field.

As they were mounted and making ready to gallop off, Quentin looked to his side and saw his son beaming at him, his young face shining with anticipation. "What is this?"

"I am riding, too, Father. That is your surprise!"

Before Quentin could speak, Toli, sitting next to the Prince, said, "We have been practicing for weeks, my lord. Your son has become a fine horseman."

"Is it true?" He stared at his son.

The boy burst out laughing. "If you could see the bruises I have endured, you would know the truth of it!"

Quentin did not know what to say. He glanced to Bria, who was attending the scene from her seat with a worried look on her face. Quentin scratched his jaw and seemed about to overrule the enterprise. He looked to Toli. "Do you think it wise?" Prince Gerin bit his lip.

"Sire, I would not allow it if I thought he would be in danger. He can handle himself and his mount, never fear. And I will ride with him just to make sure. I will not allow him away from me for an instant."

Quentin nodded, his eyes on the boy. The intense hope the youngster carried within him burned out of his eyes like a flame. How could he be denied?

"As you will," said Quentin, breaking into a grin when he saw how much his approval meant to the lad. "You shall ride. And I hope you find the biggest trophy!"

"For you, Father. I want to find one for you!"

"Toli, watch after him. And you, young sir, do as Toli tells you."

They made their way among the other riders to the end of the field—the King in the lead with Durwin on one side and Prince Gerin and Toli on the other. When they were in position, the King raised his hand and the Marshal of the Hunt blew his horn. "To the hunt!" they cried, and all at once the horses leapt away, thundering off across the plain toward Pelgrin Forest.

The thump of the horses' hooves on the plain pounded out a drumbeat, and the people cheered as the hunters flew away into the forest. Once they reached the foremost fringes of the wood, Quentin hung back and let the others go ahead. Those after game dashed ahead first, lances at the ready, searching out trails among the dark branches. Hot behind them came the trophy seekers who spread out to ride alone to secret places where they hoped a prize would be found.

"What are you waiting for?" shouted Quentin to his son, who also hesitated at the edge of the wood. "Away! Fly!"

The youngster snapped the reins, and Tarky dashed away; Toli was right behind him. "He is growing up, Sire," said Durwin at Quentin's shoulder.

"Too fast, I sometimes think." He smiled after his son. "Look at him go!"

"He reminds me of another young man I met—could it be that long ago? He also had a brown mare, as I remember."

"But he did not ride that well—as I remember."

"So it is! But he had the will to try; and a stout heart in his young frame."

"Stubborn, you mean," laughed Quentin. "How we have changed, old friend."

"Yes, changed a little. But still very much the same." The hermit snapped his reins. "Come along. Let us see how the young master fares. Keep up if you can!" With that he darted off.

"Is that any way to speak to your King, you grizzled old hermit!" Quentin shouted after him. He spurred Blazer and sped into the cool green wood.

8

"IT IS SUCH A LOVELY DAY, MY LADY. DO YOU NOT wish to join the others at the festival?" Chloe came quietly up behind Esme as she gazed unseeing out upon the plain, ablossom with scores of colored tents. "See, the hunt has already begun."

They watched the line of horses and riders galloping in a long sinuous wave over the Plain of Askelon. After a moment Esme replied absently, "You may go, Chloe, if you like. I think I will remain . . ."

"Oh, do come, my Lady. You would enjoy it. You would, I know."

"Ah," Esme sighed, "to please you. Very well, I will go."

As the day was gentle, they decided to walk, making their way through empty streets to the festival field. Chloe kept up a running banter all the way, talking of this or that small thing she had noticed in the Dragon King's household, comparing it to what she knew of other royal houses.

Esme listened with half an ear, letting her maid chirp on like a sparrow, happy not to have to think at all, but just listen. Her dark mood of the night before had returned with the morning. And though she tried to master it, she found it engulfed her more securely than she guessed. For try as she might, she could not banish it from her.

So, with no hope of ridding herself of it, and lacking the immediate strength to fight it, she merely gave herself over to the despair she felt and let it tug her along where it would.

What am I to do? she thought. What am I to do?

She had, with the death of her husband, inherited vast holdings of lands. Several small villages were under her protection, as well as a castle and a summer estate, each with a full complement of stewards, overseers, and servants. Her treasury was one of the largest in Elsendor. But all this she would have given up gladly, if only it would have offered her a glimmer of hope for happiness.

"Do not frown so, my Lady," said Chloe.

"What?" Esme pulled herself out of her gloomy thoughts.

"Promise me you will try to enjoy the occasion."

Esme smiled. "I shall try. I know it is not seemly for a lady to scowl like a haggard." She sighed again. "Oh, Chloe, what am I going to do?"

Once at the festival site, they made their way among the yellow-and-white striped pavilions, now being jostled by the roaming populace. They walked toward the King's pavilion, pausing to watch acrobats and jugglers, or to sample the treats of the vendors.

"Lady Esme! Lady Esme!" she heard a voice call out, and turned to see the two little Princesses running to her. "We are so glad you came! Oh!" said Brianna breathlessly, "there is much to see!"

"So much to see!" said Elena. "Come with us!"

"Do you want to watch us in a game?" asked Brianna.

"Oh, please," cried Elena, "you must!"

"I would love to," said Esme.

The girls were off again, quick as grasshoppers, darting toward a large ring of people gathered around a game of skittles.

"I am glad you changed your mind, Esme." Bria fell into step beside her.

Esme dropped her eyes to her feet. "It was Chloe's idea . . ." she said slowly. Bria heard the undertone of despair in her voice. "I must have gabbled like a fishwife last night."

"What is a little gabbling between friends? I welcome your confidence. If you care to talk, I will listen."

Esme did not speak again for a moment. The two women walked together in silence. "It is strange, is it not?" she said finally.

"What is?"

"Life." Esme glanced at her friend and then turned away again quickly. "Only yesterday we had so much before us—so many bright hopes for the future, so many dreams, so much joy. Those were good days—"

"And will be again."

"For others perhaps, but not for me. It seems my fate was cast from the beginning. I was never—"

"All were born for happiness, Esme. But you have seen much of pain and trouble, and it will take time to heal those inner wounds. You must not expect them to disappear in an evening."

"I thought by coming here it would be different. But I have brought my trouble with me."

"Then we shall do whatever can be done to free you— and you must also help."

"I will try, Brig. I will try for your sake."

"Not for me, dear friend. For yourself."

THE HUNT MOVED THROUGH THE THICK-GROWN TRAILS of Pelgrin Forest, and the wood rang with the voices of the hunters and the sounding of horns whenever beast was caught or trophy won. In a clearing, through which coursed a shining stream, Quentin and Durwin stopped to allow their horses to drink.

"Tired so soon?" asked Durwin. Other riders entered the meadows, also paused at the water, and then went on.

"I should return to the festival. My presence there will be required to judge the games." He listened to the crash of horses and riders through the underbrush, and felt the warm sun on his face. "It is a good hunt, eh?"

"So it is! I do not remember one better. But you go on; I will remain a little. I would like to see the young Prince ride. It is a joy to watch him. I shall try to find them."

Quentin turned Blazer and started back across the meadow; he waved to Durwin and galloped away.

Durwin struck off for the far side of the clearing where a trail entered the wood. He knew the forest well, and had a hunch where he might find Toli and Gerin, for he had seen them pushing a southerly course just before he and the King had entered the meadow.

How long has it been since I have lived in the forest? he wondered. Ah, too long! I have forgotten how peaceful it is, and how fragrant and beautiful. Perhaps I should leave the castle and come back to my old home. Perhaps. But I am content to be where the King wants me. Yes, I am content.

These and other thoughts occupied his mind as he rode along the leaf-laden byways of the forest. The green shadows were cool; yellow sunlight struck through open patches in the leafy canopy, dappling the path with dancing light. Durwin savored the solitude of the wood and felt his heart soar like a hawk on an upward draft.

Just then the air shivered with a startled cry—a sudden, sharp yelp. It hung for a moment and then was cut off. The forest deadened the sound, muffling it so that Durwin could not discern the source. But it seemed to come from somewhere very close at hand.

He spurred his steed forward, heedless of the branches reaching out for him. There was another shout, closer this time.

Durwin threw the reins to the side, and the horse careened through the underbrush. Nettles tore at his legs. He ducked branches and urged the horse to greater speed. He saw a movement through the trees just ahead. He caught a fleeting glimpse of a horse rearing, and dark shapes like shadows darting through the wood.

The next instant he was through the trees and pounding into a wider place in the trail. There before him he saw Toli and Prince Gerin on horseback, with three men in dark clothing around them. The men had short swords and were circling the riders, trying to get at them. Only Riv's flashing hooves kept these assailants at bay.

Without thinking, Durwin loosed a shout and dashed forward. The men heard the whoop and turned to see a new threat bearing down on them. The circle broke as one of the foe turned to meet the hermit.

Before the man could raise his sword, Toli whirled Riv and the warhorse's shoulder knocked him to the ground. He yelled as he went down; his two companions bolted and ran, melding back into the forest.

The man on the ground looked up, fear twisting his begrimed features. He was bleeding from a cut lip. He spat once and then lunged between the horses, gaining his feet as he made for the trail's edge. He dove into the brake and was gone.

"Who were they?" asked Durwin. He felt his heart racing in his chest.

"I do not know," answered Toli. "We merely stopped here to choose a direction—they were on us in an instant."

"Are you sound, young master?" the hermit asked.

Prince Gerin nodded slowly; his eyes showed white all around.

"What do you think they wanted?"

Toli squinted his eyes in the direction of the fleeing assailants. "That I mean to find out." He glanced from the Prince to Durwin quickly. "Stay with Durwin, young sir. He will look after you. I will be but a moment."

The Prince seemed about to protest, but shut his mouth and obeyed.

"Be careful, Toli. You have no weapons."

"Return to the field at once," ordered Toli. "I will meet you there directly." With that he urged Riv forward into the undergrowth after the mysterious men.

9

"SOME WICKEDNESS IS AFOOT," SAID DURWIN QUIETLY. "I feel it. There is evil close about."

Prince Gerin peered at the hermit closely. The boy set his jaw and stared ahead grimly. The act reminded Durwin of another who had faced trouble with the same silent resolve. How very like his father the young Prince was.

They were riding back along the trail—the way Toli and the Prince had come—when Durwin put out a hand and they stopped. "Listen!" he hissed. Both cocked their heads to one side. They heard a rustle in the bushes behind them along the path.

"Perhaps Toli is returning," offered the Prince.

Durwin felt the darkness around him increase. He could almost see it as a presence, feel its desperate strength. It occurred to him that he had encountered such a malignant force before, and in exactly the same way—a long time ago.

"We must run for it!" he whispered harshly. Gerin acted quickly and without question. With a snap of the reins the two horses leapt away. They charged along the winding forest path toward the safety of the open plain. They had not run far before they met two men in the path ahead, wearing the same dark clothing as the others they had encountered. The men waved swords in front of the horses and shouted fiercely. The horses stopped and turned. Durwin pulled his mount around and Gerin did the same, but as they made to retreat, two more ruffians stepped out onto the path behind them.

"There!" cried Durwin, pointing into the brush. He hesitated and allowed the Prince to flash past and then darted after him.

But the pony became entangled in the undergrowth and went down. Prince Gerin yelped as he was pitched over his mount's head to the ground where he landed with a grunt.

"Hurry!" shouted Durwin. "Get back in the saddle! Hurry!"

The boy leaped back to his feet and grabbed at the dangling reins as the horse struggled to its knees. He was back in the saddle even before the animal had regained its legs. "Ride!" shouted Durwin. "Ride!"

The hermit glanced down and saw hands reaching out for him. He slashed down with the reins and heard someone curse. He spurred his mount after the fleeing Prince, but felt his arm caught and held. The horse jerked away and Durwin was hauled from the saddle, struggling as he fell.

He landed on his back at the edge of the trail. There was a flash in the shadow, and he heard the air sing above his head. He squirmed and rolled to his knees and felt a sharp sting in his side. As he half-turned and threw himself backwards toward the trail, he heard the rush of air through clenched teeth and saw the glancing light arc toward him. The blow caught him low in the back; his knees buckled, and he toppled onto the trail.

Durwin put his hand to his side and felt the warm wetness seeping through his clothes. When he brought his hand away, he saw it dripping red in the dimness of the forest. The wound burned now; flames spread through him from the throbbing pain just below the ribs.

He tried to raise himself, but fell back—legs numb and unfeeling.

There was a quick movement beside him, a shout in the forest a little way off, and the thrashing of branches. He heard another shout further away and then silence.

Time gathered itself into a ball, slowed, and hovered without moving. Durwin's mind raced. He had been struck down by an unseen sword. Instead of finishing him, the attackers had gone after Prince Gerin. He must alert Toli, but how? He tried to call out, but the effort brought a flash of white-hot pain to his side. He coughed and spat. His spittle was flecked with blood.

The wound is bad, he told himself, but no matter. He lay back, panting. Toli must be summoned. The Holy Hermit of Pelgrin Forest closed his eyes and began to pray.

"God Most High, hear your servant in his time of need. Guide Toli here to save us. Bring him quickly before it is too late. Keep the Prince safe, I pray. Keep him safe . . ."

Dark mist rolled over him, engulfing him, and slowly his lips stopped moving. He lay back in the soft, mossy turf of the forest pathway, an ugly red stain spreading slowly beneath him.

QUENTIN HAD REACHED THE EDGE OF PELGRIN AND started back across the plain when he hesitated. Was that a cry he heard? He stopped rock-still.

The air was calm and warm; light breezes waited idly, lifting the leaves and blades of grass around him. Nearby a skylark warbled a song to the sun.

But to Quentin it was as if the heavens had dimmed for an instant, as if a cloud had passed before the sun, blotting out its face for a brief moment. Then all was as before, except the King's senses pricked and tingled to an unknown danger.

At once he turned Blazer back into the forest, sending his thoughts ahead to sift the wind for direction. He struck along a southerly path, sensing that the cry he imagined had come from that direction. The boles of trees, bands of light and shadow, blurred as Quentin flew along this dim corridor of Pelgrin. His heart thumped in his chest and he urged Blazer onward ever faster, choosing his course on instinct alone.

Upon reaching a small clearing, he halted. A bundle lay ahead in the trail. Was that a body?

Quentin slid from the saddle and hurried forward. He knelt down and rolled the body into his arms.

"Durwin!"

The hermit's face had gone gray as ashes. His eyelids flickered, and he focused cloudy eyes on his friend. "Ah, Quentin. . . ."

"What has happened? Who has done this to you?"

"The Prince . . . your son. They have taken him. . . ."

"Who? Here, let me help you—"

"No, no. Leave me. Find your son. They went through there." He nodded his head weakly.

"How many?"

"Three or four. I did not see them clearly. Maybe more. Toli—ah!" Pain twisted his features; his limbs convulsed and then relaxed.

"Easy," soothed Quentin. "We will find them. Rest now." He struggled to remain calm.

"Yes, I will rest." The hermit's voice was thin, but his eyes looked deeply into Quentin's. "We have traveled far together, eh?" He coughed and his eyes squeezed shut.

"Yes, and we have many roads yet to ride." Quentin held him more tightly.

"You will ride them alone, I think. But I am content—I am not afraid to die."

"You are not dying!" Quentin shouted desperately. Tears rose in his throat. "You will survive. Help is coming."

"I fear it will come too late." He gazed at Quentin again. "Do not blame Toli. It is not his fault."

"I do not understand," Quentin said.

"Be strong, Quentin. Remember, you are the King. You must lead your kingdom. This will be your sorest test, your darkest day."

"No!" Quentin could see his friend was slipping away. "You will never die!"

"So it is! The spirit never dies . . . never. We will meet again, fair friend. I will wait for you. No pain, no fear. . . ."

"Do not leave me!" cried Quentin.

A slight tremor passed through the hermit's body, and then he lay still. His breath whispered away in a sigh. Durwin was dead.

10

"Fools! Imbeciles!" Nimrood raged. "What have you done?" He whirled around the circle, thrusting a crooked finger into the grim faces before him. "You will pay for this with your lives!"

"We only did as you told us," said the leader of the temple guards. "How were we to know he would leave the Prince? They were together."

"Silence! Let me think!" He stopped to glare down at Prince Gerin, who stared back defiantly. "I send you out to strike down a man and you bring me a boy."

"He's the Prince, I say!" maintained the man.

"Is this true?" asked Nimrood. His eyes bored into the lad. "What is your name?"

"Gerin," he replied steadily. "Who are you?"

"Impudent cub!" The old man reached out and cuffed the boy, leaving a red welt on his cheek.

"My father will deal with you," said the Prince. "Let me go."

"No," said Nimrood slowly as an idea took shape in his mind. "Here is an opportunity I can turn to advantage." He smiled cannily. "Oh, yes indeed." He chuckled to himself and then snapped, "Bring him!"

They started off on foot, threading deeper into the forest. Two big men shoved the Prince forward. When he fell on hands and knees, they hauled him up by his collar and shoved him forward again. Another guard seized Tarky's reins and led the animal away.

"You two!" Nimrood said, pointing to the two behind. "Stay well to the rear of us. If anyone comes after, put them off the trail. Do you hear?"

The two men looked worriedly at one another, but nodded and dropped behind. Soon Nimrood, the Prince, and the others were lost in the dense growth of forest. The two guards watched their comrades disappear. One muttered to the other, "I do not like this foul business. Not a whit, by Ariel! We are guards of the temple, but he has made us highwaymen and kidnappers!"

"I did not hear your voice oppose him," the other replied nastily. "We are in it now and have no choice but to see it through."

"Aye, but where is it going to lead in the end? That is what I want to know. There is death here—mark my words. Death. This will be the undoing of the temple."

"Silence! There is enough to worry about as it is. If we are to get out of this with our skins, we'll need to keep sharp and stop mewling like sick cats."

"He has taken the Prince! By Ariel—"

"Shut up! We are in this as deep as he. No sense in yammering on about it. Come on, let's be about our business."

The two walked off in the direction the others had gone, listening nervously to the forest sounds, hoping against hope that no one would come after them.

TOLI ENTERED THE TRAIL AND PROCEEDED TO THE clearing. Before he even saw the huddled forms upon the ground, he knew something was very wrong. His heart jerked within him, quickening to the terrible apprehension that overpowered him.

He threw himself down from his horse and ran toward the place where Quentin held the body of Durwin in his arms.

"My lord! Oh!" He stopped short and knelt, knowing now what had happened.

Quentin raised his head slowly. His face glistened with tears. "Durwin is dead," he said softly. "Dead. Toli, I. . . ." His voice trailed off and he clutched the body to him again, his shoulders shaking with the sobs that wracked him.

Toli felt as if his heart had been cut in two. He sat back on his heels and raised his face to the sky, showing pale blue overhead through the trees. In a moment the quiet green glade hummed with a gentle sound as Toli raised the ancient Jher song for the dead.

> *"Whinoek brea faro lleani,*
> *Fallei sensi nessina wea."*

The words were simple, and Quentin understood them. Toli sang, "Father of Life, receive our brother. Grant him peace in your great home."

To the Jher people, who had no permanent home, roaming the northern forests as they did, Whinoek's great home to them meant eternal joy and safety and comfort—and peace, which to the gentle Jher was the highest fulfillment.

After a time the song stopped, fading softly away on the air. Quentin lowered the body of the hermit carefully to the ground and, with Toli, arranged the limbs. He brushed a strand of hair away from the broad face of the man he had loved, and kissed the high forehead gently. Then he rose slowly.

"They will curse the day of their birth," he murmured. "I am going after them."

"No, let me. I—"

"I am going. Ride to the castle. Bring a bier for him, and take him back. I will join you there when I have found my son."

"But—" objected Toli. He stood and approached the King.

"That is all," Quentin cut him off coldly. "You will do as I say. When you have finished, bring a company of knights and come after me if I have not yet returned."

"What are you going to do, Sire?" Toli was frightened by the look in his master's eye.

"I am going to bring back the Prince." With that, he turned away and strode to where Blazer waited patiently. Snatching up the reins, he swung himself into the saddle, then glanced back once more at the body of the hermit on the ground. "Good-bye, old friend," he said simply, raising a hand slowly in final salute. Then he was gone.

"WHAT CAN BE TAKING THEM SO LONG?" WONDERED Bria aloud. "They should have returned long ago."

Esme, sitting next to the Queen in the royal pavilion, craned her neck and gazed toward the forest. "I do not see anyone coming. But you know men and their hunting. I would not wonder but that they became caught up in the chase and have forgotten everything else."

"You are right. I am certain that is what has happened." She spoke the words, but in her heart she was far from convinced. Bria turned her eyes once more to the costumed mummers performing before her. The bright disguises glittered in the sun, and the two young Princesses giggled at the pantomime, clapping their hands with glee. Bria tried to maintain a show of interest in the performance, but once and again her eyes stole back across the plain toward the forest, watching for the return of Quentin, Durwin, and the others. But she saw no sign of anyone, so at last forced herself to concentrate on the play.

"Look!" Esme whispered urgently. "A rider!"

The Queen raised her eyes and looked where Esme was pointing. She could just make out the form of one rider approaching from across the plain.

"Oh! Only one!" An arrow of dread pierced her heart. "Something has happened!"

"We cannot be certain," Esme said lightly. "Let us wait until we have heard what he has to say. Perhaps it is only a messenger on his way to tell us the King will be late—which we already know." She laughed, but there was no happiness in her voice.

"Who is it? Can you see?" Bria stood.

"No, not yet."

They waited. Tension drew taut as a bowstring.

Queen Bria crumpled the front of her gown in her hands as the rider drew closer.

"It is Toli!" cried Esme.

"Yes, I see him now!" Bria stepped down from her chair. "Come. I cannot abide here another moment. Stay here with Chloe," she told her daughters. "I will return in a moment."

"I will look after them, my Lady," answered Chloe.

The two women dashed onto the field, scattering the actors, who parted to let them pass and then continued once more with their performance.

They met Toli at the edge of the festivities. "What is it?" asked the Queen, her intuition already answering the worst.

Toli turned grave eyes on her. He did not look at Esme. Bria felt a thin blade of terror slide under her ribs. "The King—" she whispered. "Not the King."

Toli took the Queen's hand. "My Lady, the King is well," he said softly, searching her eyes, hoping to find further words there.

"Yes, continue," said Bria. She stared steadily back.

"Durwin is dead."

"How?" Bria gasped.

"They were set upon by kidnappers in the forest. He died protecting the Prince."

"And the Prince? He is safe?" said Esme.

"Gone. The Prince has been taken—"

"No!" murmured Bria. The sound of the clattering, noisy din around them faded, and she had the sensation of the world blurring before her as she staggered beneath the force of a killing blow.

"Where is the King?" asked Esme, fighting to keep her voice under control.

"He was with Durwin when I found him. He has gone after the Prince." He glanced briefly at Esme, as if noticing her for the first time. "I am to fetch a bier and bring Durwin to the castle, then return with a complement of knights to follow the King."

"We will see to the bier. You must go at once and assemble the knights as the King has ordered. Do not delay."

Toli hesitated. Those had not been the King's instructions.

Bria came to herself. "Yes, I agree. You must not waste a moment. Go now." Bria placed a hand on his arm. "Please hurry."

Toli still hesitated. "I should have been there," he said. "I should have never left them alone."

"No," said Esme. "There is no time. What is done is done."

"Go. He will need you with him," Bria added.

"Very well. You will find Durwin in a glade along the southern trail. I will send someone to lead you." Toli bowed his head and then he was back in the saddle, racing once more for the forest where he would find the knights he sought, for most were taking part in the hunt.

Bria turned to her friend. She tried to speak, but no words would come.

Esme put an arm around her shoulders. "Come. There is much to do. We have work to occupy us while we wait. And we must pray the wait is not long."

"Yes, we must pray for Quentin and Gerin. They will need our prayers this day."

11

Toli reached Pelgrin and struck along the foremost trail leading into the heart of the forest. The hunt had moved deeply into the wood and scattered widely. He would have to keep a sharp eye for signs along the trail, and listen for any sounds of nearby hunters. He came to a place where a small stream trickled among the great trunks of ancient oaks. Along the low banks he saw the imprints of horses' hooves where several had stopped to drink before pressing on. Without a second thought he leaped across the stream and into the forest after them.

Soon he was rewarded with the blast from a horn. The long, ringing note was sounded from far-off, but the tone lingered in the air and gave Toli all the direction he needed. Alert to the minute signs of the hunters' passing, Toli followed the party unerringly through the thick, woodsy tangle. Riv charged through the underbrush, head down and ears laid back. The horse, so responsive to his master's subtlest commands, passed like a glimmering shade between trees and outstretched branches.

And then, a little way ahead, Toli heard voices. He slapped Riv on the rump once more and they jumped a fallen log, landing square in the center of a well-used path.

"Ho there!" one of the men cried when he saw Toli. "Toli! Look here!" The others with him looked up from their work. They were a party of four—Lords Galen and Bossit, Sir Hedric and Sir Dareth—and they were gutting a boar they had just killed. Toli thanked the Most High that these able and brave men were the first he met in his search for assistance.

"Lord Galen—good sirs. . . ." Toli greeted them. He reined Riv to a halt, and the horse snorted loudly. The others saw the steed's white-lathered flanks and shoulders and knew Toli had come on an errand of some urgency. "My lord, what is it?" asked Lord Bossit. A look of concern clouded his features.

"The King's minister has been struck down, and the Prince kidnapped," said Toli, his breath coming hard from his ride.

"By the gods!" exploded Sir Hedric, jumping to his feet.

"How?"

"When?"

Toli took a deep breath. "We were set upon by assassins in the wood not far from here—only a short while ago. I went after them, but they doubled back and attacked the Prince. Durwin fell protecting him."

"The hermit dead? The heir gone?" They looked grimly at one another.

Toli continued, "Mount up at once and come with me. We ride to meet the King, who is pursuing them."

"By Zoar, these rogues will pay for this outrage!" vowed Lord Galen. "We are at your command, sir!"

With that the knights abandoned their kill, mounted their horses, and fell into line behind Toli, who led them toward the place where he had encountered the attackers. They made their way as quickly as they could and at last reached the glade.

It was quiet and cool in the shaded clearing. A number of tiny yellow butterflies flitted among the leaves, darting in and out of the falling beams of light that slanted in through the trees. A hermit thrush sang in the high treetops—a clear, sparkling liquid sound, pure and sweet.

The glade seemed enchanted, and no one dared break the spell of the place.

Durwin still lay where they had left him, so still and peaceful he might have merely dozed off for a nap. No one spoke at first, overcome with the strangeness of the scene before them.

The hermit lay dead, and yet seemed in such perfect peace that those who looked upon him could but stare in awe. His presence was strong in the place; each one felt it as if he had touched them.

"Someone should stay with him," said Lord Bossit. "I will."

"No," replied Toli quietly. "He is safe here in the forest. Nothing can harm him now. Go back to the castle and lead the others here. The Queen is bringing a bier. See that all is attended to."

"As you say, my lord." He left at once.

"The King rode to the south," said Toli. He turned Riv and took up the trail. The other knights followed without a word.

QUENTIN COMBED A WIDE SWATH THROUGH THE FOR-est, working first this way for half a league or more, and then cutting back the other way. But for all his care and vigilance, he failed to uncover any sign of the fleeing assassins.

Still he pushed on, bending ever southward, with a feeling that this was the direction the abductors had chosen, though he knew they might well have taken another. The forest was huge; to cover it all would take scores of men and many months of diligent searching. As he rode, Quentin fought down the growing sense of futility and desperation that swelled within him, building up inside like a vile black broth set to the fire.

He paused periodically to listen but detected only the

normal, sleepy sounds of the wood. He went on.

Then, quite without warning, Blazer stumbled down a short, steep bank of hill, and Quentin found himself on the well-used southern road that led to Hinsenby and then bent southwest along the coast. He sat still in the saddle for a moment, scanning the road both ways. When nothing out of the ordinary presented itself to his gaze, he turned once more southward and continued on.

After riding a little way he came to a dell where the road dipped to meet a stony-banked stream. Here he found his first clue, for in the dust of the road at the banks of the stream were a number of footprints, and the hoofprints of a horse.

Whoever made those prints had emerged from the forest at this point, having followed the stream until it met the road. Across the stream the tracks led off down the way. Blazer splashed across the water, and Quentin leaned low in the saddle to examine the marks. It was difficult to tell anything for certain from these prints, for there were others all along the road.

The hunt! thought Quentin. How dull I am. These and all the rest were made by people on their way to the festival. At once his hope, so quickly born, died and shrank away. But not entirely. Of all the various tracks in the dust only a few were leading southward. All the others pointed toward the north and Askelon.

Seizing this meager scrap of evidence, Quentin once again urged the sturdy Blazer onward. The steed flew over the wide road, and the King searched along its length for any trace of his son's passing.

"LISTEN!" SAID ONE TEMPLE GUARD TO THE OTHER. "Someone comes."

Both stopped and peered back behind them on the road. They could hear the tinkling jingle of tiny bells— such as a horse would wear on its tack.

"You get off the road. If they stop, draw sword and be ready," said the first.

"But—" protested the other. His hands trembled as they touched the weapon concealed beneath his cloak at his side.

"Quickly! I will stay here and try to put them astray."

"Why were we chosen for this cursed task?" grumbled the other.

"Do as I say! Hurry! They are almost upon us!"

The frightened guard threw a dark look at his comrade, and then disappeared into the underbrush at the side of the road. In a moment the first could see horse and rider approaching rapidly.

"You there!" shouted Quentin when he came. The nervous accomplice turned and stood blinking at him, pretending to be unsure as to whether it was he who had been addressed. Then his eye caught sight of the wrought gold clasp that secured the rider's cloak—a terrible, twisting dragon, the royal blazon.

A shiver ran through the man as Quentin was recognized; color drained from his face.

"So you know your King when you see him, do you?"

The man licked his lips and said, "I am at your service, Sire." His eyes shifted unsteadily.

"How long have you been on this road?" demanded Quentin.

"Well, we—that is, I . . . not long . . . I mean—"

"Where are you bound?"

"To Hinsenby, Sire."

"Are you alone?" Quentin watched the man struggle under his questions.

"Yes, lord." The man's eyes shifted again.

"Have you seen anyone on the way?"

The man thought for a moment and then said, "Yes, I did. Only a short while ago it was. Back there—back by the stream. A group of travelers. Merchants, I think."

"How many?"

"Five, six maybe. Not more. They were bound for Askelon, I would warrant."

Quentin turned in the saddle and looked behind him. No, the prints had pointed the other way. Then he saw the tracks leading away from the road. He turned back to the man just in time to see him glance to the side and then quickly back.

"Merchants, you said?"

"Sire, I believe they were."

"And are you a merchant, too?" asked the King suspiciously.

"I am . . ."—the man hesitated—"a pilgrim, Sire."

"They were going to Askelon, you say? Was there a boy with them, a boy on horseback?"

The supposed pilgrim opened his mouth, but the words stuck on his tongue.

"Answer quickly, friend! I find your manner most peculiar."

The traveler flushed. "No, there was no boy with them. I saw none, at least."

"Liar!" shouted Quentin, scowling furiously. "In truth I saw the hoofprints at the water, and they continue this way."

The temple guard stared at the King sullenly and said nothing.

"It is no small thing to lie to your King," continued Quentin in a voice strained but in control. "I will give you one more chance. Where did they go?"

"I know not, Sire. Please . . . it is not—"

"Are you in league with them?" shouted Quentin. "Answer me!"

Just then there was a rustle in the bushes at the side of the road. Quentin whirled around as another man, dressed like the first in dark tunic and long cloak despite the heat of the day, leaped from his hiding place, sword in hand. The second man lunged clumsily forward, eyes showing terror. "Strike!" cried this attacker. Quentin turned to see a blade appear in the first pilgrim's hand as well.

Zhaligkeer sang as it slid from the sheath; the long

blade shone forth with cool brillance from its fierce inner fire. Quentin swung the mighty sword overhead. "You! You killed Durwin!" he cried.

The two men saw the terrible sword and fell back with a startled cry.

"Murderers!" shouted Quentin. "Cowards!"

"Mercy!" cried the first assailant. "Mercy . . . I beg you!"

Rage like molten metal seared through Quentin's mind; its wild fury rushed through him with blinding force. "I will show you mercy," he cried, "the mercy you showed Durwin!"

Before the man could turn and flee, the Shining One whispered in the air and flashed in a deadly downward arc. The would-be assassin quickly lifted his blade above his head to take the blow, but the sword shattered in his hand and the pieces fell to earth. He shrieked and fell to his knees, the sound of certain death whistling after him.

"Mercy!" he screamed. "Forgive me!" Bright Zhaligkeer filled his horror-stricken eyes with its unearthly light, and he threw his hands over his face. The stroke caught him at the base of the neck, cutting short his last cry of remorse. The man pitched forward into the road, dead when he met the ground.

A thin crimson ribbon trickled along Zhaligkeer's blade. Quentin swiveled in the saddle to meet the second villain, who threw down his weapon and dove headlong into the brush, disappearing into the forest.

The rage which had burned so hot in Quentin's veins left him as suddenly as it had flared. The King stared at the misshapen heap in the dust, then at the sword in his hand, and his heart froze in his chest. Zhaligkeer's fiery blade now appeared as any ordinary metal, glimmering darkly in the fading light of late afternoon.

The bright white flame of the Shining One had gone out.

12

SILENTLY THE WOMEN ENTERED THE GLADE—LITTLE more than a wide place in the trail. Esme swung down from her horse, and Bria from hers. Lord Bossit halted the small, two-wheeled wagon which carried the bier. The wooden wheels creaked to a stop, the only sound heard in the place.

"Oh!" gasped Bria as she beheld the beloved hermit. She walked slowly but steadily forward and knelt beside the body. Quietly her tears began to fall.

Esme approached and put an arm around the Queen's shoulders.

"Good-bye, fair friend," whispered Bria. Her outstretched fingers touched Durwin's folded hands, now cold. She then turned to Lord Bossit, who stood reverently nearby. "My mother is waiting," she said. "Let us take him back."

Bossit nodded to the driver of the wagon, and the two men lifted the body onto the waiting bier.

When told of the tragedy Alinea had said nothing, though her hands trembled. When she spoke, her voice was soft, yet steady; she had already mastered her grief, or had put it aside for the moment.

"Yes," she had said, "you must go at once and bring him back. Take him to his apartments. We will prepare the body there. I will await your return, and while I wait I shall pray—for Prince Gerin, yes, but no less for Quentin and for the rest of us. Now go, and may the Most High be with you."

Esme had marveled at the dowager's quiet strength; her bearing calmed those around her, removing much of the sting of the bitter news. Esme recalled another dark day long ago now, the day Eskevar had fallen in battle. Days after the King's funeral, Esme had asked the Queen how she had been able to remain so strong, comforting all around her, yet seeming never to require comfort herself.

"No, I am not strong," Alinea had told her. They were sitting in the garden among the primroses. Durwin was there, too. He had been the Queen's constant companion during those troubled days. "Though it is true I am no stranger to grief, one never becomes a friend to sorrow. But Durwin here has shown me the way of hope. This hope I carry within me makes the burden lighter, and I find I am able to help others who have not such hope."

"Then tell me, my Lady, for I would know. How can I obtain this hope of yours? Where is it to be found?" Esme had asked. She still remembered Alinea's words.

And she remembered Durwin's too. "The hope you seek is born of belief in the Most High, the One True God of all," he had told her. "Seek him and you will find him. He is ever reaching out to those who truly desire to know him."

"What must I do? Where is his temple?"

Durwin laughed. "He is not like other gods. He has no temple, and accepts no gifts of silver or gold, or sacrifices of helpless creatures."

"No?" This she found most puzzling.

"No," laughed Durwin again. "He wants *you*. All of you: your heart and spirit. He wants your love and worship, everything—he will not settle for less."

"This is a demanding god you serve, hermit."

"Yes, he is as you say—demanding. But the blessing he bestows on all who come near him are beyond all price. It is life he gives, and nothing less."

Esme wondered at the words at the time. They sounded strange to her, and so unlike anything she had ever heard from any priest. She remembered how her heart had tugged within her as the hermit spoke. Ah, she thought, but I was younger then. So young. Still, I wanted to believe what Durwin said was true. Is wanting to believe the same as believing? Yet, the time passed, and I thought no more about it, until now. Why now? Is it too late?

Esme came out of her reverie and found Bria's eyes upon her. "You are lost in thought," said Bria. They had reached the edge of the forest and were starting across the plain. Askelon shone clearly in the light of the westering sun, throwing a great shadow toward them.

"I was thinking of another sad time," replied Esme. "Of Eskevar's passing."

"Often I have thought of that dark day. When Gerin was born, how I wished he was there to see his grandson. It would have made him proud, I know. Yes, and no less proud to see his granddaughters." Her features twisted in anguish. "Oh, Esme! My son is taken from me! What am I going to do?"

"The King is searching for him, and Toli brings help. They will find him. They will bring him back safely."

"He is so young. I am afraid they will. . . ." She could not bring herself to complete the thought.

"Do not think it! No one would dare harm the Prince. No one. He will be safe." Esme forced a smile. "You would not be a true mother if you did not worry after your son. But Quentin will find him."

Bria nodded. After a time she said, "I am happy you are here, Esme. I will need a good friend in the days to come."

"I am your friend always."

They rode the rest of the way to the castle in silence, each wrapped in her own thoughts, but feeling the warmth of the other's presence.

QUENTIN BLINKED HIS EYES IN AMAZEMENT AT THE sword in his hand. One fell thrust and the fire of the white lanthanil blade had been quenched. The awful significance of what had happened struck him like a thunderbolt. And he heard once more the words spoken at the anointing of the sword:

> *"Never in malice, never in hate, never in evil*
> *shall this blade be raised. But in righteousness*
> *and justice forever shall it shine."*

That was the promise of the Shining One, and he, in one flash of anger and hate, had broken that vow. And in breaking it, the hand of the Most High was removed from him. The magnitude of his crime overwhelmed him.

"No!" he cried. His own voice rang hollow in his ears, condemning him.

The strength seeped out of his arm, and he let go of the sword. The blade spun from his hand and fell to the dust of the road, not a pace from the body of the wretch he had cut down.

Murderer! the voice of the dead man screamed at him. Murderer! Then the forest rang with accusing voices. The King is a murderer! He has broken his trust! Murderer! Where is your Most High now? Murderer!

Quentin clamped his hands over his ears to stop the voices, but they had gotten inside his head. He could not shut them out. In horror he gazed at the Shining One, now lying in the dust, and at the crumpled body beside it. His stomach churned and heaved with revulsion; a spasm rocked him backward in the saddle.

"No!" he screamed once more, a cry of utter despair. "No!"

Then he turned Blazer, sank his spurs deep into the horse's flanks, and fled down the road.

"WHAT IS THAT?" SIR GALEN RAISED HIS HAND TOWARD an object in the trail ahead.

Toli looked up quickly. They were stopped at the stream, allowing their horses a quick drink before moving on. His eyes narrowed as he turned his gaze toward where the knight pointed.

Toli's eagle-sharp vision recognized the shapeless form as vaguely human. "It is a body," he said, climbing into the saddle.

When the others reached the spot, Toli was already stooping over the corpse. Toli turned it over, and the head lolled obscenely; it was nearly severed from the shoulders. The man's shattered sword lay in pieces beneath him.

"Someone wanted this one dead," remarked Lord Galen, "to strike such a blow."

"Who could have done it?" wondered Sir Dareth. "There are no robbers abroad in this forest, surely."

"Highwaymen would not have set upon such as this. See how he is dressed?" replied Sir Hedric. "Perhaps there was a falling out among thieves."

"Or kidnappers," said Toli slowly. "Yes, I would swear this was one I dealt with in the forest earlier this day. Or another of their company."

"But to strike him down in the road—why?" Sir Dareth shook his head. "It makes no sense. They must have known we would find him."

Toli made a quick search of the immediate area, sifting among the confused tracks in the dust for a clue to what had happened. But he gleaned little for his efforts. There were far too many prints—it was impossible to tell how many men had passed, or who among them had horses and who were afoot. Still, he counted tracks of at least two horses, and one rider had apparently been involved in the fight that had ended the kidnapper's life.

"I believe," said Toli, looking southward, "the King might have passed this way."

"You think this unfortunate attacked the King?" asked Lord Galen incredulously. "It was ill-advised, though there must have been a reason."

Toli nodded thoughtfully and cast a glance skyward. The sun stretched long shadows across the road. "We must bury him quickly. We are already losing the light. I want to follow the trail as long as possible."

At Toli's command, the knights began hacking a shallow grave in the brush at the side of the road, using their swords for the task. Toli and Lord Galen examined the victim's clothing for any clue to who he might have been, or where he might have come from.

When the corpse had been disposed of, the four set off again, though the sun was well down and the first of the evening stars winked overhead. A chill seeped out of the wood as the sky deepened to twilight, but the riders pressed on, heedless of their fatigue or the hunger beginning to gnaw just in back of their belt buckles.

I am certain Quentin was back there, thought Toli as he rode along. I can sense it. But there was something else, too. Something very powerful—more than the death of that unfortunate would account for. But what? What could it be?

13

"WELL, TIP," THE ROUND LITTLE MAN SAID, "HERE'S A comely spot to rest yer bones, eh? Or shall we walk a wee bit further?"

The dog looked at her master and wagged her tail.

"Oh, quite right, quite right. We've come fer enough today. No sense getting amuch away from the road. Quite right ye are." With a clink and a clatter, Pym the tinker began shaking off his burdens, loosening packs and sacks and strings of pots, pans and tools, all of which he carried with him on his back.

But one package he placed carefully on the ground, propping it upright against a stone. His bright eyes glittered with glee, and he rubbed his hands with delight. "Now, Tipper, some firewood!" He clapped his hands. "Jest the thing, eh? Jest the thing. 'Twill be darking soon. First fetch the wood and the fire will follow, eh? Quite right."

In no time the little tinker and his dog were curled before a cozy fire, drinking their soup, watching the stars come out in the sky as night settled peacefully over the land. Every now and then the man stole a look toward the slender, rag-wrapped package that he had propped up against the stone.

"See that, Tip? There's our fortune," he would say and then chuckle to himself.

When they had drunk their broth and sopped the last of it with hunks of dry black bread, the tinker reached for the bundle and laid it across his knees. "Lookee, Tip," he said. "Old Pym has found our fortune. Yes, he has. I told ye he would, I told ye. Lookee, look!"

He carefully pulled the rags away with trembling fingers. And there revealed in the flickering firelight was a great sword: long and thin, tapering almost imperceptibly along its smooth, flawless length to a deadly point. The grip and hilt shone in the firelight as if cut from gemstone.

"Sech a beauty this 'un," he said, his voice hushed in awe. "This are no common blade, no sir. Pym can tell, he can. I know a wee bit about swords, you see, and this 'un's a royal blade if ivver I saw one. Yes, it is." His fingers traced the fine markings along the blade, hardly daring to touch it. His eyes filled with wonder at the sight of the weapon.

The big black dog watched her master, head on paws, listening to the sound of his voice.

"Oh, yes," he continued, "this blade's a beauty. Nivver meant fer common hand. Some 'un'll give good gold fer this—a fortune, ye see. As much as ivver I ask. Why, Tip, we 'uns'll have enough to buy a little wagon. Oh, yes, and another sharping stone—a round 'un with a treadle-foot 'twould be fine. I could sharp knives and shears and plowshares and . . . and anything that needs sharping. Ye know I could, Tip. Ye know it. Why, we 'uns'd make our fortune!"

The tinker gazed at the sword happily, still not quite believing his good luck. Then a shudder went through him as he remembered how he had found the sword.

"A shame 'bout the body, Tip. Oh, terrible shame, that. But I had nothing to do with 't—not a snip. Found him like that, you see. Come upon him in the road. Not long dead, I think.

"Ye saw him first, didn't ye, Tip? Yes. When ye let out that growl I knew something was amiss, didn't I? Yes. Ye don't growl without cause, and that were cause enough. Indeed. A man dead in the road. Terrible thing. Head cut near off, and this—this sword lying in the dust beside him."

He took the sword in his hand and felt its quick strength. His face glowed with admiration. "Old Pym knows craftership when he see it. Yes, sir. Someun'll give good gold to get this back—as much as ivver I ask. Enough for a wagon and a sharping stone."

A thought occurred to him. What if the one dead in the road was the owner? Who would give the gold then?

He frowned and turned the blade in the firelight, shaking his head. "That 'un nivver owned a blade like this," he said at last. "No, sir. No one ivver did—but maybe a King."

Another thought struck him, and his eyes grew round in fright. What if they think I stole it? What if they think it was Old Pym killed that man and took his sword?

"No! I nivver'd kill a man, nor take his blade. Old Pyre's a peaceable fellow. Every'un knows he is. 'Twas in the road. I found it there. How it got there, I cannot say.

"But I must be careful now, oh yes. Very careful. There's some as would steal this away from a poor old tinker. Then poor old Pym would lose his fortune." He stared woefully at his prize, and then his face brightened once more.

"We must hide it, Tip! That's what we 'uns'll do—hide it! Wrap it up in rags and hide it somewhere so not abody can find it. We 'uns'll keep our eyes and ears open—look and listen, that's right, and see what we can learn about this here sword. Yes, we 'uns must hide it well, Tip. And so we will."

DEEP IN THE FOREST, NIGHT HAD BECOME A BLACK CURtain that cut off all sight, save the occasional glimpse of the stars overhead through the interweaving branches. The moon had not yet risen, so the forest byways were difficult to follow. Prince Gerin, shuffling head down, exhausted by his long ordeal, longed to stretch out beneath a tree to rest, and let sleep steal from him the memory of this evil day.

"We will stop here to rest," said Nimrood to the others. "We should have put them off the trail by now. We will not be found, but we must be careful not to be seen."

The men were too tired to speak. They stood wearily on their feet and looked about them, wondering dully how the old man leading them found the strength to keep going. "Hate is what keeps him afoot," whispered one guard to the other. "Look at him, old as he is, and still spry as ever. He'd walk all night."

"He might, but I cannot," answered the man next to him.

"You there!" snapped Nimrood. "Stop muttering and see to our prisoner. You will take turns guarding him. Remember, your heads are forfeit if he escapes."

Prince Gerin heard only part of what was said. The next thing he knew he was being half-dragged, half-shoved to a nearby tree, to be bound there with a cord for the night. He did not fight; he was too sleepy.

"There now," said his guard. "Be good and give us no trouble, young sir. We do not wish to harm you, but you must not try to get away—that could be very painful indeed."

Gerin only looked sleepily at the man, yawned, and lay back against the tree. In a moment he was sound asleep.

"Look at him," said one guard, "not a care in the world."

"He is the Prince, by Ariel! No one would dare lift a hand against him," answered his companion.

"Keep your voice down!" the other rasped. "Don't let Longbeard hear you."

"Ah, Longbeard. Now there's a cold one. He is trouble—I said so from the start. Look what has happened: one dead, the Prince kidnapped. This could bring down the temple!"

"Shh! He watches us! Remember, we are trying to *save* the temple."

"This business is no good . . . no good at all. . . ." the guard mumbled. He yawned and then settled himself to sleep.

The other sat down on a rock, chin in hand, to wait his watch. He glanced around at the others, already sleeping. Their snores droned softly into the night air. He rubbed his neck and shook his head as he felt the weariness engulf him. Yes, he thought, Ervis is right. This is a bad business. It could well bring the temple tumbling down about our ears. But I am not to blame. I only do what I am told. The High Priest himself ordered it. What choice did I have?

He pulled his cloak around him and folded his arms over his chest; his head nodded, and soon he was sleeping like all the rest.

QUENTIN'S EYES BURNED AND HIS BACK ACHED; HE had been in the saddle all day and was not accustomed to it. He could feel his sore muscles stiffening as the chill of night seeped into his bones. Ignoring his body's plea to stop and rest, he pulled his short cloak more tightly around him and plodded on.

The trail had grown too dark to see hours ago, but still he traveled on, hoping by some miracle that he would stumble across the kidnappers. Knowing that his son was still out there somewhere in the dark, frightened, held prisoner—that thought alone kept him going.

Heartsick, numb with misery and despair, Quentin wanted only to throw himself to the ground to weep at his misfortune. A few short hours ago he had walked in the light, his realm secure, the future a bright promise. Now there was only darkness. In the space of half a day he had lost his son, his trusted friend, and—worst of all—the favor of the Most High. His mind reeled at the enormity of his trouble, his heart ached with sorrow, his body throbbed with grief and exhaustion.

How was it possible? How could it happen so quickly? Why was there no warning, no hint at what was to befall him? He could only shake his head in mute wonder.

For an instant he imagined that all he need do was turn Blazer back toward home and all would be well once more. Upon reaching Askelon he would find Durwin alive and the Prince safe in his bed. His sword would be found in his chambers, lying across its hangers below the royal device—the flame intact, the god still with him.

But it was a dream, and the grim reality remained unchanged. Hoping against hope, Quentin determined that somehow he would make everything right again. He could do it; he was the Dragon King. He *would* make it right. With that, he urged Blazer forward. The horse, head down, ambled on.

14

"THEY ARE HERE, MY LADY; THEY HAVE COME." THE maid approached quietly, lest she disturb her Queen's vigil.

"What? Quentin is back? He has returned?" She jumped up, a brief light leaping to her green eyes. Then she saw the look the maid gave her and the light dimmed. "Oh."

"No, the King has not returned." She shook her head, then added, "But Lords Theido and Ronsard are here. You asked me to fetch you as soon as they came. They are waiting in the hall."

Queen Bria left at once and went down to meet her old friends.

"My Lady!" said Ronsard when he saw her approaching from across the great room. They were the only ones in it except for a few servants readying the tables for breakfast, which would be served within the hour. "How lovely you look!" said the knight, smiling warmly.

"Just as I remember your mother," added Theido. "How is Alinea?"

"Theido, Ronsard, I am glad you are here at last. Forgive me for pulling you from your warm beds at this early hour. My mother is well. I am certain she will wish to receive you soon, but I would speak to you first."

Theido saw the dark shadows behind her smile and knew that the Queen had summoned them on a matter of great urgency. "Perhaps this is not the place to discuss important things," he said. "A more private chamber would be better."

"Yes," Bria agreed, "follow me." She led them out of the hall and along the wide corridor to a small room, a council room that contained a heavy table with bankers on either side, and a grouping of high-backed chairs in a further corner. The three entered, closed the door quietly, and took their seats facing one another.

"Now then," said Theido gently, "what has happened?"

Bria looked from one to the other of the two knights—men she had known all her life. Trusted friends of her parents, they had served the Dragon King's throne numerous times and stood always ready to serve again. Their stalwart devotion and her own need overwhelmed her, and she broke down and cried.

"I hardly know where to begin," she said, the tears streaming from her eyes.

The two glanced at one another helplessly, both feeling the depths of her sorrow.

"The words come hard, good sirs." She sniffed and willed herself to stop the tears. The knights waited for her to continue. "Durwin is dead," she said at last.

"By the gods, no!" said Ronsard. "Say not so!"

Theido held up his hand. Bria continued, "And my son has been taken."

"When did this happen?" asked Theido. "And how was it accomplished?"

His stern tone helped Bria to calm herself. She began to speak more easily. "Yesterday, during the hunt. The Prince was to ride in the hunt—he was so proud; it was his first. Toli rode with him. Quentin and Durwin went along, but were to return to join the festival after leading the hunt." She sniffed again, but kept her voice steady. "The King was a long time returning; we thought he had taken up the hunt as well. Then . . . then Toli came and . . . he told us what had happened . . . Oh . . ." She paused, gathered her strength, and continued. "They were attacked and fought off their assailants. Toli followed, but lost the trail. When he rejoined Durwin and Gerin they . . . Durwin was dead and the Prince gone. Quentin sent Toli for help. That was yesterday. I have not seen them since."

Theido did not speak, but his dark eyes and the scowl on his face showed what he was thinking.

Ronsard smashed a clenched fist into the arm of his chair. "Who would dare such a thing? It is an outrage!"

"We must organize a search at once, though—I will be frank—too much time has passed already. If the kidnappers were on horseback, they could have ridden far."

"Still," put in Ronsard, "if ransom is their game, they may not have gone far at all. Indeed, they may be close at hand."

Theido nodded sharply. "Yes, yes. There is something in what you say. But we must hurry in any case. My Lady, in the absence of the King will you give us the authority to command a body of knights?"

"Anything you require."

"Good," said Ronsard. "I know those well who served under me. We can start there."

"Go," Theido told him. "Roust them out, and see that they are outfitted for the trail. I will follow directly."

Ronsard stood and gave a little bow to the Queen. He smiled stiffly and said, "Take courage, my Lady. We will find the boy." He strode out of the room and was gone.

"Is there anything else you can tell us?" Theido asked Bria.

"I know so little. No . . . I have told you all I know. Toli could tell you more, but he is gone. Lord Bossit might know something." She reached out and took Theido's hand. "Find him, good friend. Save my child, as once you saved my father."

Theido pressed her hand, and she felt his confidence flowing into her in that touch. "One way or another we will find him, I know it. I do not know how long it may take, but we will rescue him unharmed. You may believe it; you must believe it."

"I do believe, and I pray that it is so," she said.

"Yes, pray. Your mother has taught me the power of women's prayers. The god, I think, does listen most intently to a woman's heart."

"Then he has heard mine through the night." She bent her head. "Oh, Theido, if anything happens to him I do not th—"

"We will bring him back hale and whole," he soothed. "You will see." He stood slowly. "I must go now and find Lord Bossit. The sooner we make a start, the better."

"Yes, go. And Theido . . . thank you for coming. You have no idea what it means to me."

"Would that it were a happier time, my Lady. But these days shall pass quickly and all will be right again." The lanky knight dipped his head to her and went out.

IN THE LAST HOURS OF THE NIGHT, WHEN ALL THE earth was still and waiting for the new day, Quentin had stopped along the road to rest and had fallen asleep beneath a larch tree, his cloak spread over him. Sleep offered no release or comfort; fitful, troubled was his rest, broken by dreams of futile chases and violent clashes with an unseen enemy. There descended upon him a helpless, hopeless feeling of dread and loss which pierced his heart as cruelly as any poisoned dagger, and though he slept he ached with the pain.

He awoke more wrung out than when he lay down, and rose wearily, stiff from his hard bed among the roots of the tree. In the raw red light of dawn, Quentin rubbed his burning eyes and set about saddling Blazer once more.

"Quentin!" The King turned his eyes to the shout and peered into the dimness of the forest trail. The sun was not yet fully up and the shadows still lay heavy along the road, but he perceived the forms of riders approaching some way off. He waited, then recognized Toli riding toward him out of the gloom.

"Sire, at last we have found you." The Jher's features bore the traces of a sleepless night, but his eyes were as sharp and quick as ever.

"Have you seen anything?" asked Quentin.

"No, my lord. Nothing, that is, except the body of an unfortunate lying in the road." Toli's eyes examined his master carefully.

"Yes," said Quentin flatly. He turned away and put his foot into the stirrup, climbing back into the saddle. "I saw him, too."

Toli did not pursue the matter further, thinking it better to leave it for now. The others joined them, longing for an opportunity to dismount and stretch aching muscles. No one spoke directly to the King. His woeful countenance stilled their tongues.

Only Toli had the temerity to draw him aside to speak openly. "What would you have us do, Kenta?" He used the affectionate name of years past.

"Find my son!" Quentin snapped, his mood raw as the new morning.

Toli wisely ignored the remark. "We should return to the castle for more men; we could cover more ground that way. We need fresh horses and supplies."

"Do what you will," replied the King. His jaw was set. "I will continue the search alone."

"Where will you go?"

"South."

"Why south? They could easily have turned off the trail anywhere. In the night we would have missed the track."

"What else am I to do?" shouted Quentin. The others looked at him. He lowered his voice. "I have no better choice."

"Return with us to Askelon. We will rest and ready ourselves for a proper search. We can send messengers out to all the towns and villages to watch for the brigands. We can—"

"My son has been taken, Toli!" Quentin gestured wildly to the great forest. "I will not return until he is found. I cannot return until he is safe."

Toli searched the face of the one he knew so well, and yet, at this moment, seemed not to know at all. Something has changed my Kenta, he thought. This is not like him at all. Durwin's death and the abduction of his son tormented him, twisted him. Yes, but there was something more. Then he saw it—the empty scabbard at Quentin's side. At once he understood.

"Come back with us, Kenta," he said softly. "Yesterday we had a chance of finding them quickly. But now . . . now they have had enough time to cover their trail, to double back—who knows where they may be by now? To find them we will need help, and a leader. You are the King. Who will lead if you will not?"

"Anyone!" snapped Quentin. "Anyone better than I. You lead the search, Toli!" The King's eyes burned savagely; his mouth contorted into a snarl of hate. "Durwin's blood is on your head, as is my son's if anything happens to him. They would be safe now if you had not left them alone. You are to blame for this— it is your fault!"

Toli, speechless, stared at his master and friend. Never had Quentin raised his voice toward him, never had he shown anger toward him. But then, he reflected, the King is right. It is my fault; I am to blame. I should never have left them alone and in danger like that. I am to blame.

"I am sorry," Toli started. "Sorry—"

"Find my son!" shouted Quentin, his voice shrill. "Find him, or never let me set eyes on you again!"

With that, the Dragon King slashed the reins across the stallion's neck and wheeled him around. Blazer tossed his handsome white head, and Quentin glared at Toli. "Find him," he said softly, his tone a threat. "Just find him."

Toli stood in the road and watched his King ride away. He watched until a bend in the road took him from sight, then went back and mounted Riv, and turned toward Askelon. No one spoke. There was nothing to say.

15

Nimrood sat brooding on a rock, hunched like a bent old root, twisted with age and warped by the dark forces within him. He was waiting for nightfall to undertake the final leg of their journey, for they had reached the eastern edge of the forest and the rest of the way to the temple lay through open ground. He did not want to risk traveling by day; so they waited, restlessly.

Prince Gerin, his young mind alert to all around him, was confident he would not be harmed; and since he appeared in no immediate danger, escape could wait for the right opportunity—if he was not rescued first. He also saw quite plainly that his abductors had little spirit for the task they were about. But the old one, the one with the wild white hair and the face as lined and creased as worn leather, he was one to watch out for.

Who was he? What did he want, and where were they taking him? These questions occupied the young captive as he sat on the ground beneath the tree, two guards with him at all times.

He shifted uneasily, trying to loosen the bonds on his arms. One of the guards eyed him suspiciously, glared, but did not say anything.

When my father comes for me, thought Gerin, you will be very sorry. I hope he comes soon; I am going to miss the rest of the hunt otherwise.

There was no doubt in the young Prince's mind that the King would come for him, would rescue him. All he had to do was wait.

There came a sound in the wood: someone approaching quickly on foot, and noisily with much rustling of branches and cracking of twigs underfoot. Nimrood jumped up, his voice a harsh whisper. "We are found! Draw your weapons!"

The men jumped up and drew their blades, but before anyone had a chance to position themselves for the attack, the intruder stumbled into camp. "What!" he said, startled. "No, wait!" He fell back and landed on his rump.

"You!" said Nimrood. The man was one of the two left behind to guard their escape.

He jumped up, glancing around quickly with frightened eyes. "I was not followed!" he cried. "Put away your swords!"

"You better not have been followed, or I will feed you piecemeal to the birds. Where is your friend?" Nimrood demanded, shoving aside the others.

"Dead—" The man cast a terrified look behind him, as if expecting his own death to come charging out of the woods at any moment.

"How?" Nimrood stood with hands on his hips, eyes boring into the wretch before him.

"He found us on the road. He guessed all."

"Who found you?"

The King! He knew all about us!"

"Bah!" Nimrood's countenance became threatening. The guard quaked with fear. "You said too much!"

"No, by all the gods, I swear it! We told him nothing. He knew—I don't know how he knew, but he did. We did not have a chance."

"How many were with him?"

"His Majesty—the King—was alone. I hid in the bushes in case we were forced to attack him."

"And?" Nimrood stepped closer. The guard grimaced and hurried on with his story.

"Carlin pretended to be a pilgrim, but the King knew different. We tried to put him off, but—"

"You were two against one. What happened?"

The man's eyes rolled with terror. "That sword of his—the Shining One! No man—no army is a match for that! You should have seen it flash. The flames! It blinded us, and I threw my hands over my eyes. When I looked, Carlin was dead. That sword. . . ."

Nimrood's demeanor changed abruptly; his tone became coaxing. "Ah, yes, I see. You did right to come here with the news. Yes. But tell me"—he placed a pale hand on the man's shoulder—"tell me more concerning that sword. The King's sword—what did you call it?"

"The Shining One—everyone knows about it. It is enchanted."

"Is it? How so?" Nimrood smiled a thin, sly, snaky smile. "I do not seem to recall anything about an enchanted sword. But then, I have been long away from Mensandor. Tell me more about it."

Eagerly the men told Nimrood about Zhaligkeer, the King's wonderful sword—about its burning brightness, about the magic mines wherein it was forged, about its strange and terrible powers. They told about how Quentin, still a young man, had come riding out of the mountains with the sword and, by his hand alone, smashed the invasion of the horrible Nin and turned certain defeat into resounding victory, when the Shining One quenched the fire of the Wolf Star.

Legends concerning the enchanted sword, and the King who wielded it, had already grown large in the land, and increased with every passing year. It was possessed of a holy power, they said. It was enchanted by a god—the one called Most High. Its flame was the symbol of the god's presence with the King, and more.

Nimrood listened patiently to the various stories about the sword, letting the temple guards tell him what they knew. All the time the old sorcerer was thinking to himself, Yes, this enchanted sword is just the thing. "What you say is very interesting," he said at length. "Yes, very interesting." He turned to the man who had just joined them. "Do you have anything else to tell me?"

The priest thought for a moment, desperate to please the perverse Nimrood. "Oh!" he said, brightening. "Yes. The King said Durwin—the one called the hermit—was dead."

"Oh?" Nimrood's heart fluttered in his breast. "How is that?"

"I do not know. He only said, 'You killed Durwin!' "

"No one meant to kill him, sir," explained one of the temple guards who had been there. "It was an accident. He was in the way. We had to stop him to get the Prince."

This is working better than I hoped! thought Nimrood with glee. Durwin dead! Ah, that pesky hermit out of the way. My revenge will be complete. He nodded at those around him approvingly. "Yes, accidents happen. It could not be helped. But you must tell me these things in the future. I must know everything—it does not do to withhold information from me."

"We thought you would be angry," muttered one near him.

"Angry? Why should I be angry? Am I unreasonable?" Nimrood smiled again, his thin lips splitting his lined face. "No, you will find I am quite easy to get along with if you but tell me at once. I can be quite reasonable." He clapped his hands. "Now! Get some rest, all of you. We have far to go tonight. I want to be at the High Temple by first light tomorrow."

All settled down to rest for their nocturnal journey. Prince Gerin, too, rolled up into a ball, though he did not feel like sleeping; he did so to hide his tears from those around him. He did not want his captors to see him crying for his friend Durwin.

*   *   *

AT MIDDAY, TOLI AND THE KNIGHTS WITH HIM REACHED Askelon. Upon entering the inner ward yard, they found assembled nearly a score of knights with horses and squires darting here and there with provisions and equipment.

"What is this?" asked Toli. He slid from his mount and hurried to a cluster of men standing in the center of all this activity. The ring parted as the Jher came near. "Theido! Ronsard!" he shouted when he saw them.

Both men burst into grins and clapped him on the back. "We were hoping to see you before we rode out. And the King—" Theido halted, eyes narrowed. "You have seen him?"

"Yes," replied Toli curtly. "He will not soon be returning."

"I see." Theido frowned. "We must hold council and agree upon a plan in any case. We should not delay."

"With the Queen's permission we had hoped to leave at once," said Ronsard.

"Yes, you must leave soon. I will join you as soon as I have eaten and washed."

"I will have food sent to the council chamber," Ronsard suggested, and left to arrange it. Those who had ridden through the night with Toli took their leave also.

Theido walked Toli a few paces aside to the massive inner curtain where they could talk more freely. The bustle continued in the yard around them. Theido leaned against the great wall and folded his arms across his chest. His black hair was threaded with much silver, and his eyebrows as well, but the years had not softened his sharp features—if anything, age had made his appearance even more commanding.

"There is trouble between you, eh?" Theido said calmly.

Toli looked across the yard, staring at the activity, seeing nothing. He nodded.

"What happened?"

"He . . . my lord blames me for Durwin's death and

the loss of his son," Toli replied simply.

"I see." Theido spoke gently, trying to comfort Toli. "Certainly you know such accusations to be the temper of a distraught and frightened man."

"No," said Toli, shaking his head, "it is true. It is my fault. I left him alone. After the first attack I went after the assailants. I should not have gone. I should never have left the Prince for a moment."

"You did as you thought best. What man can do more? Durwin knew how to look after himself; he was no stranger to trouble. I am certain you did the right thing."

Toli turned haunted eyes on the tall knight. "Durwin was an old man, Gerin a defenseless child. I failed, I tell you."

"No! Think what you are saying. What has happened has happened. It cannot be changed. Durwin's death is not your fault. No one could have known. If you had stayed, it might well have been you struck down to bleed to death."

"Better my blood than his!"

"Never think that." Theido placed a hand on Toli's shoulder. "It is not for you to decide such things, my friend. We are all in the god's hands. It is he who directs our steps. Durwin knew that as well—no, better—than any of us."

Toli rubbed his hands over his face. He felt his fatigue descending upon him, covering him like a heavy cloak. "I am tired."

"Yes, go wash and change. You shall rest after our council. We will leave and begin the search."

"No, I will go with you. I must."

"You will need your rest. If I am not wrong, there will be plenty of searching for all of us. Rest while you can. Also, I would have you go with the Queen and the Lady Esme."

Toli looked up quickly. "The Queen? Esme? Where are they going?"

"Durwin is to be buried tomorrow. In the forest. I would go, but now that you are here, I think it better that Ronsard and I lead the search."

"I had forgotten about the funeral," said Toli ruefully. "Yes. Someone should go with them. Very well, I will do as you suggest."

He turned to leave, hestitated, and turned back. "There is something else." Theido waited. The Jher lowered his voice and said, "The King's scabbard was empty when I found him. The Shining One was gone."

16

PYM, WITH HIS GRAY-MUZZLED DOG BESIDE HIM, stumped along the road toward Askelon. As he walked, he thought about one thing and one thing only: the magnificent sword he had hidden that very morning. Wrapped in its coverings of rags, he had placed Zhaligkeer in a hole in a great old hazelnut tree whose heart had long ago been burned out by lightning. The ancient tree was hollow, but somehow still alive. He then marked the tree with a little pile of stones, and stood a long time looking at it from all directions, so he would remember it when he came back.

Then, collecting his tools and wares, he had rattled off through the forest to the road, heading once more for Askelon.

But his mind was uneasy. With every step he wavered. "Mayhaps I ought nivver have left it," he mumbled to Tip. "Mayhaps I should fetch it back. Abody might find it back there, and steal it from Old Pym. Then there'd be no gold, and no wagon or sharping stone, neither. Oh, what to do? What to do?"

At midday he stopped in a shady nook of linden boughs to eat a few morsels. He carried a rind of hard cheese with him, which he cut with a knife for himself and Tip. They washed it down with some water and munched an apple from one of his sacks.

They were about ready to get back on the road when they heard someone approaching. "Listen there, Tipper. Someun's coming up the road, hear? Who could it be? We 'uns'd best sit tight and see who 'tis."

They waited and the sound became voices—many voices, murmuring like a millrace—a whole throng of people traveling south, away from Askelon.

The first of the group passed by, glancing toward the tinker, but hurrying on. These were followed closely by twenty or more travelers, whole families—men, women, and children, deep in conversation or exclaiming loudly to one another as they bundled along.

Pym stepped out onto the road. "I'll be vexed, Tip. Where's all these 'uns agoin'?"

He hailed the nearest traveler. "Ho there! Ho!" The man halted and looked at him. Pym scrambled up. "Where ye bound? And what's all the pother?"

"You have not heard? Where have you been, man? Asleep? The whole world's aruffle!" Others halted with the man and added their voices. "Awful!" said one. "The gods are angry!" said someone else.

"Us'n's been on this here road two days," said Pym. "I met not abody, nor noun to tell me nothing."

" 'Tis the Prince! Prince Gerin," replied the first man.

"His young lordship's been nimmed and carried off aforce!" shouted someone from behind.

"Nivver say it!" cried Pym. "When did it happen?"

"Yesterday morning at the hunt. Thieves took him, and slew the King's counselor!"

"Oh! Oh!" Pym wagged his head in dismay.

"Fifty men there were!" said a short man with a wart.

"A hundred, I heard!" another yelled. Everyone nodded.

"You seen anyone?" asked the first man suspiciously.

Old Pym blanched at the thought. "Me? I nivver did. No, sir. Nor heard aught neither. We 'uns'd seen a hundred men. But neither hand nor hair have we seen 'til now. They kilt the King's minister?"

"Dead, he is. Oh, the gods are wroth with the King for taking up after this new god of his, this Most High. They are angry, and they are showing their ire! This will teach him."

Pym muttered morosely, "This be a dark day. A dark day indeed."

"Aye," they all agreed, and then hastened off down the road once more.

Pym started on his way again, stopping several succeeding groups to inquire of them also, and all told the same sad story. It was on everyone's lips, and would surely be the topic of conversation for some time, upsetting the festival as it had.

"A deed most foul, Tip," said Pym as they walked along, still proceeding toward Askelon, though all they met were going the other way, back to their villages and towns in the south, to spread the word. In a week there would not be a single man in all Mensandor who did not know what had happened. "Aye, a deed most foul."

QUENTIN PUSHED RELENTLESSLY ONWARD. EARLY IN the day he had forsaken the road and begun combing the side trails—first this way and then the other—hoping to chance across some sign that the assassins had passed through. He found nothing, and with every league descended into a torment and anguish deeper than he had ever known. It seemed at times as if his spirit was tearing itself in two, as if his innermost self was being wracked and tortured.

Why? he kept asking himself. Why has this happened to me? Help your servant, Most High! Help me! Why is there no answer? Why do I feel alone? He has left me; the god has cast me aside.

That thought alone might have crushed him, but fear for his son and grief for Durwin added their weight until he thought his heart would burst.

Still, he kept on, pushing himself, willing himself to go further, stopping only to rest Blazer now and then, and to drink. He continued southward, and as the day bent toward evening he smelled the salt air of the sea in the breeze and knew he must be nearing the coast.

At dusk he rode out of the forest and climbed a sandy bluff overlooking the sea. Gerfallon lay dark and wine-colored in the setting sun. Overhead, a bank of vermilion clouds scudded ashore on the landward wind. Behind them darker clouds gathered; tomorrow would see rain.

Quentin dismounted and allowed Blazer to crop the sweet green grass that grew long on the bluff. To the west lay Hinsenby, though he could not see it; and to the east the Sipleth slid darkly to the sea, its waters cool from the melt of snow on the high Fiskills.

Ahead, out across the water, lay the hulking mass of the island—Holy Island it was called—rising dark from the water: mysterious, uninviting; the source of many stories and much speculation from times past remembering. The island, green with vegetation and dark with ancient forests, was uninhabited—though in older times there were those who attempted to make a home there. But these settlements never lasted long—a few years at the most, and then they were gone. The island was the dwelling of some local gods who did not wish to share their home with mortals, some said.

Local rumors maintained that the eerie island had once been a place of worship for the early inhabitants of Mensandor, the war-loving and blood-lusting Shoth who practiced their brutish religion of torture and human sacrifice within its cloaked forests, drinking the blood of their victims and eating their flesh. And it was widely believed that there were those who still followed the religion of the Shoth, that weird rites still took place from time to time in secret. Voices were heard to emanate from the island's night-cloaked shores, and sometimes the blood-red light of midnight fires could be seen.

Holy Island was also purported to be a place of power lingering from ancient days when the gods themselves walked the earth in full sight of men, when the inexplicable was commonplace: dreams, disappearances, apparitions, and miracles.

Through the gathering dusk that island seemed to beckon Quentin. Its humped shape rose from the flat sea like the head and shoulders of a lordly sea creature, regarding the land with infinite patience. Come, it said. See what is here. Do you feel my power? Do you fear it? Come if you dare.

Quentin stirred and walked down the seaward side of the bluff, still staring at the island lying only a short distance out—less than half a league. He found a trail along the face of the dune leading down to the shore. Without a thought he followed the trail, weariness guiding his steps. And with each flagging footfall his strength ebbed; he had not eaten all day, and had rested little. He felt light-headed and weak, as if he were a husk, hollow, and brittle, and light, to be blown by the wind where it willed.

Yet he walked down the winding trail to the sea, letting his feet take him, his mind and body drained by exhaustion.

On the rocky shingle the waves lapped gentle, gurgling endearments onto the shore. Birds, searching for a roost for the night, swung through the air toward hollows and nests in the bluff's pocked face, their keening night calls shrill in the stillness. The sea wind freshened, and the clouds above darkened by degrees to violet. An evening mist clung to the upper heights of the island—a shroud to discourage prying eyes. High up on the dune behind him he heard Blazer whinny, but kept his eyes on the island as if mesmerized by its presence.

Quentin walked a little way along the strand, unaware of what he was doing or where he was going. He had no thought now except to walk, to go wherever his feet would take him.

He came to a smooth, rounded form on the beach, discernible in the dying light as a dark object against a slightly less dark background. He stumbled toward it, and his mind conjured up an image of the wretch he had cut down in the road. Slowly he approached, trembling at the thought of encountering that corpse again. Drawing near, he stopped toward the thing and put out a hand. Hair!

He recoiled from the touch. Was it an animal of some sort, dead and washed up on the shore?

But beneath the shag he had felt a hardness that was not like flesh, not even dead flesh. The shape of the thing was like no animal he had ever encountered. He put out his hand again and rubbed it along the hard, bristly surface, then pushed the object. It gave against the rocks and made a hollow sound. Then he knew what it was.

Quentin bent down and grasped the lower edge of the thing and flipped it over. The ox-hide boat, constructed of a design that went back a thousand years, rocked on its keel; its oar was tied with a leather cord to the crude seat in the center of the craft, and made a thumping sound as that of a drum.

He grabbed the bow of the boat and shoved it over the rocks and into the sea, then clambered in while the water splashed over his boots. He took up the oar and began paddling toward the island.

Out from land the sea was quiet, the only sound the dip of the oar as it swirled the water. A deep sadness welled up from inside him. It had been there all along, but now, as tired as he was, he could no longer keep it down and it came flooding up like a spring. He looked into the deep blue water all around, so silent, so peaceful. How restful it would be to slip over the side of the little boat and drift down and down—beyond thought, beyond pain, beyond remembering.

But the King kept paddling, and the night gathered its velvet robes around him as the land fell away behind, still outlined by the iron-blue of the sky above. In a little while he felt a scrape along the bottom of the boat, and then a jolt told him that he had reached the shore of Holy Island.

Quentin heaved himself out of the boat and pulled it well up on shore, then stalked into the forest that came right down to the water's edge, striking along an ancient trail through the trees and bushes.

How long he walked, he did not know or care. His legs moved of a volition all their own, pacing off the steps rhythmically and slowly. There was no hurry; he had no destination. Inside, his mind, benumbed with fatigue, churned lazily, functioning ever more slowly, offering no light, no insight.

His eyes stared straight ahead but saw nothing. It was dark, too dark to see anything except the branches of the nearest trees. He listened only to his own breathing and his own heartbeat, for the island was as silent as any tomb, and as full of unseen presences.

Quentin began to feel that he, too, was but a thing of insubstantial vapors: a wraith with no corporeal existence, doomed to roam the world by night, vanishing by dawn's light; a vague, lingering presence consigned to a shadow-world where only shades walked, each wrapped in a private torment, alone and uncomforted for all eternity.

The moon rose in the trees, a cold glowing eye that watched unkindly, shedding little light. Weariness draped itself over his shoulders like a leaden garment, awakening in Quentin a dull ache that throbbed through him with every step.

I must rest, he thought. I must stop soon and rest. I am tired. So tired. But he went on, not knowing where.

After a time he came to a place where the trees stopped, and ahead, shining with the moon's silver light, spread a lawn that swept in a gentle downward curve to meet a lake. Where the lawn and water met there was formed an arcing crescent—a shimmering moon to mirror the heavenly orb.

Quentin marched down to the edge of the lake and stopped, staring across the glass-smooth surface. Here and there the water winked with the reflected light of a star. Quentin looked down into the water and saw only a forlorn and haggard face peering back at him.

A willow tree grew near the water; long, sweeping branches dipped down and limply, lightly brushed the surface of the lake. The leaves on the branches formed teardrops that fell in never-ending cascades into the lake, watering it as a fountain of sorrow.

Quentin went to the old willow and slumped down beneath the trailing limbs. It was dry here, and dark. He rested his head against the rough, knotted trunk and pulled his cloak more tightly around him.

Sleep claimed him then for its own. He did not feel his eyes closing, or mark his passing into sleep's dark dominion. To Quentin it was all the same.

17

ALTHOUGH THE CASTLE SOUNDS HAD HOURS AGO TAK-
en on subdued night voices, and the funeral party would
leave early in the morning for the burial site in Pelgrin
Forest, Toli was still awake. He lay on his bed, hands
clasped behind his head, gazing upward at the flickering
shadow of his bedpost on the wall above him. His mind
returned once and again to the painful confrontation
with Quentin that morning. He heard again the stinging
words, "You are to blame . . . It is your fault!" Like a
lash that bit into the flesh, the words tortured him, and
he could not escape their fierce judgment. In the midst
of his anguish he heard a knock at his chamber's outer
door, muted but distinct.

He rose, went silently to the door, and opened it. "Yes,
yes. Who—Esme!" He covered his surprise and opened
the door wider to let her in.

"Toli, I . . ." she began, her eyes pleading, "it is Bria."
She backed away, pulling Toli out into the corridor.

"What has happened? What is wrong?"

"She stands out on the bartizan and will not come in.
She stares as if transfixed. I do not know what to do, or
how to move her."

They hurried quietly along the wide passage to the
royal chambers, their shadows flitting beside them over

the rough walls. "How long has she been out there?" he asked.

"When I brought her supper, she was standing there and told me to leave it, and when I came back a little while ago to see her asleep, her bed was unturned and her food untouched."

Toli nodded but said nothing until they reached the royal apartments; Esme opened the door and went in quietly, Toli following. They passed through several rooms and came out onto the balcony where Bria stood motionless as carved stone, staring out into the moon-drenched night.

Toli took one long look and then turned to Esme. "Go and find Alinea," he said softly. "It may be that she can be of help here."

With a nod Esme left. Toli turned and went out on the bartizan. The night was cool and still; crickets chirped among the vines that grew up along the walls.

"My Lady," he said gently, "it is very late, and we have much to do tomorrow."

The Queen did not move or make a sign that she had heard or even noticed Toli's presence. It was as if she were under a sorcerer's spell and could be touched by nothing of the world around her.

Toli reached out a hand and took her arm. It was cool to the touch, and though she did not resist she also did not move. "My Lady," Toli insisted, "you must rest."

There was a brushing tread on the stone of the balcony, and Alinea, with a shawl over her arm, approached. "Bria, my dear, it is your mother." She took the shawl and placed it over her daughter's shoulders, speaking in soothing tones. "Come away, my darling."

Alinea glanced at Toli and Esme. Toli stepped aside and motioned for Esme to follow him. The two retreated to an inner chamber.

When they were alone, Alinea put her arms around her daughter and held her. "Dear Bria," she sighed, "I can only wonder what you must feel."

A shudder passed through the younger woman's body. Alinea continued in soothing tones to reassure her. At length there came a sigh and Bria turned her eyes, glassy from their long vigil, toward her mother. "He is out there, Mother," she said, her voice full of pain. "My little one, my son, my beautiful boy. He is gone. I shall never see him again. I know it. I . . . shall . . . nev . . . Oh, Mother!"

At once the tears welled up and began rolling down her fair cheeks. She buried her face in her hands. Alinea pulled her tightly to her and stroked her auburn tresses.

In the chamber beyond, Toli and Esme heard the long, agonized sobs and turned away, embarrassed. They crept softly to the corridor to wait.

The silence between them grew awkward; neither one could speak, though both knew that someone should. Esme glanced tentatively at Toli; he looked back. She dropped her eyes. He turned away.

At last the silence became unendurable. Toli opened his mouth and stammered, "Esme, I . . . I—"

The door beside them opened, and Alinea appeared. Her deep green eyes reflected the depths of her sorrow, but her voice was calm and comforting. "She will sleep now, I think," she said simply, having accomplished what only a mother could. "You two must also rest. These next days will be difficult for us all."

"Thank you, my Lady," said Esme. "I am sorry—"

"Shh. Say no more. I will look in again before morning, but I am certain she will sleep soundly."

"Good night," said Toli and turned away at once. The two women watched him go.

"That one bears the full weight of care on his shoulders," said Alinea. "I wish Quentin were here—he would know how to deal with him. No one else can give him counsel."

Esme did not speak, but turned mournful eyes toward the Queen.

"So much hurt in this world," Alinea continued. "How fragile our happiness. When it is gone, it seems as if it never was and is never to be regained. But all things move under heaven according to the Most High's will. Nothing happens that he does not see."

"Where is the comfort in that?" asked Esme, her voice filled with dismay. "Oh, this Most High of yours—I will never understand him."

Alinea looked kindly at the woman beside her. She gathered her under her arm much as she had done with Bria a few moments before, and led her along the corridor back to her rooms. "Ah, Esme, I thought I would never understand either. But Durwin would tell me, 'Understanding comes through faith, not the other way around.' I used to puzzle over that endlessly."

"What does it mean?"

"It means that there are many things about the Most High which faith alone can see. I have learned that all the reasons and all the thought in all the world still cannot bring one closer to belief. Belief must come from the heart."

Esme shook her head slowly. They had reached her chamber door; she turned to face Alinea, taking her hands. "This god is very different from any I know. The others require neither faith nor understanding, but are content with presents and oblations. It is so much simpler."

Alinea smiled. "Yes, the old gods are simpler. But they do not care what happens to men. They do as they will. But the Most High cares very much—more than you can ever know."

"That, at least," said Esme as she turned to go in, "is something worth believing. Good night, my Lady. Thank you for your words. Good night."

UNDER NIGHT'S DARK VEIL THE TRAVELERS MOVED with quick stealth. They kept to the road as much as possible, pushing eastward, avoiding the villages along the way, giving them wide berth in order to escape detection.

Prince Gerin trudged along with his head down, though he remained alert to any possibility of escape. He had overheard one of his guards say that by morning they would reach their destination. If he was going to escape, he reasoned, it would be best to try sooner rather than later.

He had thought about little else all day, having grown tired of waiting for someone to come rescue him. Why don't they come? he wondered. What can be keeping them? They must be looking for me. They must certainly know where I have gone. Perhaps they cannot find me. Yes, that is it! Oh, this old Longbeard is a crafty one. He has so muddled our trail that no one can find me. Yes, I must escape. Tonight.

It was settled in his mind. As soon as the attention of his guards—one standing at either side of him, and another leading his pony—wavered, or their grip slackened, he would be off. They could not catch him; he would outrun them once on horseback. That was his plan. Now he waited for his opportunity.

It came when they arrived at a crossroads. One road angled away to the north, toward the small village along the Arvin. The other led on, rising gradually as it proceeded eastward toward the Fiskill Mountains. The town of Narramoor lay straight ahead; a little further to the east and north stood the High Temple on its plateau overlooking the valley and all the realm beyond.

They paused. "We will go around the town to the south," said Nimrood, "and then to the temple."

"But there is a shorter way, to the north," protested one of the guards. Others nodded.

"Yes, shorter," Nimrood hissed, "and more prying eyes to see us pass by."

"We know a path—" started the guard.

"Silence!" rasped Nimrood. He took a menacing step forward. "We will do as I say!" He thrust a finger in the man's face. "I am your master!"

The man stepped backward, tripped, and fell over a stone in the road. The other guards watched him, their attention momentarily diverted.

That was all Prince Gerin needed. Quick as the flick of a cat's tail he leapt into the saddle and snatched the reins out of the startled guard's hands, wheeled Tarky around, and started away.

"Stop him!" screamed Nimrood. "Stop him, you fools!"

Instantly the temple guards snapped to attention. The two nearest dove for him, but the horse dodged away; they landed with a grunt in the road. Another darted toward him from the side. Gerin lashed out with the reins. The man yelled and threw his hands over his face.

"You fools!" screeched Nimrood. "He is getting away!"

The young Prince leaned down low in the saddle and kicked the horse in the ribs, urging him to speed. The guards dashed after him on either side, their dark shapes little more than shadows. The horse caught the movement out of the corner of his eye and shied, throwing his rump in the air. It was all Gerin could do to hold on. The guards now ringed them in, waving their hands and shouting, hoping to spook the animal.

The frightened horse bolted and bucked, tossing his head wildly. Gerin clung to the pony's mane, pressing his legs together, fighting to remain in the saddle. The horse neighed with fright and reared, kicking up his hooves at the dancing shapes around him.

Then Gerin saw an opening. Pulling the reins aside with all his might, he turned his steed toward the break in the ring. The horse saw the opportunity, too, and dashed for it instantly.

The next thing Gerin knew, the stars and moon were spinning crazily before him; he felt himself falling, sliding, tipping back over the rump of the horse. Then the ground came up hard and knocked the wind out of him.

He lay like a sack of grain tumbled into the road, unable to breathe. Rough hands took hold of him, hauled him to his feet, and shook him; breath poured into his lungs.

He peered around dazedly and saw Tarky bounding away riderless down the road, two guards scurrying after him. Had there been a flash of light? A noise? The sound of thunder still rang in his ears.

What was it that had so suddenly appeared in his path? What caused the horse to rear and throw him? He remembered seeing the old man raise his hand high above his head . . . then the earth and sky changed places—by what force or power, the boy did not know. Blazing violet balls of light still bobbed before his eyes; he shook his head, but they remained, fading away only slowly.

"The youngster has spirit," intoned Nimrood. "But it must be bent to our purposes. Young sir, if you wish to remain alive and whole, you will abandon any further notions of escape." Nimrood leaned close, his vile breath hot in the Prince's face. "Otherwise, when they come for you they will find nothing worth the ransom."

A guard came up, panting. "That cursed beast is gone; we cannot catch him."

"Idiots! Another mistake!" With slits of eyes glittering cruelly, the old man glared around at the chagrined faces encircling him, his long white beard glowing in the moonlight like a frozen waterfall. "The High Priest will hear of your incompetence. I am certain he will devise a punishment to suit me."

Nimrood turned abruptly and started off once more. The guards stood still and watched him. "Bring him." The voice was flat and hard. The guards fell over themselves to obey. Prince Gerin was jerked by the arms and dragged along, his feet barely touching the ground, as they continued on their way.

18

A PALE MOON POURED MOLTEN SILVER INTO THE BOWL of the lake. The water shone hard and black like glass smoked in a fire, and the willow's teardrop leaves pearled with dew. Above, the sable sky held sparks of diamond stars, tips of light as cold and sharp as ice.

Quentin awoke with a start out of a stony sleep and stared uncomprehendingly around him. Where am I? he wondered. How have I come to be here?

Then he remembered rowing to the island and walking and walking, then sinking into sleep. Though his mind was a jumble of half-formed thoughts and fragments of unfinished dreams, waking in this place, he felt strangely certain that he had been drawn here, summoned, and then awakened at the proper moment by the same force that had brought him.

His senses pricked. The place seemed alive with the presence of gods; if he listened very carefully, he could almost hear the murmur of their spirit-voices calling to one another as they plied night's distant shores.

Quentin felt the nearness of these beings, and his blood quickened. The gods had gathered close about; they watched from every shadow as from behind velvet curtains, and Quentin imagined their dispassionate eyes upon him.

He rose, stiff from his exertion, wrapped his arms across his chest, and gazed out across the lake. Mist rose like steam from the still water to thicken and drift in curling tendrils toward the crescent lawn like searching fingers. Quentin stepped to the water's edge and waited. The ghostly white mist seeped and flowed and eddied on unseen currents in the air, spreading ever nearer. He waited, stomach taut, the night chill stinging his flesh, the sense of expectancy almost overpowering. Blood pulsed rapidly through his veins; he could hear it drumming rhythmically in his ears. All around lay deathly silent.

Quentin stood at the edge of the silver lake and watched as the shifting vapors erected lacework walls over the mirrored surface. As he gazed out over the water, the mist rolled and parted and there emerged a dark shape drifting slowly toward him across the lake. Quentin saw that it was a small boat gliding silently from the wreathing vapors.

No oarsman rowed the vessel, no pilot steered. Wide of hull and low in the water, it drew nearer and came at last to rest at the King's feet, bumping softly against the grass-covered bank.

He lifted his foot cautiously and stepped into the mysterious craft—as if he thought that it might vanish into the mist once more. But the boat proved solid enough, and Quentin sat down amidships. Then, just as silently and mysteriously as before, the ghostly vessel floated away from the shore, bearing him back across the lake the way it had come.

Sitting stiffly on the wooden bench, Quentin watched as his ship entered the encircling mist. The solid world faded from view, and he was swallowed whole into a netherworld of cloud and insubstantial vapor. He might have been floating or flying, so softly and gently did the boat ride. Not a ripple marked their passage. Straining eyes and ears into the void, he saw and heard nothing.

After a time the mist thinned and parted, and the little craft drifted out into a shallow lagoon rimmed with the massive slabs of great standing stones.

There was some magic in this place; Quentin could feel it now, tingling over him, licking at his face and limbs with subtle fire.

Then he saw the figure.

Before him at the water's edge stood a man clothed in a long white mantle that glowed in the moon's radiant beams. He beckoned to Quentin to follow, and as the boat touched shore, Quentin stepped out and hastened after the figure.

They moved across the lawn to the giant stones, passing between them into a circle of smaller stones, many of them leaning or fallen. These stones, like others Quentin had seen in Mensandor, had once stood one upon another in rings at the worship sites of the ancients. The rings were erected in places of power where gods were said to touch the earth.

As they entered this sacred circle of stone, Quentin saw a fire burning brightly and meat roasting on spits. The white-clothed figure sat down on one of the tumbled stones which had grown thick with green moss and white-flecked lichen. The man smiled warmly and gestured for Quentin to sit. Though no words had passed between them, Quentin felt welcomed and unafraid. He watched while the man tended the spits.

The stranger was tall, his body well-formed and fit, his features broad, but not coarse or heavy. There was strength in the cut of his jaw and chin. His long dark hair swept back and was bound in a thong at the back of his head in the manner of prophets or seers. The man's eyes were dark, quick firebrands that sparked in the light of the campfire as he adjusted the roasting meat on the fire with his strong hands.

The fire cracked and ticked, throwing grotesque shadows over the standing stones. A thousand questions boiled in Quentin's mind, but he remained silent. No word seemed appropriate for this place. So he sat in the warm circle of light and waited.

At last the stranger reached for a nearby jug and poured from it into a wooden cup which he offered to Quentin. "Are you hungry?"

"Yes!" replied Quentin, startled that the man should speak.

"Good." He laughed, the sound deep and resonant—an earth sound, the sound of forest and hill and streams rolling to the sea.

Quentin laughed too, caught up in the delight of that voice.

"I thought you might be hungry, so I fixed you something to eat," explained the mysterious host. "It has been a long journey, and you have ridden far."

"How did you know?"

His host only smiled and replied, "I know a great many things about you."

There was something familiar, hauntingly familiar, about the man; his voice and manner Quentin was certain he had known before. But where? The memory eluded him. "There are many who might make a similar claim," said Quentin. "My name is well enough known."

"Well said," replied the man. Mirth danced in his eyes. "You are the Dragon King of Mensandor, and truly many men know your name. But I know a good deal more."

"Please continue," said Quentin. Who was this man?

"I know that you are an honorable man whose friends are many. And that you recently lost a friend, one very dear to you. I also know that you stand in danger of losing another even dearer."

"Is that all?"

"It is enough for now, I think. Here, the meat is ready." He handed Quentin one of the skewers and kept one, took up his wooden cup, and drank.

Quentin drank, too, and thought he had never tasted water so fresh and good. He pulled a piece of meat from the spit and ate it, all the while watching the stranger beside him. "What is your name?" he asked.

"Call me your friend, for friend I am."

"Friend? Nothing more?"

"What more is needed?"

Quentin ate his food thoughtfully. Who was this friend? And why did he seem so familiar? He drank again and asked, "Where am I? What is this place?"

The man did not answer, but instead asked a question of his own. "You see these stones?"

Quentin nodded.

"They were erected and stood for many hundreds of years. But now they lie abandoned and overthrown. The gods in whose honor they were raised come no more to this place. Why do you think that is?"

Quentin considered this for a moment and then replied, "Could it be that the old gods are dying, or that they never existed in the first place? There are those who say a new era has come upon us, and a new god is making himself known."

"What do you say?"

"I believe," Quentin said slowly, choosing his words carefully, "I believe that times change, yes, and new eras are born, but there is only one god who is god of all. Whether other gods exist or never did, I cannot say."

"Strange words from an acolyte," said the stranger. His smile was elusive and suggested he held some greater secret to himself.

But Quentin was stunned—it had been a long time since he had been called an acolyte. He had nearly forgotten that he ever served in the temple at all; that seemed long ago. "I was but a boy," he replied.

"Times change, as you say. But old ways die hard, do they not?"

Quentin said nothing. The man looked around the ring of fallen stones. "Why do you suppose men honor their gods with stone?"

"Stone endures," said Quentin.

"Yes, but as you see, even stone falls in the end. What is it that endures after stone has crumbled to dust?"

Quentin recognized this question as one that his old teacher Yeseph, the elder of Dekra, had asked him as a pupil many years ago. Old Yeseph, dead now and buried years before. "Man's spirit endures," said Quentin. That had been the answer Yeseph had sought.

"And love endures," the man said simply. "Would it not make more sense to honor the god with love instead of temples made of stone?"

Again a pang of guilt arrowed the King. Who was this man?

"Quentin," he said softly, "do not be afraid."

"I am not—" began Quentin. The man raised a hand and cut him off.

"And do not give yourself to despair. Your enemies seek to humble you, to mock the god you serve. Trust in the Most High, and he will raise you up."

The man stood and smiled again. "The boat will take you back across the water."

Quentin jumped up. "Do not go! Please—"

"I must. My time here is finished. I wanted to see you just once more, and to say farewell."

"No!" cried Quentin, throwing himself to his knees. "Stay with me. I would hear more!"

"It is not to be. But never fear, we will be together again. I am certain of it." The man smiled his gentle smile and laid a hand on Quentin's head.

Quentin felt a rush of warmth flood through him at the touch. The panic that had come upon him ceased.

"Before, I did not get the chance to say good-bye as I would have wished." The man raised Quentin to his feet and wrapped him in a hug. After a moment, clasping his friend's shoulders with both hands, he held the King back at arm's length and said, "Good-bye, my friend."

"Good-bye," said Quentin. He stood and watched as the man turned and walked toward the wood, passing between two great slabs of stone as through a doorway.

The mist rolled up and removed him from Quentin's sight, and he was gone.

19

THE FUNERAL PROCESSION LEFT AT DAWN AND RODE through the quiet streets of Askelon bearing the body of the beloved hermit on a black-draped bier drawn by two of Toli's finest white horses. It went to the north where Pelgrin Forest met the plain at its closest point to the castle, a distance of about a league.

The day was fair and warm, the sun rosy-gold in the treetops as it climbed into heaven's great bowl of cloud-scrubbed blue. The air, soft and still, held the sweetness of wildflowers that grew in haphazard clusters across the tableland—pink and yellow sunlilies, buttercups and bluebuttons, white laceleaves and tiny purple lady's slippers.

Toli rode Riv and led the bier; Esme and Bria followed, and Alinea came in a coach with Princess Brianna on one side of her and Princess Elena on the other. Nearly three score mourners made up the cortege—lords and ladies, knights, squires, household servants, and townspeople—all friends of the hermit, for he welcomed every man, whether of high position or of meaner birth, as friend.

And though their errand was a sad one, the day was so bright and the feeling of life so intense that it was not

121

possible for any of the mourners to remain genuinely sorrowful.

"How strange it is," remarked Bria, thinking about this very thing. "Today I feel newly cleansed. As if the past days have been an unhappy dream that vanished with the dawn."

"Yes," agreed Esme. "I feel the same way. And yet, *I* have not changed—the whole world seems to be new-born."

They continued to talk this way, and behind them in the coach the little Princesses plied their grandmother with questions. Princess Elena had never attended a funeral, and Princess Brianna only one—that of Yeseph; but she had been a baby less than a year old and did not remember it.

"Grandmother, what will happen to Durwin?"

"Nothing bad, my child. His body will rest now in the earth," Alinea answered.

"But won't he get cold?" piped Elena.

"No, never again."

"I know what will happen," said Brianna importantly. "He will turn into bones!"

"How awful!" cried little Elena, her eyes sparkling at the mystery of it. "Will I turn into bones, too?"

"Not for a very long time, my dear one. But someday, yes. Everyone dies, and their bodies turn into bones and dust."

"I do not think I shall like it," said Elena, growing pensive.

"I will!" announced Brianna, determined to make the best of any situation.

"I do not believe you will even know what has happened, nor will you care. You will begin a wonderful new life somewhere else."

"Where? Oh, tell us about it, Grandmother," they said.

"Very well. There is a great kingdom far away—the kingdom of the Most High. When you die you will go there and live with him. It is a wondrous place and more beautiful than anything you have ever seen. You will leave your body—you will not need it anymore, because you will have a new body—and go live in happiness forever."

"Is that where Durwin has gone?"

"Yes, that is where he has gone. He has gone to be with the Most High."

"Will we see Durwin again when we get there?" asked Elena.

"Of course. He will be waiting for us."

"And Grandfather Eskevar, too?" Brianna wanted to know.

"Yes, Eskevar too." Alinea smiled. The children were so trusting, so innocent and unsuspicious. They believed what she told them without needing proofs or assurances. Theirs was a most simple and indulgent faith, with room for many questions but little doubt.

"Oh," said Brianna matter-of-factly, "I shall go at once then. I should love to see Grandfather."

"It would make us sad if you went right away, dear one," replied Alinea, smoothing the girl's hair. "For then we would not see you anymore. Stay with us a little while longer, please."

"Very well," agreed Brianna, "I will. I would not like to leave you, Grandmother." She snuggled in closer.

Of all who traveled in that party only Toli did not feel the wonder of the day. He rode silently, eyes ahead, unseeing, his mind concentrating on affairs that ripped at his heart and made him want to cry out in agony, I have failed my master. I have disgraced myself and brought ruin upon the King. He was right; it was all my fault. My fault alone. Yes, Durwin's blood is on my head. I am responsible—I should never have left them alone. If I had been there, Durwin would still be alive, and the Prince would be safe. None of this would ever have happened. I failed in my duty and am no longer worthy to be called a servant. I must make it right. I must make it right, though it cost my life. My life—what good is it to me now?

They reached the site and brought the bier to the grave that had been prepared the day before. It was just a little way inside the forest, on the bank overlooking a shaded pool—the pool in which Durwin had waded many times gathering his healing plants.

Alinea had chosen the spot, remembering how he had loved to come here to wade, or just to sit and contemplate. Many times she had found him stretched out on the bank and sat with him as he talked about this or that herb, or traced his musing about the Most High.

"Quentin should be here," said Bria, "and Gerin. How they both loved Durwin. I wish they were here." She was quite over her trauma of the night before; in fact, she did not really remember it as having happened to her. It belonged to the dream, the bad dream she left behind with the new day.

"They will come here soon, I am certain." Esme watched her friend closely, looking for any sign of the malady that had stricken Bria.

Bria caught her scrutiny and said, "I am much better now." She paused and then glanced toward the grave. "It is just that it does not seem right without Quentin here."

"He would be here if he could, you know that. Quentin's first duty is to find the Prince and bring him back safely. The King cannot rest until his son and heir is safe."

"You are right." She paused and added, "But look at Toli. It tears at my heart to see him like this."

Esme observed the slim, silent Jher and nodded sadly. It touched her deeply, too. She wished nothing more than to be able to go to Toli and comfort him; and she would have, but for fear of Toli's rejection.

For his part, Toli had told no one but Theido of Quentin's harsh words. Those had been his due; he had deserved them. He signaled to several of the lords and knights in attendance, and they moved to the bier. Laying hold of the long plank on which the body rested, they lifted it to their shoulders. Bria and Esme went to the litter too, and Alinea; they took up bouquets of flowers that had been placed on the funeral wain early that morning and followed the body to the grave.

The men lowered the hermit's body into the hole dug in the rich black dirt. Sunlight filled the hole and fell on the pallid face. He seemed to be at rest, content. But he was not now the same Durwin they had known; he had changed. In death he appeared so much less himself that it was impossible for any of the mourners to look upon him now and say, "This is the man we knew in life."

Durwin—the true essence of the man they had loved—was gone. He had left only a worthless husk behind.

Alinea went to the graveside and knelt to place her flowers by him in the ground. Bria joined her, and Esme. Toli stood silently over the open pit and watched, his eyes hard as polished stone.

Others came to the grave, too, and paused briefly to pay final honor to the man. Here and there a tear sparkled in an eye, but there was no sobbing, no wailing, no evidence of unendurable grief common at so many funerals. All who had come knew that this interment was different: this was the burial of one of the Most High's trusted servants. And no one who looked upon the body in the grave felt that the man had ceased. The presence of his spirit was strong among them. It would be wrong to regard the Holy Hermit of Pelgrin Forest as having fallen into shadowy nonexistence in the underworld of the gods. Even those who had never heard of the Most High or his great and wonderful kingdom believed that Durwin had gone to a far different, far better place.

Inwardly, all who saw him in his grave wished that their own deaths could be so: assured, dignified, and peaceful. And many believed from that day forth that Durwin was right about the Most High, for they too wanted to go where he had gone.

When at last all had paid their respects to the body—Princess Brianna and Princess Elena being the last to lay flowers in the grave—Toli and five knights shoveled dirt into the hole and then, one by one, the mourners took up stones and placed them on the tomb.

"Quentin would have wanted him buried in the Ring of the Kings," observed Bria as she watched the stones being placed over the grave. "But this is better, more fitting."

"I agree," replied Alinea. "Here among the trees he loved, where wild things lived . . . this is where he belongs."

They turned then and made their way back to the castle, leaving any lingering sadness behind—all except Toli. He stayed when everyone else had gone and stood unmoving over the grave for a long time. Then at last he mounted Riv and left. But he did not ride back to Askelon Castle with the others.

"Where is Toli?" asked Esme as she swiveled in the saddle looking for him. But he was not among those who followed.

"Strange," said Bria. She craned her neck around too. "I do not see him anywhere. I thought he had come with the others."

Esme turned her eyes back toward the grave site, but there was nothing to be seen. Toli had vanished.

20

"THE PRINCE . . . HERE? BY THE GODS' BEARDS! IT IS A mistake. You have implicated the High Temple in your schemes. I will not have it! Do you hear? I will not have it!"

High Priest Pluell raved and tore at his hair as he paced back and forth in his chamber. Nimrood sat with hooded eyes, watching Pluell vent his anger, but saying nothing.

The High Priest came to stand in front of the white-bearded old man, hands on hips. "The temple is in danger now because of you. This was not in our agreement. You never said anything about kidnapping. I will not have it!"

At last Nimrood had enough. He stood, shot a withering glance at the High Priest, and stalked to the door.

"Wait! What are you going to do? Where are you going?"

"I am leaving. It is plain you have lost your nerve for our little diversion. I have no use for you. Good-bye."

"No!" shouted Pluell. "You cannot do that! What about the Prince? What am I to do with him?"

"Do anything you like with him. What do I care? He might make a serviceable acolyte, though I think his father might have something to say about that."

"Stop! Come back. You cannot leave me like this. This was never my affair!"

Nimrood stopped with his hand on the latch. "Never your affair? Ha!" He turned suddenly, his eyes darting flames. Pluell saw the change and dropped back, his mouth gaping. Nimrood advanced on him, seeming to grow in height.

"Was it my idea?"

"Who else? You are not suggesting it was mine!"

"None other's. I merely indicated to you the danger to the temple if you did not act at once. It was your men who took the boy. It was their mistake. You are High Priest—you are responsible."

"No! You tricked me! I told you to . . . to—"

"Exactly! You told me to do what needed to be done. We would not be here now if your stupid men had done their duty. I certainly never wanted it this way."

"You must help me!" wailed Pluell. The shock and rage at what Nimrood had done to him subsided in the new horror of perhaps facing the outraged King alone. Why, the Dragon King would hew him limb from limb for the attack on his son! "I am sorry. I apologize. I was not thinking clearly. Stay and help me think what to do."

Nimrood pulled on his beard. He appeared to be contemplating what should be done. Ah! he thought to himself. So easy! This pigeon is so deftly caught. He has no nerve, no backbone. He deserves his fate. But I can use him; therefore I will save him. Oh, this is working much better than I could have hoped.

"Very well, I will stay. But you must stop whimpering and do as I say. I have a plan. A very simple plan. And if all goes well, in a short while you, my pigeon priest, will hold the King in the palm of your plump hand."

WORKING OUTWARD FROM THE PLACE WHERE THE Prince was last seen, Theido and Ronsard and their search party of knights combed the forest, fanning out from that central point, probing deeper into the heart of Pelgrin. The knights rode the shaded pathways and dimly lit trails; Theido and Ronsard rode with them, meeting at prearranged spots to confer and share any news.

There was precious little news to share. No one had turned up any sign of the abductors.

"They appear to have vanished from the face of the earth," said Ronsard when they met for their final conference of the day.

"We should have seen some sign of them by now." Theido gazed at the sky overhead. The clouds held an orange tint as the sun spun lower in the trees. "It will be dusk soon, and too dark to search any further."

Ronsard scanned the sky through the open patches in the leafy canopy overhead. "Blast their bones! By the god, I had hoped to strike their trail today." He looked at Theido, whose eyes held a faraway look. "What are you thinking?"

"Nothing—it was nothing."

Ronsard shook his head. "I know that look of yours. Out with it, Theido."

Theido nodded slowly. "I was thinking about what Toli said regarding Quentin's sword."

"Now there is a puzzle. I wonder what is behind it."

"Nothing good, you may be sure. I was thinking just now that it portends a greater evil than the Prince's disappearance, and that is bad enough."

Ronsard stared at his friend knowingly. "Aye, the Shining One is not to be parted with lightly. I should have thought Quentin would fight to the death before giving it up."

"You speak my thoughts to a word. And yet, when Toli met him in the road he did not speak of it at all. Why, I wonder." Theido glanced at the sky once more and said, "One problem at a time, eh? We will start again at daybreak."

"Yes, tomorrow—and that is the last good day. The signs, if they are out there, are already disappearing."

Theido turned his horse and made to move away. "Farewell, Ronsard. I will meet you tomorrow at the same time. If we have not found the trail by then, well— just pray that we find it."

Ronsard raised his hand in farewell and watched the tall, lean knight ride away, back along the way he had come. Theido is right, he thought. Something is at work here that bodes ill for all of us. What it is we shall find out soon enough, I'll warrant.

He sighed and moved off through the deepening shadows to meet with his men once more before he rolled himself in his cloak to sleep. All around, the wood lay still and silent, as if comtemplating the coming of the night. Ronsard felt a chill creeping out with the shadows, and with it a sinister foreboding such as he had not felt in many years. He shuddered inwardly and rode on.

"IF YOU THINK IT UNWISE, MOTHER, OR IF YOU WOULD advise a better plan, please tell me." Bria watched her mother carefully, almost breathlessly. Hers had been a sudden thought, and she had gone immediately to her mother's apartments to share her idea.

"I do not say it is unwise," said Alinea slowly and with great concentration. "But I do have misgivings."

Bria frowned at the word. But her mother continued. "However, I remember another time, years ago, when Durwin counseled the same plan. Then, too, it seemed a chancy enterprise. But it was the right course, as it turned out—though even Durwin could never have guessed the outcome." She smiled at her daughter, and Bria saw the light in her green eyes. "It seems that the destinies of Askelon and Dekra are ever intertwined. Yes, my dear, go to Dekra. I will go too."

"Mother, do you mean it? You would go?"

"Why not? I am fit for a journey. And now that the King's road is complete to Malmarby the trip will be an easy one most of the way. But we must leave at once." She glanced at her daughter quickly. "What is wrong?"

"You spoke of misgivings. What are they?"

"Just that word may come to Askelon about the Prince. If you were not here to receive it. . . ." Her voice trailed off.

"I see. What should I do?"

"That I cannot tell you. You must do what any mother does; you must listen to your heart."

"Then I will go to Dekra and speak to the Elders there. We have often had reason to seek their wisdom, and their prayers may be most effective." Her eyes held her mother's. "I do so wish that Quentin were here, though."

"Quentin will return soon. We will leave behind a letter telling him what we propose. He would wish to stay here in any case to aid in the search."

"What about Brianna and Elena—I fear leaving them."

"They will come with us. Why not? They have begged to see Dekra often enough, and they will enjoy the trip. As it is, I think it would be unwise to leave them. We will take a coach and a bodyguard of knights, and travel the safer."

Bria smiled, feeling better for having talked with her mother. "Yes, naturally you are right."

"It will be better for us to have something to do. The waiting would weigh heavily on us, I fear. If word was long in coming . . . well, we will go. We must not think of anything but Gerin's welfare. The Elders at Dekra will be able to help."

Bria gazed at her mother admiringly, and then threw her arms around her neck in a hug. "Oh, thank you. I knew you would say the right thing."

Alinea patted her daughter's back. "Poor Quentin. I pray that the waiting does not distress him overmuch. I would feel better if Toli were here. Perhaps he will soon return."

"When should we leave?"

"Just as soon as the horses and supplies can be made ready."

"Tomorrow morning, then. We will rest better in our own beds tonight, and leave at first light."

Alinea nodded her assent. Bria bent and kissed her mother and then hurried away, her mind already filled with dozens of details that would require attention before they could leave. Alinea watched her go, thinking back on a time when she had planned the same journey. She smiled, nodded, and went back to her prayers.

21

QUENTIN GAVE BLAZER HIS HEAD AND LET THE ANIMAL take them home. The road was easy to follow, and the horse knew the way back to Askelon. Quentin rode without knowing or caring where they went, and Blazer unerringly led them homeward.

As the way through Pelgrin merged green and leafy with the cool blue shadows, Quentin, benumbed from lack of sleep, felt himself drifting back to the strange meeting on the island.

That he had been specifically summoned to the Holy Island he had no doubt. By whatever subtle magic, he was drawn to the lake and there waiting when the boat arrived for him to take him to the ring of stones. Enchantment, surely. But for what purpose?

Quentin could not say. As for the man—the mysterious stranger who spoke with him, knew him, called him by name—who was he? In some inexplicable way he felt he knew that man, had known him for a long time, even though he had never met him before that hour.

Or had he?

It was as if a friend had gone on a long journey to a country far away and returned after many years vastly changed, though still basically the same person underneath, and it was the change wrought in this man that shielded his identity.

"Call me your friend," the man had said, "for friend I am." I am in need of a friend, thought Quentin. Sorely in need.

He felt a loneliness take hold of him he had not felt in many years—not since as a young acolyte in the High Temple had he experienced the same crushing weight of utter aloneness. In his mind he traveled back to that time, and once again he was that gangly young boy clinging frightened to the mane of the mighty warhorse Balder, setting out on an errand which could not possibly succeed, but going anyway.

Such hope, such blindness.

Oh, to be that trusting boy again, thought Quentin. He felt the weight of years upon him, and tasted the bitter-sweet longing for that simpler, better time. He let himself drift off on waves of longing and loneliness.

WHEN HE CAME OUT OF HIS REFLECTIONS, HE SAW THAT the sun was lowering over the road, and also that he was leaving the forest. Upon returning from the island he had found Blazer waiting for him on the shore. He had beached the ox-hide boat and ridden away, not stopping all day. Now he felt the ache of the road seize him in an iron grip. His head throbbed.

He rode out of the forest and down a slight hill into a broad valley. Here in this valley were the farms of peasants and small landowners—those who sold their produce in the market at Askelon. Just a little ahead, Quentin saw the wattled house of a farmer, watched the man leading his team of oxen in from the field and his wife at the well dipping water, and decided to stop for a moment to wash the dust of the road from his throat and to rest his horse. But only for a moment, because he wanted to be in Askelon by nightfall.

"Ho there!" called Quentin as he rode into the yard scratched bare by clucking chickens. "Good day to you!"

He sat and waited for the farmer to show himself.

A face appeared at a dark window—just a fleeting glimpse and then it was gone. A moment later the farmer came around the side of the house, carrying a two-pronged wooden pitchfork in his hand.

He stared at Quentin warily, but with a certain respect. "G'day to 'ee, sir," said the farmer. His weather-browned face scrutinized the visitor frankly. If there was a trace of distrust, it was only the normal, benign distrust all simple people held for strangers who were obviously above them. Quentin smiled at the farmer and said, "It is a hot day for traveling, but good for the crops."

The farmer squinted his eyes up to the sky and seemed to lose himself among the clouds scudding swiftly toward the horizon. At length he rolled an eye back to Quentin and said, "Trav'lin's oft a thristy bi'ness."

"Now that you mention it," replied Quentin, "I would like a drink of water."

"Help 'eself," said the farmer, nodding toward the well.

Quentin slowly dismounted and walked to the well, feeling every jounce of the road in each stiff step. He settled himself on the edge of the stonework and took up the dipping gourd. He played out the braided cord, filled the gourd, and then took the brimming vessel to his horse.

Blazer, his shining white coat now dusty brown-gray, plunged his broad muzzle into the water and drank deeply. As Quentin held the gourd he noticed a movement in the doorway of the house nearby. The farmer's wife joined her husband, and Quentin fell under her sharp scrutiny. There was a mumble of whispered words behind him. He wondered what the woman was saying to her husband. When he turned around he understood, for he saw a look of awe blossom on their ruddy features—the look that accompanied him whenever he made his way in public. It reminded him that he was the Dragon King.

He looked at them and they bowed low, both of them,

awkward and self-conscious. "Rise, my friends," he said softly.

"I—I did not know as 'twas 'ee, Sire," stammered the farmer. "I be yer 'umble servant."

Quentin patted his dusty clothes. "How could you know, good man?" Little puffs of dust accompanied each pat. "I look more a highwayman than a King."

The farmer's raw-boned wife nudged her man with an elbow, and he jumped forward at once and took the gourd. " 'Low me, Sire."

Quentin was about to protest, but thought better of it and allowed the man his pleasure, knowing that for years to come the farmer would tell his friends and relatives of the day he had watered the King's horse.

Sitting on the edge of the well once more, Quentin turned his eyes to the house and noted its rude construction. Though it was a most simple structure, made from the cheapest materials—mud daubed over woven sticks on a timber frame and topped with a roof of thatch—it was clean, and all was orderly in the yard. It was identical to any number of households that stretched from one end of Mensandor to the other—from Wilderby to Woodsend.

Out of the corner of his eye he saw a quick flick of a shadow as it darted and disappeared around the corner of the house. He watched the spot for a moment and was rewarded by seeing a pair of wide dark eyes and a pale forehead poke around the edge of the house once more.

Quentin smiled and raised his hand, beckoning to the owner of those eyes to come out and join him. Presently, a grubby young boy stepped hesitantly around the corner, keeping his back pressed against the house, inching toward the stranger with the shyness of a wild creature of the forest. The dark-eyed youngster was dressed in a long, hand-me-down tunic resewn for him, no doubt, from one of his father's. The edges of this garment were frazzled and frayed, and the threads blew in the breeze like tassels. He stared at the newcomer with open curiosity and admiration—as much for the great warhorse drinking from the gourd his father held as for the horse's rider.

"Come here, boy."

The lad's mother rushed over to him and wiped his face with her dirty apron, rubbing spittle on his cheeks and chin. When the youth was presentable, she pushed him forward. The boy resisted, bashful before the King.

Quentin nodded and smiled. The boy was a little older than Prince Gerin, and though of more slender build he had the same unruly dark brown hair.

"It is the *King!*" his mother whispered harshly in his ear. "Show yer manners!"

Whether the youth understood who it was that waited for him or not, in his eyes it did not greatly matter. Anyone who rode a steed such as the one that stood in the yard before him qualified as royalty in his young opinion.

His mother prodded him to stand before Quentin, where he gazed at his unshod feet and drew lines in the dirt with his toe. Quentin put his hands on his slim shoulders. "What is your name, lad?"

The answer was some moments in coming. "Renny, Sire." The voice was scarcely audible.

"Renny, I have a boy just like you," said Quentin. A knife sliced at his heart with the words, for again he remembered that his son was gone. "His name is Gerin," he continued, forcing a smile, "and he is about your age."

"Does he have a horse?" asked Renny.

"No," replied Quentin. It was true, for although Gerin could well choose any horse in the King's stable to ride, he did not have one of his own. "But he likes to ride. Do you like to ride?"

The youngster's face suddenly saddened. "I—I've ne're been on a horse, Sire." The awful truth was out and the boy felt better for it, for he brightened instantly and announced, "But when I get big I'll have a horse an' I'll be a knight!"

Quentin chuckled at the certainty in the young voice. "I am sure you shall!" he agreed, and then added: "Would you like to ride a horse?"

The dark eyes went wide and rolled toward the nearest parent for approval. " 'Tis all 'ee's ever wanted t'do," said the farmer. " 'Tis all 'ee talks of."

"Then today you shall have your wish, brave sir!" said Quentin. He led the youngster by the hand over to where Blazer stood quietly. The horse seemed to grow in size as they approached, and Quentin felt Renny's hand grip his tightly. "This one is a well-trained mount. He will not harm his rider."

With that assurance, Quentin picked the boy up and put him in the saddle. The boy wore a dazed expression, unable to fathom his immediate good fortune or sort out the innumerable sensations assailing him in this miraculous instant.

The King handed him the reins and placed them just so in his hands. Then, when Renny was situated, Quentin took Blazer's bridle and began leading him around the yard. The farmer and his wife stood together clutching each other, beaming happily as they watched their son ride the King's own stallion.

Quentin, too, felt their joy, and he laughed out loud. It felt good to laugh, and so easy. He had begun to think he would never laugh again.

Renny, for his part, celebrated the occasion with all the solemn pomp his young frame could muster. He sat rigid in the saddle, his back straight as any lance, eyes level, shoulders square: the very picture of a knight riding into battle, full of courage, the victory sure, the foe all but vanquished.

Then Quentin showed the boy how to pull the reins to one side or the other to make the horse turn, how to make him stop and go. Renny took in this information gravely, studiously.

"Do you think you can remember all that?"

"Aye," nodded the boy.

"Then he is yours to lead. Ride him, young master."
Quentin stepped away from the horse, and Renny threw
a half-worried, half-exultant look to his parents, kicked
his heels gently into Blazer's flanks, lifted the reins, and
began to ride the horse around the yard.

Blazer, champion of battle, high-spirited and fleet as
the wind over the plain, behaved as docilely as any plow
horse. He stepped lightly around the yard, circling the
three spectators, tossing his head and snorting now and
then, to the delight of all.

When the ride was over at last, Blazer came to stand
before his master. Before Quentin could reach up a hand,
Renny threw his leg over the pommel and slid from the
saddle as expertly as any knight. He wore a look of
dazzled triumph that seemed to say, I have ridden the
King's horse! I will be a knight!

"Well done, lad!" shouted Quentin, clapping the boy
on the back. "Well done!"

Renny's parents ran forward to embrace him, as
pleased for his good fortune as if it had been their
own dream's fulfillment. Quentin was moved by this
spectacle of love between the members of this simple
family. His heart went out to them.

"Thank 'ee, Sire," said the farmer's wife. She grabbed
his hand and kissed it.

"This be a proud day, Sire," crowed the farmer. There
were tears of joy sparkling at the corners of his eye. "Me
son astride the King's charger. . . ." There were no more
words to describe the pride he felt.

"Please, it is but a little thing," replied Quentin. "I
was happy to do it."

"You must stay t' supper, m' lord," said the woman.
Then she blinked in amazement, realizing what she had
said. She had just invited the King to supper! In her
kitchen! Oh, my!

Quentin began to make his apology, but stopped and
turned toward the road. The shadows of evening were
stretching across the land. The sun had grown into a

great blazing red fireball as it touched the far horizon. He was tired, and the thought of climbing back into the saddle and riding on to Askelon seemed repugnant at the moment.

"Madame," said Quentin, as he would address any noble's wife, "I would be honored to partake of an evening meal with you."

At once her eyes grew round and her jaw dropped; she turned to look at her husband, who merely peered back at her with the same expression of absolute astonishment. Then she gathered her skirts and dashed for the house to begin preparing the meal. Quentin smiled to see her go.

"M'lord," said the farmer when she had gone, " 'low me t'look after yer steed. 'Ee must be hungry after a long day's travlin'."

"Thank you, that would be most kind."

The farmer led Blazer away to the small barn set alongside the house at the back. The horse, sensing feed was close, picked up his hooves and fairly pranced away. Little Renny watched him go, his eyes still sparkling like stars. He had relived his momentous ride a hundred times already in his mind.

Quentin sat back on the edge of the well, folding his arms across his chest. Perhaps he should not have accepted the invitation; maybe he should not delay on the road. Ah, but he could not go back on his acceptance now. Furthermore, he could leave before dawn and be in Askelon early in the morning, and he could use the rest. Here, perhaps, he could forget his troubles for an hour, eat and sleep, forget.

"Why are you sad?" chirped a young voice beside him.

Quentin stirred himself and looked up to see Renny studying him carefully. "I was just thinking, lad."

"Thinking about your own little boy? He's the Prince!" Renny informed him.

"I suppose I was. Yes, he is the Prince—"

"And you're out searching for him," said Renny, finishing his thought. "Bad men took him away, and we must all keep our eyes an' ears open so's to see or hear 'bout him."

Quentin smiled sadly. Bad news does fly with eagle's wings, he thought. Yes, they all know what has happened. All of Mensandor would know by now. His grief was not as private as he supposed. Nothing about him was private anymore. The Dragon King's life was gossip, legend, and song to them.

What would they all think when they learned he had lost the flaming sword, Zhaligkeer, the Shining One, symbol of his authority and divine appointment? What would they say of him then?

"Don't 'ee worry, Sire," said the boy. " 'Ee'll find the Prince! 'Ee're the Dragon King! 'Ee can do anything!"

"Yes," replied Quentin, ruffling the boy's dark hair absently, "we'll find him." Please, let us find him!

The farmer returned from tending to Blazer and came to stand before the King, not daring to break in on his thoughts by speaking. He just stood there silently and waited. There came a call from the house and when Quentin did not stir, the farmer announced, "M' lord, supper's set'n."

The evening sky glimmered with the sunset; the soft white clouds were tinted pink and orange. Crickets sang in the grass at the edge of the road, and swallows skipped and darted in the blue air.

The world seemed poised on a fine silken thread, perfectly balanced between night and day. Quentin sighed and stood. The thread snapped, and the world rolled on toward night.

They walked quietly to the house, dipped their hands into a basin sitting on a stool near the door, and then went in to their supper.

22

DEEP IN PELGRIN'S GREEN HEART, TOLI PAUSED BESIDE
a spring which trickled out from a hillock of white stone
into a crystalline pool. He slid from the saddle and led
Riv to drink, then knelt himself and cupped water to his
lips. The westering sun tinted the sky with evening colors of dusty gold and pale violet, flaming the woodland
greens and burnishing the boles of towering chestnut and
hawthorn with a gleam like bronze.

Soon night would cover the forest with her dark wing,
and he would have to find a sheltered hollow or a dry
thicket for the night. But something drew him on, tugged
at him gently, urging him to go just a little further.

Do not stop, it whispered in the boughs around him
as the evening breezes stirred the green-gold leaves.
Ride on.

So, after a last drink from the pool, Toli heaved himself back into the saddle and pushed on, sending his
senses ahead of him to sift the air for a clue—a sound,
a flicker of color, a scent borne on the air—anything that
would tell him what had pricked his instincts and was
drawing him forward.

It has been too long since I was in the wild, he
reflected. My skills have grown dull. Now, when I need
them most, how will I find the Prince?

He rode along, bending his trail here and there through the wood, straining into the gathering twilight. He stopped, held his breath . . . what was that?

Nothing. He lifted his hands to send Riv forward once more, then hesitated.

There it was again: a soft chirrup, faint as the whirr of insect wings on the breeze. Toli waited for it to come again, and when it did he knew beyond all doubt what it was.

How long has it been since I have heard that sound? he wondered. Then, placing his hand at the side of his mouth, he answered the call with his own—not as softly or skillfully done, but remarkably similar. He repeated the call once, twice, and climbed down from the saddle to wait, his heart thumping against his ribs.

Through a stand of slim young beeches, stepping noiselessly among the low-hanging branches they came: three Jher kinsmen dressed in skins and wearing deerhide pouches at their waists. They hesitated when they saw Toli, but he made no move toward them, so the forest dwellers advanced.

"Calitha teo healla rinoah," said Toli when they had come as close as they would. In his native tongue it meant, "You have come far south this leaftime."

"The deer," the foremost Jher replied in the lilting speech of his people. "It has been dry in the north forest." He paused and regarded Toli shrewdly. "I am Yona."

"I am Toli."

The three Jher glanced among themselves, excitement mirrored in their deep brown liquid eyes. "Yes," said the leader. "We know. We have been watching you and recognized you. Everyone knows of Toli."

"How many are with you?" asked Toli.

"Forty men and their women and children," Yona replied "It is very dry in the north."

"Here in the south," put in one of the others, "the deer are fat and run slow. Three tribes are with us."

"Have you room for one more before your fire this night?"

The three looked at each other, smiled at one another with huge, toothy grins, and hooted in amazement at their good fortune. They all but stumbled over themselves to be the first to lead him back to the Jher camp.

The campfires were lit, and vension roasted on spits over the flames, wafting a tangy scent among the trees and dome-shaped dwellings made of deerhide, bark, and twigs. Toli had not encountered another of his race for many years, and he walked into the Jher encampment as one walking back into his own past. Nothing had changed. Every detail of life for the nomadic forest people remained the same—the deerskin clothing, the meals prepared over open fires, the sparkling dark eyes watching everywhere, the timid children clutching their mothers' legs, the old men squatting before the flames instructing the young boys in wood lore—all was exactly as he remembered it, the same as it had always been.

His guides brought him to stand in the center of the camp. A good number of Jher had already assembled to see the stranger, and the sight of this Jher prince dressed in the fine clothing of the light-skinned men produced murmurs and hoots and shy pointing as they discussed him. For here was one of their own—some knew who he was and told the others—yet changed almost beyond recognition as a Jher. None of them had ever seen such a transformation.

In a moment there came a stirring at the outer fringes of the ring of onlookers, and a pathway formed through which passed a shrunken old man. He carried a long staff made from an ash sapling on which were affixed the antlers of a buck. This ancient one leaned heavily upon the staff and tottered forward to stand before the visitor. At his appearance all the other Jher became silent as they waited to see what their leader would do.

For his part, Toli waited to be received by the venerated leader, hands held loosely at his sides, eyes lowered as a sign of respect.

The old man came near and stood before Toli, drawing himself up to full height, gazing at him with quick, sharp eyes. "Toli, my son," he said at last, using the polite form of address of an older man to a younger, "I knew you would come to us again."

Toli's eyes went wide with the realization of who it was that stood before him. "Hoet?" He recovered himself and said, "It is good to see you, my father."

With that the old man threw down his staff, put his arms around Toli, and hugged him to his breast. At that moment all the other Jher, who had been watching silently, burst forth and began hugging Toli, gripping his hands and arms, patting his head and back in a great show of affection. Toli, the hero of many of their most often told and highly regarded tales and legends, had come home. Tonight would be a celebration.

A huge fire was made in the center of the village and deerskin and woven grass mats unrolled and placed around the perimeter, and upon each mat a large wooden bowl filled with fruit. Toli and Hoet were led to the place of honor to squat on their mat while the choicest pieces of roast meat were passed to them. The other Jher all found places around the fire. Little children scampered through the village whooping and calling bird sounds to impress the royal visitor.

Hoet hunched beside his guest and gazed at him thoughtfully, patting his arm or knee from time to time as if to reassure himself that it was true after all, that Toli had returned.

When hunger had been appeased, all eyes turned toward Toli and Hoet, and a chant began, slowly and quietly at first, but building rapidly to a crescendo of Jher voices. *"Thia secia!"* they called. "We want a story! Tell us a story!"

As the honored guest who had been fed and pampered with ceremonious attention, it was Toli's turn to repay the favor by telling his people a story. He stood and raised his hands above his head for silence, in the tradition of the best storytellers.

But before he could begin, Hoet stood too and laid a hand on Toli's shoulder saying, "I claim the first story in honor of our brother."

The Jher gathered around the shining fire, nodded, and whooped their agreement. Toli sat down as Hoet raised his hands and began to speak. "One day long ago, in snowtime, when all the forest sleeps in white blankets and the cold makes the deer's coat shaggy and warm, men of the white race came to the forest on horses. They ran wildly among the trees, and noisily, for the deer fled from the sound of their passing and we heard them from far away, for they had no forest feet.

"They came near our wintering place, though they did not know this. We watched them from afar, and one night encircled them as they sat before their crude fire." Here all the listeners hooted good-naturedly at the careless white travelers. "When Whinoek's fire once more filled the earth with light, we approached these white men and one of them attempted to speak our tongue." Hoet laughed and all the others laughed, too. Though they had all heard this story countless times, all strained after every word as if it were uttered for the first time.

"This one, Bushface, told us of grave danger in the forest. The vile Shoth pursued them with thirsty knives and hunting birds with poison in their talons. He asked for help. In this, Bushface showed much wisdom, for surely the white men would have sunk down to their deathsleep before one more night had passed."

At this all the Jher clucked their tongues; some smacked the earth with their hands at the mention of their hated enemy's name. "Should we help them? I asked myself. The answer was not quickly coming—it circled around me like a young deer at a forest pool. For they were white men, the same who cut down trees and kill the deer in numbers and make stone dwellings on the earth. But the Shoth are our enemy, as they are the enemy of all civilized people. So I decided to help them, for Bushface was a man with much power in him, and there was with him a woman, a *kelniki*"—the word meant wife of the leader—"whose hair shone like the dancing fire. I did not wish the evil Shoth to have such fine hair hanging from their spears. And with them also was a young boy in whose eyes I saw the look of one who is chosen for greatness. I knew I must help them. But how?"

Toli listened to the recital of the events that had changed his life forever, and it seemed that he was once again the young Jher sitting before the fire as he had so many times, listening to the tales of his elders and the deeds of heroes of his race. He remembered back over the years to the day when the white men had come into their winter camp; they looked cold and frightened and extremely awkward in his young eyes.

But the strangers had horses. Oh, how he had wanted to ride a horse! He could still feel the thrill of seeing the animals for the first time up close—so beautiful, so graceful they were, and strong. In his boyish heart he vowed he would give anything to ride one of those horses. So when Hoet's gaze fell on him he had leaped quick as a fawn to present himself for the task of leading the white men through the forest to the Wall of Stone.

Hoet had sent him then, and the rest had become legend among the people of the forest: Bushface he had come to know as Durwin, Hawknose became his friend Theido, Firehair was the beautiful Alinea, and Kenta, the boy with glory on him, he chose as his master, Quentin, now became the Dragon King.

In the eyes of his kinsmen, Toli had acceded to the highest of honors—serving a man of renown. For though he was of the white race, Quentin was also the leader of his people and that, for the Jher, gave Toli the highest acclaim; there was no higher position a Jher could aspire to than to fulfill the role of servant to a great leader.

" . . . And so he has returned this night to us," Hoet was saying, "to his own people once again. The glory of his deeds casts Whinoek's favor upon all of us, and we are accounted worthy." The old chieftain turned proudly to his guest.

If they only knew how I have failed, Toli thought. Would they still receive me with celebration and feasting? No, they would feel disgrace and shun me; my name would be no longer spoken among them. I would be forgotten.

When Toli turned again to those before him, he found all eyes on him. The fire crackled and the sparks leapt high into the night sky, glittering in all the black eyes watching him expectantly. They were waiting for him to speak now. Hoet had given him the honor of speaking last; his would be the story of Jher tribesmen carried with them to their sleep, an honor ordinarily reserved for the oldest and wisest among them, Hoet himself.

He stood slowly, unable to put his feelings that moment into words. What can I tell them? he wondered. What could I say to them that they could possibly understand?

The dark eyes watched him; a murmur arose and made its way around the ring. Will he speak? What will he say? Why does he wait? Speak, great one!

The murmur became a voice ringing in his ears: Tell them! it cried. Tell them how you have failed!

Now an awkward silence spread through the waiting crowd. Toli felt their eyes up on him. "I . . ." he began, then faltered. "I—cannot." He walked away from the circle of friends. The only sound to be heard was the fluttering of the fire as he withdrew into the darkness.

23

"YOU DID NOT THINK THAT I WOULD LET YOU LEAVE me behind?" Esme's eyes glittered in the candlelight. Outside, the sky lightened in the east to a dull gray, becoming pearl-like pink near the horizon where the sun would rise.

Bria smiled, the light softening her features. "In truth, Esme, I did not think you would care to come with me. It is a long journey to Dekra, and an uncertain errand at that. It is something I feel I must do."

"And you must do it alone?"

"No, my mother will go with me."

"And I will go with you, too. Chloe has already packed a few things for me, and as you see"—she indicated her riding clothes—"I am ready to go."

Bria laughed and hugged her friend. "Then you shall come along, by all means. Forgive me. I should have invited you. I merely thought that . . . Well, we will go together, and I will welcome the company."

Esme smiled too. "It will make me feel useful to you. And I must admit that I have always wondered about this mysterious city of Dekra. There are many strange stories about it—is it really enchanted?"

"Yes, but not the way you mean. Its enchantment grows from the love of its citizens. It is, as you shall see, a most remarkable place."

"You have been there many times?" Esme fell to the task of helping Bria ready herself for the journey.

"Not many, but a few times. Quentin and I would go there occasionally before the children were born. The last time was for Yeseph's funeral, a few years ago. Quentin talked about going back there to stay, but after Yeseph died he never spoke of it again. He is King, and the King must remain on his throne in Askelon." She shrugged, and Esme finished tying the points at her sleeves. "Now then, let us go wake the girls."

The little Princesses were already awake and chattering like squirrels when the two women entered the bedroom. Chloe was there, along with their own nurse, packing their clothes into carved chests for the journey. When they saw their mother, they jumped up and flitted across the floor to embrace her.

"Mother, oh, Mother! Is it true? Can we really go with you?" they begged. "We will be good, and we will be quiet. We promise it. Oh, please?"

Bria smiled and kissed them both, then knelt down to speak to them. "Yes, my darlings. You are coming with me. But I want you to remember that this is a long journey, and you will get very tired. You must do as I say, for we will travel quickly."

"Are we to ride horses too?" asked Brianna.

"Yes, horses?" echoed Elena.

"You will ride in a coach with Grandmother. She will need someone to keep her company on the way."

"Is Daddy going, too?"

"No," Bria sighed. "The King is searching for Gerin and will not come with us. Hurry now, and finish dressing—this stone floor is cold on your feet! We will wait for you in the yard. Chloe will bring you out when you are ready. Now run along."

Both girls scampered away to finish dressing. The two women crept back into the silent corridors of Askelon Castle and made their way down to the hall where a simple breakfast had been laid for them. There Alinea was waiting, her trim form clothed in summer green—an embroidered tunic over trousers and tall riding boots. An image flashed into Bria's mind of her mother standing just so, telling her good-bye. For a moment she imagined this had all happened before just this way.

"Good morning, Mother." The Queen paused, then asked, "Have I ever seen you wear these clothes before?" She examined them carefully.

"Yes," Alinea laughed, "I believe you have. But I am amazed that you would remember."

Then it came to her. "How could I ever forget? You were going off to rescue Father—dressed like that. You had to sneak out of your own castle."

"I thought I would just try them on and . . . well, they fit, so here I am. Do you approve?"

"How could I disapprove?" Bria hugged her mother, and then they all sat down to eat before leaving. They spoke little, each occupied with her own thoughts of the impending journey. When they finished eating, they hurried out into the ward yard where the horses and coach were already waiting for them; the coachman was tying the last bundle of provisions to the frame behind the coach.

"Wilkins!" said Bria when she recognized the man.

"My Lady," he bowed, "when Lady Esme told me of your wish to go to Dekra, I thought it best to travel with you."

"If you would rather have another . . ." added Esme.

"No, it is a fine idea. I commend it and thank you both."

"I am at your service." Wilkins bowed again and touched the hilt of his sword. Bria was once again reminded that theirs was not a pleasure outing.

From across the yard the warder, a man with short gray hair and gray eyes, whose sinews seemed made of whipcord, approached. "My Lady, I am against this enterprise." He spoke directly, not wasting any words.

Bria smiled. "I know, Hagin, but there is no worry."

"No worry? Your own son kidnapped, and you say no worry?" The man gave her a look of frank disapproval. "The King will have my hide stretched and nailed on yonder drawbridge if I let you go."

"We will come to no harm," insisted Bria. "We travel with an escort of knights, and the King's roads are safe enough."

"Then I shall go too," he announced.

"No, I would rather have you here to await the King's return."

The warder grumbled but held his tongue and said no more.

Bria and Esme were helped into the saddle, Alinea into the coach, and the horses were led out through the yard toward the gatehouse where two knights, mounted and ready, were waiting. There they paused, and Chloe and the Princesses came running out to scramble into the coach. A few of the castle servants had gathered to wish the travelers a speedy and safe journey; the little girls waved and threw kisses to all until they entered the dark tunnel of the gatehouse and were cut off from sight.

Hagin the warder, nephew of Trenn, stood rooted to the spot until they had disappeared, then shook his head and stumped off.

ASKELON LAY BUT TWO LEAGUES AWAY. WITH A LITTLE speed the tinker would arrive at midday, find himself a meal, and begin making his rounds. There were certain customers he visited every time he came to town. Milcher at the Gray Goose Inn, for example; he always needed a new pot, or a pan repaired, and always included supper too. Yes, he was one of the best customers, and there were others: the butcher's wife, the chandler's sister, the baker, and the weaver.

In fact, all the merchants needed his services one time or another. Even the King's kitchen staff occasionally bought his wares.

"A wee bit further, Old Tip," Pym told his dog, "and we 'uns'll stop a little in Askelon. What say ye there? Eh? A nice grizzle bone fer ye, Tipper. A hot pasty fer me—ah, innkeeper's wife makes the best meat pies in all Mensandor. There's a fact, Tip. The best. Makes me mouth water to think on 't."

Tip took all this in with a benign, thoughtful expression and wagged her tail with appropriate enthusiasm, and they ambled down the road, clinking and clattering as they went. As they came within sight of Askelon Castle, they heard the sound of hooves drumming along the road behind them. Pym turned around, stepped to the side of the road, and waited for the rider to pass. In an instant the white charger and its regal rider swept past them.

Pym raised his hand in greeting, and the intent rider dipped his head in acknowledgment as he rode on by. The tinker followed the horseman into the distance with his eyes and continued on his way.

"Comin' a day, Tip, an' we 'uns'll ride, too! A wagon an' a sharping stone an' treadle-foot—that's fer we!" He nodded slyly to this dog. "We 'uns've found our fortune!"

He gazed after the rider disappearing into the distance. "But ye know, I think that 'un was the King that passed by jest now. I couldn't say fer a certain, but might's been. Looked a King t' me. Would ye not say, Tipper? Eh? Quite right, quite right. Looked a King. Maybe 'twas the King."

Pym glanced at his black dog sadly. "The gods be with him, poor King. Terrible thing. Terrible. His son snatched off like that. A terrible thing—deed most foul, that. Didn't I say it, Tip? A deed most foul." The tinker raised his voice to a shout and called after the rider, now just a speck in the road far away, "The gods be with ye, Sire!"

He squinted up an eye toward the sun, gauging the time of day. The morning shone fair and bright, the sky high and wide and blue. Across the green fields farmers worked their land, coaxing grain out of the soil. Occasionally the tinker would wave to one, who would answer his greeting likewise.

Ahead the town drew slowly closer, and the sun rose higher. "Tipper, we 'uns'd best stir our bones or be too late to get our meal. Come along, now."

He put his head down, hoisted the straps of his baggage, and picked his pace; they clanged and rattled down the road to Askelon.

"YOU CANNOT BE SERIOUS," SAID THE HIGH PRIEST. HE stared at the old man as if unable to comprehend the words just spoken.

"I assure you I am." The cold eyes glared; the tongue poked snakelike between the thin scars of lips.

"But why? Why risk discovery now? It is not wise."

"Not wise? You dare to presume wisdom beyond Nimrood's?" There was poison in the voice, and echoes of cracking thunder.

High Priest Pluell paled and threw up his hands. "Oh, no! It is not that. Never." He hurried to explain. "It is just that I thought—that is . . . we are safe here. We have time now to think this through, plan our course of action. We must move very carefully, you would agree."

"I have decided," said Nimrood flatly. "There is nothing more to discuss. I will tell you what to do; I will make all the decisions from now on.

"You have nothing to fear if you do your part and see to it that your stupid priests do theirs. Leave all else to me." The old wizard glared at the priest with malevolent glee. "You want to humble that usurper King, do you not? Ah, yes. I can see it on your face. You want him and his God Most High brought low before all Mensandor. Then you will be acknowledged and the power of the High Temple increased."

The High Priest could not resist a smile at the prospect.

"Well, then, do nothing—do you hear? Wait for me. I will return shortly, and we can begin."

Pluell watched the old man—fearing him, loathing him, but his desire to flaunt his power over the throne crushed any resistance he might offer to Nimrood. Yes, to humble the proud King, to reassert the claims of the temple over the affairs of the realm—that was worth the price of putting up with the troublesome old long-beard Nimrood. It was worth the risk.

"Very well," said the High Priest. "It shall be as you say."

Nimrood nodded and winked and smiled his gruesome smile. "That is good, my pet. Do as I say and all will be well. Now I go."

The High Priest sat in his handsome chair and listened to the tap of Nimrood's footsteps receding into the temple. When it is done, I will cast the old vulture out, he thought. I have but to contend with him a little longer.

24

BLAZER'S HOOVES SOUNDED DULL THUNDER OVER THE great planks of the drawbridge; his iron shoes struck sparks from the stone flagging of the gatehouse road. Shouts of "The King is coming! Open the gates! The King is here!" preceded him, and startled gatekeepers leaped into action.

Horse and rider jolted to a stop in the inner ward yard. Squires dashed up to take the King's well-lathered mount. Without a word Quentin went straight into the castle, through the banquet hall filled with people still lingering over their midday meal, and on to the throne room.

He flew up the steps to the Dragon Throne and threw off his soiled cloak as he collapsed into the throne. Quentin called angrily for his High Minister, his voice booming out into the quiet of the deserted throne room. His call was answered with a flurry of footsteps, but no sign of Toli.

Quentin seethed inside. He had risen late—later than he had planned—and had started his journey to Askelon after the sun was well up. This put him in a raw mood. Every stride was too slow after that, and he arrived in Askelon harried, fuming, and out of patience.

He had slept well enough, curled in his cloak on the

farmer's own bed—the farmer's wife would not have it any other way but that the King should have their bed—and awakened feeling better than he had in days. But his tardy start, and the dark thoughts of what awaited him in Askelon, soon destroyed the fragile peace he had achieved.

As a result, he now raged about the lack of respect for his person and the slipshod attention his interests received.

"Where is the High Minister?" he bellowed. His voice echoed back to him from the far corners of the empty hall.

There was no answer.

Quentin sank deeper into his melancholy. He shouted again and this time heard answering footsteps.

"Well?" He looked down to see Hagin, the warder, coming resolutely toward him.

The man bowed when he reached the dais and said simply, "My lord, you have returned."

"Yes, I have returned," Quentin snapped. "Where is everyone? Tell me quickly if you value your tongue."

Hagin appeared unperturbed. His clear gray eyes regarded Quentin unflinchingly. He was man enough for any monarch's moods. "They are gone, Sire," he related simply. "All are gone."

"All? What do you mean all?"

"Everyone."

Quentin stared sullenly at the man. "What are you babbling about? Send for them at once."

"It may not be, my lord."

"The Queen—where is she?"

"Her Highness and the dowager and the children have left Askelon, the Lady Esme with them. They ride for Dekra."

"What?" He had not expected that answer. To Dekra? Why? "When did they leave?"

"Just before sunrise."

Quentin struck the arm of the throne with his fist. While he had dawdled on the road, his wife had left the castle. If he had not stopped, if only he had ridden on to Askelon, he would have been here in time to detain her. She would not have gone if he were here.

"Where is the High Minister?" Quentin growled.

"He has disappeared, Your Majesty."

Again an unexpected reply. "Eh?"

"He was last seen in attendance at the hermit's funeral, Sire. After the burial he disappeared. He did not return to the castle. It is believed he slipped away from the procession on the way back to Askelon. No one has heard from or seen him since."

Toli has disappeared? Well he might. If the Prince is not found, it would be better if he never returned.

Who else was left? "Theido and Ronsard—have they arrived?"

"They arrived, my lord, and immediately took responsibility for the search party for the Prince. They have gone."

That was it, then. All were gone—those he needed most to see. He was alone.

The gnawing loneliness he had felt on the road was upon him once more. It was true: everyone he cared about was gone.

Here was a loneliness deeper than that of the temple. Then he had not known any different life, but now . . . He had not been so deserted in years. Every day he was surrounded by his closest friends and loved ones— every single day. He thought it would never end, that the closeness, the love would go on forever. But sadly he was wrong. In three short days—already it seemed a lifetime—his world had been shattered and the pieces scattered by some cruel fate. Nothing remained now of the happiness he had so recently possessed.

"Sire?"

Quentin stirred himself. The warder was looking at him strangely.

"I asked if that would be all, Sire."

"Yes, that will be all. Go now. Leave me." He heard

the man's steps diminish as Hagin left the hall. A door closed, and a boom rang in the silence like a pronouncement of doom.

There in the dim interior of his throne room, the King gave himself over to the hopelessness that assailed him, sinking deeper and still deeper beneath the crushing weight of despair.

WITH A ROUND WOODEN BOWL TUCKED BETWEEN HIS knees, Toli sat on a woven grass mat outside the summer hut of Hoet. The Jher went about their daily business around him, but he was aware of their constant sidelong glances which told him that he was still very much in their minds. No one would ask him about what had happened last night as he stood before the fire unable to speak—that would be too impolite. Still, they would wonder, and the gentle Jher would watch him when they thought he was not looking. So Toli, aware of their scrutiny, pretended not to notice and slowly dipped his hand into the bowl for the sweet mulberries that were his breakfast.

A shadow fell over him as he squatted in the sunlight listening to the chirp and twitter of the early morning forest, the soft soughing of the upper branches in the breeze, drinking in the musty fragrance of earth and bark and growing things. Toli glanced up at the figure which had come to stand before him.

"You are leaving again," Hoet observed.

Toli nodded. "I must."

"I knew that you had not returned to stay. You are needed, for there is trouble in the land."

Toli cocked an eye to the old chieftain. "You know about the white men's trouble?"

"It is not only the trouble of the white race; when darkness falls, it covers all. Yes, we know there is trouble in the land. Wind is a swift messenger, and the forest holds no secrets from the Jher."

"Then you know the King I serve needs your help.

His son has been taken from him by force."

Hoet nodded and leaned long on his staff before he spoke again. When at last he did, he replied, "And you carry the blame for this deed."

Toli looked away. "How did you know?"

"How else can it be that you are not with your master in his time of need? He blames you, or you blame yourself, and that is why you ride alone."

"Yes," replied Toli softly. "Your wits are as sharp as your eyes, Wise One."

"When you did not speak last night before the fire, I knew—though I guessed even when you came riding alone to our camp."

"Then you knew why I could not speak."

"Come with me," said Hoet, and started away.

Toli rose, set the bowl aside, and followed the aged Jher leader through the village among the trees. The glances of his kinsmen followed him as they walked the length of the camp to where Toli's horse waited, already saddled, grazing in a clump of sweet clover at his feet.

"You do not belong here, Toli. Go now."

Toli felt the color rise to his face; his shame burned within him. "You are right to send me away. I have dishonored my people."

"It is not from dishonor that I send you, my son," said Hoet gently. Toli's eyes darted to his elder. "Why does it surprise you? You have not turned away from your master—*that* would be dishonor. No, I send you for yourself. Go, my son, and find the white leader's son. Your life will not be your own until you have found the boy."

Toli smiled and gripped the old man's arm. "Thank you, my father. The knife in my heart does not hurt so much now."

"Yes, go. But come again one day, and we will sit together and share meat."

Toli took up the tether peg and gripped the reins, swinging himself easily into the saddle. Riv snorted, eager to be off. "I will ride more swiftly with your blessing."

"I have no blessing to give you that Whinoek has not already given." Hoet paused, regarding the slim man before him. "It is said the King raises a temple to the One Most High."

"Yes," replied Toli. "The Father of Life is not widely known among the white race. My master seeks to make the name of the God Most High known to every man alive under the great heavens so that they may worship the only true god."

"That is most worthy," replied Hoet. "But it seems to this old one that where one temple stands, another may not also stand. Is this not true?"

Toli stared at his tribesman for a moment before the implication of what Hoet had said broke in on him. "Yes, your words are true, Wise One, and I would hear more."

Hoet shrugged and lifted his antlered staff. "It has been reported to me that there has been much night traveling in the forest by men from the east, who also returned that way. I did not see them, so I cannot say how it is, but the white men's great temple of Ariel lies to the east, does it not?"

"You know well that it does," said Toli with a grin. "Thank you, my father. You have given your son a great blessing." He turned Riv into the forest and stopped before entering the shaded trail to raise his hand in farewell.

Hoet raised his staff and said, "Go in peace." He remained gazing into the forest long after Toli had disappeared, then turned and shuffled back into the Jher village.

25

NIMROOD CACKLED WITH MALICIOUS GLEE AT HIS GOOD
fortune as he flitted through the shadowy passageways of
the High Temple like an overgrown bat, his black cloak
billowing out behind him like wings. Such a stroke of
luck! The gods had sent the meddlesome Jher to the very
steps of the temple.

That ridiculous High Priest wanted to turn him away,
thought Nimrood. Would have turned him away! But I
was there to stop it, and before the dog could run away I
had him bound and beaten and thrown into the cell with
that mewling Prince! Ah ha! Ha, ha!

At first the sorcerer had to fight down the impulse to
finish the deed begun in Pelgrin Forest on the day of the
hunt—to strike down the Jher at once. Even now the old
hatred fired his thin blood, but he was compelled by a
greater prize to turn away from his long-nursed wrath at
the one who had shorn him of his power, his precious
magic, and had very nearly stripped him also of his life.

The image of that day still burned in Nimrood's black
brain: Durwin, a far inferior wizard, stood before him
and would not even protect himself, would not lift a
finger to summon the power at his call—not that it
could have saved him. No, thought Nimrood, nothing
could have saved him.

And then, as Nimrood lifted his rod to deliver the lethal bolt and so blast that cursed hermit's bones to powder . , . that arrow! From out of nowhere it had come, striking deep into his flesh, sending the rod from his hand. Then, there was the Jher notching another arrow onto his bowstring. The sorcerer had pleaded for his life—those miserable pleas still echoed in his skull. "Don't kill me!" he had screamed, and the words had mocked him every moment since that day. He had been humbled before the bow of the Jher, but the young warrior had withheld his pity, had sent another arrow into his enemy's heart.

It has exhausted every last living spark of Nimrood's power to transform himself into a raven and wing to safety. It was a long time before he could once again take mortal shape, for he had not even the magic left to change, but was forced to wait until the spell wore off of its own accord.

And a bitter exile it was, trapped in that feathered body, prey to the elements and living on scraps of dead, rotting meat. But though he regained but a thread of his former power—the rudiments of mere child's dabbling still clung to him, the ability to make noise and light— yet he had returned to seek his revenge equipped with an older and more pernicious art: treachery.

The name of Nimrood the Necromancer had perhaps died from men's memory; so be it. His lies would do what enchantment could not—of that he was certain. Yes, at long last he would have his revenge.

Oh, the gods were fickle and full of mischief! It took all one's cunning to outsmart them. Nimrood had done it all his life. And now they had finally delivered the victory into his hand. Yes, oh, yes. Soon the upstart whelp of an acolyte king would suffer as he, Nimrood, had been made to suffer all these years.

Nimrood allowed himself one whoop of demented joy at the impending consummation of all his dreams. Yes, the Dragon King would fall; and that barbarous god of his, that brutish Most High, would fall with him.

The wizened old sorcerer clenched his fists and laughed out loud, throwing his head back and letting the sound pour forth from his wicked throat. It was a sound to chill the marrow of anyone passing by. But no one heard it; he was alone and savored the moment to the full, his black heart lifted in exulation.

PYM STOOD BEFORE THE SIGN OF THE GRAY GOOSE, A strolling heap of scrap metal and tools, bags and bundles and barter enough for any two tinkers. The hand-painted sign of a long-legged, long-necked plump gray goose wobbled on its chain, the windows of the inn dark now, the door open, but silence within.

"Tinker!" he cried. "Tinker, ma'am!"

He waited, winking at Tip. The dog winked back with both eyes.

In a moment he heard footsteps coming toward him across the planked floor. Then appeared a round, flushed face and the plump form of Emm, the innkeeper's wife. She waved her apron when she saw him, exclaiming, "Pym! You are a sight, you are! Come around again, have you? Give me a hug."

She threw her arms around him, and he around her. They were old friends and good ones. "It's good t' see ye, Emm. You know me—I been afancy for one of yer meat pasties and a noggin o' yer best. We 'uns jest had t' come back soon's we 'uns finished away south."

"You missed Emm's cooking, eh? Well, come in, come in with you. We'll set a fork and trencher at the board and put you to it."

Pym followed the matron inside, rattling like a calf in a cupboard with every step. "Milcher!" she called. "Otho! We got us a guest. Look lively, now!"

Milcher poked his round bald head out from behind a cask he was rolling across the room. "Oh ho! Pym it is! Oh ho! Pym, good to see you, old friend. Come to visit, eh? Glad to have you. Glad to have you!" He called over his shoulder, "Otho! Hurry up now! We have a guest!"

A tall boyish-faced man came into the room carrying two small kegs under each arm. He grinned at the tinker and put the kegs down, then went to the cask his father was straining at. With ease the overgrown Otho hefted the cask into place. "Pym and Tipper is it?" He grinned boyishly.

Milcher wiped his sweating face on his sleeve. "Whew! I've been at it since dawn this morn." He shook his friend's hand. "Come and sit down with me. We'll drink a sip and fill our bellies."

"Don't you 'uns trouble yerselfs fer we," said Pym. Tip wagged her tail amiably, knowing that this was the place where she recieved those juicy tidbits and gristly beef bones. She barked once in anticipation of such a morsel.

"Yes, Tip," laughed Otho, stooping to pat the dog. "We won't forget you. Good old girl."

Pym threw off his implements and wares and trundled them into a corner. He sat down with the innkeeper, and Emm served them up a little stew and bread. Otho fetched frothy ale in crockery jars and joined them.

They talked of all that had happened since Pym's last visit, and all the customers who would need Pym's services. Before long, however, their conversation turned to the one subject on everyone's minds and on the tips of everyone's tongues in every gathering place in Askelon.

"Shocking!" said Emm, clucking her tongue. "Simply shocking. I can't imagine who would want to harm that beautiful boy, poor Prince Gerin!"

"Nor who'd be fool enough to go agin' the Dragon King. There's the mystery," nodded Milcher knowingly. "Him and that sword of his, enchanted and all."

They all shook their heads in bewilderment at the affairs that had befallen their King. "*You* were on the road," continued Milcher. "Did you see anything?"

Pym merely shrugged. " 'Pears I come too late." He was of half a mind to tell them about the dead man in the road, and about the sword. But even though they were his

friends, he thought better of it and kept that part secret.
" 'Twas over before we 'uns got to Pelgrin, tho a' course
we met lots abodies on the road to tell 't."

"Oh, there's talk aplenty, there is," agreed Milcher.
"Most of it not worth a thimble o' mud. They say
it was the Harriers got the boy Prince. Others say it
was some of that swill-belly Nin's cravens who've been
hiding up in the mountains all these years. Bah! That
lot was driven into the sea at lancepoint—every last one
of 'em."

"Strange though how nobody has seen hand nor hair
of them that took him. 'Tis very like the earth opened up
and swallowed them whole, quick as you please. Nobody
seen nothing," said Otho.

"I saw the King," volunteered Pym. "This mornin' on
the road. Least I thought 'twas the King. Looked a King
t' me."

"Likely did. Likely did," said Milcher, slapping the
board with his hand. "Ham the butcher says the King
rode in this morning all alather. Been riding like a wraith
for days."

"Did he have his sword when you saw him?" Otho
asked Pym.

"What a question!" Milcher cried. "Of course he did.
The Dragon King never goes anywhere without that
sword. That's what makes him invincible."

Otho did not back down. "That's not what I heard."
He lowered his voice and leaned forward across the table
so no one would overhear him, though there was no one
else in the place. "I heard from Glenna, the Queen's
maidservant—"

"Glenna's his sweetheart," put in Otho's mother, smiling a knowing smile. "Works in the royal kitchen."

Otho threw a warning glance in her direction but
hurried on. "—that there's talk in the castle that the
King has lost his sword!"

"Lost his sword?" Milcher gasped, staring wide-eyed
at his son. "Bah!"

"He never would!" said his mother in a hushed tone. "Lose the Shining One? Never!"

Otho only nodded; his eyes squinted. "He rode out with it the day of the hunt. Everyone in Mensandor saw it—its great golden hilt gleaming from the scabbard at his side. We all saw it." He put his finger in the air for emphasis. "But no one saw it when he returned."

"What happened t' it?" asked Pym. His heart raced faster.

Otho licked his lips. "No one knows." His voice was a whisper. "But they say that if the Zhaligkeer is gone, the kingdom is ruined."

"Pshaw!" said his father uneasily. "Who would believe it?"

"It could well be," maintained Otho. "Could well be."

The King is still King, isn't he?" Emm glanced at her son apprehensively.

"Aye, as long as he holds the sword. That sword is his power. Without it he is doomed."

"Doomed?" wondered Pym.

"Aye, and you would be too. There's some as says that Quentin isn't the rightful King, not being blood and all."

"He was chosen, by the gods!" cried Milcher.

"Chosen he was. But it was the sword that backed it up." Otho inclined his head conspiratorially. "It is the work of the gods. They are angry with this new temple of his; they don't like his chasing after that new god— that Most High. The old gods are going to humble him as an example to the whole kingdom to return to true worship with gifts and supplications."

Otho crossed his long arms and leaned back in his chair, smug in his rightness in the matter. The others looked at one another helplessly. Who was there to dispute what they had heard?

If this was a matter between gods, who could intercede on behalf of mere mortals? Who could contest the gods?

Once there was a resolute young man with a flaming sword who had the very hand of a god upon him. He was strong, invincible. But he, too, had proven only human, subject to the wounds and errors of all flesh.

How fickle the gods were. They had allowed him to prosper for a season; now they wanted their tribute, and even the Dragon King would have to bend before them. Blazing sword or not, they meant to have their due, and the King could not refuse them.

The glittering dreams of the Priest King and his wonderful City of Light were just smoke after all. Men were just the playthings of the gods.

So it had ever been, and so would ever be.

26

IF NOT FOR THE URGENCY OF THEIR ERRAND, BRIA would have enjoyed the journey to Dekra. The days wore the golden-green mantle of fair summer; peace clothed the land and seemed to blossom from every bough. The dark deeds of only a short time ago—a few days—receded into the past, more and more remote with every league.

Only the throbbing ache in her heart reminded her that all was not well, that her son had been taken from her, that her world would never be right until he was returned.

By day she rode with the others, keeping her spirits high—talking, singing, or steeping herself in the beauty of the day. By night she prayed; her prayers were not for herself, but for her son and her husband, that the Most High would keep them safe wherever they were. And sometimes in the night, when no one could see her, she wept.

The Queen and her companions, though unused to the rigors of the road, were well looked after by Wilkins and the other two knights, and were made as comfortable as possible. And owing to the smoothness of the King's Highway, they moved swiftly toward their destination.

"Today we will cross beyond Celbercor's Wall," declared Alinea. Several leagues from their camp of the night before, though the sun was only a few hours up, they had stopped to eat some breakfast, and to let the Princesses gather wildflowers.

"Have we come that far?" asked Esme with some surprise. "I thought the journey would be much longer."

"Before the King's Road, yes. Quentin's work in extending the highway has made travel to this part of the kingdom the easier and more quickly done.

"We may reach Dekra by evening tomorrow if we hurry," said Alinea. She pointed to the east and south where the mountains lifted their heads to the clouds. "Celbercor's Wall runs from the sea into those hills of rock. Once beyond it, Dekra is only two days' ride."

"Oh, then let us hurry by all means," cried Esme. "I have always wanted to visit Dekra. You have told me so much about it, I cannot wait to see it."

"It is indeed a most remarkable place," said Bria. She gazed into the distance as if she were looking for the sweeping towers of the city to rise above the horizon. "The Ariga were a noble and beautiful people. Theirs is a city like no other."

"Yes, and much changed since I first saw it," Alinea said, and began to tell them about the occasion of her first visit—the flight to Dekra in the dead of winter with Theido and Durwin, Quentin and Trenn; the wild midnight ride to the wall just ahead of the Harriers; Quentin's near-fatal tangle with the poisoned talons of a Harrier's hawk and their anxious vigil over him as he lapsed into deathlike sleep upon reaching the ancient ruined city; the extraordinary love and kindness of the Curatak who healed him.

When she finished, Esme's lovely features held a mesmerized look. "I have never heard the story before—oh, a piece of it here and there. But to hear it now like this . . ." She turned admiring eyes upon Alinea. "You were very brave, my Lady. You and the others. It is a most remarkable tale. Now I want to see Dekra all the more."

They rode on, following the road through wooded hills and pleasant lowlands, green and fragrant in the sun. Sometimes they met farmers leading ox-drawn carts, or other travelers—merchants on foot or in wagons, riders speeding on hurried errands to distant parts of the realm. But most often they had the road to themselves for long stretches.

Celbercor's Wall, that singular, enduring feat of strength and cunning, grew as they approached: first a thin line crossing the far hills, gray in the distance, with no more substance than a bank of low-lying clouds. Closer, it loomed high and strong, rising from the crown of hills with solid force, the sun shining full on its blank stern face.

The road bent along the face of the wall toward the Malmar Inlet. The travelers rode down the long wooded slope to the rocky shore of the inlet. There they stopped, watered the horses, and waited.

"How will the ferryman know to come for us?" asked Esme.

"Watch," replied Bria. One of the knights had made his way along the shore to a tall pine pole standing in a heap of stones. There he fastened a red pennon to a cord attached to the pole and raised the pennon to the top where it waved smartly in the breeze. "You see? We have only to wait a little. The ferryman will see the signal and come at once."

"Clever!"

"It was Quentin's idea. When he used to travel frequently between Askelon and Dekra, it was often difficult to find a boat on this side of the inlet. So he established the ferry hoping, I think, that one day travel to Dekra would much increase."

They sat on the warm rocks, listening to the calls of seabirds wheeling overhead and the lap of water murmuring to the rocks at their feet. In a little while they saw a wide flat boat plying toward them across the water.

"Good day, my ladies," greeted the ferryman when he had brought the boat into the narrow rock-lined channel that had been cut into the shore. "A good day for travel. Going to Dekra, is it?" He eyed them each with good-natured curiosity.

"Yes, we are," replied Alinea.

"Allow me to fetch you across first, if you please. Then I will return for the coach and horses."

"Thank you, Rol," said Bria.

The man turned and looked at her carefully. "My Lady? Do I . . . it is! I am sorry, Your Highness! I did not recognize you!" He bowed quickly, reddening with embarrassment. The Princesses tittered happily.

"It has been some time," laughed Bria. "And I am hardly dressed the part of a Queen."

"No, my Lady," Rol bobbed his head. He said no more, but went quickly to his work. In no time the passengers were sitting on the broad benches at the bow. Wilkins stayed behind with the animals and the coach.

Rol worked the long oar with his wide strong hands, and the ferry moved out slowly into the deeper channel, floating to meet the current that would carry them across the water.

At Malmarby their arrival was greeted by a score of barefoot children who had flocked to the docks to see the strangers. Travelers were still not so common an occurrence that they did not draw laughter from inquisitive youngsters, as well as amiable stares from their elders.

"I was deeply distressed to hear what happened to young Prince Gerin," said Rol as he led them up a long, planked ramp.

"You have heard then. Now you know why we ride to Dekra," replied Bria.

"Everyone has heard, my Lady. Some of us had gone to the hunt. I was there when . . . we know what you must feel. But the Dragon King will find the evil snakes that did this, I know."

"We are praying for the Prince every moment," said Alinea.

"Yes, my Lady," said Rol. "Perhaps they can help at Dekra. There is much power there."

"Thank you, Rol," said Bria.

"If you would excuse me, my Lady." He bowed again and shoved the boat back out into the inlet. In no time at all he was back with the coach and horses.

The Queen and her entourage remounted and moved on. "I will be here when you return!" shouted Rol, who raised his arms and clapped his hands, shouting and scattering the children in front of him like chickens.

The travelers passed through Malmarby and entered the marshy lowlands beyond. The country in Obrey was wilder, more spare and open. It changed at once from that on the other side of the inlet, becoming a more forbidding place so that the traveler might well feel he had left the hospitable world behind and entered a land untamed and unpredictable, where anything might happen.

"The coach can go no further," announced Wilkins. Little more than a league out of Malmarby the track had all but vanished. Wilkins had just returned from surveying the trail ahead. "Even on horseback it will not be easy."

"I had quite forgotten how wild this land is," said Bria. "What do you advise?"

"Leave the coach," the driver replied. "One of your bodyguards can ride one of the coach horses and I the other. Alinea can take the knight's mount, and the Princesses can ride with me."

"Let me take one of them, at least," offered Esme.

"And I the other," said one of the knights.

His comrade dismounted and offered his saddle to Alinea, who accepted. "Thank you. It has been too long since I have ridden bareback, and I do not think I could manage the feat now."

Wilkins and the first knight began unhitching the horses, then rearranged the baggage, distributing the necessary items among the riders and abandoning the rest along with the coach, which they hid in a bower of young maple saplings and wild ivy. When they had finished, all were mounted once more and they continued on their way happily, if more slowly.

"MY LORD," SAID THE CHAMBERLAIN SOFTLY AS HE rapped on the door, "Lord Theido and Lord Ronsard have come. They ask that you receive them at once, Sire."

Quentin sat slumped in his huge chair, staring into the cold ashes on the hearth before him. His eyes were red from lack of sleep. His hair was in disarray and his features coarse and haggard.

"Send them away," he croaked. "I will see no one."

"But, Sire, they insist!"

"How many times must I tell you?" the King shouted, seizing a silver cup from the table at his hand and heaving it at the chamberlain's disappearing head. The cup struck the door, splashing red wine, like blood, over the embossed wood and onto the floor.

He heard voices in the anteroom and then quick steps. His door was flung open and in came Theido, with Ronsard close on his heels.

"My lord, we would speak with you," said Theido tersely.

"We did not think it right that you closet yourself thus, receiving no one," added Ronsard.

"It seems you give me no choice," said Quentin. He did not so much as turn his eyes toward them, but continued staring into the ashes as if they were the ashes of his own life, now dead and spent.

"This is not like you, Quentin," said Theido, deliberately using his name.

This brought nothing but a mirthless smile to the King's lips. "See? The truth: I am no King and never was. I only played at being King, and my friends humored me as they would a child." He laughed, an aching, hollow sound. Then he turned his face toward them and asked, "Where is my son?"

One look at his fearful countenance and both men inwardly gasped—so great was the change that had occurred since they had seen their friend last. Gone was the youthful man full of vigor and quick strength, keen-eyed and alert, always sharp as the point of a lance, and eagerly winging through life, with the reckless vitality of an eagle soaring above the clouds for the sheer joy of soaring.

This man before them appeared as one who had lived in darkness for years, bereft of hope and brittle with despair. One wrong word and he might collapse upon himself in tears or fly into a foaming rage.

"The men are combing the hills and villages beyond Pelgrin. We will find him, Sire." Theido was the first to recover his voice. He tried to sound matter-of-fact, though the sight of his distraught King disturbed him greatly.

"We would have come sooner . . ." began Ronsard. His voice failed him, and he turned away.

"Go away," said the King.

"My lord, we would speak to you as friends." Theido took a step toward him. "Please, I ask as a friend, hear us."

"Friends," Quentin mumbled. The word was a curse upon his lips. He passed a hand over his eyes and then asked again, "Where is my son?"

"He will be found. Trust in it; he *will* be found."

The Dragon King shot an angry look at the two knights. "Trust in it! He says to trust that my son will be found!" His voice rose higher as rage leapt up in him like a flame. "Trust, eh? Trust what? Trust you? Trust the Most High? Ha! There is nothing that a man can trust. Everything deserts him in the end. Youth fades. Love grows cold. The works of his hands disintegrate—or are torn apart by his enemies!"

The King lurched up out of his chair and took up the long iron poker from the hearth as he began to pace back and forth. "The gods, my friends, the gods! Sooner trust in the weather; it is less fickle than they. The gods taunt a man, build him up so that they may laugh at him when they dash him under the wheels of misfortune. Great sport! See how he writhes and tears at his flesh! See how his heart turns upon itself; see how his pain devours him!"

Theido and Ronsard could only stare at this tirade.

"The Most High!" continued the King. "Do not speak to me of the Most High. He is more subtle and more wicked than all the rest! He tortures his victims with dreams and visions of glory. He prophesies and promises. He delivers their enemies into their hands and raises them up far beyond their rightful place.

"And then he takes it all away! Takes the man's very heart out of him, strips him of all he holds dear in life and casts him bleeding into darkness! That is the Most High, God of gods! And fool is he who trusts in him!"

With that Quentin threw the poker. It smashed into the table, knocking over a tray of food which had been sitting there cold and untouched. Silver utensils scattered and clattered to the floor.

Quentin staggered, holding his head, and fell back into his chair exhausted.

A stunned silence hung like a pall over the room. Ronsard touched Theido on the arm, nodded toward the door, and the two left quietly, closing the door behind them.

27

"Never have I seen him so." Ronsard gestured with his hand toward the chamber they had just left. He spoke in an astonished whisper. "He is not himself."

"The weight of his dreams has fallen upon him, and he is being crushed beneath it." Theido shook his head sadly.

"Dreams are one thing, but he raves as one gone mad!"

"If he feels the depths of his sorrow more deeply than other men, it is because he has trusted the Most High more than most."

"If he falls the farther, it is because he flew the higher, eh? Would that Durwin were here. He would know what to do." Ronsard sighed heavily. "I miss that old hermit."

"Aye, and so do I. But we must do the best we can. The kingdom depends upon it, I think."

"What shall we do?" Ronsard shrugged helplessly. "Until the Prince is recovered, there is nothing to be done."

"No," said Theido slowly, "I perceive there is more to his torture than the Prince's disappearance."

"Or Durwin's death?"

"Or Durwin's death. Though both of those weigh heavy on him now, I believe he could rise above them if not for his loss of faith in the Most High."

"What can we do about that?"

"Find the sword." Theido looked steadily at his friend. "Find the sword and return it to him before someone else takes it for himself."

"I am all for it, sir. Only tell me how to do it, and it will be done."

"I would tell you if I knew, count on it. I only know that we must recover the sword—and soon." Theido put his chin in his hand and stood for a few moments in deep thought. Ronsard watched him and waited.

He said at last, "Ronsard, you must go alone and begin the search."

"And you?"

"I will stay here, close to the King. He may need a stout companion nearby."

"As you say, Theido. But where shall I start?"

"That is the puzzle. But I think I have a plan that will be useful to us. Are you game to try?"

"I will do anything."

"Good; then come with me. There is no time to lose."

THE FIRST THING HE FELT AS CONSCIOUSNESS RETURNED was something cool running down the side of his neck. Blood? He raised a hand and felt the side of his head where the trickle started.

The movement brought a throb of pain to his aching head. He moaned.

"Toli? Are you alive?"

The voice was hushed, but nearby. He opened his eyes carefully, then squeezed them shut again quickly, the light sending blazing fireballs through his brain.

"Ahhh!"

"Just lie back. Do not move," the voice urged. Toli tried to place it.

In a moment the throb in his head eased somewhat and he opened his eyes, shielding them with his hand. The bare stone room was dim. The light slanted down in a single brilliant band from a narrow window high up in the wall. He lay on a straw pallet on the floor opposite the window.

He turned his head to the side; his vision wavered, but he made out the form crouching beside him on folded knees.

"Prince Gerin! Oww! What did they do to my head?"

"They dumped you in here. I was afraid you were dead."

"When was that?" Toli pushed himself up slowly on his elbows. Each small movement brought a new stab of pain through his head.

"Do you not remember?" asked the Prince. He offered again a bit of cloth soaked with water that he had applied to Toli's head.

Toli took it and placed it against his forehead. "I remember nothing," he said. "No—I remember coming to the temple and asking to see the High Priest. I saw him, I think—talked with him. The next thing I know I am waking up here."

"The High Priest?"

"Yes."

"Is that where we are? The temple?"

"It must be," replied Toli. He looked around the cell and at the door, which was not the door of a castle dungeon, though it was heavy oak and strong enough to keep a prisoner from breaking free. "Did you not know where you were taken?"

"No, it was dark. And they blindfolded me. It seems we walked for days. Then I was shoved in here. Days ago. That is the blindfold you are holding." Gerin indicated the damp rag.

"I see. How many days?" Toli studied the Prince carefully, searching for any signs of mistreatment.

"Three, I think—maybe four. Yes, four. Two before you came."

"I have been here two days?" It did not seem possible.

"This is the second. How do you feel?"

"I will live." Toli reached out a hand and patted the young Prince on the shoulder. "You have done well, young sir. I am glad to see you alive. How have they treated you?"

"Well enough. I am fed from their table and have good water." Gerin looked eagerly at his friend, glad to have someone he knew with him, though both were prisoners. "Toli, what has happened?"

"I scarcely know." He shook his head slowly. How do I tell him? he wondered.

"I know about Durwin. I have been worried for Father."

"He is well. He is searching for you—for us. Ronsard and Theido, too."

"Poor Durwin," said Gerin. Tears came to his eyes. "Oh, poor Durwin."

"Your father was with him when he died. He died at peace."

Gerin sniffed, trying to hold back his sorrow. But he had been brave so long; now that a friend was here, he could let down. The sobs came, and the tears washed down his face.

Toli put an arm around the boy's slim shoulders. "It is good to cry. He was your friend. There is no shame in tears of mourning."

When Prince Gerin could cry no more, Toli gathered him close, speaking softly. "I do not know why this has happened, but there is some evil behind it, you may be certain. Priests do not leave the temple to murder and kidnap the innocent—that is, they have never done so before. Why they should start now, I cannot say." He looked at Gerin closely. "But we must find out what it is they plan. Think now, what did you see?"

The Prince was silent for some moments, then raised his eyes to Toli and said, "There were six of them, five of them swordsmen and one other—the leader. I heard them talking about him."

"What did they say?"

"They do not like him much. That is all." He thought for a moment, and added, "And the one who told about Durwin—he said that the King had killed one of them in the road." He looked at Toli questioningly.

"It is true. In his grief and rage your father struck down one of the kidnappers on the road. That is on his heart, too." Toli was silent for a moment, then added, "Well, it is done. Perhaps there is yet some better purpose behind it. We must hope so."

The two talked and comforted each other. The day, measured by the slanting band of light as it moved across the floor and up the opposite wall of the cell, stretched on. Toward evening a priest came with two bowls of water and a large trencher of food. The door was opened, the food slipped in, and the door closed and bolt thrown—all in an instant.

"This is how the food is brought?" Toli asked.

"Yes, every day. I think they are afraid I will try to escape."

"Have you tried to escape?"

The Prince nodded. "Once—on the road. Tarky reared and I fell, or was grabbed. That is when he ran away. It was not far from here."

"A horse with Tarky's sense can find his way back home, or someone will catch him and take him to the King. Either way I believe someone will soon think to look for us in this direction; the King will find us, you will see."

Gerin nodded, but said nothing.

Toli patted his shoulder, saying, "Never fear, young sir. I will not let anything happen to you." The words almost stuck in his throat. Though it cost my life, he thought, I will not fail you again.

28

"WHAT FOR YOU, MY GOOD FELLOW?" MILCHER RUBBED his pudgy hands on his sopping apron, and grinned good-naturedly at the stranger. "Are you new to Askelon?"

The sandy-haired man, dressed in the clothes of a common laborer—leather jerkin over a brown tunic and baggy brown trousers—leaned against the bar. "A jar of your dark, if you please, sir," he replied. "Are you the inn-master?"

"Aye," said Milcher. "I am the keeper. But my wife is the master." He gave the man a great wink. "Dark it is, and the best in all Mensandor, some say. I myself prefer it."

The innkeeper turned away for a moment to fill the jar, and the man took advantage of the lapse to study the interior of the inn. The Gray Goose was filled tonight. There was a hubbub of conversation, which was normal, but this overlaid a churning current of excitement. An atmosphere of expectancy thickened in the place as dense as the smoke from the pipes of the patrons, which curled toward the low-beamed ceiling. Ale jars clinked, and men drank and talked in strained, nervous voices.

Ronsard had felt it the moment he walked in—this tingly, anxious suspense. It was as if they were all gathered there waiting for something to happen, knowing that something would happen, wanting it to happen.

Secure now in his disguise as a peasant, there was little chance of discovery; he was not a frequenter of inns and did not live in Askelon any longer, so it was unlikely he would meet anyone he knew. Ronsard turned back to Milcher, who was laying the pewter jar on the board. "Strange mood tonight, eh?"

"Aye—for the last two nights." Milcher nodded slyly.

"How so?"

"Have you been out of the country, man? The kidnapping! The King's sword lost!" Milcher rolled his eyes and leaned close. "There is wickedness about, my friend. Folks do well to look to themselves, if you know what I mean."

"I heard about the kidnapping," said Ronsard, sipping from his jar, "but what is this about the King's sword? I know nothing of that."

"Oh!" cried Milcher. He leaned close again in the air of a man discharging a secret it burned him to keep. "The King's sword is gone. No one knows where. It is said the King will fall. Without the sword he cannot stand."

"You cannot mean the Shining One—"

"One and the same! Yes, that's the one. What other sword would it be?" He turned to the other man working at the bar. "Otho! Come here."

Otho lumbered up and fixed Ronsard with a look of benign appraisal. "Yes?"

"Otho, tell this fellow about the King's enchanted sword."

Otho was not tired of relating his knowledge, though he had done little else since he heard it. With enthusiasm he embroidered on the scant details he possessed, embellishing them to lend his tale extra color.

"Aye, I see what you mean." Ronsard nodded solemnly when Otho had finished. "This could be bad. Very bad indeed. I am glad I am not the King."

"His fish is flayed, as they say. I do not think he will be King for long. There is much talk against him now."

"I have not heard such talk."

"It is just beginning. There was a man in here last night, a white-bearded fellow from the north, out of Obrey. He said that people there are afraid of the Dragon King's new god—this Most High of his. They are arming to protect their temples."

"Protect their temples? From what?"

"From the King! The Dragon King has sent men to pull down the temples." Otho nodded knowingly, his round face glowing with pleasure at having such a dull-witted and uninformed listener.

"Aye, I have been hearing the same," put in Milcher.

"Who is this man—this one who is saying these things?"

"He was in here last night. Told us all about it. If you wait a bit he may be back. I think he said he would come back tonight if he was still in Askelon." Milcher swept his eyes over the crowds lining the benches and hunched over the tables of his establishment. "I do not see him now, but he may come later."

Ronsard took up his jar and said, "I will wait in that case. I want to hear what he has to say. Point him out to me when he comes."

THEY HAD COME UPON THE RUINED CITY IN THE SETting sun. The red stone of Dekra glimmered like ruby in the crimson twilight, its delicate spires and finger-thin towers rising toward the deep blue heavens. The city seemed to have magically appeared, dropped out of the sky into the wilderness, a thing of charmed creation.

"This is Dekra," said Esme. "I have never seen anything like it. It is so . . . so different."

"It is a strange beauty," replied Bria. "Very unlike the cities we build. The Ariga used many building methods unknown to us."

"There has been much accomplished here since last I set eyes upon it," said Alinea. "That was long ago. But

Quentin has told me that the work goes on apace. Yes, much has been done."

They rode to the gates of Dekra, now closed against the night. But upon reaching the huge tiled gates a boy appeared, popping his head through the smaller gate-door cut in one side of the much greater panel. He disappeared again, quick as a blink, and they heard his voice calling on the other side. "Visitors! Open the gates! Visitors!"

They waited, and in a little while heard the creak of the gates opening. The stoop-shouldered man who met them smiled and ushered them through the gates, saying, "I am sorry to have shut you out. We did not expect visitors this night, or I would have left them open for you. Come in, come in. Welcome to Dekra!"

The travelers all dismounted, glad to be free of the saddle. The man closed the gates once more and then hurried to them. "Have you ridden far, good people?"

"From Askelon," replied Alinea.

"All is well in Askelon, I hope. It is a far ride; you must be very tired." He peered at them with kindly eyes, glad to see these visitors who would bring some news of the rest of the kingdom. "I have sent the boy to bring an elder. I am sure he will want to receive you properly."

At that moment there were voices; they looked up to see the young boy followed by a man in a long mantle coming swiftly toward them. Behind him were several others who had dropped what they were doing in order to come and make the visitors welcome.

"Ah, Alinea! Bria! How good to see you again! Oh, this is a joyous surprise! Look," he called to those around him, "the Queen has come! And Alinea!"

Alinea looked at the man, trying to remember him. Bria stepped up just then. "Mother, you certainly remember Elder Jollen."

"Oh yes, I remember him well. It has been a long time. I am much surprised you remember me!"

"Not as long as all that—to look at you, you have not changed a bit. You are still as lovely as ever you were." The elder bowed to the ladies graciously. "And, Bria, if not for your mother standing here beside you, I would declare you were her. So much alike you are. Flowers of the same bud. Speaking of flowers. . . ." He winked at the Princesses, who giggled.

"You do flatter us, sir."

"No flattery, my Queen. It is the truth." His eyes turned to Esme, standing nearby. "And you must be the lovely Esme, of whom so many good things have been spoken."

"I am honored, sir, and much impressed, for surely we have never met."

"No, but it is not difficult to guess your identity. I remember an occasion or two when Bria told me about her friend. I knew when I saw you that you must be she. Welcome." He turned his eyes to Wilkins and the knights. "Welcome, good friends all." Elder Jollen paused, regarded his guests carefully, and added, "May you find in Dekra that which you seek."

There was silence for a moment, then he clapped his hands and said, "Now then, the Governor's Palace is ready for you. My wife instructs me that you are to dine with us this night. But take your time; refresh yourselves from your trip. Some of the young people will go along to help you settle your belongings."

"Thank you, Jollen," said Bria. "But I feel already revived having just set foot in Dekra. We will join you soon."

"Excellent! Go along now. I will invite the other elders to join us after the meal and we will talk—with your permission?"

"Yes, please do. I would have suggested it. I think it will be best."

"It is good to be here again," remarked Alinea. "I had forgotten how it lifts the heart, and how much I have missed it without knowing what it was I longed for."

"Then I am glad you have come. Perhaps you may stay a long while, my Lady." Jollen beamed happily at his weary guests. "Yes," he said again, "I am glad you have come."

The visitors were immediately swept up and away by the happy inhabitants of Dekra, and led to the old Governor's Palace in the heart of the restored section of the city in a procession that wound through the narrow paved streets of the ancient ruin. All along the way Curatak stopped to watch them pass, greeting them enthusiastically or joining in the throng.

Esme gazed in wonder at all she saw; everything appeared so foreign and so strange. The walls of buildings all aglow in the setting sun shone with colored tiles—mosaics of the life of the vanished Ariga. Great arches and long colonnades of graceful spiral columns—all carved from the same gleaming red stone—gave the appearance of a majestic, exalted race. The simple sweeping lines of their architecture spoke to her of lofty purpose and a nobility of heart and mind.

The effect was singular. So simple and yet so right. Yes, that was the word. There was a rightness about things here, she decided. A wholeness. A wholeness of what? She did not know yet. It was only upon seeing and experiencing Dekra that one noticed the aching lack in the rest of the world.

All around her the Curatak chattered like happy children, glad to see them, to receive visitors. She felt their eagerness splash over her like spring rain, reviving her, warming her. She felt the great lump of buried ice she had carried so long in her heart begin to thaw and melt.

Oh, she thought to herself, what a wonderful, fantastic place. I am glad I came. By the time they reached the Governor's Palace she was thinking, Truly this is the city of gods. I never want to leave.

29

To Pym, the inside of Askelon Castle was utterly and inexpressibly remote—like a castle of the gods in the far mountains. He had often seen the high, forbidding walls rising from the great crown of rock on which the castle was founded, and had as often wondered what the inside looked like.

Of course he had been through the gates on occasion—on his visits to the kitchens where he did his business with the King's staff. But never had he been invited into the castle itself, and the close proximity served to heighten, rather than diminish, his curiosity.

But now it appeared he would be allowed through the inner gates and into the halls and chambers beyond—perhaps even to stand in the Great Hall of the Dragon King. Reluctantly he said good-bye to Tip, being forced to leave the dog in the inner ward yard, and turned to wait for the chamberlain who would conduct him inside. He had come at dusk, after his day's work was finished, thinking that Kings worked sunup to sundown like other men, and that he would have a better chance of an audience when the King's daily labors were done.

Ordinarily Oswald—son of Oswald the Elder, who had died some years ago, following the death of Eskevar—would not have dreamed of letting the little tinker inside the castle, but would have sent him straightaway to the kitchens. But he was overwhelmed with anxiety for the King. Quentin had sunk further into depression and did not stir from his stuffy chamber, which he now kept sealed and dark as a tomb.

Oswald feared for the King. Even Theido had been powerless to effect any change in the King's behavior. So anything was worth a try—even a tinker who came to the gates insisting on seeing the King, saying he had important information for him, information which only the Dragon King himself could hear.

"I am Oswald, the King's chamberlain," he had explained. "What do you want?"

Pym, sitting on a stone bench just under the archway of the main castle entrance, stood up quickly and came forward. "Good sir, if ye please, be s' kind as to bring me to the King, We 'uns've a pressing matter t' set afore His Highness."

"The King," informed Oswald coldly, hoping to draw information from the man, "sees no one who will not state his business to me."

Pym scratched his jaw. "That I cannot say, sir. It is fir the King." He leaned forward and confided, "But I kin tell ye this much. . . ."

"Yes?" Oswald glared at the man, but he seemed not to notice.

"It be veery, veery important. That's what 'tis, yes."

"And what does this important information concern?"

"That be fer the King, sir. Not fer noun else."

Oswald could see that the man was adamant about an audience with the King. He looked harmless enough, and who could say but that the tinker might indeed have something that could be useful to his master, though that seemed highly unlikely. Still there was a possibility, and in this dark time even the minutest chances might be snatched at.

"What is your name, sir?" asked Oswald.

"Pym, sir. Pym 'tis, and Pym 't always will be."

"Very well, Pym. Although it is not my proper course to admit you like this, I will. But if you waste the King's time and my own with worthless drivel or idle rumor such as is heard in any village market or inn, I will have you removed promptly. Do you understand? You will never be welcome in Askelon again!" He looked at the tinker sharply. "Now, then, do you still want to see His Majesty?"

"I do, sir." Pym swallowed hard.

"Do you still maintain that your information is vital to his ears alone?"

" 'Tis, sir."

"Follow me."

With that Oswald the Younger turned on his heel and walked away. Pym hesitated. "Well?" asked Oswald. "Are you coming?"

Pym nodded and hurried after the chamberlain. They marched along a wide, polished corridor where servants moved, hurrying about their chores. To Pym, the smooth stone walls and oak-beamed ceilings seemed things of enchanted origin. He marveled at even the most commonplace furnishings he glimpsed along the way, for they were royal furnishings. This was the home of the Dragon King, and these were the Dragon King's chattel.

Past countless doorways they went, past halls—each with huge carven doors—and galleries hung with giant tapestries of rich design. Up stairs and down stairs they went, deeper and deeper into the heart of the castle, and with every step Pym grew more excited. He was to see the King!

Finally they stopped in a short passageway of paneled oak—the royal apartments. Oswald led them to a door which bore the carved and red-lacquered figure of a terrible, twisting dragon. The chamberlain put his hand to the latch and said, "Wait here; I will announce you."

Pym, with palms sweating now, wiped his hands on the backside of his pants, shifted first on one foot, then on the other. Perhaps it was a mistake—perhaps it *would* be better to tell the chamberlain and let him decide if the King should hear his story. Yes, without a doubt. Let the chamberlain decide.

But before Pym could change his mind, Oswald reappeared, and he was yanked inside. Oswald took him through this first room—there were chairs and a great long table piled high with many scrolls of plans for buildings and a gleaming suit of armor standing on its frame—and to a door at the further end, to the King's inner chamber.

Oswald knocked softly, opened the door, and pushed Pym in. "Sire, Pym the tinker to see you." The door was closed quickly and quietly behind him, cutting off his only escape.

Pym tottered forward on shaky knees, his eyes unused to the darkness, his mind reeling in the awesome knowledge that he was in the presence of the mighty Dragon King. It was almost more than he could endure.

As EVENING CAME ON, THE INN GREW CROWDED AND the conversation more intense. Amidst the clink of ale jars in the hazy, murk-filled room, Ronsard, in his disguise as an ordinary laborer, listened and watched all that took place around him.

Something was at work; he could sense it, feel it. What is more, all gathered at the Gray Goose could feel it too. A heightened impatience, a simmering restlessness seethed just below the surface. Expectation, at first casual, had been drawn tighter and tighter until it hummed like a bowstring. Anticipation quivered in every voice, danced in every eye.

Tonight there would be trouble.

Ronsard had seen moods like this before in crowds of men. On the battlefield it could send troops into a foaming fury to drive the enemy into flight. It could just as easily turn back on itself and ignite flames of fear, causing even field-proven veterans to abandon their arms in mortal terror. Which way it turned depended on the leader.

But who was the leader here? He wondered. That white-bearded traveler the innkeeper had mentioned?

Ronsard drifted unseen from table to table, listening here and there to what was said, trying to determine not only what sparked this unnatural mood, but also what course it would take when it broke.

"I tell 'ee," said a man, "the gods er angered."

" 'Tis the fault o' the King. Any man, blind or not, can see that plain enough," said another.

"It is no good going against them. No good at all."

"Dangerous it is! Dangerous!"

"Something must be done!"

"The sword is lost, did you hear? The Zhaligkeer is lost."

"Aye, there's trouble coming. It has brought us nothing but trouble. What's wrong with the old ways?"

"Old ways are best! By the gods!"

"The Shining One gone? What can it mean?"

"The kingdom is without a King! That is what it means!"

So the voices went. And of all the gossip Ronsard heard, one item concerned him more than any other: they knew about the missing sword. The King's enemies would know soon, if not already, and then the infighting would start.

Would Quentin be equal to it? Ordinarily, yes. But not now, not in his present condition.

Ronsard settled back along a rear bench and watched the room, as one would watch a caldron beginning to boil. Would this stranger, this Longbeard show himself? What if he did not come—what would happen? Ah, what would happen if he did appear? That was more to be feared.

Ronsard stood and was about to return his long-empty ale jar to the bar when Longbeard entered. Ronsard did not see or hear him. Rather, he knew the man had appeared by the sudden tension in the room, the thrill that tingled in the dank, smoky air.

The inn grew hushed.

"He is here!" said a voice close by.

"There he is. That's the one I told you about."

"Ah, yes. Here he is."

"Now we will find out what to do."

"Longbeard will tell us what to do!"

The whispers swirled around the gnarled old man like dry leaves around a bent old tree. Longbeard moved into them easily. If he understood the sensation his sudden appearance had caused, he showed no outward sign of it.

Ronsard watched him walk to the center of the room, making his way to the bar. The inn was completely silent now. All eyes were on the old man with the flowing white hair and beard. Watching. Waiting.

Then came a shout. "Longbeard! Have you seen him?"

Seen whom? wondered Ronsard.

Longbeard turned toward the voice and replied, speaking normally, but so every ear could hear him, "Yes. I have just come from his chambers."

A man standing near him asked, "Will he change his mind?"

"No." Longbeard shook his head slowly, with infinite sadness. "He will not change his mind."

"Then we must take matters into our own hands," shouted someone from across the room.

"Tell us what to do," said another.

Longbeard held up his hands. "It is not for me to tell you what to do. I am a simple man like yourselves. I know not the ways and minds of gods or kings."

The knowledge stung Ronsard like the blow from the flat of a sword. The King! He was talking about the King! Quentin was the "he" this Longbeard mentioned.

But how was this possible? It was improbable that this white-bearded old stranger had been allowed to see the King. The Dragon King had shut himself in his rooms and would see no one—not even his closest friends, as Ronsard well knew. Yet, the implication was plain: I have been to see the King and he will not change his mind. Change his mind about what? What game was this twisted old root playing? What was his aim?

I must speak to him alone, thought Ronsard. I must get him out of here some way and take him where we can talk without being overheard. There are too many people here. The situation could get out of hand.

But before Ronsard could form a plan in his mind, someone shouted, "Tear the King's temple down!"

"By all the gods, yes! Tear it down!" answered another.

Other voices took up the shout and added their agreement. Benches were thrown over as men jumped up. In an instant every man in the room was on his feet, fists in the air, crying for the destruction of the King's Temple.

This, then, is the spark that ignites the flame, thought Ronsard. *But there must be a way to stop it*. He glanced around for a place to stand, saw an empty table nearby, and jumped up on it.

"Friends!" he cried in his sternest, most authoritative tone. "Friends, listen to me!" The clamor which shook the inn died down somewhat. "Listen to me!" He held up his hands for silence and looked around him at the upturned faces. He had their attention now.

"Friends, what you propose to do is wrong. It is very dangerous as well. Some of you could get hurt—hurt very badly. Maybe even killed. It is no small thing to go against the King. Do you think he will not defend his temple? How many of you would make your wives widows this night?"

Ronsard noticed that some of the eyes slid away from his uneasily. Good, he thought, this is working. But I must give them something now.

"Let us instead send a petition before the King," suggested the knight. "We will demand that he account to us for the raising of this temple. The petition can be our voice."

There were mutters of agreement all around. Hot heads were cooling under Ronsard's sobering logic. He drew a sleeve across his face to wipe away the sweat.

"Please," he continued in a more reasonable tone, "for your own sakes, and for your families, let us all sit down together and draw up the petition."

"When?" said someone close by.

"At once—here and now!"

"And then?" the same voice asked.

"And then I will take it to the King personally." Yes, thought Ronsard, this is working. A disaster has been averted tonight.

But just as he framed the thought, there came a shout from across the room. He glanced up to see old Longbeard standing on a table pointing at him.

"Lies!" Longbeard screamed. "Lies!" Before Ronsard could speak the old man shouted, "Do any of you know this man?"

The crowd grumbled its answer: no one knew him.

"Ah, you see!" shouted Longbeard. "He is one of the King's men. I saw him when I went to see the King this evening. He was there. The King has sent him here as a spy among us!"

"No! It is not true! I only want to help you."

"King's·man!" a burly peasant shouted behind him.

"It is true, I am a friend of the King. But I am no less your friend. I am warning you: do not go against him in this matter. Do not take th—"

Before Ronsard could finish speaking, he felt the table on which he was standing rise up, tilting away from him.

"Lies!" they shouted. "Liar! We'll do for you!"

The table tipped, and Ronsard was pitched to the floor. He landed on his side, and the fall knocked the wind out of him. He rolled to his knees, gasping for breath.

A boot lashed out and struck him in the ribs. A fist caught him behind the ear. He struggled for his feet.

The room spun crazily. The air was heavy, and Ronsard found it hard to breathe. Loud voices buzzed in his ears, but he could not hear what they were saying. Feet and fists pummeled him.

Ronsard rolled into a ball to protect himself, throwing his arms over his head. A table crashed to the floor nearby, scattering ale jars. A heartbeat later, light exploded behind his closed eyelids. His limbs jerked convulsively, and he lay still.

30

THE MEAL HAD BEEN SIMPLE, WHOLESOME FARE: BROWN bread and white cheese, braised meat, early vegetables and fruit. Esme, enraptured with Dekra, thought each dish a delicacy, and savored every bite.

She spoke little during the meal, but listened to all that was said around her. There was a quality to the voices she heard—a song which rang in the air, faintly but noticeably; it was music to charm her soul. Upon reaching their rooms in the visitor's quarters of the Governor's Palace, they had bathed in fresh, sun-warmed water and changed clothes, accepting clean new gowns of white with light summer mantles of blue, tied at the waist with long blue sashes. They had rested then on clean featherbeds, awaking refreshed when their young guides came for them.

When they reached Elder Jollen's dwelling, the stars were beginning to light the twilight sky, and the sound of laughter and music drifted out of the courtyard adjoining his home. Many of Dekra's people had been invited to make welcome the important visitors. There were candle lanterns all around—lining the tops of the walls and hanging from the trees. A long table had been brought outside where they could sit; others made themselves comfortable on cushions or benches along the wall. After they had eaten, songs were sung and the Elders told stories to the amusement of all.

The evening passed like a dream, a dream of happiness and light, of fullness and peace. Flowing peace, thought Esme, like a river. Not merely the absence of care, but a deeper all-absorbing trust in the ultimate rightness of things. Like a river that runs along its course, be it rocky or smooth, accepting both with equal ease, never allowing the rocks to stanch the flow, filling the deep and shallow places alike, covering all and flowing on.

All this Esme received from looking and listening: looking at those around her and listening to her heart.

When at last they were alone with the Elders—the little Princesses were carried back to their beds sound asleep—Bria began to tell them why they had come. Esme waited to see how the Elders would receive this news, and what they would do about it.

They were unusual men, these elders, she thought as she watched them nodding their heads gravely; their very presence invoked an aura of wisdom and trust. Only moments before they had been telling funny stories and laughing the loudest of any. They sat or moved among their people without regard for their exalted position— indeed, more like servants than leaders. But now they sat in solemn council, entering into the troubled events that Bria described with empathy and compassion. Not as judges, but as sympathetic friends, they listened with all attention, sometimes nodding, sometimes shaking their heads sadly, but listening until the Queen was finished.

" . . . And that is why we have come to you," Bria was saying. "We did not know what else to do."

Elder Orfrey, the man chosen to replace Yeseph, spoke gently in answer. "You have done well to come here. We will help you all we can."

"Ah, the many shapes of evil," said Elder Patur. "Darkness is most inventive in its combat with the light."

"But powerless in the end," added Elder Clemore.

"Yes, as long as men refuse to give in to it," said Elder Jollen.

"The battle rages on all sides," said Patur, "and men are drawn into the meleé whether they will or no. I see that the battle has come once more to Askelon and to the King. But it is ever thus—darkness fears the places where light burns the brightest, and these the darkness would destroy."

"What can be done?" asked Bria. Esme wondered the same thing.

"That is the responsibility of the Most High," replied Clemore. "We will seek his guidance."

"Through prayer?"

"Yes, through prayer," said Patur. "We will hold a prayer vigil for Quentin and young Gerin, Toli, and the others. Concerning Durwin, though we mourn his passing, we will rejoice in his entrance to the kingdom of the Most High, and pray that his reward is great. We will begin at once."

With that the men joined hands with the women and began to pray. Esme, who had never prayed in this fashion, felt awkward at first, but relaxed and turned her mind to the prayers of the Elders. As she listened, she felt a moving within her; her heart quickened, responding to the words, but also to something more: a presence unseen, but distinct. It was as if the Most High had come to sit among them, entering into their prayer.

Esme's scalp prickled at the thought—a god who walks among his people! How strange. Gods were remote, disinterested, living in their mountains or in their temples, served by man, but never serving, as likely to harm as to help if it pleased them.

At that moment she gave herself to the God Most High, saying to herself, "I know not of your ways as others here; but, Most High, if you will receive me I will follow you. For I, too, would learn of you and serve you."

In response Esme felt a slight rising sensation, as if her soul were being lifted up. By this she knew that her prayer had been heard and accepted. She gripped the hand on either side of her more tightly, and felt life begin to trickle through her heart once more, after being dried up for so long.

PYM STOOD IN THE DARKNESS OF THE KING'S CHAMBER. He could hear him breathing slowly, rhythmically, like an animal in its lair. Should he speak? he wondered. Should he wait until addressed?

The moment stretched to an awkward length and still the King said nothing. Pym cleared his throat hesitantly. He waited.

"Well?" asked a voice out of the darkness. The voice rasped like the voice of an old man. "What do you want?"

"I've come . . ." began Pym.

But before he could continue the King shouted at him, "I do not care why you have come! Go away and leave me!"

The tinker saw the hulking form before him suddenly lurch to its feet and stagger toward him. He took a frightened step back. "Sire, I meant no harm. I meant—"

"Get out of here! Can you not see I want to be left alone?"

Pym made a move toward the door.

"No! Wait! You have news of my son?" The Dragon King asked. He came near and gripped the tinker by his shoulders, blowing his breath in the man's face.

Pym recoiled from the grasp and from the King's foul breath. "Nay! I have no sech news," Pym managed to stammer.

"Ach!" cried the King, and released him with a shove that sent him flying.

Pym slammed against the door and stayed there, petrified. Surely the King would not kill him, would he?"

"What is it?" spat the King savagely. "Well? Tell me! Have you lost your tongue?"

Before Pym could reply, there came a hasty knock behind him and the door was shoved open, sending the tinker sprawling.

"Sire! Come quickly. Something is happening! Trouble, Your Majesty. Come quickly."

In the light from the open door Pym saw the King—face as gray as ashes, dark circles under his eyes, cheeks sunken and hollow. He looked like a wraith who had come back from the grave, not a flesh-and-bone man with warm blood in his veins. Was *this* the great Dragon King?

Without a second glance, the King swept by him and out the door. Pym scrambled to his feet and peered through the doorway. There were other voices now ringing down the corridors. Pym paid them no attention; his only thought was to leave at once and get as far away as possible before the King came back and found him still there.

He crept out of the chamber and back along the now-deserted passageways of the castle, coming at length to the entrance. He stepped out into a cool night, bright with stars. Tip lay waiting for him with head on paws.

"It's home fer we 'uns, Tipper," said Pym, still shaken by what had happened to him. Tip wagged her tail. "Back t' the Gray Goose we go right enough."

He cast a last look behind him and then made his way across the inner ward yard and through the gate into the outer ward yard and toward the castle gatehouse. The great gates were closed, but a keeper stood near the smaller door, which was still open within the larger.

Pym said nothing, but hurried on by, through the gatehouse tunnel, lit with torchlight, and onto the huge drawbridge. Upon reaching the ramp he slowed, feeling like a malefactor escaped from the castle dungeons to freedom. He walked along the streets and as he turned toward the inn heard a rumbling like the sound of distant thunder carried on the wind. He stopped and listened.

A group of men came around the corner—a dozen or more, shouting loudly and carrying oily, smoking torches. They brushed by him in the narrow street, hurrying away. One look at their wild, twisted faces, and Pym knew that they meant no one any good.

He shivered as he watched the men disappear down a side street. Shouts echoed in the empty streets afar off. Pym shook his head dismally. "Aye, there be trouble, Tip. Master Oswald spoke aright. Come along, old girl. 'Tis no night fer we 'uns to be about."

They hurried back to the Gray Goose. In the distance the rumbling could still be heard intermittently; not thunder now, but the drums of battle just before the inevitable clash.

31

By the time Theido reached the site with his small force of knights, the destruction was almost complete. Three walls had been toppled, and the fourth was wobbling under the stress of ropes and poles in the hands of scores of frenzied townspeople.

"My lord, we have come too late," said the knight at Theido's right hand. His face flickered in the blaze of torchlight around them. "Do you want us to disperse them?"

Theido watched the men screaming and leaping to their task, obviously caught in the rage of destruction. At that moment the upper layer of stones on the last wall gave way and tumbled to the earth—thudding with such force that the ground shook and reverberated like a drum.

"No, not yet," replied Theido. "Someone could get hurt. I do not want anyone killed; the damage is already done."

"We should do something," the knight insisted. "The King's Temple. . . ." His voice trailed off as he gestured hopelessly to the ruin.

"What would you have us do?" snapped Theido angrily. "The deed is done! Broken heads will not save anything. Look at them out there—the whole town has gone mad!" Theido stared into the mob. Ropes snaked out through the air, poles thrust against stone, shouts became a growling chant as another whole section of the wall caved in. A cheer went up. It was the cry of a beast.

Theido said wearily, "Send the men around the perimeter to ring them in. When it is done, disperse them. We will not have this insanity spread. Do not hesitate to use the flat of your swords. But I want no unnecessary hurt done to anyone—is that understood?" The knight nodded. "See to it, then. I am returning at once to the castle."

FROM THE HIGH BATTLEMENTS QUENTIN WATCHED THE assault on his new temple in mute agony. The hill on which the temple was being constructed blazed with torchlight, and he could hear the shouts of the townspeople clearly in the night air, though the building site lay some distance away from the castle. He saw the churning mass around the walls, and he saw the stones of his great temple fall.

Those around the King held their tongues, afraid to speak, fearful of what he might do. The cold, unnatural light on his haggard face created a ferocious, almost savage aspect. Muscles tense, limbs rigid, the veins in his neck and forehead standing out, eyes staring from his head in horror—he appeared ready to leap over the battlements at any moment, or of a disposition to tear the limbs from any who came near him.

Quentin stood as stone and watched the desolation of his dream take place before his very eyes. With every stone that fell to earth, a piece of him was laid waste, and he could do nothing but watch and feel the wound in his soul knifing deeper with every section of wall that thundered down.

When the last wall came crashing onto the pile of rubble, he turned without a word and went back to his chamber. Theido found him there, sitting in the dark.

Taking a candle from a holder in the outer chamber, the stalwart knight approached the King. He lit the candles on the table and several others on their stands around the room, moving quietly as if he feared disturbing his monarch's meditations.

When he finished, he put his candle in a holder on the table and went to stand before the King. Quentin did not look at him; his eyes were trained upon a scene far away.

"There was nothing to be done," said Theido gently. "They will be dispersed and sent home."

The Dragon King said nothing for a long time. Theido waited, uncertain whether the King had heard him or not. Silence stretched between them like a web.

"Why?" asked Quentin at last. His voice was raw. The single word spoke volumes of misery.

Theido watched his friend, knowing that he was being devoured inside. When the hurt grew too much, the knight looked away. He could think of nothing to say which would ease the pain.

"Always before there has been a sign," said Quentin, speaking more to himself than to Theido. "Always before the way was shown clearly—when I most needed to be shown. Always." In the candlelight the years seemed to roll away from the King's face. He appeared once more the young temple acolyte Theido had met in the hermit's hut so many years ago. Even his voice took on the plaintive note of a young boy who had lost his way. "Where is he now? Where is the sign? Why has he abandoned me?" The words hung in the silence, unanswered.

"I saw it, you know, Theido." Quentin glanced at his friend, acknowledging him for the first time. The next words were spoken in a rush. "I saw it all. In that moment when the Zhaligkeer struck the star, when the light of the new age blazed on earth, driving the darkness before it—I saw it."

"What did you see, Sire?" Theido asked the question as one would ask a child.

"The temple. The City of Light which I was to build. The Most High showed me his Holy City. I felt his hand upon me. . . ." He paused and looked at Theido forlornly. "But no more. He has gone from me. I am condemned."

"Condemned? Who could condemn you, Sire? Certainly you have ever done what the god required. You above all others have lived according to his way. Durwin has said you were chosen."

"Marked, you mean! Marked for failure. Durwin is dead. The god is gone from me. I stand condemned by my own hand. I killed him, Theido. I did—I, the Dragon King, cut him down with as little thought as one would give a rabid dog. I killed him, and the Most High punishes me with my failure."

Theido could only think it was Durwin that Quentin referred to. "Sire, you did not kill him. How can you think such a thing?"

No, it is true! I am telling you the truth!" screamed Quentin, throwing himself from his chair. "I killed him, and the flame went out! The flame died in my hand! The light is gone, Theido. Gone."

Theido stared at the king, mystified by the outburst. He could make nothing of it; it was the incoherent raving of a madman.

Quentin threw his hands over his face. His shoulders started to heave, but at first there was no sound. Then Theido heard the sobs come forth.

"Darkness," he cried, "all is darkness!"

"Ooo!" Ronsard moaned. He tried to open his eyes. Only one would open; the other was swollen shut where he had been kicked. He ached in a dozen different places, and his ribs sent stabs of pain through him with every breath.

"There, now . . . take it easy. Do not be too quick to get up, sir," said the voice in his ear.

Ronsard turned his good eye toward the sound and saw the face of Milcher the innkeeper bending over him, holding him by the shoulders. "The wife has gone to bring a cold cloth for your head. Don't you worry, now. Just sit back."

Ronsard looked around the room. Benches were overturned and tables stood on edge, but no one remained of the mob that had been there before. "Where are they? Where have they gone?"

"I do not know, nor do I want to know." Milcher reached for a jar and held it up to Ronsard's lips. "Drink some of this; 'twill clear the cobwebs from your head."

Ronsard took the jar and sipped the cool ale, and felt the tingle on his tongue. The drink revived him a bit; his head cleared. "Who was he?"

"Sir?" Milcher blinked back at him.

"You know who I mean—Longbeard. Who is he? Where did he come from?" Ronsard made to get up, but the effort sent pain booming through his head. "Ooo!"

"Careful there, sir." Milcher held him under the arms and helped him to his feet.

Milcher's round wife returned, sat the knight down in a chair, and pressed the cool cloth against his bruised head. Ronsard sipped some more ale. "Look at this mess!" She clucked her tongue in disgust.

"What happened 'ere?" a new voice asked. Ronsard looked up to see the tinker enter the inn and come toward him.

"There was a riot," explained Milcher. "They worked themselves into a fit—a roaring fit! I never have seen a thing like it."

Emm frowned. "And just the moment my back is turned, too." She said it as if her husband was somehow to blame for all that had happened in her absence. "This gentleman"—she indicated Ronsard—"tried to talk sense into them, and look what happened. He got his head broken for his trouble."

Pym only nodded sadly. Tip held her head to one side and whined sympathetically.

"Well," replied Ronsard, "it will not be the first time I have had head broken in the service of the King.

Probably not the last time either, the truth be known."

"How's that, sir?" asked Milcher suspiciously.

Ronsard remembered his disguise, shrugged, and said, "I am a King's man. My name is Ronsard."

"Lord High Marshall!" gasped Milcher. "I remember you."

"No longer—but I am on an errand for the King. I meant no harm in my deception. I only came to hear the talk here in town and thought that tongues would wag more freely than if there was a nobleman about." He fixed Milcher with a stern look. "Now, then, what of this Longbeard? I would hear all you know."

"There is nothing you have not already heard, good sir. He came here much as any stranger might. Drank little, talked to some, and left, saying he might be back. He had business that would keep him in Askelon a while, he said—as I have already told you."

"Then what was that they said"—a jerk of his head indicated the now nonexistent crowd—"all that about 'Have you seen him? Did he change his mind?' That referred to the King, I'll warrant."

"I know not, sir. I only know what I have told you. An innkeeper cannot be responsible for all the talk that goes on within his walls. I keep a good house."

"I am certain you do," replied Ronsard. Milcher was getting worked up, and he saw no reason to keep at him; the strain of the night's events was telling on them all. "I will inquire after this Longbeard elsewhere. But you must let me know if you hear anything more."

"He will," said Emm darkly, and helped Ronsard to his feet. "Never fear, he will. I will see to it."

"I am sorry—" Ronsard began.

"No damage done, at least none that cannot be fixed right enough. Get you home to bed and give your head a rest," said Milcher, leading him to the door.

The knight stepped out into the cool night air. The street was empty and very quiet—an unnatural quiet, it seemed to Ronsard. He knew that some violence had been loosed on the world; he could feel it deep within him, as surely as he felt his bruises. He started off down the street and then remembered he had left his horse at Milcher's barn behind the inn.

32

BRIA WAS AWAKE LONG BEFORE THE SUN ROSE ABOVE
the green mountains around Dekra. She dressed and
went quietly out onto the balcony to stand in the liquid
dawn, now showing pale gold in the east.

A new day, she thought. What a wonder. Somewhere
my child will wake to this day. Most High, be with
him. Comfort him, and give him strength to endure.
And give my husband strength as well. Thank you. Yes,
thank you.

Bria felt with unutterable certainty that her prayer was
heard and answered even as she spoke. Here in Dekra,
she mused, it was easy to believe that prayers were
always answered. Nothing evil ever touched Dekra; it
alone remained ever safe from the world's troubles.

They had stayed long with the Elders, praying together. There would be more supplications throughout the
day and every day thereafter—as long as they were
needed. For that she was grateful, and for the uplifting
love she felt from the gentle Curatak.

But it seemed strange to be here in this city, Quentin's
city, without Quentin. Always before they had come
together. She smiled as she remembered the way he
had dashed here and there showing her the things he
was doing, pointing out all he saw and planned that

first time he had brought her to Dekra. They were young and in love and soon to be married. Quentin was newly crowned, and his vision for the realm burned in him with such fierceness he could not stand still for a moment.

They had come often in the early days, and then when the first child was born they stopped. One child and then another, and then one more . . . it had been a long time since they thought about a trip to the ancient ruined city, even though now it could easily be managed since the children were old enough.

But Quentin had his temple now. He was so intent upon building it—throwing all of himself into it—that he forgot about Dekra, would have forsaken it completely except for Yeseph's death. What a sad time that was. If not for Durwin, Bria wondered what Quentin would have done. The funeral of the Curatak elder was a simple affair, and not at all sad, not in the way one usually thinks of funerals. As with Durwin's burial, there had been a pervading sense of relief, even joy. Here was a servant of the Most High, finally released to stand in the courts of the One, to walk with his Creator and glory in his presence. What could be sad about that?

For Quentin, however, it was a time of confusion—mostly because Yeseph's death was so unexpected. They found him at his table in the great library he loved so well, head down upon a manuscript as if merely taking a little rest from his work. The day before he had spoken with every one of his closest friends, as if he knew that he would die soon and wanted to say good-bye to each one.

But Quentin was not there. Yeseph died without seeing Quentin again, and it was this, perhaps, that caused Quentin the greatest grief. "I should have been with him," Quentin repeated again and again. And as often as Bria had pointed out that he had kingly duties and matters of state to attend to in Askelon, and that there was no way he could have known, Quentin often grew sullen and replied that he had never wanted Askelon.

Bria had breathed a great sigh of relief when Quentin began the new temple, for almost overnight the old fire was back. But, too, he never mentioned Dekra again, at least not in the same way as before.

"Is it really a different place?" The voice behind her started Bria out of her reverie. Esme came up to sit beside her on the parapet.

"I did not hear you! I was daydreaming," replied Bria absently. She sighed and smiled at her friend.

"Nothing sad, I hope."

"Sad? Why sad?"

Esme shrugged. "The look on your face seemed sad to me, but surely no one in this place is ever sad." She turned her deep brown eyes upon the Queen. Bria saw the kindled glow in their shaded depths.

"Yes, it is a different place," said Bria. "They say it is one of the last places of power on the earth, but that, I think, has less to do with it than people believe."

"Oh?" Esme put her chin in her hand and gazed dreamily out over the glimmering mountainside, the dew beginning to glint in the first rays of morning light. "What, then, is it that accounts for what I feel here? For there is some glamour here that weaves its magic with the soul."

"That is easy," said Bria. "It can be told in one word."

"Then say the word, for I would hear it."

"Love."

"Love?"

"Yes, there is a love here which is rarely found on earth. Perhaps in families, certainly between a husband and wife on occasion, but almost never in the world at large. Love governs everything here. Everything. Love and the continually practiced presence of the Most High."

Esme glanced at her friend questioningly.

"Yeseph explained it once to me. He said that the Most High is indeed ever-present with his creation, with us. But we often lose sight of him—we fall away from him unless we practice his presence. By that he meant we must keep him with us in our thoughts and deeds, lest we forget.

"For it is not the One who forgets us, but we forget him. It is how we are made, a defect perhaps, but one that makes belief necessary. And belief is the Most High's greatest gift. So even there he has rescued us."

"Rescued us from ourselves. I see." Esme watched the daylight rise to the sky and the night shadows withdraw from the tree-thick lowlands like a fine, transparent veil pulled away. "Is it love that transforms even the common things—the sunrise yonder for one—into such works of beauty? Is it love that makes me feel as if all my life until now was a life lived in shadow?"

"Oh, yes! Love, and knowledge of the Most High."

"But I know very little of the Most High. How can it be that I feel as I do?"

"In your hearts of hearts you know him. Durwin used to say that all men were born with the knowledge of the Most High in their hearts. The trick is to spend more time remembering, and less time forgetting what we already know."

"From now on," said Esme resolutely, "I will spend all my time remembering."

QUENTIN RODE TO THE RUINS OF HIS TEMPLE AS SOON as it was light enough to see. The sky was dark; low gray clouds formed a hard shell over the earth, keeping out the sun's light. A misty drizzle fell from the clouds and dampened all it touched.

Though Quentin already knew what he would find when he reached the site, he was still stunned when he viewed the finality of the destruction.

Not one stone was left standing upon another. The walls had been pushed inward on top of one another—whole sections of quarried rock, all toppled, crumbled, and broken by the force of stone crushing stone. The wooden scaffolding and wall supports were splintered kindling. Here and there a jagged beam poked out of the debris, snapped like a twig trodden underfoot. The gray-white rubble lay in a great heaped mound like a huge grave, the grave of the Most High. Or a grave for a King.

Quentin waded into the ruins, stepping over fallen rock, climbing onto the mound. Scattered in amongst the wreckage he saw tools—a stonecutter's axe, a mason's trowel, a level; the tools were undamaged. Surely there was a lesson in that, but what it could be escaped him.

When he reached the center of the mound, he stood and surveyed the damage. It was complete, save for a single column as tall as a man that had marked an outside corner of the temple. Quentin picked his way to this lone surviving remnant of his dream, looked at it sadly, placed his hands on it, and felt the cool, smooth surface.

How was it still standing? How had it been saved? Most likely it had merely been overlooked in the fever of destruction.

Quentin leaned against the column, pushing his full weight into it, straining against it until the column groaned, tilted, and toppled into the pile. The stones broke apart and rolled with a dull thudding to their rest.

It is done, thought Quentin. The ruin is complete. With that he turned away and walked to the place where he had left his horse and climbed at once into the saddle without looking back. As he galloped down the hill, it started to rain—a slow, miserable rain, as if the gods ridiculed him by pouring false sympathy over the wreck of his once-glorious vision.

AS THE SLANTING BAND OF SUNLIGHT BEGAN ITS CRAWL across the floor of their cell, Toli got up and began pacing. Prince Gerin still slept peacefully, as if he were in his own safe bed in his father's castle. Toli watched the boy and smiled, thinking how wonderful to be a child and to have only a child's limited tolerance for trouble. Was it that their tolerance was so limited, or that their endurance was greater? he wondered. Either way, children simply would not allow trouble to dominate them for any length of time. They shrugged it off like an unwanted cloak on a hot summer's day. When was it that they learned to wear that stifling cloak?

Upon waking, a plan had occurred to Toli. He thought about it now, thrashing it out in his head, examining it from every possible angle until he was certain about it. When at last he had settled himself with it, he went to the heavy oaken door of their cell and pounded the flat of his hand against it. He waited and pounded again.

In a moment he heard someone hastening to the cell. "What is it? Be quiet," said the voice on the other side.

"I demand to see the High Priest!"

"No! Be quiet—I have my orders."

"I demand to see the High Priest! As a prisoner within his walls it is my right!" Toli began pounding on the door once more.

"Be quiet, do you hear? You will get us both into trouble. Shut up!" The man's tone was frightened.

"I demand to see—" Toli began, but stopped when he heard the bolt sliding away.

The door creaked on its iron hinges and opened a crack, into which a temple guard thrust his head. His sleep-swollen face glared angrily at the captive. "Shut up! Do you want to wake the whole temple and get me in trouble?"

With the quickness of a cat, Toli sprang forth and shut the door, pinching the guard's head between the door and the jamb post. "Ach!" said the guard as the door squeezed his neck.

"Now you shut up and listen!" instructed Toli firmly. "If you value your worthless head, you will do as I say. I want to see the High Priest at once. Arrange it. Do you hear me?"

"Ugh . . . what if I refuse?" the man gasped.

Toli pressed the door more tightly against his neck; he heard the guard's hands scrabbling for a hold on the other side. "Then," he answered, "I will be waiting for you when you come with the food next time. And the next time I will crush your throat with this door."

"Gack!" the man croaked. "Let me go—I will do it!"

"Good. You had better, or next time. . . ." He let the threat trail off.

The guard made a face and Toli slowly eased the pressure, backing away from the door. The man wasted no time in pulling his head free, slamming the door, and ramming the bolt home.

Toli heard the man's bare feet slapping the stone as he hurried away, and felt he had won his way. Yes, the guard was a coward and would do what he was told. Of that he was certain. But the High Priest? He would not be so easily persuaded. The man was as oily as the sacred stone the priests so diligently anointed. He would have to be dealt with in a different way entirely: not with threats, but with promises. And Toli knew what he would promise.

33

"It is just as we feared," said Theido. "They have come in force."

"How many?" asked Ronsard. His cheek was purplish-black from a bruise below his left eye. He held himself stiffly, for his muscles ached.

"Six. And they have ridden all night, by the look of them." The tall knight spoke softly though the door to the council chamber was closed and the guests within could not hear.

"They did not waste any time," sneered Ronsard. "They are carrion birds, Theido—vultures come to feed on the flesh of the suffering." He shot an angry look through the stone wall to those who had just arrived and were waiting inside. "What are we going to do? The King cannot attend them; that is out of the question in his present condition."

"Perhaps," replied Theido thoughtfully.

"You cannot be serious! Are you thinking of allowing the King to face them?"

"It might do him good. A round with those jackals might shock him out of his despair.

"It might crush what little is left of his spirit, too."

Theido nodded gravely. "You could be right. But I do

not know what else to do. We cannot keep them waiting in there forever. They will see the King soon or late; we cannot prevent it. I am afraid Quentin has no choice but to face them."

"He might succumb. . . ."

"Not to them." Theido jerked his head toward the council chamber door. "Not like this. But they have the power to convene a Council of Regents. If they sway but five more to their cause, it could be done."

Ronsard nodded gravely. "Has such a thing ever been accomplished?"

"Not in recent memory—but yes. Once or twice. They would declare the King incompetent—"

"As of now that would not be difficult."

"And they would have to join forces behind one of their own number. That might prove more difficult—getting them all to agree on who the new King should be. There are many proud lords who believe themselves the only reasonable choice."

"We have an ally in vanity—thank the Most High for that!"

Theido nodded and ran his hand through his hair with the air of a man who does not welcome taking the next necessary, and possibly fatal, step across a treacherous bridge.

"Go on," nudged Ronsard. "It must be done. I will wait here and keep an eye on them until you return."

"And pray, Ronsard. Pray the King has enough wits about him to fend off this attack."

PYM WALKED ALONG MORE QUICKLY FOR THE LACK OF his usual baggage, but he missed the bang and clang of his pots and tools—his own musical accompaniment wherever he went. He wiped the damp from his face. At least the rain had stopped, and the sky showed signs of clearing before long; it was already shining blue away to the east.

"Ah, Tip, d' ye see?" said the tinker. "We 'uns'll have

the sun soon enough. Yes, sir. Won't have to walk in the rain no more, eh?"

The black dog raised her head to her master and barked once to show that she was glad to be traveling again.

"Yes, fearful it were, Tip. Fearful, I tell ye. Ye should'a seen the King—should'a seen him. All dark and broken was he, more monster than man to look at him. Nivver seen abody looked like that! No, sir. Nivver have, Tip. Him locked away in his own chambers a prisner. That's what he were—a prisner."

Pym's eyes grew round as he remembered his audience with the Dragon King. "What could make a man like that, Tip? I ask ye, what could make him like that? I'll tell ye—that sword! Yes. The loss of it drives him mad. I know it, yes I do. Don't I, Tip? Yes, sir.

"He's lost this son and now his sword, and it drives him mad as a weasle-bit dog. Yes, it does. We 'uns've got to bring the King his sword, Tip. The sword we found, it must be his—or, if not, mayhaps 'twill do fer another. We must bring it to him, Tip."

The tinker and his dog had left the Gray Goose after one of Emm's delicious breakfasts, and struck off along the southern road to Pelgrin and the place Pym had hidden the sword he found in the road.

"The King needs a sword, Tip. We 'uns'll give him a sword, won't we? Yes, sir," he said as they strolled along. He had heard that talk in the inn and around the town—about the King losing his sword—and had become convinced that the blade he had found in the road belonged to the Dragon King. Pym had known it to be a valuable weapon from the moment he had seen it glimmering in the dust of the road. Now he meant to retrieve the sword from its hiding place and carry it back to the King; that was the message he had meant to deliver to His Highness.

"But the King were in a'state, Tip. He was. Couldn't talk to him—raving mad he was. Then Master Oswald come and told us there were trouble and I left. I got right out of there, Tip. 'Twere no place for a tinker. No, sir. Glad to go I was.

"And trouble all right—hoo! They teared down the King's temple last night, Tip. Tumbled the walls to the ground, they did. That's why we have to bring back the sword, Tip. The King needs it now, he does. He needs it now."

Pym, in his simple way, blamed all the sorry events taking place in the kingdom upon the loss of the King's sword. He reasoned that if he returned it, all would be made right again somehow. In this belief, he was no different than the rest of the common folk of Mensandor, who held that the King's power lay in the Shining One and possession of the flaming sword gave him the right to rule.

The fact that Eskevar himself had chosen Quentin as his heir and successor had long ceased to have any significance in the popular imagination. It was Zhaligkeer, the enchanted sword, that made Quentin King. Without the sword . . . well, who was to say what might happen?

TOLI WAITED WITH HIS BACK TO THE DOOR OF THE CELL, watching the oblong patch of sunlight as it advanced across the floor. It was starting its climb up the further wall before he heard the footsteps of the guard returning. Prince Gerin sat dejectedly in the corner of the cell they used for their bed, his chin resting in his hands, shoulders rising and falling with every breath. "I will return shortly," said Toli. "Perhaps with freedom."

The bolt scraped and the hinge creaked, and the guard shoved his foot into the crack. "Stay back," the guard warned. Toli stepped away from the door. "That is better. He will see you now. Follow me—and if you try any tricks, I have orders to stop you by any means. Hear me?" The temple guard rubbed his sore neck; there was a red welt where the door had squeezed it earlier.

"I hear you," replied Toli. "Take me to the High Priest now."

The guard jerked his head for Toli to march ahead of him, waited behind to bolt the door once more when the Jher was out of the cell, and then led him off to Pluell's chamber. Another guard had been sent to accompany them in case Toli entertained any notions of escape.

Through corridors cool and dank as a dungeon—for sunlight had not shown inside the temple in a thousand years—the guards pushed Toli, until at last they came to stand before a wide, arching door. The guard rapped once upon the door frame with an iron ring that was attached to a sconce. "Enter," said a voice from within.

The guard opened the door and pushed Toli ahead of him into the chamber. Pluell waited for them, sitting in a high-backed chair, dressed in a priest's robe of fine velvet with his hands folded meekly in his lap. "You wish to see me?" he asked. He might have been addressing one of his priests who had come seeking guidance in a matter of conscience.

"Do not think you can hold yourself above this trea-son, priest," said Toli. He spoke firmly and with author-ity, and saw the effect of his words in the tightening of the skin around the High Priest's eyes.

"Leave us," snapped Pluell to the guards looking on. "Wait outside, but do not wander away." When they had gone, he looked at Toli with a long appraising glance. "You cannot think that this is any of my doing."

"Snake!" said Toli. "You would do well to abandon your disguise; I see through it. You are not an innocent instrument of your god. Your hands are as red with the blood of the hermit as those who slew him!"

Pluell stared in sullen silence, then heaved himself out of his chair as if it had suddenly become too hot to sit in any longer. "You do not know," he cried. "You do not know . . . If he thought I was even talking to you, why, he'd—" The High Priest broke off sharply, glanced around as if frightened that he had been overheard.

"Who is with you in this?" demanded Toli, taking a step toward the priest.

Pluell's hands came up quickly as if to ward off blows. "No—I . . . there is no one."

"Then you own the deed as yours alone."

"No!" He shot a sly look at the prisoner before him and then seemed to remember who he was. "You forget the position you are in," he said in a more subdued tone. "I am the High Priest, and you are here under my protection."

"Protection!" Toli exclaimed. "You dare abduct the Prince and hold the High Minister against his will and call it protection?"

"None of that was my doing," High Priest Pluell retorted. "Have you been harmed? Has the boy? No! You see—I have protected you."

"Let us go!" Toli's eyes kindled with a fierce inner flame.

Pluell turned away and paced slowly to one of his hanging tapestries as if examining it.

"You must know," Toli continued, "that with every moment that passes, the King's anger against those who have wronged him grows the stronger. It is a fire that will consume all in its path."

Pluell still stared at the arris, but said nothing.

"Think! You can divert some of the King's wrath and lessen the severity of his judgment."

"How?" asked Pluell, his voice soft and weak.

"Let us go," said Toli simply. "Let us leave at once."

"So you can tell the King where you have been and who had kept you? No! I would be a fool. It has gone too far."

"Not too far—not yet. Let us go now. Do you think that the King will not soon learn where his son is hidden? His men are searching the hills and villages beyond the forest now. They will come to the temple as I did." He waited for his words to have effect. "Let us go."

The High Priest seemed on the verge of making a

decision and then drew back from the course he had chosen. "No," he said again. "I dare not let you go."

"Then let the Prince go, at least. I will stay in his place. This the King will count to your credit; it will greatly appease him."

Pluell considered this, but hesitated.

Toli pressed his advantage. "Set the boy free. Let him go now before the King learns where he is and comes with his knights in force. Free the Prince. I will stay; I do not care what happens to me as long as the boy is freed safely."

High Priest Pluell turned toward Toli once again; he had made up his mind. He opened his mouth to assent to Toli's plan, but before he could speak a voice from the door scoffed, "A pretty speech for a Jher dog!"

Toli and the priest whirled around; neither had heard anyone enter the room. There stood a twisted old man whose face was lined and creased as the bark of the oak. White hair started out from his head, and a long white beard flowed down his thin chest.

"You worm!" shouted the old man at the priest as he approached menacingly from across the room. "You were about to let the princeling go, eh?"

"No! That is, I—"

Toli watched as the mysterious old man advanced on the priest and the priest shrank away. Who was this ancient who held such power over the High Priest?"

As if reading Toli's thoughts, the stranger stopped and turned to him and gave him a flesh-withering grimace. "So? You do not recognize your old enemy. But then, you never thought to see me again, did you? Look at me!"

The realization struck Toli like the kick of a horse, rocking him back on his heels. His mind reeled.

"Nimrood!"

"Yes, Nimrood! Ha, ha! Nimrood has returned to settle his accounts. And you will pay for the torment I received at your hands, Jher. Oh, yes. You should have killed me when you had the chance long ago, for I mean to kill you—but not before all Mensandor learns to fear the name of Nimrood!"

"The King will stop you. You will fail."

"Oh, I have plans for the King. Great plans. His subjects will see him grovel on his knees before me; the whole world will see him humbled. Yes, your brave King will lick the dust from my boots; he will acknowledge me before his realm." Nimrood threw back his head and laughed loud and long, then shouted, "Guards!"

Two temple guards burst into the room, fairly stumbling over themselves to obey the summons. "Take the prisoner away," ordered Nimrood. "I have finished with him for now. Take him away!"

They seized Toli by the arms and hauled him roughly from the room and back through the corridors of the temple. Behind them Toli could hear the insane cackling laughter of the wicked old sorcerer ringing after them down the deserted halls.

Nimrood! thought Toli, still stunned by the knowledge. Nimrood has returned!

34

DESPITE THE GNAWING ACHE IN HIS HEART AND HIS utter disinterest in official duties, Quentin still possessed the foresight to demand that the nobles attend him in his throne room, rather than in the council room where they were already assembled. In this they would be subtly reminded that he was still King; they would come to him and stand below him while he sat in his royal seat of authority. They would argue from an inferior position.

"So they have come," remarked Quentin when Theido told him. "Yes, I will see them, but not yet. Let them wait first."

"Sire, they have been waiting," replied Theido.

"Let them wait a little longer!" he roared, then added in a softer tone, "You know why they have come, Theido?" Quentin studied the knight. "Yes, of course you know— but even you are afraid to say it outright. They have come for my crown. So be it!"

"Sire, you cannot be thinking of giving it to them!"

"I will give them nothing!" muttered Quentin darkly. "If they mean to have my crown, they will have to take it by force."

This is more like the Quentin I know, thought Theido. "What is your pleasure, Sire?"

"My pleasure?" Quentin spat the words and glared

dully at his friend, but then said, "I will attend them, but not in council. Bring them to the throne room instead. If they have backbone enough for this fight, then they will stand on their feet. I will not sit with them and have them denounce me to my face."

Theido bowed, then left the King's apartments thinking, It is good to see some fire in him once again. Perhaps he will not fare too badly after all.

WHEN THE NOBLES WERE USHERED INTO THE THRONE room some time later, they found the Dragon King waiting for them. And though he appeared gaunt, weary, and haggard, his face wore a violent scowl and there was anger in his eyes. He called them by name as they entered one by one. "Lord Kelkin . . . Lord Denellon . . . Lord Edfrith . . ." he intoned, pronouncing each name coolly, "Lord Lupollen, ah yes! . . . Lord Gorloic . . . Lord Ameronis, I might have guessed you were behind this."

The lords glanced at one another uneasily. Surely their information regarding the King's disposition could not be wrong. But the Dragon King's demeanor shocked them and made them nervous. What was he up to? Did he really know why they had come?

The noblemen went on one knee before the King's throne. Quentin allowed them to kneel, then said, "Oh, do not make a pretense of doing your King homage . . . Ah, but it is not the King you honor—it is his crown." With that he lifted the crown from his head and held the thin gold circlet before him. "Who would be first to snatch it from me? Well? Who among you wants it the most, I wonder?"

Guiltily the assembled lords glanced at one another. Lord Ameronis found his voice first, rose, and said, "My lord, you apparently misapprehend the reason for our audience. We heard the news, and have come—"

"Have come to see for yourselves how best to bury your King, is that it?"

"No, my lord," replied Ameronis smoothly. "We have come to lend whatever aid we may in your time of need."

"Liar!" roared Quentin, gripping the armrests of his throne, ready to leap out upon them. "I know you for what you are! In Eskevar's time you played your hand and failed. You think now to try with me."

This outburst brought a murmur from the noblemen, who dared stricken looks toward their unacknowledged leader. Ameronis, however, appeared unruffled. His voice took on the tone of a physician calmly reasoning with a reluctant patient. "You greatly misjudge our motives, my lord. We are concerned for your health." He looked at his friends for support, and they nodded grimly. "We have heard rumors, Sire. . . ."

"Rumors. There are always rumors."

"The people say that you are ill, that you have fallen under a spell of magic. This concerns us, naturally."

"Naturally," replied Quentin sarcastically.

"We thought merely to ride to Askelon as soon as may be to discern the truth of these rumors for ourselves."

"Stop it!" shouted Quentin, leaping from his throne and starting down the steps. He caught himself half-way down and halted, throwing an accusing finger in Ameronis's face. "Stop it, I say. I know why you have come! Do you think your King blind and feeble-minded? I know why you are here: to see a raving madman and to wrangle among yourselves for his crown!" He pointed his finger at each one in turn; the finger crooked and the hand balled into a fist which he shook defiantly in their faces. When he spoke again, his voice was a whisper. "You shall not wear this crown, my noble friends. Not one of you." He turned his back and ascended once more to the throne.

The lords backed away a pace as if to withdraw— all but Ameronis, who was more ambitious and more determined than the rest. "Stay!" he said to the others. "We have not yet come to the heart of it." To Quentin he said, "Word speeds throughout the land that you have lost your sword. I see that you do not wear it."

"Yes," spat the Dragon King bitterly. "Now we come to it."

"Answer me. Where is it?"

"I owe you no answers, Lord Ameronis, and will give none."

"Do you deny that it is missing?"

"I deny nothing." The King leveled his piercing glance upon the ambitious nobleman.

"It is true then; you no longer possess the Shining One." His words were an indictment. "Or prove me wrong and show us the sword."

The Dragon King, lips drawn into a thin, hard line, said nothing.

"Very well," said Ameronis to his friends, "you have all seen. He refuses to answer for the sword and will not show it. I say that the rumors are true, that he does not have it! I say that he who finds the sword and holds it is the rightful Dragon King of Mensandor!"

Without waiting for a reply, Ameronis dipped his head curtly and spun on his heel. The others, silent all this time, bowed. Lord Edfrith found his tongue and said, "By your leave, Sire." The remaining lords started to life, made hasty leave, and marched out. The King was once more alone.

"Yes, leave me, you hounds! Go! Follow your chosen leader, and find the sword if you can!" Quentin called after them. The huge door boomed shut behind them, and the sound filled the near-empty throne room like the crack of doom, or the axe falling upon the head of a deposed King.

A YOUNG CURATAK GIRL CLEARED AWAY THE DISHES from the women's midday meal while Esme, Bria, and Alinea talked with Morwenna, Elder Jollen's wife. Over their meal the conversation had touched upon the continuing work of the Curatak at Dekra, and the progress being made in restoring the ruined city once more to glory.

Esme said little, but found the talk fascinating. She listened intently and turned her eyes this way and that over the city from the balcony where they sat. Yes, she could almost imagine what it had been like, for out of the jumble of stones and pillars there rose wonderful buildings under the hands of skilled masons and carpenters who worked from ancient drawings found in the great Ariga library.

"You must see the library," Morwenna was saying. "I am certain you would find it interesting."

"I would very much like to see it," replied Esme at once. "All that I have seen of this magnificent city enthralls me."

"If you would like to go there now, I would be most happy to show you."

Before Bria could reply Esme said, "Oh, would you? I can think of nothing I would rather do!"

"Yes," agreed Bria. "I think I would like to see it once again." She made to rise, but Esme was already on her feet. "You and I must hurry, Morwenna," laughed Bria, "or Esme will be the one to guide us!"

They started off together, walking along the wide winding cobbled streets of Dekra. Grass grew thick and green between the stones, and moss roses of pink and yellow poked up through chinks in the paving. Blue-feathered birds hopped along the tile rooftops, or flitted from street to eaves as the ladies passed.

"Is the library as large as men say it is?" asked Esme. They had turned and passed beneath a standing arch which stood before a narrow courtyard lined with doorways opening onto a common area dotted with neatly pruned trees and small stone benches.

"That you must decide for yourself," replied Morwenna. "I do not know what men say of the Ariga library, but the Ariga were very fond of books and were great scholars." She waved her hand to include the whole courtyard. "There are thousands of books here."

Esme blinked and looked around. "Here? Where? I see no building capable of holding even a hundred books, let alone thousands."

Morwenna smiled and Bria explained, "You are standing on the library, Esme. It is underground."

"The entrance is there." Morwenna pointed across the courtyard to a wide arched doorway between two slim poplars standing guard before it. They crossed the commons and entered a great circular room of glistening white marble. On the walls were murals of imposing robed figures who watched the visitors with large, dark, serious eyes. "These we believe are some of the more renowned Ariga leaders, or perhaps the curators of the library."

"Where is the entrance?"

"Beneath that arch," said Morwenna. "Come." She led them to where the marble steps descended into the underground chamber and pointed into the darkness. "There it is. Esme, would you like to lead the way?"

Esme peered doubtfully into the darkened stairwell, but gamely placed her foot on the first step. Instantly the stairs were lit from either side. "Oh!" she cried in surprise.

"Mine was the same reaction when Quentin showed me," laughed Bria. "It does seem most magical."

"Indeed!" called Esme, already springing down the steps to the chamber beyond.

When the Queen and Morwenna caught up with Esme, she was standing at the bottom of the stairs, gazing with open mouth at row upon row of towering shelves, each shelf bearing the weight of dozens of scrolls. Young men moved between the shelves with armloads of books, taking scrolls from among the shelves, or replacing them.

"These are our scholars," explained Morwenna. "We are translating the books. All we have learned about the Most High we owe to our scholars. The teachings of the Ariga are contained in the books."

"They are priests, then, your scholars?"

"Yes, but not the way you mean, Lady Esme. The Ariga believed, and so do we, that the God Most High dwelt among his people and permeated all of life with his presence. Therefore there was no need for a separate priesthood—each man could be his own priest."

Esme cocked her head in an attitude of puzzlement. "That must be very confusing."

"Not at all! Though I will admit that it does require men to take responsibility for learning the ways of the god and living before him accordingly. This is why we have elders, to help us and instruct us and lead our worship of the Most High, Whist Orren."

The three began to walk along the rows of shelves in the immense underground chamber. Esme had expected a dark and musty dungeonlike place, and was surprised to discover how dry and pleasant the immense library was. As the other two talked, she wandered alone among the books, stopping now and then to finger an interesting scroll, or to try to make out the words written on the hanging ribbon that identified each one. The words, though she could not read them, charmed and fascinated her, so gracefully were they written.

She came to a nook lined with more honeycombed shelves containing extremely large scrolls rolled in fine red leather. A low wooden bench sat within the nook; so Esme, feeling herself invited, stepped in and withdrew one of the bound scrolls and settled herself on the bench to unroll it.

She could still hear Bria and Morwenna talking in low tones nearby, so she thought she would take a quick look at the book for curiosity's sake. It was bound with a leather thong, which she untied; then she carefully drew off the cover to reveal a fine white parchment, yellowed at the edges with age, but undamaged for its years. With trembling fingers Esme took up the carven wooden knob at the end of the rod and began to unroll the scroll. She held her breath, for there before her eyes were the most beautiful drawings she had ever seen.

The drawings, she guessed, were illustrations taken from the accompanying text, for beneath each was a double column of the wonderful Ariga script. Each illustration had been rendered in delicate colored inks, the colors scarcely faded since the artist had dipped his brush to them long ago. There were exquisite renderings of tiny colored birds and forest creatures, depictions of everyday life in the Dekra streets, a long scene of a river alive with fish of many different kinds, and quaint little boats with fishermen in them trying to catch the creatures with nets, and many other delightful images.

Esme gazed at the scroll in rapt wonder, feeling as if she were a child once again and had been given a rare and costly gift of a book from a far-off land. As a little girl growing up in her father's house, she had had many picture books which she loved dearly and pestered her nurses to read to her constantly. At this moment she entered once again into that special time. Her surroundings faded from view, and she became once more the little girl transported to a distant time and place.

35

When Quentin returned to his apartments, he found Oswald the Younger waiting for him in the ante-chamber. One glance at his servant's deathly pallor told him that some dire event had overtaken them which he now must hear.

"Well, what is it?" the King demanded. Theido entered behind him at that moment and Oswald, relieved not to have to deal with his foul-humored monarch alone, breathed more easily. He shot a worried glance at the gaunt knight, who returned it with a nod as if to say "proceed."

"I am waiting," said Quentin. "Out with it!" He then saw the flat, folded packet the chamberlain carried and snatched it out of his hand.

"It came only a moment ago," said Oswald, fear making his voice hollow. "A messenger, Sire."

"Whose messenger?" Quentin raised the packet and studied the seal. "The High Priest?"

"He did not say, Sire. I thought it from one of the noblemen, but . . . he was already gone when I saw the seal."

Embossed in green wax at the fold of the message was the cipher Quentin knew well: the bowl with tongues of fire above, the symbol of the High Temple employed by the High Priest.

The King broke the seal and tore into the packet, unwrapping it to find a lock of hair, a bit of blue cloth, and a note. Theido stepped close and Quentin, staring at the objects he held in his hand, thrust the note at him. "Here, read it!"

Theido took the note and opened it. With an effort he held his voice steady as he began to read:

Your son is well for the present. What happens to him now remains for you to decide. We are holding him captive within the High Temple, and are prepared to release both the Prince and the Lord High Minister Toli upon receiving your sword, Zhaligkeer, called the Shining One. You are required to surrender the sword in person to the High Temple at midday on the last day of this month, or the Prince and the High Minister will be killed in that same hour.

"Is that all?" asked Quentin, his tone hard and flat.

"There is no signature," replied Theido.

"The messenger is gone, you say?"

"Yes, Sire, gone before I could stop him." Oswald looked helplessly at Theido, who watched the King closely, fearing what he might do. "I sent one of the gatemen after him, I. . . ."

"He must be found—put more men on his trail." Quentin turned, and his eyes held a distant look. "Leave me now. Both of you."

"I would stay, Sire," replied Theido. "Allow me to help—"

"No! Go and find that snake of a messenger if you would help. Leave me!"

Without another word Theido and Oswald left the antechamber, shutting the door quietly behind them. "What are we going to do?" whispered Oswald fearfully.

"Do as he says," replied Theido absently. He was already deep in thought at the unexpected appearance of the ransom note. "Find the messenger. He cannot have gone far. I will send some men to you at once."

"What are you going to do, my lord?"

Theido glanced up quickly. "Do not worry after me! Get moving! Hurry!"

Oswald opened his mouth to speak, thought better of it, and closed his mouth again with a snap. Theido called after him as he dashed away, "Oswald! Tell no one what was in the note. Do you hear? Repeat to no one what you heard in the King's presence." Oswald nodded and scurried away as fast as his feet would take him.

"Now, to work," said Theido to himself, taking the folded message once more from his hand where he had hidden it. "Ronsard must see this."

"THE VIPER'S BROOD!" EXCLAIMED RONSARD AS HE quickly scanned the ransom letter once again. "The cold-blooded arrogance! We should pull down that serpent's nest upon their wicked heads!"

"And upon the heads of Toli and the Prince as well?" replied Theido. "No, they have doubtless considered that in their plan, my friend. They know that as long as the King's own son is tucked out of sight within their walls, the King can do nothing against them."

"Then what can be done?" asked Ronsard, raising hopeless eyes from the crumpled message in his fist.

"Find the sword," said Theido.

"Aye, find the sword. The whole kingdom will soon be searching for the Shining One—if not already!"

"We must pray, brave sir, that we are the first to find it—and soon. You saw the date? Only five days hence."

"Little enough time to scour the whole kingdom—we'd have a better chance of finding a pearl in a pigsty!"

"Then we waste time talking. Assemble the men at once—every household in Askelon, and the villages beyond, must be searched."

"If we do that, the whole world will know the King has lost his sword."

"He will lose his son and servant if we do not. The world will know soon enough anyway, my friend. Lord Ameronis will see to that!"

Ronsard nodded sadly. "We must pray that there are still those loyal to the Dragon King. We can count on the common folk to help, I think."

Theido turned to leave and replied, "The common folk destroyed the King's temple not two nights ago, remember. We may have a difficult time convincing them to help him now. But we shall do what we can."

ESME STILL SAT WITH THE SCROLL IN HER LAP, HER eyes drinking in the marvel of the colored drawings of the Ariga book. As she studied the tiny intricacies of each picture, she began to grow sleepy. Though Bria and Morwenna still talked somewhere nearby, from her nook Esme could not see them, and their voices began to drone like the buzzing of pollen-laden bees on a lazy summer day.

She yawned, suddenly overcome by the need to sleep, as if a thick, woolen blanket had been drawn over her. She yawned again, lay the scroll on the floor at her feet, and then stretched herself on the bench, her cheek resting on her arm. Her eyes closed, and she was instantly asleep.

To Esme it seemed as if she had entered another world as soon as her eyes closed upon this one, for she found herself standing atop a high plateau in a dark and featureless land. She turned and saw men laboring nearby, bearing heavy burdens on their backs, passing by her to the very edge of the plateau. She followed at a distance and soon came to a great pyre; the men carried bundles of firewood which they dumped onto the mound and then took their places in a ring around it.

Next to the pyre stood a man with a torch in his hand. When all had thrown their wood upon the stack, the torchman thrust his torch into the tinder; but though the flames from the torch licked out and leaped among the ricks, the fuel did not ignite. The torchman withdrew his flame in frustration and called out, "More wood!" The laborers disappeared in search of more firewood, leaving Esme alone with the torchman.

"What are you doing, sir?" Esme asked.

"I am building a beacon fire," answered the torchman, "that the people of the valley may see it, for they travel in darkness with no signal to guide them."

"Why did you not light the signal, then?"

"I have tried, but the fuel is old and damp, and will not catch," the torchman told her sadly. "I have called for more wood, but it is sure to be too wet as well."

Esme was overcome with the utter futility of the enterprise and turned away. At once the landscape shifted. The dark land faded, and she found herself on a cliff near the sea where the waves rolled endlessly, tearing themselves against the rocks and washing onto the shore with a sigh. She looked and saw a tower rising up and workmen on scaffolds laying stone, building the tower higher.

She moved closer and watched as the masons raised row upon row of stonework, while the quarrymen piled fresh materials beneath them on the ground. Then, without warning, a portion of the wall leaned out precariously and split away from the tower wall. The men on the scaffolding screamed in terror as the stone rained down.

The whole tower quivered, and portions began crumbling away; the workmen leaped from the scaffold and ran to get clear of the falling rock as the walls collapsed with a thunderous crash and stone plunged into the sea.

When the catastrophe was over, Esme approached the ruin and spoke to one of the workmen. "Why did the tower fall?" she asked.

He shook his head and pointed with his finger. "See, the foundation is old and soft; it crumbles away when we build on it."

"If the old foundation will not hold, why do you not build a new foundation?" It seemed obvious to Esme, though she knew little about such matters.

But the workman threw up his hands and wailed, "We have no master to show us how to lay a new foundation!"

"Where is your master mason?" Esme glanced around and saw no one who seemed prepared to assume leadership of the workmen. The man did not answer, only shrugged and shook his head. So Esme told him, "I will find a master mason who will show you how to build aright, and I will bring him to you—" Esme stopped speaking, for the workman and the tower had vanished like smoke on the wind, and she stood now not on a cliff by the sea, but in a busy marketplace where farmers sold their produce and merchants their wares.

The market bustled with buyers and sellers, and she heard around her the babble of voices haggling over prices and the quality of goods bought and sold. She passed by the butcher's stall and saw him cutting up a carcass, slicing meat from a large bone. With a wink to her, the butcher, dressed in a long dark robe, took the bone and tossed it out of the stall where instantly it was pounced upon by hungry dogs who came running from every corner of the marketplace.

The dogs fell upon the bone and began fighting over it, first one dog snapping at it, then another. One dog would succeed in snatching it up in his jaws, only to have it taken away by another, larger dog.

A crowd gathered to watch the fight as savage snarls and growls filled the air. "Stop it!" shouted Esme. "Please, somebody stop it!"

But the onlookers did not heed her, and the dogs fought ever more fiercely. She buried her face in her hands and turned away, but the terrible sounds grew louder and when she looked again she saw not a long, clean length of bone on the ground, but a square of cloth in the jaws of the dogs. Each had a corner of the cloth and was pulling on it, worrying it in his teeth in furious effort to free the cloth from the other dogs. And on the cloth Esme saw a device: a red writhing dragon.

"Stop it!" she cried. "Stop!"

36

"BLESS ME BONES, TIP, BUT THIS TRIP IS FERTHER THAN I remember, eh? Yes, quite right. It always seems ferther when ye're in a hurry. Quite right." Pym cocked an eye skyward and gauged the day by the sun. "Nearing middleday, Tip. Right enough, an' I'm hungry. We 'uns'd ought to athought to bring a bite to eat. Some of Emm's fresh-baked bread and a noggin of the dark would hit the spot, eh? And a soup bone for ye, Tipper. Yes."

The black dog wagged her tail to the sound of her master's voice and walked along beside him, lifting her ears now and then when a rabbit or squirrel rustled the leaves of a holly bush near the road as they passed. But Tip did not give chase, content merely to pad peacefully alongside her master, to press her head into his hand now and then to receive a loving pat on her head or a scratch between her ears.

Presently they came to a place in the road that looked to the tinker somehow familiar. "Ho there, Tip. This be the place, I'll warrant. What say ye? Looks the place to me, eh? Yes, it does." Pym gave a quick glance both directions along the road to see if he had been followed, or if any other travelers were about to see him.

They were alone, so he stepped quickly into the forest, pushing through a yew thicket to where the forest thinned somewhat and a trail wound among the trunks of trees.

"Is this the place, Tip? I tell ye, I don't know. Thought 'twas, I did. Now I'm not acertain." After some time wandering among the trees, Pym decided that they had not remembered the right place after all and so retraced his steps to the road once more and set off.

"Ah!" he cried a little further down the way. "This must be it! Yes, how could I forget?" Again they pushed into the forest only to become disoriented before going very far. "No, sir." Pym stood with hand on hips, craning his neck up at the tall trees surrounding him. " 'Tweren't here. This's nivver the place, Tipper. Back we go."

The noonday sun shone down through the interwoven branches above, casting a fretwork of cool shadow upon them as they trudged down the bare earth road yet again. The further they went, the less certain the tinker became. "I don't know how I'll ivver find it, Tip. I don't seem to recall the place—ivverthing looks so unlikely here-abouts." He stopped and stared around him. "I don't know what to do, Tip. What we 'uns need is a sign. That's it, yessir. A sign!"

So taken was he with the notion of a sign that Pym clasped his hands right then and there and raised them up to the heavens. "Here me, ye gods!" At a sudden thought he added, " 'Specially whativver god it is the Dragon King serves. I'll warrent ye'd be more concerned with the King, so hear me, whativver yer name might be."

Pym paused here to consider how to proceed, nodded to himself, and then continued, "Ye see, the King has lost his son—snatched away he were, yes. And he needs his sword to get the boy back with. Now, I don't know fer acertain that the sword we 'uns found belongs to the King, but might do—'tis a handsome sword.

"Now," explained Pym carefully, "I have put this sword by in a safely place, ye see. Trouble is, I can't remember me where. Don't recognize the place no more, ye see—and me who's been atraveling this road fer a score of years, too. That's why I am calling on ye fer to help. I need a sign to show the way to the sword—where I left it, that is."

The tinker lowered his hands, thought for a moment, then raised them again and added, "It's not fer me, it's fer the King, ye see. He's in trouble bad, he is, and likely needs his sword—leastwise it couldn't hurt. Since yer his god, maybe ye could send the sign. That is, if ye have a care fer mortal troubles."

Pym stopped speaking and lowered his hands. "Well, Tipper—" he began, but before he could finish the big black dog began barking. "Shh! What is it, lady girl? Eh, Tip? What is it?"

Out from an immense gorse hedge stepped a black stag. Tip barked furiously, but the deer, moving slowly, regally, head high and antlers glinting in the sun like silver, remained calm and unperturbed. The graceful animal crossed the road, passing not more than a dozen paces in front of them, and then stopped to look at the man and dog watching him.

Tip barked, her tongue hanging sideways out of her mouth, legs stiff, hackles raised. Pym laid a hand to her collar. The stag moved with lordly pomp once more into the forest, paused to eye the spectators one last time—as much as to say, "Follow me, if you dare"—then lifted its forelegs over a bayberry bush and leapt away, its tail bobbing white behind.

Tip could not stay still any longer. She barked wildly and shook her head, pulling free of her master's grip; the chase was on. "Tip! Come back here!" shouted Pym after the bounding dog. Tip reached the bayberry bush, paused to yap once at her master, and then wriggled through the bush and after the deer.

"By the gods' beards!" muttered Pym, "I don't know what's come on that dog." He could hear Tip yelping excitedly as she crashed through the brush after her game. Pym sighed and trudged off into the woods to retrieve his pet, knowing she could never catch the stag but would not give up easily.

He shrugged through the brush and stumbled into the trail, hastening after the sounds of the impromptu hunt. The trail widened as he went along, broadening as it reached a place where giant old trees grew tall, clearing all other trees from beneath their overarching limbs: huge old chestnuts, oaks, and hickories. He did not stop to gawk at the trees, but rushed along head down, calling for Tip to come back. Then, without warning, the dog's yapping ceased. Pym plunged down a shallow bank and through a patch of creeping ivy and glanced up to find himself in a secluded hollow.

Before him, on her haunches, sat Tip, wagging her tail and panting. A little way off from them stood the stag, head lifted high, bearing its crown of antlers as regally as any King, gazing calmly at them with its great dark liquid eyes. As the tinker watched, the stag lifted a hoof and nudged a stone at its feet—a white stone from a neat little pile of white stones.

"Tipper," whispered Pym, hardly breathing. "Lookee there! The stag has led us to our spot!"

The deer turned and regarded them casually once more, then lowered his head and trotted smoothly away, his flowing shape blending with the forest around him and vanishing from sight.

Pym crept forward to the place where the deer had stood. "Yes, sir. This be the spot, Tip. Lookee, here's the stones we 'uns left to mark it, and here's the hazelnut." He tilted his head to regard the lofty tree, then walked around it to the hole in its hollow trunk. Taking a deep breath, Pym thrust his hand through the hole and grabbed.

His hand closed on thin air. His heart leaped to his throat. Gone, he thought. Someone's taken it! He shoved his hand deeper into the hollow space and stretched his fingers, feeling the soft, damp interior of the tree, but no sword. Frantically he thrust his arm in again and searched the depths of the hidden space, feeling nothing but the spongy, rotten wood. "It's gone, Tip!" he cried hopelessly. "The sword is gone!"

Just as he was about to withdraw his arm, the tips of his fingers brushed against something hard. "What's this?" he said, and pushed his arm back in up to the shoulder, as far as it would go, standing on tiptoes, straining so hard that sweat beaded up on his face and rolled down his neck.

His hand closed on an object cold and hard. He gulped. Could it be? Yes! It was the sword! The tinker withdrew his hand slowly, and the hollow tree gave up its prize— a long, narrow bundle wrapped in tatters of rags.

"Here 'tis, Tip! We 'uns found the sword! Yes, yes! Lookee, Tip, here 'tis at last!" He cradled the bundle to him and then, just to make certain, peeked between the folds of the rags. He saw a dull gleam of metal and part of an inscription on the blade. " 'Tis the veery sword, Tip. The veery one as we 'uns left behind. Yes, sir." He glanced guiltily around him like a miser who fears discovery with his treasure. "But we 'uns dare not stay here, no sir. It's back to Askelon and give this sword directly into the King's own hand, eh? Quite right, yes. Directly into the King's own hand."

So saying, the tinker took a length of twine from his trousers pocket and wrapped it around the sword's concealed hilt and tied a loop through which he put his arm. He started off at once, slinging the mighty weapon over his shoulder, making for Askelon Castle to give his present to the Dragon King.

SOME WAY FURTHER AHEAD ON THE ROAD TO ASKELON, where Pelgrin thinned and gave way to farmland hills, a brown pony wandered riderless across a field of young corn, pausing now and then to nibble at the tender tops of the shoulder-high plants. This intrusion did not go unnoticed, for a pair of quick, sharp eyes had seen the animal from a distance, and the boy who looked out of those eyes was slowly and with utmost caution making his way across the field to intercept the horse.

Renny forced himself to steal along stalk by stalk, row by row, all the while his heart screaming at him to run and capture the wonderful creature before him. A horse! Who would have believed it? A horse wandering loose through his father's field. If he could catch it . . . no, he *would* catch it, and then he would have a horse of his very own!

Now he was close, very close. The pony stood nipping at the new leaves, unaware of the boy's presence. Renny crept near and waited. The brown horse plodded a few steps nearer and paused to munch some unripe ears of corn just forming on the stalk. "Shhh. . . ." said the boy, as quietly as a sigh. "There, now. Shhh. . . ."

He put out his hand to snag the animal's bridle. Tarky saw the movement, tossed his head up quickly, and backed away with a loud whinny. "Easy now," soothed Renny. "Easy . . . I won't hurt 'ee. No need to fear. No harm'll come to 'ee." He approached slowly, the pony backing away step by step, tossing his head stubbornly.

Renny moved closer, whispering endearments to the animal. But Tarky, skittish from his days of running wild in the forest, kept just out of reach, and at last tired of the game and turned to prance away. The boy realized it was now or never and lunged at the beast, diving headlong at it. Tarky gave a startled neigh and dodged away. But the youngster, with quick desperation and deft fingers, snatched up the dangling reins. The horse neighed in fright and reared, jerking its head away; but, it was caught in the grasp of a most determined young master, and Renny refused to relinquish his find. He scrambled to his feet and grabbed the bridle, his heart thudding against his ribs with excitement.

Then, as if he had been doing it all his life, the farmer's son led his captured prize down the low sloping hillside to the house. Tarky gentled under the lad's touch and allowed himself to be led away peaceably.

When they reached the rude farmhouse, the boy loosed one wild whoop which brought his parents into the yard. "Look what I've got here," Renny said proudly.

"Where did 'ee get that?" asked his father when he recovered from the sight of his son holding a fine horse, both saddled and bridled, in his own yard.

"Where on this green earth?" echoed his mother.

"I found him," replied Renny. "Found him eating corn in our field."

The farmer stared speechless at his wife, who returned his look with one of equal amazment. If the horse had materialized before them out of thin air, they could not have been any more surprised. And there stood their own flesh-and-blood son holding this creature—it surpassed all belief.

Lest there should be any misunderstanding of his claim or intent, Renny announced, " 'Ee's mine. I found him—'ee belongs to me, and I'm keeping him."

His father came close and raised his hand to stroke the pony's flank. " 'Tis a fairly fine horse—no doubt. But 'ee don't belong here."

" 'Ee's mine now." Renny tightened his grip on the reins and thrust his jaw forward with determination. "I'm keeping him," he repeated firmly.

"This be a nobleman's mount," said the farmer, examining now the fine leather of the saddle and tack. "Doesn't belong here."

The boy darted a quick glance at his mother for help, his lower lip quivering. The kindly woman came close and placed her hand on her son's shoulder. "What your father means, Renny, is that this one must go back to his rightful owner."

"Sooner the better," added the farmer.

"I'm his owner now," maintained Renny, his dark eyes filling up with tears. " 'Ee's *mine*."

"No, son," said his mother gently. She patted the slim shoulders and brushed his shock of hair from his eyes. "Someone's bound to come looking for him. If you keep him, they'll take him away."

"Take him by force, they will. 'Ee can't stay."

"But . . . I *found* him!" wailed Renny. The injustice of it stung bitterly. To have his horse so swiftly taken from him in the moment of his triumph—it was too much to bear.

The farmer frowned and turned stiffly away. Renny sobbed and his mother soothed, trying to ease the hurt. "I know what 'ee can do!" she said, brightening. "Take the horse to Askelon—people there will know who his master is. Methinks if 'ee return him hasty, there will be a reward in it for 'ee."

At the mention of the reward Renny stopped sniffling and rubbed his eyes with the heels of his hands. "Reward?"

"Maybe."

His father turned and added, "Why, that's the answer! Take him to Askelon and claim your reward. Might bring a coin or two, a fine animal like this. A man'd be most hearty grateful to get him back, might give a good reward."

"I could ride him?" asked Renny tentatively. "Ride him to Askelon?"

The farmer glanced at his wife and scratched his jaw. "Well, now, Renny, I don't be—"

"I know how to ride!" Renny said quickly. "The Dragon King himself taught me, remember?"

"By my lights, 'ee did," agreed his father. "But it's a far ride, and you'd have to walk back all alone."

"I don't care," shouted Renny. "Could I take him? Please?"

"If your mother says so, I say so," hedged his father.

The woman looked at the light dancing in her son's eyes and did not have the heart to dash it out. She nodded slowly. "I'll fix 'ee a rucksack to take with 'ee so's 'ee won't get hungry on the way." She turned and went into the low-built farmhouse.

"I'll ride him all the way to Askelon!" crowed Renny. "And I'll claim the reward!"

37

"ESME! ESME, WAKE UP!" BRIA EXCLAIMED, SHAKING the arm of the sleeping woman.

"What? Oh!" Esme said, jerking awake with a start. "Oh, my! It was a dream!" She turned and gazed at Bria and Morwenna bending over her, and raised a shaking hand to her temple. "I must have fallen asleep . . . but it was so *real*—not like any other dream I've ever had."

"You cried out." Bria glanced at Morwenna, who nodded and took one of Esme's hands in her own.

"We did not know where you had gone, my dear," said Morwenna. "When we turned around, you were no longer with us. We were looking for you when we heard your cry. How are you feeling now?"

Esme shook her head slowly, but the images of her dream remained as vivid as before. "I believe I am well. I was looking at the pictures and became sleepy; I rested my head on the bench for a moment and dreamed a very strange and unsettling dream."

"Tell us, if you wish," offered Bria. "Can you remember it?"

Esme nodded vigorously. "I am not likely to soon forget. I can still see it as if it had happened right here moments ago." She paused; her eyes looked past them and into the world of her dream once again. "I was standing on a high plateau. . . ." she began. But Morwenna held up her hand.

"Wait, my Lady," Morwenna said. "There is one among us who is highly skilled in the unraveling of dreams and their meanings. Come, we will go to him at once, and he must hear your dream."

Esme rose to her feet. "It is important? It was just a dream."

Morwenna stopped and took Esme by both arms. "There are many ways in which Whist Orren chooses to speak to his children. Dreams are one of his most important means of revealing himself, and they are not treated lightly in Dekra." She smiled quickly and added, "But come, we will hear what our dream reader has to say."

The three left the Ariga library, passing among the tall ranks of honeycombed shelves and tables stacked with scrolls, back up the stairway and through the narrow courtyard to the street. Morwenna led them a little way further along the street to a blue-tiled arch in a white brick wall. She pushed open the gate and ushered them into a green expanse of garden filled with flowering shrubs of many kinds.

"What a wonderful garden," said Bria. "Who lives here?" She indicated the tiny house that joined the wall at the far end of the garden pathway.

"That you will see soon enough," replied Morwenna. She raised her hand toward a huge, spreading sycamore standing in the center of the yard, and beneath it a figure propped up in a high, wide bed. Beside the bed another figure, that of a woman, bent near the one on the bed. This second figure Bria recognized as that of her mother.

"Mother, what are you doing here?" asked Bria with some surprise when they came up. Then she glanced at the figure lying in the bed beneath cool white linens. "Biorkis! Oh, forgive me," she blushed, embarrassed, "I meant to come to you sooner. Please forgive me for shunning an old friend."

Biorkis, bald as a knob now, but his beard longer and whiter than ever, squinted his eyes merrily and replied, "No need, no need! You have been very busy since you came, I know. A Queen's time is not her own. Alinea has brought me your greetings, and I've met your daughters—lovely little creatures, I must say. Just like their mother."

"I have only just sent them away with the other children to play," said Alinea. "Biorkis and I were talking about"—she hesitated—"about the news of the kingdom."

Biorkis started forward. "I am no stranger to trouble; there is no need to shelter me from its pain. I have lived long enough to know that fretting over it does no good." He paused and favored them each with a long, appraising gaze. "Yes, here you are. And though trouble brought you, I am glad to see you, my friends. It has been a long time."

"Too long," said Bria, "and for that I am sorry. Sometimes we do not remember how much our friends mean to us until we see them again."

"Do not be sorry for this old badger!" protested the aged priest. "I am not sorry for myself, nor should anyone be who is loved and cared for as I am here. Look! I am old and cannot walk anymore, so what do they do? They carry my bed outdoors for me! And in return I tell them stories and read to them from the old books. This, they claim, pleases them; so I am allowed to stay."

Morwenna smiled and settled on the edge of the bed. "This one is a most highly regarded servant of the Most High. We would sooner turn out an elder than Biorkis. We would have made him an elder long ago, but he would not hear of it."

Biorkis replied gleefully, "Preposterous! The former High Priest of the temple of Ariel an elder? That would never do! No, I am content as I am. But please, my Ladies, sit down. I will have more chairs brought."

"We can find places here," said Bria, perching on the arm of her mother's chair. Esme sat down on the bed beside Morwenna. "The King—Quentin—would like to see you. I am certain he would have come with us, but—"

Biorkis held up his hands. "Your mother has already told me what has happened, and my prayers are with you all. I, too, feel the loss of Durwin even now. How much more must Quentin feel it?—not to mention the abduction of your son, my Lady. But as I will be joining Durwin soon, I do not feel such grief as a younger man might. I cannot but think that the old rascal of a hermit will have some great work already in scheme for us to do when I get there. And so I will tarry here a little longer and rest up for it."

The old priest spoke so assuredly and with such calm conviction that Esme wondered at it. "You make it sound as if he has only gone on a brief journey to his home in Pelgrin Forest."

"Aye, and so he has!" cried Biorkis. "But his journey was never to a place so humble as Pelgrin. No, my Lady. He has joined the court of the Most High, Lord of All. If I feel sadness, it is only for the cruel way in which he was cut down. For all the goodness that was in him, Durwin should have ended his days like me, here, surrounded by friends and loved by all."

Morwenna smiled and patted the pale hand that rested on the sheet. "I am glad to hear that you have decided to remain with us yet a little longer."

Biorkis nodded happily, his clear eyes dancing at the sight of the women gathered around him. "I would remain always if I could be surrounded by such beauty as I see now." He paused, then glanced around him, adding in a more solemn tone, "But this visit, as pleasant as it is, shares some more urgent purpose than merely to cheer a babbling old rattlepate. What is it that brings you to me?"

Morwenna spoke first. "A dream. We would like you to hear it and tell us what it may mean."

"Ah, a dream." He nodded knowingly, and then turned to address Esme directly. "Why don't you tell me your dream, then, my Lady, and we will see what can be learned from it."

Esme's jaw dropped. "How did you know it was me?"

Biorkis's eyes narrowed. "I saw it the moment I laid eyes on you. I said to myself, 'This one wears the cloak of vision.' "

"You can see it?"

"These old eyes have lost none of their sharpness; in fact, they have gained some into the bargain. The veil between this world and the one beyond grows ever more transparent. Indeed, lately I have difficulty contenting myself with only looking at this world.

"But yes, I saw the aura of your dream still clinging to you when you entered the garden. A most powerful dream it must have been. A vision!"

"Do you think so?" Esme pondered this and then said, "It is true I have seldom had such an unusual and forceful dream. Perhaps it was a vision." She seemed taken with this notion.

"Why not tell me and we shall see?" prodded Biorkis gently. The others looked on quietly as Esme gathered her thoughts, closing her eyes and entering once again into the dream that had so frightened her.

As she began to speak she saw again the vivid events of the vision, taking place once more even as she spoke, only this time there was no sleep, only the images playing out before her as before. The garden and those around her faded from mind as she recounted her dream of the high and lonely place where men labored in vain to light the soggy pyre; of the tower built on a crumbling foundation that would not support it; of the bone thrown down in the market square which became a banner of the King. . . .

"I see," said Biorkis softly as Esme opened her eyes. All was silent in the garden, save for the faint buzz of insects among the flowers. How long had she been under the spell of the dream? she wondered.

She read the anxious expressions on the faces of her friends and knew that her dream had disturbed them as much as it had unsettled her. "Do you think it means anything—anything important?"

"Oh, aye. Undoubtedly! It is a dream of power, as I have already said. It carries within it seeds of truth. . . ." He hesitated, then said quietly, "But what that truth is, I am not now able to say." He frowned. "No, I must have time to think about this and discover its meaning."

"But surely it is most apparent," said Esme, and shocked herself with her own boldness. "Forgive me, sir. I meant no disrespect."

Biorkis cocked an eye at her. "Speak, my Lady. The god may have revealed its meaning to you already."

Esme licked her lips. "The dark land must surely be our own, where men wander aimlessly without true light to guide them."

"Yes, so I would say. I agree."

"The beacon cannot be kindled without proper fuel— the flame will not take hold—"

"The flame of true faith cannot be kindled on the fuel of the old religion—I ought to know," said Biorkis. "But continue, please. You are doing wonderfully."

Esme wrinkled her brow. "This next is a most difficult part. I don't know what it can mean: the tower that cannot stand."

"Oh, but that is the easiest part," explained the former priest. "The god often presents the same message in different ways." Esme frowned, so he explained by saying, "The tower of the new god will not be built on the foundation of the old ways, the old religion. One cannot build something new without clearing away the old."

"I see," said Esme, "but I still do not understand what the last part can mean."

"It is plain enough," replied Biorkis.

"How so?" asked Bria, who had remained very quiet since Esme had told her dream.

"Ah, I think you already know, my Lady. Yes, you would," said Biorkis. "Do you not see? This part of the dream means exactly what it says! Esme saved me from looking at it too closely; I would have spent all night pondering it and missed the meaning completely! As it is, I think we need look no further than what has already been revealed."

"You mean that this part of the dream says its own meaning?" asked Esme.

"I believe so, yes. It wears its meaning in the events it describes: the bone of contention thrown down by a man in priest's robes—"

"The butcher?"

"You said the man dressed in dark robes—a priest, then, or one who hides behind priestly garb to do his work."

"The bone became a royal banner," said Alinea. "The dogs tore it to shreds!"

"The kingdom!" gasped Bria. "It is being rent asunder! Can anything be done?" Her green eyes pleaded for an answer.

"Oh, yes. Yes. It must be hoped above all hope that the events foretold in Lady Esme's vision can be turned aside." He raised a finger in the air. "No doubt it was for this reason the vision was given."

"Then we must return to warn the King at once," said Bria.

"Yes," agreed Alinea. "But tell me, you mentioned nothing of the Prince in your dream. I wonder why?"

"I cannot say," replied Esme, a puzzled expression on her face. "Unless . . ."—she glanced at Biorkis, who nodded encouragement to her—"unless the welfare of Gerin is not in doubt."

"Very good!" exclaimed the old priest. "I could not have said it better myself. My Lady, you show a fine talent for interpreting dreams. We must talk more about this before you leave."

"We will go now," suggested Morwenna. "If Esme's vision is true, the Elders will want to hear of it immediately."

"Yes, yes, go at once," said Biorkis. "You must speak to them. No doubt they will discover something we have missed entirely. I was about to suggest it myself."

Bria stood, saying, "With your leave, good Biorkis, we will go. But I hope we may see you again before we must return to Askelon."

"Come back if you have time, but do not worry if you cannot. I understand completely. Go, all of you. It is time for my midday nap. Shoo!" Grinning, the old man folded his hands across his stomach and closed his eyes.

Bria bent over him and kissed his bald head, and they all crept away quietly, leaving the garden to its lone occupant, and him to his rest.

38

"WE'UNS'LL REACH THE CASTLE BY NIGHTFALL, TIPPER. Yes—leastways not long after. Still a fer road, though. Almost too fer on two legs in a day. But I don't mind, Tip, I don't." The tinker patted his dog and ruffled the fur behind her ears as they sat on a hickory stump beside the King's Road.

The afternoon sun slid lower in the west over fields of ripening grain. They had left Pelgrin behind and upon emerging from the shaded wood, sat down for a few minutes to rest in the warmth of the day. The sword leaned against the stump for the moment; the weight of it had caused the thin cord to dig into its bearer's shoulder.

"Ah, what a day, Tip. Eh? Lookee yonder to that cloud o' dust rising. Some'uns coming and coming quick by the look of it. Not one only, maybe two or three or more. We'uns'd best stay put right here out of the way. They'll pass right by us so we'uns'll see who 'tis." Pym watched the dusty ochre cloud rising from the road beyond the next hill. In a moment he heard the drum of hooves on the earthen track, sounding a dull rumble, then saw the riders themselves as they crested the hill and came on toward him.

Soon Pym could see the bearing of the men in the saddle and their fine clothing and knew that they must be knights or lords. He could hear the clink-chink of the steeds' tack as they trotted along.

The foremost riders—two men riding abreast—drew near where he sat on his rough hickory stump. Eyes straight ahead, looking neither right nor left, they passed him in a flash. Three more dashed by in an instant, and one of these raised a gloved hand in greeting, while one of his companions glanced at the tinker and nodded as he galloped by. Pym got to his feet and took up the sword. He stepped into the road and was in the act of hoisting the sword onto his shoulder once more, his eyes on the backs of the retreating horsemen, when a sixth rider approached.

Before Pym could think or move, the rider was upon him. He jumped back, dropping the sword as the horseman jerked the reins hard, bringing his charger to a hoof-clattering, dust-churning halt.

"Out of the way, you fool!" growled the angry rider. "If you cannot watch where you are going, you should stay off the road! Next time I will trample you!"

Pym threw his hands in the air. "Sorry, yer lordship! I beg yer pardon, master! Oh!" He scrambled out of the way as the ill-tempered rider and his fidgety mount cantered closer. Then, remembering the sword, the tinker turned quickly, stooped, and picked it up.

"Ho! Stop!" said the rider. "What have you there?"

Pym raised frightened eyes. His mouth worked the air, but his voice was some time in coming. "N-nothing, sir," he managed to sputter at last, his features convulsing in anguish.

"Hold, peasant! If you knew who it was that addressed you, you would do well to keep an honest tongue in your head."

The tinker lowered his eyes and said nothing; he brought the bundled sword behind his back, away from the prying eyes of the lord before him.

At that moment Pym became aware of a sound behind him. The other riders, having seen one of their party stopped in the road, had come back to discover what the trouble was. All five of them rode up behind Pym. "What is the trouble, Ameronis?" asked one of the newcomers, eyeing Pym in his shabby clothes suspiciously.

"This rascal darted out in front of me and nearly threw me from the saddle," replied the quarrelsome Ameronis.

"I am certain he meant no harm," said Lord Edfrith—the one who had previously nodded to Pym as he rode by. "I noticed him on the stump here a moment ago. Leave him, and let us be off." The nobleman made a move as if to ride away, but none of his friends followed.

"What are you holding there?" asked Ameronis again, his voice cold and menacing. "I will see it before I ride hence."

Pym glanced at the ring of faces around him, his heart leaping to his throat. "I—I . . . nothing, my lord." He pulled the sword to him. "I am a poor man. A tinker. Please let me go."

"Let him be, Ameronis," said the one who had spoken before. "He has nothing to interest us."

"Nevertheless," roared Ameronis, "I will see it! If it is nothing, let him show me." His piercing eyes fell upon Pym with keen determination. "But," he continued slyly, "if that is a sword he holds wrapped in those rags, I mean to find out where this tinker came by it."

This brought a murmur from the others. "Well? said Lord Gorloic. "Show us, then, for I too would see it."

"I discern the shape of a weapon beneath those rags," added another—this was Lord Lupollen, Ameronis's closest friend. "Show us, tinker; it is our right."

"No! wailed Pym helplessly. "I cannot!" His black dog flattened her ears and growled. One of the horses stamped the ground and snorted.

"Give it to me!" demanded Ameronis, thrusting out his hand suddenly.

Pym clutched his prize to his chest and refused to give it up.

"Come," said Lord Edfrith, "let us be about our own business."

"Go!" shouted Lupollen. "We do not need you. But as this interests me, I will stay to see it through."

Edfrith pulled his reins and his mount backed from the group, wheeled, and galloped away. "I will have nothing more to do with this ill-advised plan," he shouted over his shoulder.

"Please, sir. I have done nothing," pleaded Pym, sweat dripping down his neck, staining his shirt. "Let we 'uns go in peace. I beg you, ple—"

"Silence, peasant! Shut your mouth!" With that, Ameronis leaned down from his saddle and grabbed the bundle.

Terrified, Pym hung on and was pulled off his feet. Lord Ameronis struck him a blow across the face with his studded glove, raised his foot from the stirrup, and kicked the tinker in the stomach. Pym released the sword and fell writhing to the ground. Tip barked and snapped at her master's attacker.

Ameronis tore at the rag coverings, shreds of cloth falling from his hands. "No!" cried Pym, rolling up to his feet once more. "Please!" He looked to the other noblemen for help and saw their cool, impassive faces. They were with Ameronis. "I beg you, sir! Give it back!" He lurched for the blade, but was not quick enough. The haughty Ameronis lashed out with his booted foot, caught the tinker full on the jaw, and sent him sprawling backward in the dust.

"I am in your debt, tinker," crowed Ameronis, pulling the last of the tatters aside. "You have delivered the prize into my hand!" He raised the sword high. "And also the crown!"

"By all the gods!" gasped the noblemen, looking on. "It is Zhaligkeer, the Shining One!"

"For this service I will give you a reward, tinker," said Ameronis, his eyes shining with the light of his greed. "What do you think of that?"

Pym stared in horror at the sword in the usurper's hand and said nothing.

"I will grant you your worthless life," said Ameronis, laughing. His lords laughed too, nervously, still amazed that the sword had come to them. "For surely you have stolen this sword, tinker," continued the lord, lofting the sword and swinging it, enjoying its cold, resilient strength in his hand, the blade so finely crafted that it seemed alive.

"Now get up on your feet, scum," he ordered.

Pym, his mouth bleeding and the skin along his jaw swelling an ugly violet-red, dragged himself to his feet.

Ameronis flicked the point of the Shining One at the tinker's throat. "You will tell no one of this, tinker, do you hear me? I have ears everywhere, and if you tell I will know about it and I will have your head on a spike over the gate of my castle. Do you understand?"

Pym felt the cold kiss of the sharp blade against his flesh. He knew the ambitious Lord Ameronis would not hesitate to kill him, and within his heart he burned with rage and shame: he had let them take the King's sword. What could he do? How could he prevent them?

"Ye might as well kill me now," said Pym sullenly. "For I will not keep quiet about this." Now that the words were said he stood by them. "Yes, we 'uns mean to go to the King straightaway and tell him as what's happened."

"You care so little for your life then, tinker?"

"I care so much fer me King," replied Pym. "It be his sword ye hold there as ye well know. We 'uns were taking it to him—it been lost, ye see."

"I warn you for the last time," Ameronis menaced. He raised the sword to strike. Tip growled savagely and barked at her master's attacker.

Pym stood his ground and closed his eyes. If it was to be his last moment . . . very well, let it be in the service of his King. He waited for the sound of the blade singing through the air.

Instead he heard a shout—far-off and high-pitched.

"Wait!" said one of the others. "Someone is coming!"

When a sound of hooves came thumping up behind them, Ameronis cursed and said, "I will finish with this one even so!"

"Do not be a fool!" said Lupollen, his voice tense. "We have what we want; let us leave the field clean."

Pym opened his eyes a peep and saw the violent lord's face, black with rage, still towering above him, the sword still raised in his hand. The hooves pounded closer, and another shout reached them.

Ameronis glanced up, then hovered for a moment in indecision.

"Come!" urged Lupollen, his horse wheeling around. The others turned their mounts and started away.

"The god bear witness," muttered Ameronis thickly, "blind luck has saved you, tinker. But if ever we meet again, your life is forfeit." With that he spurred his charger forward, directly at Pym, who jumped to the side. He was not quick enough, and Ameronis swung the sword hilt down on his skull.

The heavens darkened, stars swung from their courses, and Pym collapsed in the road.

39

RENNY, RIDING THE PRINCE'S BROWN PONY, JOGGED along the well-used track leading to Askelon. He sat erect in the saddle, pretending to be a knight returning to the realm from quests and adventures in faraway lands. He fancied himself returning to the King's service after a long absence to find his name on the lips of his countrymen and peers, his deeds sung in halls great and small throughout the kingdom.

Yes, to be such a knight, he thought, would be any man's greatest dream. He would give his life for it—for one hour in the armor of a knight in the saddle of a genuine warhorse. Tarky trotted easily along, Askelon Castle showing misty in the distance over green fields. The world seemed calm and lazy in the warmth of the day, and Renny despaired of finding any adventure on the way, for with every step the castle and its city drew nearer.

Then, as horse and rider reached the bottom of a hill and started up the opposite side, they met another rider galloping fast the other way. The stranger passed by them in a flurry of hooves, his short cloak blowing out behind him, the charger's tail streaming. He did not so much as glance in the boy's direction, but thundered by, eyes ahead and hard.

"That'd be a nobleman most like," said Renny to his mount. "An' one fleeing something by the look of it. Maybe highwaymen!"

At once his young head was filled with images of a fierce conflict with a band of ruthless robbers in which he, Sir Renny, bested the whole pack and sent the brigands scrambling back into the Wilderlands where the cowards belonged.

Enticed by such impossible heroics, Renny urged the brown pony to a faster pace as they climbed the hill. Then as they reached the crest and the road stretched out before them once more, Renny saw the scene he had just imagined: a group of brigands menacing a helpless traveler. The only difference he could see was that the highwaymen were on horseback and the poor traveler afoot. He loosed a wild yelp, kicked his heels into Tarky's flanks, and galloped to the rescue, never thinking that he had no weapon and would not have known how to use one if he had it. Nevertheless, Renny dashed for the thick of the fray with visions of glory dancing before him.

It was about this time that Lord Ameronis and his friends heard the young rescuer approaching. Renny saw a sword lifted up about to strike and gave vent to another war whoop, urging Tarky to greater speed as they came flying down the hill, elbows flapping, legs akimbo.

Here it was that the lords prevailed upon their leader to spare the tinker and to make clean their retreat with the King's sword. They all turned at once and galloped toward Renny, who swallowed hard, put his head down, and charged into them.

At the precise moment of collision, Renny squeezed shut his eyes. He felt the air buffet him as the riders swept by, and then heard the sound of their retreat behind him. When he opened his eyes again he was alone in the road, the highwaymen sprinting away and disappearing over the hill. Ahead of him, the wayfarer lay in a heap at the side of the road. Renny clattered to a halt, threw himself from the saddle, and dove to the man's aid, rolling him over in the dust. Blood ran freely from the cut on his mouth and a raw bruise welted on his jaw. Tip licked her master's face, cleaning away some of the dust and blood.

Pym's eyelids fluttered open weakly. "Ohh. . . ." he moaned.

"Good sir, are 'ee alive?" asked Renny, eyes wide as pot lids.

"Ohh . . . me head. Ow! They've kilt me good," he said, struggling to get up.

"Easy there," said Renny, raising him to a sitting position. "I come to help 'ee."

Pym, eyes watering from the throbbing in his head, squinted at his young savior. "Who are ye?"

"Renny, sir," he replied as if the name should have preceded him and would explain all. "I came upon 'ee here beset by brigands."

"Eh?" Pym turned his head and saw that his attackers were indeed vanished. "Ye saved my life! They meant to carve me to a treat. Yes, sir. Ye saved me, young master! Thankee, oh thankee!"

Renny glowed with this admission. Yes, he *had* saved the man's life, just as a knight would have done. He had faced a band of cutthroats and, unarmed, routed them and sent them fleeing for the Wilderlands to escape his justice. "Who were they?" he asked seriously.

"Oh, a bad lot, young master. A bad lot they were—all of them evil. They were going to put me head on a spike, they were. Yes. I stood a dead man 'til ye came arunnin'. Oh, thankee."

"Did they steal anything?"

At this the tinker began to tremble. "Ohh! They took the sword!"

" 'Er sword?"

"Not mine. No, nivver mine! Oh, no. The *King's* sword! They took it—one called Ameronis; he's the very one as did it. He wanted to carve me up and put me poor head on a spike."

"Ameronis? Lord Ameronis? I have heard tell of him."

"A bad one. Oh, yes. Very bad."

Renny thought for a moment. "How could 'ee have the King's sword?" he asked, scratching his head. " 'Ee mean the Shining One itself?"

"None other." Pym nodded solemnly. "We 'uns found it in the road a few days ago. Didn't know it *was* the Shining One then and hid it. Yes, hid it in a tree. We 'uns went back fer to fetch it early this morn and were bringing it back fer the King. He needs it something powerful."

Renny studied the situation carefully, weighing what the man had told him. "Well," he said at length, "there's nothing for it but to ride straightaway to the King and tell him what happened."

"I agree." Pym rose unsteadily to his feet, placing a hand on the boy's shoulder.

"Can 'ee ride? The pony is sturdy, and we're not terrible far from the castle."

"I think so," nodded Pym, and then squeezed his eyes shut with pain. "Oww! He caught me a good 'un then, he did. That 'un I'd like to repay."

With Renny's help Pym clambered into the saddle, then let down a hand to hoist the boy up behind him. They swayed uncertainly and started off, Tarky bending his head low with the extra weight, but making surefootedly for Askelon.

THE SHADOWS OF THE HIGH CURTAIN BATTLEMENTS stretched across the inner ward yard by the time Theido and Ronsard had assembled their men to begin searching for the sword. All afternoon the ward yard had been in turmoil as knights and men at arms were outfitted for a search such as Mensandor had never seen. Ronsard spared no one from the task who could not serve better in some other way, and horses were saddled and provisions laid in for many days on the trail.

"This is war," said Ronsard to Hagin, when the warder protested the plundering of his stores. "If we fail, the Dragon King falls. I see no reason to hold back a reserve—we would only be inviting our own defeat."

"Do not speak of defeat," replied Theido, overhearing. "It will be difficult enough as it is. War you said? Worse than war—our foe is time, and time wins all in the end."

"Not this battle," replied Ronsard grimly. "I mean to win this one."

Just then a gateman came running up, saluted Hagin, and blurted out a message. "Warder, sir, there's someone at the gate demanding to see the King. I told them the King sees no one, but they insisted. I didn't like to trouble you, but they will not go away."

"What do they want?"

"They will not say, sir."

"Then send them packing," ordered Hagin, "with the edge of your sword, man."

Theido and Ronsard, about to turn away, heard the gateman say, "There's two of them on one brown pony, and—"

Ronsard spun around. "A brown pony?" His senses prickled.

"What is it, my lord?" asked Hagin.

"Bring them," ordered Ronsard. "And the pony. At once."

The gateman dipped his head and ran off to fetch the visitors as instructed. "You have a reason for this, I'll warrant?" said Theido. Hagin looked on quizzically.

"It may be nothing," replied Ronsard. "But I seem to remember someone saying that the Prince rode a brown pony the day of the hunt."

"Aye, he did. It was his favorite," offered Hagin. "What of it? There must be dozens of brown ponies in the region hereabouts."

"As you say, but two do not ride unless there is some urgency, and they do not arrive at the castle with demands for the King."

"I see what you mean," said Theido. "But do you think this can possibly have anything to do with us?"

"That we will quickly discover, I think." He looked across the yard where the gatekeeper approached leading a pony; two hesitant figures trailed behind.

In a moment the gateman had brought the visitors—a thin, gangly boy and a slump-shouldered man—and their mount to stand before the knights and the warder. "Here they are, sirs. As you requested."

"Tinker, we meet again," said Ronsard. "Hagin, would you examine the horse? I think some of us may know this animal."

"We 'uns did not steal it, yer lordship," replied Pym. "But how do ye know me?"

"I was the wretch whose head was broken at the Gray Goose the night the King's temple was pulled down."

Pym's eyes opened wider in recognition; he nodded knowingly. "Same as what happened to me not three hours ago."

"This is the Prince's mount and no doubt." Hagin patted the pony's neck. "That's the Prince's saddle and tack. The animal came from the King's stables—that is a fair certainty. If you like, I will call the stablemaster. He would know better than anyone else."

"That will not be necessary," said Ronsard. He looked at the two before him. "Well? You had better tell us all about it."

"I found him, sir," said Renny in a small, awed voice. Here he was in the inner ward yard of Askelon Castle where knights and horses, squires and men-at-arms hurried to ready themselves as for battle; he could hardly take it all in. "He came into our field below the forest. I caught him."

"The pony?" Ronsard smiled; light twinkled in his eyes. "I see. And then what did you do?"

Before the boy could answer, Pym broke in. "I'll tell ye what he did. He saved my life, that's what he did. We 'uns—"

"You and the boy?"

"Me and Tip, sir," said Pym, motioning to the dog.

"I see. Go on. . . ."

"We 'uns were bound fer Askelon and were set upon by highwaymen and brigands—leastwise I thought they were highwaymen and brigands, I did."

"Highwaymen?" asked Theido. "In this part of Mensandor?"

Pym nodded vigorously. "They caught me and took the sword."

"They took your sword?" asked Ronsard. "When does a tinker have need to carry a sword?"

"Not my sword, yer lordship," explained Pym. "The *King's* sword!"

40

THEIDO WAS THE FIRST TO REACT TO THE NEWS. "YOU found the King's sword?"

Pym nodded solemnly; Renny nodded, too, and Tip wagged her tail. "We 'uns found it in the road days ago now. . . ." He lapsed into silence remembering what else they had found.

"Next to the body of a man—isn't that right?" prompted Ronsard.

Pym nodded slowly and thrust his hands out. "But we 'uns had nothing to do with that! No, sir. Nivver lifted hand against any man me whole life long. No, nivver did."

"We believe you, tinker," said Theido. "What you have told us fits with what we already know. What did you do with the sword when you found it?"

"Hid it, sir. We 'uns hid it in a hollow tree, we did. A hazelnut tree in the forest. But we 'uns did not as much as know it were the King's sword—not at first."

"But when you found out, you went back for it. Is that right?" Ronsard had formed a picture in his mind about what must have happened—the tinker coming upon the sword in the road, frightened, hiding the weapon and coming to town, hearing the talk, and determining to bring back the sword. "You intended giving it back to the King?"

"Yes, sir, very much. That's what we'uns planned all along—well, maybe not at first. Didn't know it was the King's sword at first. No, didn't know that."

"Who took it from you?" asked Theido. "You mentioned highwaymen."

"Six of them there were. Two passed while we'uns rested aside of the road. Then three more—nivver paid me no mind—but the last one nearly knocked me down in the road, he did—came a'charging along that way. We'uns nivver seen him 'til he pitched to a halt. Then 'twas he saw the sword and took it. I hanged on as mighty as I could, but he caught me a blow or two on the jaw." Pym rubbed the swollen bruise gingerly. "This 'un here"—he indicated Renny—"saved old Pym's hide, he did. He rescued me, and him just a lad—but with spunk, yes sir! Lots o' spunk has he. Yes, and he flew into them and sent them slinking away like a pack of mangy curs!"

Ronsard regarded the boy closely. "Is this true, young master? You defended the tinker here from the brigands?"

Renny nodded, too overwhelmed to speak.

"Brave lad," remarked Theido. "Well done. Not many would take on six armed men alone and with no weapons. What made you do it?"

Renny opened his mouth, and the words tumbled out. "I'm going to be a knight, sir. Knights are brave and help those as needs help."

"Indeed!" Ronsard agreed. "But were you not afraid?"

"No, sir. Not until Pym told me who they were."

"Oh? You know who they were, Pym?" Theido leaned forward.

"We'uns heard a name—the one as took the sword. It was—"

"Let me guess," put in Ronsard. "Ameronis?"

"The very one!" cried Pym. "That's the very one. And

a mean one he is, sir. Mean as the night is long. Yes, he is."

"I thought so!" said Ronsard. "Well, here is our battle, already drawn for us. There can be no doubt where the rook has taken his prize."

Theido pulled his chin and gazed out across the yard. "To that snuggery of his on the Sipleth." He turned to Ronsard. "That is settled, then; we prepare not for a search but a siege!"

AFTER RECEIVING THE LETTER OF RANSOM, QUENTIN had taken to his bed in despair; he had not moved all day. Paralyzed by a crippling helplessness, he lay as one stricken with the disease which turns the limbs to stone. The letter had been his son's death foretold, for he no longer had the Shining One to give the kidnappers, and not enough time to find it in any event.

Now, because of his transgression, because of his striking down the wretch in the road, he would lose his son and heir, and his throne as well. But what did that matter? He had already lost his truest friends: Durwin dead, Toli driven away and captured; even his Queen left him alone in his hour of greatest torment. But beyond all this, the pain that cut him deepest was the knowledge that the Most High had removed his hand from him and was now pouring out a heavy judgment upon him.

The judgment was more than he could bear.

There came a rap on his chamber door, and though Quentin did not move or attend the sound in any way, the door swung open. A tall, lanky figure entered the darkened room and came to stand beside the bed.

"Sire, said Theido, "all is in readiness."

The King did not answer.

Theido stood looking sadly down on his friend for a moment, then said, "We are waiting for you to lead us." He had been about to say that they were leaving now, but Quentin's condition shocked him and he thought to try to rouse the King. For an instant he thought the ploy might work.

Quentin turned his head on his pillow; his eyes focused on Theido's face. "They are going to kill my son," he said softly, "and I am to blame."

"Nay, Sire. I have come with news: the sword has been found. We go now to claim it."

"Zhaligkeer found?"

"Lord Ameronis has stolen it from a tinker who found it in the road the day of Prince Gerin's abduction."

"Then he has won. He will never give it up."

"Not without a fight, no. But we mean to give him a fight the likes of which he has never seen. In the end he will give the Shining One back, and gladly. That is why you must ride with us."

"There is no time, Theido. No time. Already it is too late."

"It is not too late, lord. But it will be if you delay."

"Go, then, and see what can be done."

Theido was about to agree, hesitated, and instead replied, "I will not give the order, Sire. That you must do. And you must ride at the head of your troops if we are to show Ameronis and his friends that we will brook no treason in this realm."

Again Quentin lay silent. Theido could not tell if his words were finding their mark or if his listener was so far given to his despair that nothing could reach him. The knight said a silent prayer to the Most High to move the King once more to action. "Defend your throne, my lord," Theido said. "Come. Ride with us. Lead us."

Quentin sighed and passed a hand before his eyes. "No, I am no King. Leave me."

"Who will lead the troops if you will not?"

"You lead them."

"I will not."

"Ronsard, then. Anyone. I do not care."

Theido knew he was beaten then, turned away, and walked to the door. With his hand on the latch he paused and said, "There are those who will give their lives for you and your throne. And many more will brave any danger in service to you. Durwin did, and Toli—and others you know nothing of. Will you not lift a hand to save yourself?" With that he closed the door.

The King heard his footsteps diminishing in the corridor, and lay staring up into the darkness of his blackened room. He did not move.

"WELL?" RONSARD ASKED, ALREADY GUESSING THE answer, for it was written in the gray, weary lines of his friend's face.

"He will not ride. I fear we have lost our King even before a single blow has been delivered."

"If our King gives himself over to defeat, then our kingdom is in disarray. The jackals will tear it to pieces."

Theido drew a deep breath. "That, at least, we can hold off for a little longer. We will ride to Ameron-on-Sipleth and do what we can." He cast an eye skyward. "If we ride all night we can be there by morning."

As twilight tinted the bowl of heaven the color of dark wine, the Dragon King's army left Askelon. In all the times of leaving, in all the wars when Mensandor's men-at-arms had answered the call and marched forth into battle, in all the frightful days when foe threatened and peace would be won only by lance and sword, there had never been a more silent departure.

The troops filed through the outer ward and gatehouse, over the immense drawbridge spanning the dry moat, and down the long ramp to wend through the streets of the city. The knights came first on horseback, their armor bundled beneath netting behind the saddles of their squires. The footmen were next, marching together in long ranks, not speaking—for word had spread through the file that the Dragon King had not the heart to lead his men. After the footmen came the heavy wagons loaded with provisions and weapons for the footmen and knights; smiths' and surgeons' wains with supplies and tools for mending broken men and their armaments formed the rear of the train.

The silent army passed through the streets of the city like a ghostly phalanx whispering off to some forgotten battle on the mists of time. No one came out to mark their passing; no citizen cheered their march. The streets remained empty of all but a few mongrel dogs, hungry-looking and scabby, who ran yapping at the horses' hooves.

At the head of the troops rode Ronsard and Theido side by side, upright in the saddle, eyes ahead. They did not speak, but wrapped themselves in their own thoughts like cloaks against the night. And though the night was warm, there was an atmosphere of melancholy and futility that chilled the air. All felt it who followed the banner of the Dragon King this night.

For, without the enemy so much as lifting blade against the throne, Mensandor had lost her King.

41

ELDER JOLLEN SAT STROKING HIS BEARD IN THE firelight, staring into the glowing embers on the hearth; next to him sat his wife, Morwenna, and Alinea beside her. Bria and Esme, opposite the esteemed elder, watched him carefully, waiting for what he would say. Shadows flickered on the walls, and in one corner a cricket chirped its nightsong. Finally, his chest rising as he drew air deep into his lungs, he looked up and said, "Yes, I agree. You must go back at once. The dream, as Biorkis suggests, has been given as a warning for you to return—or a sign that you must be present to witness the event which is foretold and will take place soon. Either way you must go."

"Thank you, Elder Jollen. Your words make my heart rest easier in its decision," Bria answered.

"I could discuss this with the other elders if you like, but I have no doubt that they will say what I have already said. Yes, go. I know that you have hardly had time to rest from your journey and now must leave, but we will pray that the god will give you strength for your travels."

"I hate the thought of leaving," said Esme. "In so short a time I have come to feel very comfortable here— almost as if I belong here."

Jollen looked at her, nodding to himself as if he could see something in that young woman that no one else could. "Perhaps the god is speaking to you, Esme. It may be that he has a place for you here among us. In any event, you will always be welcome in Dekra. Return when you may, and stay as long as you care to; allow your heart to find itself again."

The elder's last words surprised Esme. "Did Bria tell you about my . . . my troubles?"

Jollen's smile was gentle. "No, my Lady. I did not need words to tell me that you have been a party to much pain and sadness of late. From the moment you came through the gate I saw much in you of the little child lost."

Esme lowered her eyes and stared at her hands in her lap. "It is so apparent, then?"

"No!" replied Bria.

"No, no—perhaps not to everyone," admitted Elder Jollen. "But it is part of my gift that I see most clearly the shape of the inner soul. I do not speak to shame you, Esme. Only to tell you that we know of your hurts and have been praying for you since you entered here."

"I thank you for your prayers. And I have felt more at peace here than at any time since. . . ." Her voice faltered and she paused, letting her words trail off.

Morwenna rose and put an arm around her. "Come back when your work is done, and stay with us. It would be an honor to have you here."

"My work?" Esme looked around at the group. "What do you mean by 'my work'?"

"Of us all, Esme," replied Alinea, "you are the one who had the vision; you are the one to whom the Most High has spoken."

"I have some part to play in this?"

Elder Jollen chuckled lightly. "We all do, to be sure. But yours is a special part. The Most High has revealed to you alone something of his plan. Yes, his hand is on you, Esme."

They talked a little more then, about commonplace things and the preparations that had been made for their departure early the next morning. But nothing more was said of Esme's dream or its possible significance, though all knew that some word of power had been spoken among them and that it would result in some great deed as yet unforeseen, and that this was what sent the women hurrying off once more. When they rose reluctantly to go to their beds, Morwenna led them to the door, saying, "I will come to bring you breakfast and to see you away in the morning."

"Please do not bother," said the Queen. "You have all done so much for us already."

"It is no trouble." Morwenna dismissed Bria's comment with a whisk of her hand. "I only regret that I have not had the pleasure of spending more time with your little ones. They are charming! You must bring them back soon, and Quentin too. He has been too long away."

"He would agree with you, I know." Bria took Morwenna's hands as Jollen came up to stand behind his wife. "Pray for him. Please . . . pray for him, and for my son."

"You may trust in it that we will," answered Jollen. "Our prayers have not ceased since you came to us. Yes, until we hear that all is well with you once more we will remain in prayer." He paused and regarded the women with a long, appraising gaze. "But be encouraged," he said abruptly. "Your task here, the reason for your coming, has been fulfilled, and the Most High is pleased to give you his blessing. You have been faithful to your hearts, and even now the things which he has promised are coming to pass. Go, so that you may witness them and know that he is ever true to those who follow him."

Silently the visitors embraced their hosts and stepped from the warm, firelit room into the cool summer night ablaze with myriad stars. They hastened to their beds, too full of private thoughts to speak, but feeling each one closer to the other, conjoined with a strength of love and purpose that held them secure. And though they might be forced to ride through the darkness of evil days ahead, none doubted the light which had been promised at their destination.

"TOLI? ARE YOU ASLEEP?" ASKED PRINCE GERIN. THE boy slid closer to the man's huddled form beside him.

"No," replied Toli, rolling over. "What is it?"

"I heard something; someone is coming."

"I heard it as well. It is the guard again, making sure we are still here and have not vanished through the cracks in the wall."

"They have been watching us closely this day, and the last—closer than before. Why?"

"They have sprung the trap, I believe. They do not want anything to happen to us until they know if they have caught anything or not."

"But what do they want?"

"Revenge. Nimrood tried to steal the throne once before, and—"

Before Toli could finish, there came a scrape at the door and it creaked open. Flickering light from a torch thrust in through the crack illumined the room. Toli rolled to his feet. "What is it now?" he asked as the visitor entered the cell.

"Resting comfortably, my pets?"

"Nimrood!" said Toli darkly. "So you have slithered in to taunt your prisoners?"

"Oh, my, no! I have come to tell you just how high a price I have set on your worthless heads. The ransom letter has been sent and received. The King has no choice but to comply."

"What have you done, snake?"

"Merely suggested that I would be willing to free my captives in exchange for a certain object of value to the King." Nimrood paused and laughed wickedly, "Ha! An object soon to be of little value to the King!"

"What are you talking about?" Toli got to his feet.

"Stay where you are!" Nimrood shouted. Then, in a calmer voice, "That is better. What object?" He shrugged, the torch throwing his black shadow huge against the walls. "I see no point in keeping it from you. His sword—that is the object I will have."

"The Shining One!" gasped Prince Gerin, who had come to stand at Toli's side.

"Yes, I believe that is what they call it. A fine weapon I am told, though I have never seen it myself."

"No!" cried Gerin. "The King cannot give up the Shining One!"

"We shall see," Nimrood chuckled. "We shall see."

"The Prince is right. The Dragon King will never surrender the Zhaligkeer. It would mean humbling the throne, and he will not do that."

"Pity," sniffed Nimrood. "But perhaps he will see it differently. What is a throne worth? The life of his only son and heir, and that of his closest friend as well?"

"I see," replied Toli coolly. "You would force the choice. But you are forgetting that a King is King first and a man second. He must do what is best for his realm."

"In any event, the choice should prove interesting. And we will soon have the opportunity of finding out."

"How soon?"

"Five days' time. At midday five days hence you will be led to the temple courtyard and bound. If the King does not bring this enchanted sword of his, you will be killed on the altar of Ariel. Oh, the gods do not require human sacrifices these days, I know. But this time I think the High Priest will insist. What will the courageous King Quentin do with the blood of your deaths on his hands? How will he live with himself, I wonder?" Nimrood stepped back a pace and lifted the torch high. "And now you will wonder, too!"

Toli stood as one made of stone, fists clenched at

his sides, muscles rigid, and watched the old sorcerer disappear. The cell door closed, the bolt scraped in the lock, and the room was dark and quiet once more. They heard Nimrood chuckling to himself as he stalked back along the corridor to his foul nest.

"Is it true?" asked Gerin when the wizard's cackling could no longer be heard. His voice trembled as he spoke.

"Yes," said Toli, wrapping an arm around the boy and pulling him close. "I am afraid it is true. He might have come here to taunt us with it, but I think not. The old vulture wants us to share the poison of fear between us; he hopes that this knowledge will fester in us like a belly wound. But we must not let it. We must not give up hope for a moment."

"I am afraid, Toli. What will happen to us?"

"I cannot say, young master. It is out of our hands now."

42

A DULL, GRAY-WHITE DAWN BROKE OVER PELGRIN, bringing mist from the turbid, muddy waters of the Sipleth River. On the riverbanks, at a place where the ground rose to form the rocky crag of a bluff overlooking an expanse of gray water, stood Ameron Castle. Below the castle the Sipleth flattened and widened as it curled around the bluff in its stony bed, giving Lord Ameronis a natural barrier on two sides; the forest, wild and thick in that part of Mensandor, protected him on a third side. This left the only clear approach from the front, an approach made difficult for any attackers by rough terrain and a rising slope.

Theido and Ronsard leaned heavily on the pommels of their saddles and surveyed the fortress in the fitful light of the new day. "It is rockier than I remember it," said Ronsard, "and better fortified."

"We will take up our positions there and there," indicated Theido with a sweep of his arm, "just out of bowshot. A man like Ameronis will be prepared for battle at any time, so we must not delude ourselves that we will catch him napping."

"There is one thing we may do before they know we are here—send the sappers to scout a location for a mine beneath the walls."

"Order it at once, and send archers with them in case the castle awakes and offers battle."

Ronsard swung himself wearily down from his mount and walked back into the fringe of trees where the army waited. He talked to several knights who would act as field commanders and gave them their orders. Theido, too, dismounted and paced along the perimeter of the wood, studying the lay of the land and the situation of the castle upon it. While he looked on, a score of men dressed in rough hide clothing came running out of the forest toward the castle carrying long pointed rods in their hands. Behind them came bowmen with longbows and quivers of arrows on their backs.

When they reached the very feet of the towering curtains, the men split off into groups of two or three and began probing the ground and examining the stone all around the outside walls, jamming their rods into the ground, or thrusting them into cracks and seams in the stone at the foot of the outer curtains.

After a while Ronsard came up to stand beside Theido as he watched the activity of the sappers. "It will likely take some time. I suggest we both get some sleep if we can, before Ameronis awakes and discovers that he is besieged. I have already given the order to the troops."

Theido rubbed his eyes with his fists and turned to his friend. "My heart is not in this fight, this raising sword against one of our own, even if it is Ameronis. He is still a lord of the realm."

Ronsard shrugged. "He ceased being a lord of Mensandor when he willfully defied his King. He is a renegade and must be dealt with. Treason is no little thing."

"I do not disagree. I only wish there was some other way."

"Every moment he abides within, holding the King's sword, he holds the King's heir in his hands."

"I wonder if he knows that."

"Would it make a difference to him, do you think?"

"Perhaps not. But I will see that he is informed as soon as may be. That, at least, will make him think twice before he forces this issue further."

Ronsard frowned. "He will not bend. Ameronis is too proud and has waited too long. The siege will begin, and let us pray that it is a short one. We do not have much time."

With that the two turned and went back to attend to the establishment of the camp, and to find themselves a place to stretch out for some much needed sleep.

IN AMERON CASTLE, LORD AMERONIS AND HIS FRIENDS slept in their high soft beds beneath fine linen in rooms hung with exquisite tapestries embroidered in silk. Ameronis was accustomed to the very best things, and styled himself a King, so hot did the flame of ambition burn in him.

Now he slept soundly in his broad bed, dreaming the day close at hand when he would ascend the Dragon Throne in the Hall of the Dragon King. It was a vision long cherished and nourished in his heart, and soon he would see its fulfillment—now that he possessed the storied Zhaligkeer. The sword itself lay in a locked casket at the foot of his bed; he did not trust even his own armorer to keep it for him, but wanted it near him at all times.

On the wall walk outside the lord's tower window men ran shouting, their footsteps slapping the stone flagging. Their cries stirred Ameronis from his dreams of kingly glory and he awoke. "Chamberlain!" he cried, and his call was answered at once by a slight, weasel-eyed man with brown, rotten teeth.

"My lord?" the servant said, thrusting his head in through the doorway.

"By Zoar, what is going on? How is a man to sleep with such a clatter? I have guests in my house and will not have them awakened."

"Some disturbance outside the castle, my lord. Its nature has not yet been determined."

"Blazes! I will see to it myself!" With that Ameronis threw back the coverlet and strode out onto the bartizan and mounted a flight of steps to the battlements. The lord's chamber was in the foremost west tower and overlooked the gate and the approach from the forest.

It took him only an instant, once the sleep had been rubbed from his eyes, to ascertain the cause of the disturbance which had roused him from his bed. "By all the gods of heaven and earth!" he cried. "We are besieged!"

At that moment a young knight, who was Ameronis's commander, approached. "My lord, we are besieged."

"I can see that! How many are there?"

"We have not had time to count. I have just come from fortifying the gates. One of the watchmen sounded the alarm only minutes ago at the southern battlement. Sappers, my lord, are looking for a weakness to exploit."

"King's men?"

"They wore no badges, my lord. Nor have I seen any."

"Very well. Rain arrows down on their foolish heads. That will teach them to come sniffing like dogs around these walls!"

"Bowmen have been ordered, my lord. But the sappers ran off as soon as they arrived at the battlements."

Ameronis turned and gazed out toward the wood where the Dragon King's army waited. "So," he murmured to himself, "it begins already." Then he barked an order over his shoulder to the young knight. "Post archers, and inform me at once if they show themselves again."

"Yes, my lord." The commander dipped his head, and Ameronis strode from the wall walk on bare feet, back down the steps and across the bartizan to his chamber. There he dressed hastily, throwing on his padded tunic in the event he would be required to don his armor before the day was out. Then he hurried to the armory to order the disposition of the weapons; from there he went to the warder to inquire into the castle's provisions: food, water, grain, and fodder for the horses; next he went to the gates to personally oversee the reinforcement of their immense timbers with wedges and crossbeams.

All this Lord Ameronis did without fluster or anxiety, but as one well accustomed to war and its preparation. In truth, he had been waiting for this day all his life. If he went about his business with the clear-eyed dispassion of a battle-tried veteran, it was because he, like his father, was a man whose ambition for the throne schooled him well in the use of power and its attainment.

He would be King, he vowed, or die trying.

AT MIDDAY RONSARD AWOKE FROM A TOO-SHORT NAP and made an inspection of the camp, visiting with his commanders and men, all of whom had been busily transforming the woods round about into a small village—a village of fighting men.

"Sir Garth," said Ronsard, hailing a thick-sinewed knight who was directing the construction of a tether line for the horses. "What word from the sappers we sent out this morning?"

The big man drew air into his great barrel of a chest and puffed out his cheeks; the air whistled through his teeth. "Nothing good, my lord. Castle Ameron is as secure as the rock she sits upon. The sappers found no breach point, nor any soft footing around the entire perimeter—at least three sides, I mean. The fourth side is the river."

Ronsard frowned. "Nothing?"

Sir Garth shook his head. "Her roots are stone, my lord, hard as her master's heart. We'll find no tunneling place beneath those walls."

Ronsard nodded and walked off. So be it, he thought. If we cannot go under the walls, we will go over. There is no time for a lengthy siege; the matter must be settled in four days if we are to reach the High Temple before . . . Well, one way or another we will reach it in time. With the true god's help we will reach it in time.

Just then he heard footsteps behind him and turned to meet Theido. "You look the better for a bit of sleep, my friend. We are getting too old to be chasing through the forests all night, eh?"

Though Ronsard's tone attempted cheer, Theido remained heavy-hearted; his voice was gruff when he spoke. "Is there any sign from the castle?"

"None. I spoke with the watch commander a moment ago—he said there has been no signal from towers or battlements, though it appears a few archers have been posted. They are waiting."

"Hmph!" said Theido. "Then I will give them something to think about while they wait." With that, he spun on his heel and called for a squire to bring his horse.

"What is your plan?" Ronsard hurried after him.

The squire came running with Theido's charger, and the tall knight caught up the reins and put his foot in the stirrup. Ronsard placed a hand on his shoulder. "Do not go alone."

"Come with me, then. It makes no difference to me." Theido swung himself into the saddle and wheeled his horse.

"Wait!" called Ronsard, and then sent the squire scurrying after his own mount.

When Ronsard caught up with his headstrong friend, he was halfway to the castle across the stony escarpment. Granite outcroppings pushed through the mossy turf, making the way more difficult. The sun shone down from directly overhead, glancing off these rock faces with a harsh light. Ameron Castle stood before and above them at the top of the slope, and Ronsard studied the walls carefully as they approached.

They rode to within bowshot of the walls and halted. Theido raised his hand to his mouth and called to the watchers. "I am Lord Theido, friend of the King. I would parley with your master. Bring him."

The two riders waited while the men on the battlements debated this request, ultimately deciding that they could not refuse. One of the men said something, a head disappeared from the crenellation, and the first watcher called back, "We have sent for our lord, sir."

They waited; the knights' horses stamped and snorted impatiently, tossing their heads and shaking their manes, eager to move on. But the wait was rewarded with the appearance of Lord Ameronis at the battlements.

"So, Theido, it is you!" Ameronis called down from his wall. "And is that Ronsard?"

"I want to speak to you, Ameronis. Face to face."

"I am sorry, but it seems that the gates have been closed and fortified. I cannot open them for you." Ameronis spoke with good humor, as if he would gladly forget that the men before him bore anything but friendship and goodwill.

"Then allow us to approach, for I have something to tell you that you should know before blood is spilled on either side."

"You're wasting your time," muttered Ronsard. "The only thing this wolf understands is the broad side of a blade."

"I know," replied Theido. "But those with him are not of the same stamp. We may be able to sway them. See? Here they are."

Ronsard saw several more heads join Ameronis to peer over the wall. "I do not see Lord Edfrith among them."

"Perhaps he has had the good sense to withdraw before entangling himself further in this greedy one's plots. That shows, at least, that this pack is not of one accord."

"You may approach," shouted Ameronis down to them. "I will listen to what you have to say."

43

"I DO NOT LIKE THIS, AMERIONIS," SAID LORD KELKIN. "If it is true we hold the ransom for the King's son, we must give it. I do not want the Prince's blood on my head."

The friends of Ameronis were gathered with him in his council chambers, a room high in the tower keep above the dungeon. The windows were open so that the breeze might stir the air, which lay still and heavy in the room. Ameronis sat on a sill gazing out across the escarpment toward where Theido and Ronsard had retreated only a few minutes before.

"You had stomach enough for it when we rode to the King himself," said Lupollen. "I did not hear you complain then. If it is true that he who holds the sword is King, then here is our King!" He gestured to Ameronis, who placed his hands on the sill and rose, facing them, silhouetted in the narrow window.

Lord Denellon muttered beneath his breath, "If he is King, why are we hiding behind bolted doors, waiting for a fight?"

Ameronis ignored the remark. "Do you not see that this is exactly what they wanted?"

The others looked at him askance. "What do you mean?" demanded Gorloic. "Speak plainly."

"Then believe me when I tell you it is nothing but a trick to make us relinquish the sword without so much as an arrow exchanged. Theido is a crafty old fox; he knew this would cause dissension among us, and that is why he spread the lie."

"You doubt him—after all that happened in Askelon?" asked Denellon.

"Oh, I do not doubt that the Prince was abducted—that is true enough. Most likely he was abducted by simple highwaymen who only want a few ducats of gold to let the boy loose. For all we know, the lad may be free now, the ransom already paid.

"No, this story about the sword being ransom for the Prince and his life forfeit if the Shining One is not delivered four days hence—why, it is a ruse, and a shabby one at that."

The lords listened to this speech of Ameronis's, spoken calmly and with assurance, and frowned—not convinced, but swayed somewhat by the sly reckoning. At last Kelkin stood and said, "I think we make a grave mistake, sirs. And one we will long regret. But we are already enjoined and must see the matter through. Aye?"

"Aye," echoed the others. "It is the only course left to us."

"Yes," said Ameronis, nodding as if he, too, had been finally convinced by Kelkin's address. "It *is* the only course open to us. They"—he pointed out the window—"they have forced us to it, and we must see it through."

"What answer will you make to them, Ameronis?" asked Lupollen. "It is nearly time for them to return for your reply."

"What answer can I make?" Ameronis spread his hands. "I will tell them that we cannot give over the sword. I will offer to forgive the affront on my honor which has been served me by their presence if they will leave. If not? Well, it is out of my hands."

With that, the lords rose and filed out one by one onto the battlements. On the ground below Theido waited alone, having returned for the reply to his demand to give up Zhaligkeer.

"Lord Theido," called down Ameronis, "before I give my answer, I would ask a question of you." The other lords on the ramparts with Ameronis looked at each other. What was the devious lord up to now?

"Ask it then," replied Theido from below, leaning with an arm on the pommel of his saddle.

"What guarantee have I that if I give up the sword to you, you will not turn and use it in your own bid for the throne?"

"Only a man such as yourself would think such a thing," snapped Theido angrily. "You who are true to none believe all men to be as disloyal as yourself."

Ameronis merely shrugged. "What guarantee?"

With an effort Theido held down his temper. "I can offer no guarantee save my word of honor. But if you prefer, you may ride with us back to Askelon and place the sword in the hands of the King yourself."

"With you and your knights as escort?" Ameronis scoffed. "I would be cut down before I rode a half a league."

"Theido's word is good enough for me," replied Lord Kelkin. "As good as a King's seal and promise."

"He is offering a chance to save honor without shedding blood," put in Lord Denellon. "I say we should consider it."

"He is offering to have us flayed like trout, my friends. Do you suppose he would not seek to punish us once the sword was his?"

"He said we could deliver it into the King's very hands," argued Gorloic. "I say we should reconsider."

"And find ourselves in Askelon's dungeons as soon as the sword is handed over?" said Lupollen.

"The Dragon King would not do such," said Kelkin. Gorloic and Denellon nodded with him in agreement. "We could ask for safe conduct."

"Safe conduct! Ha! The only safe conduct we would

receive would be safe conduct to the headsman's block!" Ameronis frowned. "No, we dare not give up the sword now. As long as we hold it, we hold our lives—give up the sword and we are dead men."

"I am waiting," said Theido. "What is your answer?"

"You have my answer," said Ameronis. "I will not give up the sword. If the Dragon King wants it, let him come and take it from me himself!"

"You realize this is treason—"

"Do not speak to me of treason, sir! When I am King, your effrontery will be counted treason and we shall see who squirms then! Leave this place, and take your men with you."

"We are charged to bring back the Shining One, and we will achieve our purpose. If you have no thought for the King, at least think of the life of his son."

"A ruse! Be gone; I am tired of talking to you."

"I am leaving," replied Theido coolly. "When next we meet, it will be at swordpoint. You have forced us to declare the siege begun." Theido snapped his reins, turned his horse, and galloped back down the slope. Ronsard was waiting for him at the edge of the encampment.

"How is it with them?" asked the sandy-haired knight.

"You were right, my friend," replied Theido hotly. "It *is* a jackal's den. Though the others with him—Gorloic, Kelkin, and Denellon—seem inclined to reason, they allow themselves to be led astray by his smooth tongue."

"So the siege is begun." Ronsard stared off at the castle rising before them. "Those walls will not be easy to breach. And we cannot starve them out. We must go over the top."

"Perhaps it will come to that," replied Theido, following Ronsard's gaze. "But not yet. I want to examine that fourth side of the castle, the west wall on the river."

"How do you propose to do that?"

"It will have to be tonight, under cover of darkness."

"Very good. I will arrange a diversion as well; that will mask our true purpose. But what do you hope to find?"

"A postern gate. I have never yet been inside a castle that did not have a rear entrance of some kind. A man like Ameronis will have a secret gate if nothing else—if only we can find it."

Ronsard nodded and added, "If only we can find it in time."

FOR THE REST OF THE AFTERNOON AND INTO THE EARly evening, the camp bustled with activity. The woods nearby rang with the sound of axes as trees were felled and stripped of their branches; men combed the forest gathering dry pine needles by the armful; the forge and bellows of the smiths sent black smoke rolling up through the trees and into the sky.

By nightfall all was in readiness. A pale half-moon rose in the treetops, casting a glimmering light upon the escarpment, bleaching the castle walls and the granite outcroppings on the field white as dead men's bones.

"All is in readiness," said Ronsard. He came to stand beside Theido who was instructing a group of knights he had chosen for the night sortie.

"Good. We are ready here too." Theido dismissed the men, saying, "Rest now. I will sound the call when it is time to go." The knights departed into the darkness, leaving Theido and Ronsard alone with the embers of a slowly dying fire. "Now to wait. The moon will be well down in a few hours; it should be dark enough then to move without being seen."

"Once we start in, not a soul in Ameron Castle will think to look for you. I will make certain of that."

"How long can you keep up the diversion?"

"As long as you require it. We are well-provided."

Theido sighed, "Ah, well, then all is ready. We may as well take some rest too. We must have our wits about us if we are to beard the lion in his den."

44

AT THE EDGE OF THE WOODS THE TWO PARTIES ASSEM-
bled: one a force of two score men-at-arms, the other a
dozen handpicked knights. The moon had climbed the
night sky and sunk down behind the trees of Pelgrin,
and full darkness lay upon the land. The castle rose
before them on the slope, a massive black shape in the
greater darkness. But for the blazing stars shining down
like the fires of a celestial host encamped, the besiegers
would not have had enough light to find their way.

"We will give you enough time to get into position,"
said Ronsard. "You will know when the diversion starts,
I daresay. With any luck the whole castle will soon be
awakened to the alarm."

Theido nodded. "We will be ready. Do not get careless, and stay well out of arrow range. There is no need
for anyone to get hurt tonight. Yours is not the risk—at
least not yet."

"We will keep out of bowshot, never fear," Ronsard
assured him. "See that you do the same."

With that the two men parted company, Theido leading his knights off into the woods, making for the river
bank where the slow Sipleth flowed dark and silent.
After walking what seemed a lifetime through the wood,
the knights came upon Sipleth's east bank. The sound of

moving water eddying and curling as it slipped along its shores told them that they had reached the first stage of their journey.

Walking silently, their tools and weapons muffled to prevent any sound, the small force turned and filed along the river bank, proceeding toward the castle. Presently the river broadened, flattening as it bent around the castle rock. The bank rose to form a cliff above the black water, unseen except for the winking glint, here and there, of starlight on a ripple in the current.

The knights made their way up the rising cliffside, fighting through tangles of nettles and bramble thickets along the way. Their labors were rewarded when Theido at last halted their progress and passed the whispered word back along the file: "The castle is just ahead. We wait."

Ahead, right to the very edge of the cliff, stood the west wall of Castle Ameron. The raiding party knelt down in the path to wait for the signal. It was not long in coming, for as the knights waited silently below the curtain, there came a shout from above, far-off. "Fire!" This call was echoed by another and another all along the battlements. Then the knights heard the clatter of feet racing along the high walls directly over their heads as the cry resounded, "Fire!"

Still Theido waited, holding up his hand to stay his men. "Hold," he whispered. "Give it time."

Now the alarm cries could be heard echoing through the castle yards and along the furthermost battlements. But nothing more was heard from directly above; so Theido, moving stealthily, crept forward to the western wall beneath the tower and along the curtain, walking the entire length, gazing upward as he passed.

He was back momentarily, saying, "It worked. The watch has withdrawn to the far side of the castle. We have little time, so let us work quickly. Go."

The knights leapt to action at once. Coils of rope were produced and heavy stakes driven into the ground. The ropes were attached to the stakes, and knights began lowering themselves over the edge of the cliff to the river below. Theido and two archers remained beneath the walls to protect the ropes while their comrades were vulnerable below.

When the last knight had disappeared over the edge Theido said, "Now we wait once more. Stay back close to the wall in case the tower watch returns, and keep sharp for my signal."

The two knights melted back into the darkness beneath the tower wall. Theido, too, stepped back from the edge of the cliff, sitting down with his back against the immense curtain of stone to wait, praying that the watchmen would not return soon.

THEIDO NEED NOT HAVE CONCERNED HIMSELF, FOR AT that moment every available man under Lord Ameronis's command was either lofting buckets of water to quench the fires burning in the ward yards, or lining the eastern wall with bow and arrows, in an attempt to prevent the siege force from sending more fireballs their way.

For when Theido's party departed, Ronsard and his force had waited until they were well away and then moved out upon the field, dragging with them the crude catapults that had been constructed that very day. There were two of them, ungraceful machines of rough timber and rope; long poles of ash with slings at one end and counterweights of stone at the other were lashed to sturdy sledges of pine. Along with the catapults were two wagonloads of baled pine needles, tinder dry and awaiting the spark which would set them roaring into flame.

Teams of horses positioned the catapults—one below each facing tower on either side of the gatehouse just out of reach of the most determined bowman. Once in position, the horses were unhitched and led back to camp, and the war machines securely anchored to the ground with ropes and stakes. At Ronsard's signal two riders came galloping from the campground with flaming torches, and the firestorming of Ameron Castle began.

The first bales were loaded into the slings, the catapults set, and the torch applied. Instantly the bale of pine needles burst into flame and the catapult released. Fwshh! The fireball soared through the air, describing a perfect arc toward the wall. In almost the same instant a second fireball swooped in from the opposite side.

The first missile cleared the wall and battlements and fell into the ward yard. The second missile fell short, striking the upper section of the stone wall and sliding back to earth at the foot of the wall.

"Take over, Sir Ban," commanded Ronsard. "And keep them coming." He dashed off to help realign the second catapult; it took a few minutes to shift the counterweight and lengthen the throw pole, but before the alarm had spread very far through the castle, the second catapult was hurling fire through the skies with deadly accuracy.

"There!" remarked Ronsard proudly, watching a fireball burn through the air to fall well inside the inner ward yard. "This should keep them busy most of the night."

Archers took to the walls and sent arrow after arrow streaking toward the dimly-outlined men tending the catapults. But Ronsard had correctly estimated the distance, and arrows fell spent to the ground, short of the mark. This brought cries of outrage and frustration from those on the battlements, and jeers in reply from those on the ground, as missile after missile lit the night sky with roaring flames.

LORD AMERONIS WAS SUMMONED FROM HIS BEDCHAMber as soon as the first flames appeared in the ward yard— a fireball had fallen on the stable roof and burst, scattering flames among the straw and fodder below. Frightened horses screamed and bucked as squires and footmen braved the flames in an effort to bring the horses to safety, thus turning the entire inner ward yard into a sea of

churning chaos. Another fire burned near the kitchens.

Ameronis stood with his fists on his hips, barking
orders to those around him, all the while seething with
a rage at the attack under way. Up to now, the ambitious
noble had considered the contest something of a game
where the spoils went to the winner. Now he saw that
the King's forces were in dead earnest, and his demeanor
changed abruptly.

"More buckets!" he bellowed. "Bring more buckets!"
He stood in the midst of the riotous confusion, shouting
above the noise as men darted everywhere in an attempt
to save the stables.

The fire was not large; it had been caught in time and
was soon under control. Ameronis left the inner ward
yard and mounted the battlements, bristling with anger.
"Any luck with the archers?" he asked his commander,
Sir Bolen.

The young knight turned, his face ruddy in the
torchlight and the lights of several small fires in the
outer ward. "No, sir; the enemy is too far removed."

"Any damage?"

"None in the outer ward. The fireballs seem intended
mostly to harass us. There is no real hurt. The fires are
easily extinguished."

"Not so easily!" snorted Ameronis. "If you had been
with me in the inner ward yard just now, you would have
seen the 'harassment' these missiles can do." He glared
out between the merlons at the torchlight glimmering
on the field; this marked the position of the catapults.
Just then a fireball smashed into the gatehouse turret
and rolled down its pitched roof onto the wall. A dozen
warriors threw down their weapons and dodged away.

"I could send a contingent out to put a stop to this,"
suggested the young commander. In the dancing firelight
his eyes glittered with the excitement of a man ready to
brave any danger in order to distinguish himself and win
favor in the eyes of his superior.

"What? And open the gates to them? That is just what they want us to do!" shouted Ameronis. "Use your head, man! No! You will do no such thing. We will weather the attack as best as we can and wait until morning."

"I am sorry, sir," muttered the young knight. "I only thought—"

"Wait!" said Ameronis, glancing up and down along the battlements. "Who is standing watch on the other walls?"

"No one. . . ." replied the commander hesitantly. "When the alarm was sounded, they must have come to help—"

"Send the tower watch back to their posts at once! Have them report to me immediately if they see anything amiss! Hurry! Who knows what these dogs of King's men may be about!"

"DID YOU FIND ANYTHING?" THEIDO LAY ON HIS STOM-ach at the edge of the cliff and called down to the man dangling on a rope below him.

"There is a narrow shingle along the water's edge, sir. It runs all along the bank below the cliff. We have sent men to scout it both directions, but have found nothing yet."

"Continue," said Theido, rising to his feet. Just then there came a voice from the battlements above.

"Halt! Who is there?"

Theido's heart clenched in his chest.

Half-crouched, half-standing, he remained rock-still, hoping that whoever was above him would not see him directly below, an easy target for even the poorest marks-man.

"Hey!" called the voice above. "Bring your torch over here! I think there is someone below."

Theido heard footsteps come running as a second guard joined the first with his torch. He held his breath, fully expecting an arrow to come singing to its mark at any second. One heartbeat . . . two . . . three. Then—

"There's nothing down there, maggot-brain," said a second voice drifting down from the battlements. "You are seeing shadows and thinking them soldiers. Get to your post, and do not call me again unless you see something more than a shadow on the rocks."

The first soldier grumbled and moved on to his place in the tower. Theido released his breath and drew back to the wall to wait. From either side of him at a distance of no more than twenty paces, he heard the soft footfall of his archers withdrawing and realized that as soon as the guard had discovered him, two arrows had been notched to their strings and those strings drawn taut. Had either guard so much as squeaked a warning, the man would have been dead before the words were out of his mouth.

Theido drew his cloak over him and leaned back against the hard curtain. Random shouts still echoed from beyond the walls of the castle, but the initial frenzy which had greeted the first volley of fireballs had died away. To the east the sky held a lighter hue, tinting the sky iron-blue against the black. Hurry, whispered Theido to himself. Hurry! Dawn is coming, and we must soon be gone or be discovered. Hurry, there is so little time.

45

STARS DIMMED IN THE EAST, AND THEIR NUMBERS DWIN-dled as the sky lightened to dawn. Ronsard and his force still manned the catapults, but the fireballs soared less frequently now. "We are running out of bales," reported one of his men. "These are the last."

Ronsard cocked an eye skyward and said, "The others should have returned by now. Hold as long as you can. With any luck they will come before first light."

Hurry! thought Ronsard. Hurry, before they find out. . . . For one fleeting heartbeat he wondered, What if they have already found out? He dismissed the thought instantly, telling himself, Somehow we would have known.

The sandy-haired knight turned his eyes toward the ragged line of forest as it sloped down to meet the river. From here Theido and his party would return. But he saw no one. No figure hailed him from the trees, and no messenger came to tell him that all was well, that the raiding party had returned safely.

"Come on," whispered Ronsard. "It will be daylight soon!"

The catapults flashed, hurling their flaming missiles to the castle walls which could be plainly seen now, showing dull and imposing in the feeble light. But the interval between projectiles had stretched to several minutes, and though the enemy still lined the walls and scurried to put out each new blaze, they did not shout and rail at the foe anymore, but merely watched with casual interest as if bored by the long-running spectacle.

There was a shout and a man came running up from the second machine, saying, "Sir, the bales are gone, and we have nothing else to throw at them." He waited for Ronsard's leading.

"We must continue a little longer. Send some men back to camp, and ready some more bales; have the others there help. We will need enough for both catapults. Meanwhile, we must keep the attention of those on the wall; so have your men move to a new position while you are waiting for your amunition." He pointed across the field. "There—more toward the center."

The soldier hurried off to carry out his orders. Ronsard crossed his arms on his chest and frowned at the sky. "You should have been back long ago, Theido. Shall I send a search party after you?"

He decided to wait a little longer and began pacing back and forth between the catapults, glancing now and again toward the fringe of forest where he expected his comrade to emerge at any moment.

The sun burned nearer the horizon, flaming the sky bright red beneath the gray clouds. The outlines of the castle could be made out clearly now, and black smoke drifted on the rising wind from the numerous small fires they had set through the night. At least, thought Ronsard grimly, we have kept them busy this night, and none of our own have been hurt.

When the men returned, carrying more bales of pine needles and branches, Ronsard ordered the troops to be changed. Fresh soldiers took over for those who had worked through the night, relieving them so they might go to their well-earned rest. The new contingent fell to with a zeal, and the catapulting continued.

Ronsard, increasingly anxious over his friend's delay, placed command of the machines in a subordinate's hands and returned to camp to form a search party to go after Theido and his band. He had assembled the men, and they had armed themselves accordingly and were about to start off on the trail Theido had himself taken when a voice hailed them from the forest. "Ho! Ronsard!"

The knight spun on his heel and met the returning party coming toward them through the forest, their faces drawn with fatigue, but adopting a jaunty air for their comrades.

"We were just setting off to look for you. You were due back long ago."

"I began to think we would never leave. The watch returned to the towers and wall, and we were trapped below the cliff. We had to wait until the guard changed before we could move."

"Well? Am I to guess the rest?"

"We found it: the secret postern entrance. Ameronis is clever, and it took us all night, but we found it."

At this Ronsard and his search party broke out in cheers for their comrades, clapping them on the backs and shaking their hands. "Where is it? Tell me everything you know about it."

Theido dismissed his men to their rest, and he and Ronsard walked to the tent that had been raised for them as their command post and private chambers. Inside, they sat down on benches facing one another across a rough-hewn table. "At first it did not appear that we would find an entrance—secret or otherwise. The cliff below the west wall is smooth-faced and drops away at a sharp angle to the water. But below is a narrow shingle a man may walk along—" He paused and pointed to a jug. "I could use a drink of water."

Ronsard snatched the jug, poured, and handed Theido the cup. "Go on, go on. What did you find?"

"That is much better," Theido replied. "Now then . . . yes, the river bends around the castle rock, and if you follow it far enough you will find that the shore widens as it passes the rock. Here"—he traced with his fingers on the table before them—"and here the forest comes down to the water's edge. I sent the men up along this lower bank as far as it went before it flattened out to the waterline again.

"We found nothing at first. On the second sweep along the bank, one of the men found a cave well up on the cliff face—small, but large enough for a man to squeeze through. It was hidden by juniper scrub, so was impossible to see from the northern approach. But from the opposite direction it could be spotted. They climbed up into the cave mouth and found that not more than half a dozen paces inside, the cave becomes a tunnel."

"No!"

"Yes," Theido affirmed. "The tunnel, though long and winding like a snake, leads to a portcullis of iron and a gate beyond."

"Right into the heart of Ameronis's lair. Well done! Well done, indeed!" He beamed at his friend. "This was a night well spent." Immediately the knight's mind began making calculations, racing ahead to make plans for the campaign to follow. "Can we cut through the ironwork?"

"Yes," replied Theido with a yawn. "I did not see the gate, and we had no torches to properly examine the tunnel—all had to be explored in the dark—but the tunnel is not large, so they were able to at least reach the portcullis without difficulty. But yes, it can be cut through through—given enough time. The iron is thick, and appears to be well made. It will take time."

"Then we must begin at once." He saw the look on Theido's face and asked, "Can we reach the tunnel in daylight without being seen?"

"No." Theido shook his head wearily. "At least not by land. But there is a chance that if we go by water, hugging close to the riverbank below the walls, we can reach it without being seen from above."

"Swim?"

"Too difficult. We could not carry the tools we would need."

"We have no boats."

"Rafts. We must construct two rafts of size enough to hold a dozen men each with equipment and weapons."

Ronsard stared across the table. "That will take a day at least, maybe two."

"We have no better choice that I can see. Scaling the walls without help from inside is our last resort. The foe is well-equipped—certainly better provisioned than we are—and we cannot wait for them to be weakened by the siege. No, the secret gate is the only way."

Ronsard fell silent as he turned the matter over in his head. Finally, he admitted that Theido was right and said, "In that case, I must not waste time sitting here. I will have the carpenters begin constructing the rafts at once." He stood to leave. "You look weary to the bone. Sleep now; I will attend to the raft building and summon you if there is any need." He moved to the entrance and held back the flap, hesitated, and said, "We will win, Theido."

Ronsard's statement begged confirmation. Theido, always so certain before, so sure that the right would win out in the end, could not muster that same strength of conviction now. For once it seemed as if despite all they might do, they would not prevail, that the evil which had poisoned the realm so swiftly had achieved its end already and they were powerless to turn aside its effects.

Ronsard lingered, watching him. Theido rubbed his face with his hands, and yawned. "It has been a long night," he said. "I am tired."

For a moment the two held each other's gaze, each trying to read the other, to plumb the depths and find there some hidden reserve of assurance or hope. At last Ronsard turned his face away, looking out into the camp, but not seeing the men moving there, cooking their breakfasts before the fire, carrying firewood and water, looking after their weapons and the horses. The light shining on his face, his jaw flexed and set, Ronsard stepped outside, leaving Theido to his sleep.

46

QUENTIN STALKED THE HIGH WALL WALKS OF THE CAS-
tle. Restless, unable to sleep, he paced the bartizans and
battlements, his short cloak flying out behind him like
wings, his unkempt hair streaming back from his head
in wild disarray. To any who saw him, the King appeared
as one gone mad, roaming the high places in the dead of
night like those unhappy spirits who haunted the desolate
places.

The King himself was not aware of what he was
doing. He only knew that he could not remain still any
longer; he must move, walk, go, and keep going lest he
fall under the weight of the blackness which had crept
into his heart. He had wrestled with it often enough in
the last days to know that he could not win against it. It
held him in a death grip, and meant to drag him down
into the dust of oblivion.

So, to hold the inevitable at bay yet a little longer, he
prowled the walls by night, in the light of a pale sickle
moon, like an animal half-crazed with pain. Quentin felt
the night press in upon him, enfolding him in its velvet
embrace, smothering him. He stared out across the land
eastward and saw the dark line of Pelgrin hedging the
broad, flat plain. Beyond Pelgrin, further east and north,
lay Narramoor and the High Temple on its flat table of

stone, overlooking the entire kingdom.

Somewhere within that temple his son waited for him to come and rescue him, waited as he himself had waited as a boy for someone to carry him away from that place. And he had been rescued—by a dying knight who placed in his hands a charge that he alone could fulfill. In those days it had been easy—easy to believe, easy to follow without asking for signs or assurances, or at least without requiring them at every turn.

Now it was much harder. He was no longer the simple, trusting acolyte with neither home nor family, and nothing much to lose. He was the Dragon King, leader of his people, protector of the realm.

Sadly, he had not been much of a protector of late. He had not been able to prevent Durwin's death, nor his son's kidnapping, nor any of the host of problems that so beset him. The god had removed his hand from him, had taken the blessing that was given to him and had departed, leaving him alone and helpless.

So be it. The god had moved away, had abandoned him as gods will. He could do nothing about that; he was only a man, after all. The business of the gods was for the gods; mortals could not influence or change affairs once the gods had spoken. And though Quentin had believed wonderful things, incredible things about the God Most High, and had trusted him with his life and the lives of those he loved, the god, like all gods, had ultimately disappointed him.

Still, he had a choice. He could abandon his faith in the Most High and reclaim his life for himself, or he could continue believing, continue serving and trusting, even though there was no good reason to continue, even though all good reason said to cast off the belief that had so long bound him in blind trust to a god who lied when he claimed to care about his children. Where was there ever a god who so much as pretended to care for his followers? None of the old gods, surely. None that he had ever learned about in the temple. If the ways of the gods were beyond the reckoning of men, then at least it made more sense to believe in the only one who held out the hope of something greater than the pitfall rituals played out by the scurrilous priests of the High Temple.

The old gods? Those ancient ethereal impostors? Those vague, capricious forces men called upon, worshiped, and revered with the names of gods? How could he believe in them, knowing them for what they were? As an acolyte, he had served long enough in the temple to learn that a priest's fleshly lips applied to a hole in the stone brought forth the god's oracle, and a priest's avaricious whim became the god's demand.

At least the God Most High shunned oracles and objects of silver and gold as sacrifices to win his favor. When he spoke it was directly, and with power. Yes, Quentin had felt the power. Even if he did not feel it now and would perhaps never feel it again, he would forever remember the time when he had known beyond all doubt that the god had spoken and empowered him.

This was more than mumbled words whispered through a speaking hole hidden in a stone. There was hope here, and that was something the old gods of earth and air, of crossroads and high places, of flowing water and seasons, could never give. Quentin could still remember what it was like to live without that hope, could still remember the aching despair that would come on him when as a boy he lay on his straw mat in his temple cell and prayed in the night to be shown the truth. He would wait, listen, and wait some more, only to have his words fall back upon him, mocking from the silent void.

No, having found the hope he had so long sought, Quentin would not abandon it now. He could not live without hope, for without it there was no life at all. Better a life without sight, or touch, or taste, or any of a dozen other faculties, including love, than a life without hope. He knew that road for what it was and would not travel that way again.

At Dekra he had seen the difference for the first time, had seen the sharp contrast between the hollow sham of the old religion and the true faith. Ah, Dekra . . . with her good, caring people and her quiet ways. Was he never destined to return and live out his days in peace, surrounded by love and beauty? Sadly no. His course had been chosen for him, and it did not include Dekra; Quentin knew that now.

But somehow it was enough merely to know that such a place existed on the earth, and that he could go there on occasion to revive his spirit. Yes, that was enough; he could accept it. For he would always carry a part of Dekra with him wherever he was.

If the god chose to move in him or if he did not, so be it. He could not rule the Most High—what kind of god would allow himself to be so ruled? But Quentin could believe. That he could do, and even the Most High could not prevent it. He could believe and hope though it cost him his crown, though it cost his life!

In that moment the choice became clear. Quentin no longer cared what the god could do for him. He would believe though it proved to be his downfall; he would continue to trust though the god himself proved untrustworthy. Yeseph had believed, and he had died believing. Durwin had believed and he, too, carried his faith to the grave. Very well; Quentin would do no less than the men he had loved, and who had shown him how to believe. He would believe and would follow with all the strength left in him.

That settled, Quentin turned his eyes once more toward the High Temple. Though he could not see it in the distance, he knew that it was there, perched on its plateau like a carrion bird awaiting its next feast of dead meat. Yes, his son waited within those walls, waited for him to come. He would go to him. Could he call himself "father" if he did not? If it meant giving up the sword, he would go. What kind of King would he be if he allowed his only son, heir to the throne, to be killed while he had strength and will to prevent it?

THE TWO LARGE RAFTS, MADE OF LOGS LASHED TOgether with rope, slid into the night-dark water of the Sipleth while a dozen soldiers clambered aboard each, taking with them weapons and tools for breaking through the iron portcullis and gate guarding the secret rear entrance to Ameron Castle.

Once each raft was loaded and the passengers settled in the center, the polemen shoved the ungainly vessels out into the river's sluggish current. Traveling against the flow would not be easy, but along the bank the water's pull was not strong, and the polemen were able to work their rude crafts slowly up the river.

Theido sat with his men in the center of the foremost raft as they laboriously made their way upstream to the place below the walls where the bank offered them a footing so they could disembark and make for the cave entrance.

Throughout the day the carpenters had slaved over the building of the rafts, and though they were far from elegant, Theido was relieved to discover that the crude, lockish platforms floated well enough. By nightfall they were ready and he ordered them launched in order to take advantage of night's protection to further veil their activities. He had no doubt that if even the smallest sound aroused the night watch posted on the wall, they would be discovered and their plans ruined. If Ameronis as much as suspected that they had discovered his secret tunnel, defending it would not be a problem: a trio of archers could keep any number of knights pinned down.

Now Theido crouched with his knights and listened to the water sloshing and splashing by them as they slid along the brush-covered banks, hoping against all hope that they would not be heard or seen passing beneath the walls. The polemen worked the poles and drove the rafts forward, keeping as close to the shoreline as possible. After what seemed like hours, they came to the place where the castle rock rose up and the river pushed its way around it, carving into the cliff of stone. Moving cautiously and with agonizing slowness—for the towers rose unseen directly above them—the rafts inched forward. Straining into the night, Theido scanned the cliff face for the sign he sought—the juniper bushes concealing the cave.

As they rounded the bend of the rock, Sir Garth, who had been with him the night before when they discovered the tunnel, and had himself been inside it, raised an arm silently and pointed to a spot along the bank halfway up the cliff. There it was; Theido could just make out the place as a dark spot against the lighter stone of the cliff. He nodded silently. Yes, they were almost there.

The first raft nosed into the stony shingle, grating softly as it came to rest. The nearest men scrambled ashore and began unloading the weapons and equipment, and then the others followed. The second raft pushed up behind the first, and those aboard made to disembark, but an overanxious departure by the first soldiers dangerously unbalanced the craft and the raft tipped, throwing the remaining passengers into the river with a tremendous splash.

Those on shore froze, hearts pounding, while their comrades swam to shore and dragged themselves out as quietly as possible. Each man held his breath and prayed that the sound would go unnoticed.

They waited.

From somewhere high up on the wall above them they heard a shout which was answered by another shout. The words were not distinguishable, but Theido guessed that one watchman had called to another to ask about the commotion. Then there came the sound of voices drifting down from above—someone was leaning over the battlements to see what had caused the splash.

Theido raised his hand to indicate that everyone remain as still as stone. For a dozen heartbeats he relived his adventure of the night before when he had nearly been discovered. Then there came a call; those below heard it plainly. "All clear," the voice said. The men huddled below breathed a sigh of relief.

Theido signaled for the men to resume their work, and the rafts, unloaded now, were poled up river a little way and hidden among the brush of the bank where the shore flattened and the forest grew close to the water. The rest of the soldiers formed a human chain and began passing the equipment from hand to hand up the side of the cliff and into the mouth of the cave.

Sir Garth and Theido climbed to the cave and crawled inside. Garth produced a flint and steel and found one of the torches among the supplies being stacked at the entrance. In a moment he had the torch flaming brightly and said, "Now we will see what we are up against."

Holding the torch high, he led Theido deeper into the cave. They passed along narrow walls—no wider than a gallery corridor—and came to the furthermost wall of the cave. Here an entrance had been opened and a tunnel cut into the soft rock. "Ages past, the river hollowed this cave. When the castle was built here, someone discovered it and connected it with this passage," said Garth, pointing to the smooth-chiseled surface of the stone.

He lowered his head and stepped into the tunnel. Theido followed. It was narrow—narrower than the cave, with room enough for only one man to pass comfortably. The secret passage led upward and in a slight incline as it made for the castle above. The floor was dry and dusty for the most part, but as it neared the gate Theido noticed water seeping down the sides of the walls. Garth indicated this with his torch, saying, "We are passing beneath the castle cistern, no doubt."

Presently they came to a place where the tunnel walls widened a span and there just ahead stood the iron portcullis, glimmering darkly in the torchlight.

"There it is," said Garth, placing the torch in a sconce set into the stone at the edge of the gateway. "And now that I see it in the light, I see that it is much sturdier than I had first imagined." He ran his hand over the iron, feeling its thickness and strength.

"Yes," agreed Theido, "it is well made, as anyone might have guessed who knew Ameronis and his kin. And it looks in good repair."

"Not a speck of rust, my lord."

"The smiths have their work ahead of them. All the more reason to get them at it."

"Right away, sir." Garth turned and started back through the darkened tunnel.

"And, Garth," said Theido, "have the weapons brought here. I would have them close to hand." The knight left, and Theido returned to his scrutiny of the iron barrier before him. Could they cut through it in time? And once through, what would they find on the other side?

47

BRIA HAD RISEN LONG BEFORE DAYLIGHT, AND ROUSED their bodyguard to begin readying the coach and horses for the day's journey. In two days they had made good time through the soggy moorland between the low mountains of Dekra and Malmarby, and by nightfall had reached the place where they had abandoned the coach. There they made their camp for the night.

Upon leaving Dekra, there had settled over the Queen an unspoken urgency. With every step closer to Askelon she seemed to hear a plaintive voice. Hurry! Hurry, it whispered, before it is too late! And Bria, heedful of this inner urging, pressed the group to a greater speed.

Alinea, sensing this change in her daughter, had questioned her about it when they stopped the day before to eat along the trail. "What is it, dear? What is wrong?"

Bria confessed, her green eyes staring off toward Askelon, "Wrong? I cannot say. But I feel as if something is about to happen, and I must be there to help it or prevent it somehow, I know not which. But my heart tells me to hurry, and I feel we must pay it heed. We must not be slow, Mother."

"Is it Gerin?"

Bria considered this in the way of a mother who

knows when something is happening to her child though he be far away and removed from her sight. "No, it is not Gerin. I am at peace with him. It is more Quentin, I think."

"Has it to do with Esme's vision, then?"

"Yes, that must be it—at least in part. But what I am to make of that I hardly know. Still, I feel we must go with all haste and return to Askelon as soon as may be."

Now, at the dawn of a new day, the feeling of urgency pressed Bria even more strongly, causing her to awaken and rouse the others so that they might break camp the quicker. The little Princesses, still yawning and rubbing sleepy eyes, splashed their faces with water and made a game of getting ready. Alinea herded them together and kept them out of the way of the men hitching up the coach. Bria flew to the task of repacking their sleeping bundles and helping the men stow the provisions on the coach once more.

Esme, for her part, helped too, if a little absently. Since leaving Dekra she had retreated more and more into herself—brooding, contemplative, and given to long periods of silence, her lovely features wrinkled in fierce scowls of concentration. What it was she was feeling inside or so fiercely thinking about which made her seem so sullen and aloof could not be determined. For when Bria attempted to draw her out, she simply replied, "I am a bit preoccupied. I am sorry; forgive me." But following an attempt at rejoining the conversation of the others, she would slowly drift off into her intense reverie once more.

When at last they were ready to travel again, the sun peeped above the rim of mountains to the east behind them. Esme turned and stared longingly in the direction of Dekra, then abruptly turned, mounted her horse, and fell in line behind the coach. By midmorning they reached Malmarby and, after greeting the entire village, arranged for Rol, the ferryman, to take them across the inlet to where the King's Road awaited them beyond Celbercor's Wall.

The coach was taken across first with the horses, and two of the bodyguards, whereupon Rol returned for the remaining passengers. Esme took a seat alone at the bow of the wide boat and turned to face outward, staring across the water. Malmar Inlet flowed deep and dark, its waters silent and clear. As Esme stared down she felt herself drifting off, floating on the water as it stretched its mirrored surface to the great wall rising out of its depths on the far shore.

The wall, she thought. There is something about the wall, but what? As she sat gazing at it the wall seemed to change, rising higher and higher, stretching across the entire realm, extending its mighty length until it encircled all Mensandor with a smooth, seamless face of black stone. And it grew ever higher and higher, blotting out the sun.

Oh, no! she gasped. We are cut off. Trapped! Soon there will be no more light. She looked again and saw robed priests walking along the top of the wall and realized that it was the priests themselves who caused the wall to grow, who encouraged its ever increasing girth. She saw the wall change, forming other walls and pillars and a roof of stone—a temple, the High Temple. And there was a multitude of people moving along the road toward the temple, wending their way up the long, winding trail to the top of the plateau where the High Temple stood. Then there came a roar like a rushing wind and smoke rolled up, blotting all from sight; she peered through the smoke and saw not a temple any longer, but a field of stones and rubble, a desolate place overgrown with weeds and thorn tickets, where owls keened their lonely, spectral call. . . .

"Esme!"

The Princess started at the sound of her name. She turned and saw Bria sitting beside her; she had not noticed her friend approach.

"Esme! What is happening to you?"

Esme grasped Bria's hands and held them, turning her

eyes once more toward the wall. "I have had another vision; the god has spoken to me again." She stared at Celbercor's Wall rising bold and impervious before them and then shuddered as if with cold, looked around at Bria, and said earnestly, "We must go to the temple, Bria."

Bria searched her friend's face for a sign, for anything which would explain her words. "Are you certain? The temple? Why?"

Esme pressed Bria's hands harder. "I am certain. Please, we must not return to Askelon. The temple— I saw it clearly."

"What else did you see?"

"Just that. The wall changed and became a temple— and priests. Twice I have seen priests. This is the confirmation of my vision. Something is to take place at the temple, and we must be there."

Bria nodded and said, "I, too, have felt uneasy since we left Dekra, as if I were being prodded along and urged to haste. But the temple—what about Quentin?"

Esme shook her head. "I do not know. I did not see him, but there was a throng assembled in the courtyard of the temple, and I knew that we must be among them."

Bria bit her lip, then weighed the decision.

"Please," said Esme, "the certainty of what I have seen is strong in me. I know it is a sign from the Most High."

"Very well," replied the Queen slowly. "We will turn aside and ride for Narramoor and the High Temple. And let us pray that we arrive in time to do whatever it is that the god intends for us."

"Yes," said Esme, "that will be my prayer."

ALL DAY LONG RONSARD WAITED AT HIS POST ON THE edge of the field. He watched as the sun rose in the treetops, crossed the vault of the heavens, and began its downward descent toward evening, and still no word came from Theido. The main body of knights and fighting men waited restlessly, burnishing lance and sword and tending to their armor, making sure it was in good repair. When the signal came from Theido, Ronsard would lead his troops into battle to storm the walls of the castle.

For his part, Theido and his men were to come up through the castle by way of the hidden passage, sneaking in behind Ameronis's troops to open the gates for their comrades. But the signal had not come, and that could only mean that the secret gate had not been breached.

So, as twilight lengthened the shadows of the forest encampment, Ronsard gave the order to stand down. "We cannot attempt the walls in the dark," he said. "But tomorrow—secret gate or no—we must fight. There is no more time to wait." He turned to his commander, gave him instructions for the men, and turned away from the field, saying, "I will be in my tent if any messages come."

Throughout the camp men began taking off their armor and laying aside their weapons. Ronsard, too, removed his breastplate and gorget upon entering the tent, went to the basin standing on its tripod, dipped his hands into the cool water, and splashed his face.

Another day gone, he thought, and now there are no more days. It must be tomorrow. Tomorrow or the King's son will die. He stood over the basin, his hands dripping, and stared through the side of the tent, picturing the little Prince captive in the clutches of the loathsome High Priest. He saw the boy bound and placed on the altar and the dagger plunged into his trusting heart.

"No!" he cried aloud, slamming his hand into the basin. Water splashed everywhere and sloshed over the rim. "Not while I have breath in my body will they harm that boy!" he vowed. He heard a sound behind him and said to his squire, "Hand me a cloth," putting out his hand to receive it.

"I, too, have made a similar vow."

Ronsard looked up and noticed for the first time who his visitor was. "Quentin! You—Your Majesty! I thought—"

Quentin smiled thinly. "I know what you thought. But never mind. Here"—he handed the dripping knight a strip of clean linen—"dry yourself and we will talk."

The King threw off his riding gloves and cloak and sat down on one of the benches at the table. Ronsard ran the towel over his face and dried his hands, all the while studying the man before him as a physician might study a patient who has suddenly and unexpectedly arisen from his sickbed. "I am tired, Ronsard. It is a long ride from Askelon. I wonder that Ameronis has the will to make the trip as often as he seems to. But then, he always did sit a strong saddle."

"Sire, allow me to send for something to eat. I was about to get some food for myself."

"Yes, do that. I am hungry as well. I have eaten nothing all day."

"I will see to it at once!" Ronsard fairly shouted, for here before him sat the King, who to all appearances seemed in his right mind. Ronsard could detect none of the melancholy that he had so recently seen in his friend. True, his manner was grave beneath the forced civility of his aspect; clearly the King struggled to show himself composed. And fatigue sat on his shoulders like a burden, bending him over, draining his features of color.

But he had come, and he spoke as one who knew what he was doing, who had purpose and reason behind his actions. Surely this was the very best sign.

Ronsard crossed to the tent flap and called to a squire to bring food and drink, then returned a moment later. "Sire, it is good to see you. We thought . . . that is, we were afraid—"

"You were afraid your King had deserted you completely." To Ronsard's look he added, "Well, you were right. I *had* deserted you. I sent you out to fight my battle for me while I stayed within my own walls and ate out my heart with self-pity and grief. But no more. Though I have but one more day to be King, then King I will be—not a coward."

It heartened Ronsard to hear Quentin talk this way—with fire in his voice, and his tone resolute. "Sit, my friend," said Quentin, "and tell me how the matter stands."

Ronsard lowered himself to the bench opposite, leaned on his elbows, and began to recite all that had taken place since they had come to Ameron-on-Sipleth. While they talked, the squire entered with their meal and laid it on the table before them. Ronsard motioned the young man away, indicating that they wished to be left alone and would serve themselves.

Quentin listened intently, nodding now and again as he ate, dipping his hand to his trencher. He raised his cup and drained it when Ronsard had finished and said, "You and Theido have done well. I am pleased."

"Sire, will you lead the troops tomorrow?"

Quentin considered this and then inclined his head in assent. "Ameronis must be made to face his King if he would wear the crown. Yes, I will lead. He must see me riding at the head of my army, and know who it is he would overthrow."

Ronsard smiled. "Excellent! Yes, that is the Quentin I know! Those jackals will turn tail and run!"

"You know that I would not lift blade against them if it could be avoided. I would not that a single man were hurt. But my son's life is at stake, and I must not fail him."

Ronsard opened his mouth to speak, thought better of it, and closed it again. But Quentin said, "What is it? Speak—we know each other too well to hold back."

"As you say, my lord," Ronsard began, then hesitated once more. "Sire, the words come hard."

"They will come no easier for holding them."

The stalwart knight turned his face away and said, "What will you do if we fail to regain the sword?"

"That I cannot say. If I thought riding with an armed force to the High Temple was the answer, I would have done it without delay. But I dare not risk the danger to my son, Ronsard. We must in all events try to recover the Shining One." He paused, adding in a quiet voice, "Failing that, we must trust in the Most High to work his will. That is all any man can do."

"HOW MUCH LONGER?" THEIDO ASKED, SWEAT DRIP-ping from his forehead and running down his neck. Sir Garth looked back at him and shook his head sadly.

"No telling yet, my lord. Another few hours at least; likely more." The brawny knight jerked his thumb over his shoulder to where men labored to cut through the iron bands of the portcullis with various implements.

"Put new men to the task, and spell them regularly from now on. We still have to fight once we are through the gate; I do not want the men exhausted before they must lift their swords."

"It is the heat in this blasted tunnel," said Garth. "It drains a man's strength. We would have cut through long ago if not for that."

Theido turned and walked to the barrier. For all their efforts, they had succeeded in removing only one small section of the thick iron gate. A second section was nearly freed, but a third and a fourth must be cut away to ensure that an armed man could pass through quickly. There was nothing to be done but continue hacking away at the structure at the same maddening, slow pace.

Abruptly Theido left the chamber, passing back through the narrow tunnel to the cave mouth and the cool night beyond. The ping and chink of the workers' tools echoed through the passageway as their chisels bit into the iron. Below the cave the soldiers whose services were not now required at the grate rested on the shingle beside the water. The moon had risen and shone sparkling on the dark river, illuminating the cliff and the castle walls above with a ghostly light.

The soldiers glanced up as Theido made his way down to them. Progress? the glance asked. None, Theido's look answered as he sat down among them.

One of the men, a knight by the name of Olin, leaned close to Theido and asked, "What will happen if we do not breach the grate? What will we do?"

"The grate will be breached," Theido answered stiffly.

"Yes, I know—eventually. But what if dawn comes first?"

Theido turned cheerless eyes upon the man and replied, "Ronsard will attack at dawn. He has no other choice. With our help or without it, he will go against the walls."

Olin stared at Theido in silence.

"You asked for the truth; I told you."

"It is a hard truth, my lord. It is sure death to go against those walls. Catapults and rams—"

Theido cut him off. "We have no time for catapults to wear down the walls or rams to splinter the gates. No time."

"Then if we fail here, we die."

"Yes, and more. If we fail, the realm dies with us; the kingdom is in ruins." Theido nodded slowly, gazing out over the smoothly flowing water. "You did not know so much was at stake?"

"No, my lord," answered the knight. "I thought it was just to save the Prince."

"The Prince, ourselves, our nation."

Sir Olin said nothing more for a long time. Then, without another word, he rose to his feet and climbed back up the side of the cliff to the cave and went back to take his place at the portcullis with the other workmen.

Then, as Theido watched, one by one the others who had been resting, having just come out from the tunnel, got up and climbed back to the cave to pick up their tools once more.

48

As DAWN BROKE FAIR AND CLEAN IN THE EAST, THE Dragon King raised his gauntleted hand and urged Blazer forward. The mighty warhorse jigged sideways and pranced, smelling the scent of battle in the air, feeling his bold blood race in his veins, eager to gallop with his master into the fray. Quentin, with Ronsard at his left hand, rode out onto the field, his armor glinting in the early light.

He wore the battle dress made for him by the legendary Inchkeith, the armor he had worn against Nin the Destroyer on the day he had become King. Polished smooth, bright as water, the pale silver shimmered in the sun's first rays, throwing beams of light from its clean, flat surfaces like the facets of a gemstone. On his head he wore the silver helm without a crest, except for the thin gold circlet of a crown that he had placed there on the day of his coronation. From his shoulders hung the exquisite cloak of chain mail, its tiny links rippling like quicksilver with every jouncing step.

Ronsard, too, was arrayed in his best armor, and rode beside his King with eyes ahead, visor up, surveying the formidable walls rising before them on the escarpment. His hand rested easily on the hilt of his sword; his shield hung down from the pommel of his saddle, ready to be snatched up in an instant when need occasioned. His battle steed shook its mane and pawed the earth as it pranced out into the morning.

Behind them came the King's knights mounted on their chargers, their armor clinking in the silent dawn. No drums beat time; no trumpet sounded the call to arms. The army of the Dragon King would march unheralded into battle this day.

After the knights came the footmen with their pikes and ladders, and grappling hooks on long ropes to aid in scaling the walls. They wore short, heavy swords thrust through their belts, for in the close fighting on the battlements there would be no room to swing a longer blade; and any who were lucky enough to reach the heights of Castle Ameron would need a stout weapon.

The advancing forces reached the catapults, and teams of men ran out and began readying the machines, loading stones and fireballs into the slings. This done, the men waited for the King's command. Quentin scanned the high ramparts, raised his sword—a sturdy blade which he had chosen from among others in the armorer's wagon—and lowered it in a swift movement.

The catapults sang through the air and the footmen raced toward the walls with a mighty shout, flooding over the rising ground to the very feet of the enormous stone curtains. There they flung their ladders against the walls and sent their grappling hooks snaking through the air, while archers positioned themselves to offer what help they could.

At almost the same instant, a cry went up from the walls as Ameronis's men leapt to the embrasures and began hailing arrows, stones, and timbers down upon the men below. The first men on the ladders fell screaming to the earth, but others appeared to take their places, and others behind them, each with a shield over his head to stop the deadly rain. But arrows found their marks, stones struck down with bone-shattering force, and brave soldiers fell.

As the attack began, Ameronis and his noble friends, sitting in the banqueting hall over their breakfast, heard the cry go up from his men on the battlements. Ameronis rose from his chair and said, grinning, "So, the King's army has no patience, eh? It sounds as if they mean to tumble these walls with their wailing. Come, my friends, this will be rare sport. These walls have never been breached in living memory. Let us see how the Dragon King's army fares."

With that he turned and hurried from the hall, Lupollen following after him. The others sat in silence, looking awkwardly at one another for a moment, and then followed. "He did not seem to think it worth mentioning that his walls have stood secure all through the years because of the Dragon King's favor and protection," muttered Gorloic.

"Aye," agreed Denellon. "I am sorry we ever listened to him. We will pay for our error before this day is through. Mark my words, sir. We will pay."

They found Ameronis striding the wall walk, barking orders to his men, exhorting them to a fighting frenzy. Heedless of his own safety, he dashed here and there to join in the worst of the fighting, leaning out over the crenels and shoving the ladders away with his bare hands.

"See how he rages!" cried Lord Kelkin, holding his head in dismay. "He is like a wolf, blood-drunk and ravening for the kill!"

Catching sight of them, Ameronis shouted, "Look! Here is a sight for you! The Dragon King has joined the contest!" He thrust out a hand and pointed below.

The other lords rushed to the embrasure and peered fearfully down into the moil; and there, amidst the writhing, seething mass of men struggling to mount to the walls, they glimpsed the white flanks of the King's charger, flashing here and there among his troops, and the Dragon King himself riding with his sword uplifted and shield held high.

"Bring me a bow!" bawled Ameronis above the clamor. "A bow! Bring me a bow!"

"Stop!" bellowed Gorloic. "Think what you are doing!"

But Ameronis would not listen; he snatched up a longbow from one of his archers and notched an arrow to the string and let fly at the King. Gorloic and Kelkin rushed forward and grabbed Ameronis by the arms. "Let me go!" he screamed. "Let me go!" He struggled free of their grasp and backed from them. "If you have no stomach for the fight, get below and hide with the women in the scullery! I mean to wear the crown, and I will take it however I must!" Horrified, the noblemen backed away and withdrew to the gatehouse turret where they could watch the battle in safety.

Once the fighting began, Ronsard allowed the main force of footmen to establish themselves before the gates of the castle before leading his own small force to the lesser defended northern wall. Ladders were thrown up and secured. One knight gained the battlement without being seen, and another as well before the alarm was sounded and Ameronis's men came running with sword and halberd to repel the invaders. But Ronsard's knights fought well and held their own while their number was strengthened from below. Ronsard was the third man over the wall and was soon joined by others until there were twelve of the King's knights on the wall.

Together these twelve labored to cut through to where their comrades fought to gain the western wall. They inched along the northern curtain toward the northern tower; from there they could cross over to the west. Once in the tower, however, they encountered strong resistance. Ten of Ameronis's knights, hearing the alarm from the northern curtain, had come running up from the ward yard below to meet them.

The foremost of these, a giant of a man in an iron morion and carrying a two-handed axe in one hand and an ox-hide shield in the other, came crashing in through the door of the tower, swinging his weapon in a deadly arc around him. Ronsard, with two of his knights, managed to force the giant back out the door, which they sealed at once.

"Can you hold the doors?" asked Ronsard, throwing open his visor.

"I think so," replied his second-in-command. Just then there came a fearful crash at the door they had just sealed as the giant's axe thundered on the planks. "For now," he added.

"Hold out as long as you can," said Ronsard, "and then join us below. I am going to try to fight through to the gates. Perhaps we can force them open." So saying, Ronsard led the other knights down the spiraling wooden steps to the tower keep below, which was as yet unguarded.

With swords singing they forced their way across the outer ward to the gatehouse, encountering little resistance since most of the castle's defenders lined the wall walks above. Once inside, they overpowered the frightened foe easily.

"In the King's name, open the gates!" demanded Ronsard, his sword at the throat of the quaking gatekeeper.

The man wailed and rolled his eyes in terror. "Though you sever head from shoulders, I cannot!" cried the man.

"Open them, or I will drop you where you stand!"

"I cannot!" screamed the gatekeeper. "Brave sir, believe me! The doors are fortified and cannot now be opened by anyone—leastways, without removing the timbers and chains."

"My lord," shouted one of Ronsard's knights, "he speaks true. The gates are bound in chains and reinforced with timbers. To remove them would take us half a day!"

Ronsard was about to make a reply when behind them on the staircase leading to the parapet they heard a shout and the sound of many feet pounding down the wooden stairs. "We are discovered!" cried one of the knights.

In the space of three heartbeats the loyal besiegers were swarmed by knights as the gatehouse filled with troops from the ramparts above. And though Ronsard and his men stood toe to toe against the defenders, they were sorely outnumbered and were forced to retreat back across the ward yard to the northern tower. There they rejoined their comrades who still held the doors leading out onto the wall walks.

"Seal the doors below!" ordered Ronsard. "We will go above and win the turret!"

They clattered up the stairs to the turret, which was defended by archers. One look at the armored knights boiling up out of the tower, however, and the archers, assuming that the King's forces had breached the walls, threw down their weapons and begged for mercy. "Take their weapons," said Ronsard, and the archers were herded together at the further rim of the turret and made to sit down while a knight stood over them with a sword.

Ronsard then strode to the embrasure and stood up in the crenel, waving his sword over his head. Men on the ground below recognized him and cheered, swarming at once to the tower with their ladders and hooks.

This minor victory proved short-lived, however, for Ameronis too saw Ronsard's signal and sent a force of his best knights to the northern tower. In moments the knights had rushed to the tower and were hacking at the doors. At the same instant, the giant on the wall walk succeeded in battering the door to splinters with his huge axe; he came charging through, followed by others, and they all came thundering up the stairs to the turret.

"We're trapped!" hollered one of the besiegers. "We are cut off!"

"Here!" said Ronsard, motioning to the archers who had given themselves up. "Sit on the hatchway—all of you!"

The prisoners scrambled together and sat down on the planks, holding the door closed with their combined weight. "That should keep them out for a while at least," said Ronsard. "We can only wait now. The fight is taken from us for the moment."

IN THE SECRET PASSAGE DEEP BENEATH THE CASTLE, the clash and clamor of the combat could be heard, muted through the heavy gate beyond the portcullis. "Listen!" said Theido, and the hammering halted. Into the silence drifted the eerie sound of heated battle—as if the echoes of an ancient war still lingered in the rocks of the cave and now came drifting out from the stones that had held them.

"By the One!" cried Theido. "It has started! Hurry, men, or we come too late!"

At once the hammers rang out on the cold iron, filling the cave and tunnel with a horrendous din as chisels bit deep in an effort to free the last section of the grate, for now they did not have to worry about the noise; any racket they made would be drowned in the battle roar above.

With shouts and curses the soldiers threw themselves at the unrelenting iron until, exhausted, they fell back panting into the tunnel. When one man faltered, another took his place as the assault on the portcullis continued.

49

ALL AROUND HIM ON THE GROUND LAY THE BODIES OF the wounded, broken, and dying, some crushed beneath timbers and stones, many more pierced through with arrows. Still the King strove to rally his flagging forces to remount the assault. But, disheartened by their lack of success in gaining the walls and dismayed at the loss of their numbers, the Dragon King's army shrank from the walls, and Quentin was forced to withdraw to regroup his forces.

At the first sign of the King's retreat, a cheer went up from Ameronis's men on the wall. The lord himself joined in the exultation, and called after the receding troops, "Have you had enough, and so soon? Come back; let us finish it for once and all!" This brought more cheers from his men. So Ameronis leaned out over the wall and called still louder to the delight of his army, "The Dragon King slinks away like a scalded hound— with his ears bobbed and his tail between his legs! Come back and fight like a man of honor!"

Up in the gatehouse turret Lords Kelkin, Gorloic, and Denellon watched as the King's forces retreated from the field. "It is going badly for them," remarked Kelkin. "Would that I had my knights with me now; I know which side I would join."

"I, too, would add my aid to the King," said Denellon. "I have seen enough of Ameronis's ways. His true face is revealed in war, and it is not a face I would care to see under the crown."

"Nor I," put in Lord Gorloic. "But though my knights guard my own fortress and are far from here, I still have a sword, and an arm to use it! And while I live, both belong to the Dragon King!"

"Aye!" agreed the others. "So be it!"

"But," said Kelkin, "we are only three. Ameronis and Lupollen have the advantage over us. We would be cut to pieces before we put hand to hilt."

"Then we will have to find another way to better them. We cannot do that here. Come, my friends," said Gorloic, "time is fleeting and we have work to do!"

"ARE YE FAIR CERTAIN THIS BE THE WISEST COURSE, young master?" asked Pym as the two rode along through the forest. "What will yer mother say when she learns we'uns 'as let ye follow the King to battle—and we'uns without so much as a stick to shake at the foemen."

"Be quiet," replied Renny. "I'm thinking."

"Yer *lost!* We'uns've been riding these woods fer near a day and no sign of the King. We'uns'd best go back."

" 'Ee go back if 'ee want to," said Renny stubbornly. "I mean to fight for the King."

Pym sighed—as he had sighed a hundred times in the last twelve hours—and scratched his grizzled head. "Well, if ye have yer heart set on it, there'll be no persuading ye—not as I haven't tried, neither. But ye must admit it: we'uns is lost."

"Not lost," replied Renny. "We just lack direction."

They had left Askelon the day before when the King rode out, following him as he himself had followed his army. But the two of them on Tarky were no match for the spirited Blazer and were soon outdistanced and left behind. Pym had been for turning back, but his young companion pursued his course with single-minded determination, bent on serving the Dragon King beside those noble knights he had met when they tried to return the horse.

The two were resting along a little-used pathway through the southeastern reaches of Pelgrin when they heard the jingle of a horse's tack and the murmur of voices on the trail ahead.

"Someone's coming!" Renny jumped up and peered into the green shadows. "A horse and rider! We'll ask him how to find Ameron Castle."

Closer, they saw not one, but two riders trotting lightly along the pathway. Boldly Renny stepped out into the center of the trail so that they would stop, and in a moment he looked up into the face of a black-bearded nobleman astride a sleek black charger.

"Ho! Who goes there?" said the nobleman with a wink to his companion, a knight with a broadsword on his thigh and a shirt of mail.

"A highwayman by all appearances," returned his companion.

"Please, my lord," said Renny, speaking up with all the courage he could muster. "We need help."

"We are true men," replied the lord. "You have but to ask, and if it be within our power it is granted. But ask quickly, for we are about important business."

Seeing how the lord received the lad, Pym brought Tarky and came to stand beside Renny. "This is my friend," said the boy. "We are on our way to join the King's army at Ameron-on-Sipleth."

"We'uns've lost our way, yer lordship," added the tinker. Tip barked once to affirm their plight.

The nobleman leaned forward in the saddle and studied the travelers closely. "What do you know of the King's army?"

Pym grew tentative. "Only that they marched out from Askelon two—no, three days ago sunset time. The King followed last night, and we'uns followed him."

Renny nodded. " 'Ee goes to claim his sword back from them that took it!"

The lord glanced at his companion, then back at the two before him. Recognition came to him like a flash of lightning out of a clear blue sky. "Why, I know you," he said, looking Pym up and down. "You're the tinker in the road."

"And I know ye, too, yer lordship. Ye were the one as didn't want a poor tinker to come to no harm."

"That bruise on your jaw, man—did Ameronis do that to you?"

"To say he didn't would tell a lie, yer lordship. That he did, right enough." Pym rubbed his still-swollen jaw. "When he took the sword."

"Ah, so it *was* a sword you held under those rags, was it?" He watched Pym carefully. "The King's sword?"

Pym nodded. "I don't know if it be the Shining One or no, but there's no end of them that thinks it, sir."

"It must be!" said the nobleman to the knight beside him. "And Ameronis took it, you say?"

Pym nodded. Renny spoke up, "And we mean to help the King get it back. 'Ee needs it to save the Prince!"

"What's this? What about the Prince?"

"It be the ransom, yer lordship. The sword must be delivered to High Temple tomorrow middleday or the young Highness is to be killed."

"Does Ameronis know about this?" asked the nobleman.

"We'uns can't say if he does or he don't. But all Askelon knows now. It's all anyone talks of, ye see. The word went out yesterday when the Dragon King rode out. Folks 'as said he went to claim his sword to save his son, ye see."

"Yes, I see." The lord rose up in the saddle and turned to the knight. "Ride back and call out my men— all of them, and my tenants, too. As many as have weapons. If any lack, let them be equipped out of my armory."

"Yes, Lord Edfrith," replied the knight, taking up the reins and turning his mount.

"Meet us at Castle Ameron. I go there at once."

"Alone?"

"I will hardly be alone, sir. I have two stout comrades with me here; no man in the realm could be better served. Go and bring my troops. The King will need all the help we can provide if he goes against Ameronis. Hurry!"

"RONSARD AND HIS CONTINGENT ARE TRAPPED, SIRE. A few of our men managed to reach the turret to join him before the tower was taken again," explained one of the King's commanders. "They fight now just to stay alive; we cannot look for any aid from them."

Quentin nodded gravely and dismissed the knight, turning his eyes toward the battlefield. His surgeons carried litters bearing the wounded and dying. Ameronis's troops looked on from the wall, awaiting the next assault, content for the moment merely to watch and wait and conserve their strength.

So, thought Quentin, it has come to this. Ronsard trapped, Theido rendered useless, and I am here alone. His mind turned to the others he had depended on throughout his life: Durwin, Bria, Alinea, Yeseph, Eskevar, Theido, Ronsard, and Toli perhaps most of all. But now, at this moment, all were gone. When he needed them most there was no one to turn to, no one to say to him, "Yes, go on," or "No, turn aside." No one to give counsel, confer with, or share the aching anxiety of this moment.

Even the Most High stood far off, his hand removed and his presence withdrawn.

Quentin squared his shoulders. I am the Dragon King, he said to himself, and it is time I learned to accept what it is to be a King, to be a man whose choices must be his own, and who must live or die by his decisions. Oh, but it is hard. Look at all these others here, watching me, trusting me to lead them, to save them, laying down their lives at my command. Such faith they have, trusting me with their lives. I never asked to be a King, but I was chosen. And I will lead these last faithful men as truly as I know how.

Quentin swung down from his saddle and handed the reins to a squire. He walked among his troops resting on the ground, speaking to them, rebuilding their courage for the next sally.

"HURRAH! THE GRATE IS BREACHED!" THE CHEER ECHoed along the secret passage beneath Ameronis's castle.

"Good!" said Theido. "At last! Now for the gate beyond. Come on, men. We are almost through!"

With axes and wedges the soldiers ran through the gaping hole in the portcullis and went to work on the timbers beyond. In moments the planks were shivered by the sharp blows of the axe and split by the thrust of the wedge.

"Ready yourselves!" called Theido to the others waiting behind him. "We will be through the gate in no time. Be armed and keen for the fight."

GORLORIC, KELKIN, AND DENELLON CREPT ALONG through the castle corridors and galleries, having armed themselves from the hands of fallen and expired warriors. Now they moved quietly toward their objective: the gatehouse.

"I will see to the gatekeeper," said Gorloic. "You two take care of his men."

"What if Ameronis or Lupollen discover us?" asked Kelkin. He glanced around nervously, as if expecting the treacherous lords to appear at any moment.

"They will not," replied Denellon.

"Aye," agreed Gorloic. "If we wait until the attack renews, they will have enough to think about. But we must work quickly. See? The gatehouse is through the antechamber before us. Are we ready?"

"Listen!" said Denellon, for at that moment a tremendous crash was heard in the ward yard outside.

And another shook the outer curtain. "The catapults! The attack has begun!"

From up on the wall walks above, the lords heard the roar of a shout from the troops lining the ramparts as the Dragon King's army came rushing to the walls once more. "We go!" said Gorloic, and laying a hand to his hilt he rushed forward through the antechamber and into the gatehouse, his friends coming hard on his heels.

"Gateman!" Gorloic shouted. "Open the gates!"

The gatekeeper and his men, some of whom had been crouching behind barrels in the corner, turned to meet the noblemen, their eyes showing white all around. "But, your lordship," he complained, "we cannot! The gates are fortified! It is Lord Ameronis's order that they remain sealed."

"Silence, fool!" shouted Gorloic. "It is his order that they be opened now. The battle is turned, and he expects the enemy to break ranks and run at any moment. He wants the gates opened so that he can give chase!"

The keeper shook his head slowly, peering doubtfully at Gorloic. "Sir, I dare not without an order from my lord himself."

Denellon dashed forward. "Do you hear the shouting? Hurry!"

Kelkin added, "Think how angry your master will be when he learns you disobeyed his order."

This rattled the gateman. His eyes bugged out, and he threw up his hands. But still he refused. "I dare not go against my order."

Gorloic turned on him angrily, grabbed him by the shoulders, and whirled him around. "If you and your men will not help us, we will do it ourselves! And I will personally tell Ameronis that you defied him!"

"No! Oh, I—"

"We have no time!" insisted Gorloic. He nodded to Denellon and Kelkin, who rushed to the gates and began hacking at the shackle-bolts with their swords. "Are you going to help us?"

"You will take responsibility?"

"Yes! Yes, gladly!"

The gatekeeper waved his men forward and produced a ring of keys. "Here, with these it will go faster." And he proceeded to loose the shackle-bolts while his men threw off the heavy chains binding the timbers that had been jammed against the gates.

50

WITH EVERY OUNCE OF STRENGTH REMAINING, THE King's troops threw themselves at the walls, planting their ladders once more and struggling to mount them. But wherever they attempted to gain a foothold—choosing a portion of unprotected wall, or establishing themselves within the protection of archers—always that attempt was repulsed. The enemy rushed to the edge to hurl stones and beams down upon them, or archers darkened the air with arrows and drove them back.

The Dragon King rode fearlessly through the fray, arrows glancing now and again from his armor and shield, shouting to his men, heartening them, urging them on. But the tide of battle was against them.

"Sire!" Quentin turned to see one of his commanders riding up. The knight threw open his visor, saying, "We have lost the left flank. Too many men have fallen, and we cannot continue alone."

"Join with Sir Heldur's men in the center!" ordered Quentin. "We must hold the center." The knight rode off again, and Quentin was hailed from the other side. The report was the same; the right flank had been weakened and was in danger of falling. His army teetered on the brink of defeat. In only a few minutes the rest of his soldiers—overcome with fear and futility—would retreat, and once in flight would not return again to the field.

Even as Quentin thought this, the first ranks broke and fell back, shrinking from the fight. "Hold!" he cried, riding forward with upraised sword, though in his heart he knew that there was no good reason now to hold on. More and more troops were falling away as others, looking about and seeing their comrades withdrawing, joined the retreat. Soon soldiers were streaming from the field by the score.

Just as the foremost ranks of footmen faltered and fell back, someone shouted, "The gates! The gates are won!"

Quentin looked up to see the castle gates swinging open, pushed from within by figures he vaguely recognized. Then, as they were thrown wide, one of the figures sprang out and beckoned to him with a sword. "Gorloic?" shouted Quentin as he rode for the gate.

"Sire"—the nobleman dropped to one knee—"forgive me for my faithlessness. Allow me to earn back your trust with my sword."

"And I," said another.

"And I, as well," replied another coming close.

"Denellon, Kelkin, Gorloic—yes!" shouted Quentin as already his knights surged through the gates and into the outer ward yard.

Those in retreat, seeing the gates swing open and their King standing in the breach, halted, turned, and came running back with a tremendous shout and pressed forward into the castle, sweeping their King and comrades before them.

"WE ARE BETRAYED!" BELLOWED AMERONIS. HE STOOD with clenched fists and pounded the rough stone of the crenel as he saw below him the King's army flooding in through his gates.

"Rally! Rally!" cried Lupollen beside him. "We can match them blade for blade. We have superior numbers now."

It was true. The assault on the walls had weakened the Dragon King's forces, depleting their ranks severely. "Yes! We are far from lost!" said Ameronis. "And I will welcome the chance to exchange blows with the King and best him with his own sword."

In the space of a dozen heartbeats, Ameronis's troops came flying down from the battlements to engage the enemy in the outer ward yard. Instantly the air was shattered with the clash of arms as sword beat upon shield, and axe and mace smashed steel armor. "For the Dragon King!" cried the King's warriors as they forced their way forward through the press.

But Ameronis's men were tough and well-trained. They held forth and did not give ground. Fierce battle raged on every side. Quentin dodged here and there into the fray, striking again and again, until he seemed to be everywhere at once. Those of his men who were pressed hard to the point of breaking, those who slipped and were about to fall had only to raise their eyes to see the Dragon King's blade swinging to their aid. And if it was not the Shining One that men had learned to fear and respect, it was at least a sword in the strong hand of a deliverer.

The archers on the battlements threw down their longbows, ran to the armory, and took up crossbows—a weapon better suited to the close infighting of hand-to-hand combat—and began hurling deadly bolts into the thick of the meleé, driving the King's forces back. For none could stand against the lethal missiles which pierced even the heaviest armor, and none could get close enough to strike at the assailants.

High up in the turret above the northern tower, Ronsard and his knights, who had cheered wildly when the King's men shoved through the gates to win the outer ward yard, now stood mute while Ameronis's forces turned the battle once more against them.

"We must help them!" cried one of the knights.

"Here!" shouted Ronsard. "Take up the prisoner's

bows—all of you! Aim carefully, sirs—there are friends among the foe down there!"

With that, the trapped knights loosed a volley into the chaos below. Ameronis's men, so confident only seconds before, now drew back as death came whistling after them from the skies.

"That has helped, but unless we receive more substantial aid soon, the day is lost. See? Ameronis has our forces outnumbered two men to one."

The words were scarcely out of Ronsard's mouth when there rose a cry from out on the field before the castle. Ronsard dashed to the far embrasure and stared down upon the escarpment and at the host of knights and footmen running forward.

"Who is it?" asked one of the knights. "I do not recognize the blazon."

"The crest is Lord Edfrith's, I'll warrant."

"An enemy! We are lost!" It appeared that Lord Edfrith and his men were swooping in behind the King to cut him off, thus crushing all hope of victory or even honorable retreat.

"No, wait!" said Ronsard. "He rides before the King's troops!" For an instant the lord was cut off from view as he passed beneath the curtain and into the gatehouse. "Look! He has come to our aid!"

"We are saved!" shouted the knights, and the turret erupted in shouts of jubilation as Edfrith and his knights came pounding in through the gates, swords flashing, voices raised in a battle chant for the King. And all who heard it took heart.

"For Mensandor! For honor! For the Dragon King!"

Ameronis, who at that moment was cutting a swath toward the King with Zhaligkeer, glanced up and saw the army of Edfrith streaming in through the gates. He heard the chant and turned to Lupollen who labored beside him matching thrust for stroke. "Edfrith rides for the King! We are twice betrayed!" Despair rushed upon him, and he staggered back.

"We are not vanquished yet!" Lupollen said, grabbing him by the arm and shaking him. "You hold the sword—let us escape while we still may. With the sword we may raise an army elsewhere."

"Good counsel. Let us fly!" Ameronis turned and fled back through the thronging soldiers and into the castle with Lupollen after him.

SURROUNDED AND DISADVANTAGED BY NOW-SUPERIOR forces, Lord Ameronis's commanders threw down their weapons and begged for quarter. Cries of "Mercy! Mercy!" and "Give quarter!" rang out in the castle yard where before the shouts of "Hold forth! We win!" still hung in the air, so quickly had the battle ended.

Pym and Renny, astride Tarky, peered fearfully in through the gate. Lacking weapons and armor, they had hung back from the battle at Edfrith's command; but upon hearing the cries of the vanquished they had come close to see the struggle ended and discover which side had won. "The King has carried the day!" shouted Renny. "Hooray! The Dragon King has won!"

"So he has for a fact," replied Pym sagely. "We 'uns nivver doubted it fer a minute, eh? No, nivver fer a minute." They slipped in through the gate and rode into the press around the King.

Denellon, Kelkin, and Gorloic also pushed through the mob and came to stand beside Edfrith, who had dismounted, and all four stood before the King. "It is over. We declare the victory yours, Sire," they said, and all around them raised a victory chant.

Quentin held up his hand for silence, and when the cheer died down, said, "It is not over until I hold the sword." He stood in his stirrups and scanned the crowd. "Where is Ameronis? I will have him here before me."

Ronsard, who wasted no time in abandoning the turret once the tower was taken, shouldered his way through the crush around the Dragon King. "Ameronis has escaped!" he called, breathless from his run down the tower stairs.

"I saw him and his cunning friend fly the battle and disappear into the castle."

"Then he has taken the sword with him!" said Gorloic. "Our efforts have been for naught!"

"Curse him!" spat Kelkin. "There is no catching him now!"

"Why?" asked Quentin, sudden panic flooding over him, twisting his stomach. "Where has he gone?"

"There is a secret passage beneath the castle," explained Kelkin. "It leads out onto the Sipleth and to a trail along the shore. Upriver he keeps a boat in readiness. At least, his father always did. I suppose Ameronis does as well."

At this, Quentin and Ronsard threw back their heads and laughed heartily as relief chased the dread from their faces—just as sunlight removes the shadows when the clouds have moved on.

"You find this humorous, Sire?" Kelkin asked.

"You do not know the fears your words have slain just now, my friend," replied Ronsard. "You may just have performed your greatest service to your King."

"How so, sir?"

"Look!" said Ronsard, raising his arm. "I think friend Theido escorts two most reluctant prisoners."

A wide avenue parted in the company as a group of knights came marching up, pushing Ameronis and Lupollen—much chagrined, yet still defiant—before them on the points of their swords.

"Sire!" exclaimed Theido. "It is heartening to see you. We did not expect—"

"Did not expect me, I know. But did you really think I would allow the likes of Ameronis to challenge me without a fight?" asked Quentin with a smile.

Theido grinned readily. "The battle is won, and none too soon." The tall knight placed a hand on Ameronis and pushed him forward to kneel before the King. "We caught this one and his friend trying to escape through the secret passage."

"Give me the sword, Ameronis." Quentin glared down at the humbled lord. Ameronis put his hand to his side and withdrew the sword from his scabbard. Laying the blade across his outstretched hands, he offered it up to the King with his eyes averted and head bowed.

Quentin took up the sword and raised it in the sunlight, then slid it home to its sheath. He said, "I do not have time to deal with you now, traitor. But I will, and soon— you may count on it. And let your contemplation of your punishment add to its severity." He turned to the others. "My friends, at midday tomorrow my son will die unless I meet the ransom demand. I ride at once to the High Temple."

"I will go with you," said Theido.

"And I," said Ronsard. His words were echoed all around, so that when the Dragon King rode out from Ameron Castle there followed behind him a great train made up of lords and soldiers and people from the countryside who had been drawn to the scene of the battle. And all made their way northward through Pelgrin Forest toward Narramoor and the High Temple beyond.

51

RAIN PATTERED IN THE TEMPLE YARD ALL THROUGH THE night. Toli lay awake, listening, praying for deliverance for himself and the little Prince, and for the courage to face whatever awaited them. When morning came, the sky remained dark and overcast although the rain had stopped and a fresh wind had risen from the west.

When Prince Gerin awakened, Toli stood over the place he had occupied all night during his long vigil. At the moment the boy's eyes blinked open, he sat upright on his straw mattress and said, "Today is the day of our freedom! Isn't it, Toli? Today my father will come for us!"

Toli nodded and smiled to see the faith of the boy, undimmed by the long, numbing days of captivity. "Yes, today we will be free." He looked at the Prince for a long while, then sat down beside him on the bed. When he spoke again, it was in a more serious tone.

"Gerin, I have something to tell you."

The youngster waited for him to continue.

Toli turned toward him. "You know that I love you as my own son. That is why I would not have you ignorant of what may take place today."

"I am no longer afraid, Toli. I was before, but only for a little while. But my father is King, and he will not allow anything to happen to us. I know it."

Toli smiled again and said, "Yes, I believe he will come. But . . . there are times when even Kings are powerless over events. Your father is King, yes, but he is also a man and may not be able to change all that he would like. Sometimes things are done that no one can undo."

Gerin remained silent for a time, thinking on Toli's words. "Will they kill us?" he asked at last. Without waiting for an answer he blurted ahead, "I am not afraid to die."

"There is no shame in being afraid. There have been times that I have feared for my life. But courage comes in not allowing your fear to win over you."

"Yes, but I am not afraid now. I have been thinking. The Most High has his purpose—that is what Durwin always said—and if it is that I must die for the kingdom to be saved, then I will do it."

Toli marveled at such simple, wholehearted trust. "Yours are brave words, young sir, and wiser than you know. And yes, it may be that our lives are required. I know that I will go easier with such a strong comrade beside me." He pulled the boy close in a tight hug. "But we are not dead yet, and the end is not yet revealed. We must still believe that the King will save us, Gerin."

"I know he will, Toli. He is my father."

THEY TALKED NO MORE OF THE IMPENDING CONFRON- tation, but turned to other themes, remembering happier times. When the temple guards came for them, they found the cell ringing with laughter as Toli recounted his recent recollections of the Prince learning to ride and jump.

"How heartening to hear our prisoners enjoying their last moments so pleasantly," said Nimrood, stepping into the cell. "Would you agree, Pluell?"

The High Priest ducked in behind Nimrood. His face was white and his eyes and lips set in a fierce scowl. "This has gone far enough, Nimrood. Too far! Let them go now before the King gets here. There is still time."

"Time, yes—time to groom our captives and make them presentable. We must not let anyone think that we have mistreated our guests. No, that would not do at all." He beckoned to the guards still standing in the corridor, and they came forward carrying basins of water and clean linen towels and the prisoners' clothes, which had been taken from them the day before. "See? Freshly laundered. Fit for the King himself. Oh, I hope he appreciates the trouble we have gone to on your behalf, Princeling. But then, I am certain he will understand."

"Please," begged Pluell, his face contorting in a grimace of pain, "please, let them go. There is nothing to be gained by going through with it!"

"Silence, fool!" flared Nimrood. "We have been through this time and again. You weary me with your whining. I will hear no more of it! Do you understand me? No more. It is decided."

Toli watched the two warily as he washed himself and shed the filthy robe he had been given. "What does he mean—nothing to be gained by going through with it?" asked Toli as he pulled on his clothes.

"See?" said Nimrood, turning on the High Priest. "You have ruined our surprise."

Toli advanced on the old sorcerer. The guards drew their swords and held them at ready. "You do not plan to let us go whether the King meets the ransom or not, do you?" said Toli flatly. "You mean to kill us regardless."

Nimrood leveled his eyes upon him, and Toli saw the depths of hate within them. He knew he faced a being of pure evil. Still, he did not shrink back. "You, Jher dog, should have known that I would never allow you to escape twice. I, Nimrood, will have my revenge—on you and that grasping, spineless master of yours. And it has not been magic that has overthrown you, no— you saw to that long ago when you robbed me of my powers. It has been my own cunning, my superior wits, that have brought you down."

Nimrood walked across the cell to where Prince Gerin stood. Toli started to move toward him, but felt the sharp point of a sword in his back. The old necromancer placed his hands on the boy's shoulders. "But you do not have to be sacrificed, boy. Look at me." The Prince raised his eyes. Nimrood gazed down at him, saying, "I will offer you a choice. Come with me. Become my pupil, and I will teach you secrets such as no man, save Nimrood only, has ever known. I could give you such powers, boy—power over fire and air, earth and water, life and death. Come with me, and let me be your teacher." He raised a hand and stroked the youngster's fair head. "Eh? What say you, lad?"

"No! In the name of the Most High God!" cried Toli. "Leave the boy alone!"

Gerin shivered and, as if awakening from a lulling sleep, shook the sorcerer's hands from him. "No!" he shouted and ran to stand with Toli.

Nimrood's eyes narrowed to hate-filled slits. "I gave you a choice; remember that when your blood runs out upon the altar-stone, impudent young cub. I could have given you powers and wealth unimaginable."

"The Most High will reckon with you, Nimrood," Toli said firmly. "He watches over his servants and remembers the injustices practiced against them. He will repay and bring you to account."

Nimrood whirled on Toli and his hand flashed out, catching him on the side of the face. The blow resounded in the stunned silence that followed. "Shut up!" spat Nimrood savagely. Fire burned from his eyes; his lips dripped spittle. "Shut up! Do you think I care anything for your petty god? Ha! He is less than the worm that crawls through the dung heap to me. Little men"—Nimrood glared into every face before him—"today you will see how your little gods behave when challenged with true power!"

The necromancer turned and strode to the cell door. "I am finished, and it is time. Bring them."

High Priest Pluell threw a frightened look behind him at the prisoners and then fled after his demented master. The temple guards, six of them altogether, some with lances and some with swords, prodded the captives with the points of their weapons and marched them off down the corridor.

"I do not know what will happen, Gerin," whispered Toli as they walked along, guards ringing them in on every side. "But stay alert to any possibility of escape. I, too, will be watching, and if I say 'run,' you fly as fast as you can and do not look back. Agreed?"

"Agreed." Gerin nodded resolutely, and Toli knew he would do as he was told.

When they reached the entrance hall of the temple, the great doors were thrown open and the prisoners were led out onto the steps of the temple. Before them on the flagging of the temple yard stood the great altar which had been moved from its place in the temple near the sacred stone and established at the foot of the steps in full sight of the onlookers now crowding into the space within the walls.

People from as far away as Hinsenby, Persch, and Woodsend, and not a few from Askelon, streamed into the yard, jostling for a place to stand, for word had gone out that the Prince was held in the High Temple and that the King would seek to ransom him there. And as many as could travel quickly on horse or on foot came to see their King humbled and the temple exalted and its supremacy reasserted. For though they loved their King, they feared their god more. The simple people believed that the Dragon King had angered the god Ariel of the High Temple by commissioning a new temple to be built to a strange new god; and for this the King, though King he was, must be punished.

Many, to look at them, had walked all night; their clothing was still wet from the rain they had endured to be present at the moment the King laid his enchanted sword aside. They waited reverently, whispering behind their hands to their neighbors, while others talked openly, laughing and joking about what was soon to take place.

But at the moment when the temple doors opened and the prisoners were led out to stand on the steps before the altar, a hush spread over the throng, and the people stared expectantly as the captives' wrists were bound with braided rope.

Overhead the sky glowered down with dark menace, threatening more rain at any moment. The sun could not be seen at all, and its absence cast a heavy gloom over the scene in the temple yard. Thunder rippled in the Fiskills far off, growling ominously, like a hungry beast stalking its prey.

Toli and Gerin stood side by side on the temple steps surrounded by armed guards in scarlet cassocks. Below them, near the altar, stood the High Priest and the white-haired, white-bearded Nimrood, his long black robes wrapped around him like a cloak of darkness.

"Make way for the Queen!" called a voice. The populace shifted, and a pathway opened in the mass of people crowded to the very steps of the temple. Through this avenue came the Queen, followed by Lady Esme and the dowager Alinea, with Princesses Brianna and Elena between them. With them were the knights who had accompanied them as their bodyguard. All came to stand before the High Priest.

"Release my son!" demanded Bria. "For the good of the realm and the people of Mensandor, release him now." Relief and anger roiled inside her, making her voice quaver: relief at seeing her son at last, safe and sound; anger at what he had been made to suffer.

High Priest Pluell threw up his hands and looked at her fearfully. "You do not know what you ask, woman. Stand aside."

"If you will not release him, allow me to take his place."

Pluell's eyes darted toward Nimrood. The Queen saw the look and turned toward the wizard. "I see that it is you who I must appeal to. Allow me to take the place of my son if you will not release him."

"I am not inclined to accept a bargain at this late hour. Stand aside and watch with the others."

"Sir!" said Bria, starting forward. The guards snapped to attention and lowered their lances toward her; others leveled swords at the Prince and Toli. Instantly the swords of the knights came whistling from their sheaths and met the lances of the guards. "No!" shouted Bria. "I will wait if I must. I will not be the cause of bloodshed this dark day."

Fearing for the safety of her son if she pressed her demand, she withdrew with the other women to stand off to the side. Afraid of what was to come, she asked one of the knights to take the Princesses to the carriage and sit with them there. Temple guards were placed with crossed lances before them, ensuring that there would be no further interference from that quarter. The women joined hands together and bowed their heads silently.

"It is time," said Nimrood. "The King is not coming."

High Priest Pluell turned his eyes to the sky and said, "No, it is not time yet. It is not yet midday. You said we would wait until midday."

Nimrood drew breath and seemed about to protest, but held his tongue and instead said, "As you will, priest. We will wait yet a little longer. I am not so anxious that I cannot savor the waiting."

The yard fell silent all around. Not even the wind stirred the leaves of the trees lining the wall—trees into whose branches the curious had climbed to better see what would take place.

They waited.

Toli glanced down at Prince Gerin, standing beside him. He nodded as if to say, "Courage; he will come." The boy returned it with one of his own which replied, "I know, and I am not afraid."

The clouds rolled overhead, angry and swollen, hard and black as smoked amber, flying away on swift storm wings. An unnatural twilight descended over the temple yard, as if the sun had withdrawn and refused to shed its warmth and light on the proceedings.

Still, they waited.

At last Nimrood could stand it no longer. "There is no more time. It is midday, and the King is not here. He is not coming. Bring the prisoners."

The guards looked at one another and hesitated.

"Bring them!" shouted Nimrood, his voice shrill. The High Priest, shaking visibly now, nodded and turned his face away. The guards thrust the captives down the steps with their weapons.

Toli started forward, lifted his foot, and then stumbled, rolling down the steps. "Run!" he shouted to the Prince as he went down. Young Gerin leaped down the steps and dashed forward into the crowd.

"Stop him!" roared Nimrood. "Bring him back!"

Before the knights standing with the Queen could lift a hand, one of the temple guards whirled around and seized the Prince by the nape of the neck, hauling the kicking lad off his feet.

"Gerin!" cried the Queen. "Gerin!" She struggled forward, thrusting out her hands in a desperate attempt to reach him, but was stopped by the lance of the remaining guard. "My son!"

Toli was hauled to his feet and shoved forward. "A very clumsy effort for a nimble Jher," clucked Nimrood. "For your trouble you will be allowed to witness the sacrifice of the boy. I had planned it the other way around."

With that, Nimrood swooped down and lifted the lad onto the altar, where he fought to free himself. One guard held his feet and another pulled his bound hands over his head. Toli shouted and dove toward the altar, but the guards around him grabbed his arms and held him fast.

"No!" shrieked the boy's mother, her features twisted in horror. Esme threw her arms around the Queen and held her tightly.

"The knife," said Nimrood to the High Priest. "Take up your dagger."

52

"DAGGER?" HIGH PRIEST PLUELL'S FACE BLANCHED even whiter than before. He patted his robes absently. "I seem to have misplaced my dagger. I do not have it with me."

Nimrood smiled maliciously. "I thought you might have forgotten yours—conveniently, too, I might add. So I brought my own." He withdrew a long thin poniard from beneath his robe and, taking the High Priest's hand, placed the knife in it. "Now then, High Priest. Do your duty!"

Pluell, eyes glazed and the sweat of fear glistening slick on his brow, turned a stricken countenance upon the Queen, whose face was hidden in her hands, and upon his evil accomplice, who smiled thinly and nodded. "Do it!" Nimrood croaked, his eyes sparkling with glee.

The dagger shook in the High Priest's hand, but he turned to where the young Prince lay on the altar and raised his arm above the boy's heart. Gerin closed his eyes and drew his mouth into a tight pucker so that he would not cry out.

The knife hung in the air, hesitated, and—

"Stop! The King is here! Wait! The Dragon King is coming!"

With a sigh the air rushed through the High Priest's teeth; his arm wavered and dropped to his side, and he fell back away from the altar.

Across the yard there came the sound of horses and men pounding up the winding road below the temple, as well as the voices of those outside the temple walls who shouted and hailed the King as he came.

In a moment the crowd parted, and the King's stallion came clattering into the yard. Quentin reined Blazer to a halt, the courser's hooves striking sparks from the paving stones, and threw himself from the saddle.

He advanced toward the temple as those with him— Theido and Ronsard, Lord Edfrith, and a host of knights and men—came pounding from behind into the already overcrowded yard. The people drew away from the King, giving him wide berth as he approached the altar.

"I have brought the ransom," Quentin called out boldly. "Let my son go!" He directed this challenge at the High Priest, who drew back among the other priests at the edge of the temple steps.

"That will not do, my King," replied Nimrood coolly.

Quentin turned to face him across the distance between them. "Who are you?" He stepped closer, his eyes on the old man's face, struggling to read some recognition there. "Do I know you?"

"We have never met," the old man replied. "But I think you know me."

"I ask again. Who are you?"

"A name? Very well, I shall give it. You see before you none other than Nimrood, known as the Necromancer once long ago, before my power was shorn from me."

"Nimrood!" It took all Quentin's strength not to stagger backward as the knowledge rocked him to the core. "You rise from the dust of death like one of your ghastly creations!"

"Yes, and I have come to claim my revenge." He stepped behind the altar and motioned to the guards holding the boy to remove him. "Your sword, proud King, the Shining One—that was to be the ransom. Where is it?"

Quentin drew the sword; it whispered as it slid from the scabbard. He held it up for all to see and started for the altar.

Nimrood held up a hand. "Not like that!" he screamed. Quentin halted. "On your knees! I want all your subjects to see you bow to me. I want you to acknowledge me before all these witnesses."

Quentin advanced two more steps and came to the altar. "On your knees, proud King!"

"Never!" shouted Quentin. "You ask for the sword; here it is. You will get nothing more from me."

"Bow to me on your knees, or the boy dies!" Nimrood whirled around and snatched the dagger out of the startled High Priest's hand. In a flash the knife blade lay against the young boy's throat. "Kneel, great King, or lose your son and heir." The rasping voice dripped venom.

Quentin, every fiber of his being rebelling at the act, dropped slowly to one knee. He glared frightfully at Nimrood, who smiled wickedly as he held the knife against the Prince's neck. The people were silent as death watching the humiliation of their King.

"Now the sword," said Nimrood, breaking the unearthly silence. "Lay it on the altar." His words stabbed like dagger points, penetrating to the furthest reaches of the temple yard so that every man there heard plainly what was said.

The Dragon King raised the sword once more and held it by the hilt. This sword, he thought, is the Shining One promised me in the dream long ago, and given to me by the hand of the Most High. It is the sword of the Most High himself; I cannot give it up to Nimrood. I cannot lay it upon that altar; to do so would be an act of worship to that depraved monster. I will not forsake the true God—not to save my life or the life of my son.

Quentin turned the sword in his hand and looked at it, and then at Nimrood. He rose to his feet once more.

"On your knees!" screamed Nimrood. "Bow down to *me!*"

Quentin raised the blade above his head in both hands and turned his face toward the heavens. "Most High God," he said, his words ringing in the silence of the temple yard, "hear your servant. Show your power now; exalt yourself in the midst of your enemies. Let your justice burn like a flame in the land, that all men may worship the true god."

"Your god is deaf, it seems," scoffed Nimrood. "Ha! There is no true god. Pray to me, Dragon King! Perhaps I will grant your prayer!"

Quentin, eyes closed and face turned upward, did not listen to Nimrood's mocking laughter, but instead prayed as fervently as ever he had in his life, pouring himself out before the Most High. And in that moment he felt the blade grow warm in his hand. He opened his eyes and looked skyward as the heavy black clouds parted and a single shaft of light fell upon him, striking the blade in his hand. He stood in a circle of golden light, and as he looked the light played along the tapering blade, winking in the gems at the hilt. The light was alive, and out of it a voice spoke, saying, "Throw down the altar! It should have been thrown down long ago."

Suddenly fire fell from the sky, dropping through the air like burning rain to strike the sword. Zhaligkeer flashed, its flame rekindled and blazing with white heat into the gloom roundabout. The people could not bear the piercing brightness and threw their hands over their eyes to shut out the awful splendor of that holy fire.

The flame is back in the sword! thought Quentin. The Most High has not abandoned me! He is still with me; he never left! The realization burned through Quentin just as the flame burned in the sword.

"The sword! The sword!" howled Nimrood. "Give me the sword!"

"No!" shouted Quentin. It flashed with terrible brilliance, and fire seemed to leap from the shimmering blade, scattering light all around. "You shall never hold this blade." With that, the King raised the Shining One over his head and brought it down with all his strength onto the massive stone altar.

There came a blinding flash and the sound of hot metal suddenly plunged into cold water as the scent of burning stone seared the air. The ground rumbled deep in the earth, and the stone slab of the altar tipped, tilted, and then slid sideways, cloven in half, the stone jagged and smoking from the place where the Shining One had bitten deep into the rock.

A cry went up from the crowd, a gasp from a thousand throats, and they drew back as one from the sight of their King standing before the crumbling altar with the flaming sword in his hand.

The High Priest threw his hands upward in horror and ran back up the steps into the temple, his priests fleeing with him. The temple guards threw down their weapons and ran after.

Nimrood's arm went up; the dagger flashed in his hand. Toli, seeing his chance, lowered his head and charged into the sorcerer, knocking the boy from his grasp. Gerin sprawled forward, rolled to his feet, and dashed to his mother's open arms. Bria swept him up and hugged the boy to her. The crowd surged forward around them.

"You!" screeched Nimrood at Toli. "Twice you have cheated me. Never again!" Toli leaped to the side, but with his hands bound could not keep his balance and fell backward onto the steps of the temple.

Like a cat the old wizard pounced on him and plunged the dagger into Toli's chest, then fled up the steps to the High Temple.

53

THE GROUND RUMBLED AND TREMBLED UNDER THEIR feet, and the crowd in the temple yard screamed in terror as the ground shifted, cracking paving stones and tearing great gaping rents in the earth. The crevice which had opened beneath the broken altar spread toward the temple. Heedless of all else, Quentin flew to the temple steps shouting, "Theido! Ronsard! Hurry!" He reached Toli's body, now crumpled upon the steps, and bent over it, plucking the cruel dagger from his chest and flinging it away.

From above him on the steps there came a rattling laughter. He glanced up and saw Nimrood standing over them, his head thrown back, the hateful sound bubbling up from his throat like the shriek of a carrion crow. Ronsard reached Quentin first. "Take Toli to safety," the King ordered. He leaped to his feet and flew up the temple steps.

"Sire! Come back! It is falling!" cried the knight.

The fissure in the earth had now reached the steps and split them. The air trembled with the sound of churning earth and shattering stone. Roof tiles rained down, smashing on the flagging. The pillars swayed dangerously as the lintels cracked and gave way, sending huge chunks of stone careening downward. Quentin scrambled up the heaving steps, the sword bright in his hand. Nimrood saw him and screeched, "Stay back!" He whirled away and Quentin raced after him, catching the sorcerer by a trailing edge of his priest's robe.

"Ach!" Nimrood fought to free himself from the robes, but only entangled himself further. Quentin held on with all his might and yanked, jerking the wizard off his feet. Desperately the old sorcerer writhed, squirming on the tilting floor like a snake. "Save me!" he hissed. "I will do anything—anything you ask. I can give you wealth, bring you glory! I will destroy your enemies! Save me!"

The blade flashed in Quentin's hand, and the Shining One sang in the air, descending in a deadly arc, striking down upon the sorcerer's neck. With one last shriek he fell back into a shriveled heap and lay still. Nimrood the Necromancer was dead.

Now stones and brickwork tumbled, and the pillars groaned as pieces of the roof caved in. Quentin could hear the thunderous roar as the heavy stone slabs collapsed, and the foundation beneath his feet shook with the cataclysm. The great heart of stone on which the High Temple stood shuddered and convulsed.

Those inside the temple fell on their faces before the sacred rock and called upon the gods of old to save them: Ariel! Azrael! Zoar! Heoth! But the names fell from their lips dead and devoid of power. The floor rolled under them, and they watched in horror as a seam opened in the anointed face of the sacred rock. The stone splintered and popped as it crumbled before their eyes. The priests wailed and prostrated themselves, covering their heads with their robes.

IN THE TEMPLE YARD THE TERRIFIED POPULACE SWEPT through the gates and streamed down the winding trail to safety in the valley below. Dodging broken flags, Quentin ran back across the courtyard to where Toli's body had been removed.

Theido and Ronsard looked on as Quentin sank to his knees beside the body of his friend. "Toli, forgive me!" he cried, snatching up a lifeless hand and clutching it to him. "I drove you from me. I blamed you for all that happened, and it was not your fault. I have wronged you, my friend. I am sorry!" The King wept, tears flooding his eyes and splashing freely down his face.

The others came to stand by him; he felt Bria's hands on his shoulders. "He is gone!" sobbed Quentin. "And I am to blame!"

Esme knelt down beside Quentin and laid a hand on his sleeve. "In Dekra I had a vision—a vision of what would happen here today."

"You knew?" The King raised sorrowful eyes to the Lady beside him. "You saw all and did not try to prevent it?"

"Not all. I saw the temple brought down—but not the fate of Toli and Gerin," she said. Quentin only stared sadly at the body of his friend. "The Most High showed me what would come, and I did not see the death of our friend. That was never in his purpose."

"That may be," said Theido. "But many things happen in this world contrary to the Most High's purpose. It is the way of the world."

"Aye," agreed Ronsard, nodding sadly. "No man rises from the bed of death."

"Why not," Esme asked, "if it pleases the god?"

Just then another tremor shook the yard, and all turned to see the last remnants of the High Temple come crashing down in a thunderous roar. Smoke and dust climbed toward the sun in a thick gray-white column. "You see this?" said Esme. "The temple is destroyed just as it was revealed to me. It is gone, and its evil is destroyed with it."

They looked on in wonder as Esme, her face illumined with a glowing inner light, stretched her hands over Toli's body. She touched the crimson wound in his chest with her palm, then pulled back his tunic.

The cloth around the wound was sticky with blood and ragged where the dagger had slashed into the flesh. But though the skin was stained a deep red from the flowing blood, there was now no wound to be seen.

"Look!" said Queen Bria, who was clutching at her mother's sleeve. "Toli is awaking!"

"He is alive!" shouted Gerin happily.

"Toli?" said Quentin, peering into his friend's face. Toli's eyelids flickered and opened, revealing quick black eyes which gazed upward at the ring of faces above him. "Toli, you are alive! Alive!" Quentin fell upon him and lifted him in a powerful embrace.

Theido and Ronsard stared in disbelief at the scene before them, then leapt forward to pound Toli on the back. Bria and Alinea wept, their eyes filling with happy tears. Gerin jumped and whooped for joy.

"What did I do to deserve all this?" asked Toli when they released him at last.

"I would not have believed it if I had not been standing here to see it!" Ronsard shook his head in amazement.

"I am not sure I believe it yet," added Theido.

Esme threw her arms around Toli's neck and kissed him. "How do you feel?"

"Feel? I feel. . . ." He paused and glanced around him at the ruin of the temple, and then down at his own blood-soaked clothing, "I feel as if I have missed out on something . . . Nimrood! Is he—"

"Dead. They are all dead," said Quentin. "But you have rejoined the living."

"Did Nimrood do this to me?"

"A mortal wound, sir," said Theido. "I saw him strike you down. Do you remember it?"

Toli shook his head dazedly. "I remember knocking Gerin free and falling backward. I remember his face above me . . . then nothing—until I woke up here."

"The Most High has restored your life to us, Toli," declared Alinea. "Great is the Most High!" They all joined in praising the god and thanking him for raising up Toli. Their joyous cries rang in the empty yard and echoed among the heaps of fallen stone as they started down the winding trail to the valley below. Above them the smoke and dust still ascended from the ruin, drifting and fading on the wind as the clouds rolled away to reveal a sky of sparkling blue.

By the time they reached the valley and passed before the wondering stares of the people lining the trail, word was already winging throughout Mensandor proclaiming the triumph of the Dragon King and the power of the new god, the Most High, the only true god, who caused altars to crumble, temples to fall, and dead men to rise up and walk.

54

IN THE MASSIVE GREAT HALL THE DRAGON KING SAT on his high throne. Dressed in his most regal finery, he wore a royal blue cloak with the insignia of the dragon worked in gold; the cloak was secured by a gold dragon broach and chain. On his feet were high boots of soft red leather; and his gold ring—the ring Eskevar had worn—sat high on his finger. Across his lap he held the Shining One in its sheath, his hand resting lightly on its bejeweled hilt. The great carven doors of the hall had been opened wide to allow all who would come to crowd in to witness their King dispensing justice. The people stood in ranks among the gleaming black columns, lined the balustrades of the upper galleries three deep, and pressed forward to the steps of the dais.

When all had gathered in, the trumpeter sounded a call. The noise died to a whisper in the hall and Quentin said, "When I was a boy I stood in the court of King Eskevar and watched him mete out justice and favor with a wise and generous hand. And I vowed that if ever such a task fell to me, I would try to be at least as righteous and good as Eskevar.

"A King does not often have the opportunity of rewarding those who serve him as they deserve. But today I will do my best. First, however, I will punish the offenders."

He nodded to the trumpeter standing on the dais, wearing a tabard emblazoned with the royal device. The youth blew a strong, clear note, which was answered by the sound of marching feet.

Into the great hall came a contingent of knights dressed in their best armor, their breastplates burnished bright and their long scarlet cloaks billowing as they approached. Between them marched Lord Ameronis and his friend Lord Lupollen, both in chains. Both were gray-faced with dismay and kept their eyes lowered, not daring to look at the King.

"Lord Ameronis," said Quentin when the knights had pushed them forward to the foot of the throne. "Look at me, sir." The chagrined lord raised timid eyes. "It is with a distinctly altered attitude that we meet again, eh? You have had time to think on your crimes, and so have I."

At this Lord Ameronis trembled visibly, expecting the worst.

The King continued. "Your crime is one of ambition, which I can understand and forgive—for I, too, have been ambitious in my own way. You wanted this crown and throne for your own, but that is nothing more than any lord dreams of one time or another, and so I forgive you there.

"You caused me anguish and inflicted hurt upon me while I was suffering under the grief of great loss. You took the sword, Zhaligkeer, which you knew to be mine and which you knew would have saved my son, and yet you withheld it. These are hurts practiced against me, and as one man to another I will forgive them, for you were blinded by your power-lust.

"But your actions caused great hurt and injury to soldiers who had no choice but to defend their King with limb and life. Many brave men fell in battle, some never to rise again; and their blood calls me to do justice.

"I could have you executed"—here Ameronis flinched—"but what would the shedding of your blood accomplish? Very little, I am persuaded, though there are those among us who would take some measure of satisfaction there.

"No, I have decided that you shall live, and that the support of all the aggrieved widows you have left without husbands, and all the children you have left fatherless shall be placed in your hands."

"Ahh!" cried Ameronis. "I will have to sell half my lands; and all my gain for the rest of my life will be forfeit!"

"So be it," said the King flatly. "At least you will live to see the wrong you have done redressed. The families of the slain will become your families, the maimed will become your brothers. And so you will treat them, for if ever complaint is raised against you hereafter, your life will be forfeit.

"And you, Lord Lupollen," continued Quentin, "you chose to throw your substance to the support of your friend Ameronis. As you thought to share in the spoils of his victory, so will you share in the loss of his defeat. For the sentence I have pronounced upon him shall be yours as well. I have no doubt that Ameronis will welcome your aid now and in the years to come."

Next the remaining lords were brought before the throne. They paid homage respectfully, but remained grave and stolid. "My lords, I am of two minds about you," said the King. "You had it within your power to turn Ameronis aside before he carried out his scheme, and you did not. Yet, unlike Lupollen, you saw clearly enough who to serve once the issue was forced.

"Therefore, Lords Edfrith, Gorloic, Kelkin, and Denellon, I do hereby condemn your disloyalty. But I stand ready to call you friends again if you will swear fealty once more to the throne."

The lords went down on one knee and swore before all the assembly an oath of loyalty to their monarch. When they had finished, they took their places with the rest.

"As for the others," continued the King, "Nimrood, the High Priest, and their foul flock—their punishment has been delivered by the Most High, the final judge of all; and let no man say they received more than their due." The pronouncement brought a murmur from all gathered there.

"Now then," said Quentin, "bring forth my new friends that I may reward them." The trumpeter sounded his call again, and the onlookers craned their necks to see a small boy, not much older than Prince Gerin, approach the throne timidly, followed by Pym the tinker and Tip, his dog. Quentin beckoned to the youngster's parents who hung back meekly in the ranks. "Come closer, good people." The farmer and his wife crept forward shyly and came to kneel beside their son and the tinker.

"Rise, my friends," said the King. "For you are my friends—as true as any who have ever served the Dragon King's throne.

"Renny, your young heart yearns for knighthood, but you have already shown yourself as brave as any knight in the realm, though you possess neither horse nor armor. Is it still your wish to be a knight?"

"Yes, Sire," came the small voice in reply. "More than anything."

"Then so be it. On this day your name shall be placed on the roll of the King's knights. When you come of age, you will enter into the knighthood in service to the realm." Quentin paused. "But a knight must learn to ride, and he must have much skill at arms. Therefore, you may keep the pony Tarky which you found and tried to return; keep him until such time as you are able to handle a charger from the King's stables. Then you shall choose a mount of your own. What do you say to that, Renny?"

Words escaped the boy, but the light in his eyes said all.

"My son has asked that you be allowed to take instruction with him under the master-at-arms of Askelon Castle. A knight of the King, even a knight in training, must be housed and fed in a manner worthy of his master. So, Sir Renny, the crown will endow you with an annual stipend which your parents will use for you as they deem fit."

The joy which shone on the faces of the three could not be contained, and they bowed their thanks again and again as they returned to their places in the crowd.

"And you, good tinker," said the King. Pym folded his hands over his knee and gazed upward expectantly. "You found the Shining One and kept it safely hidden away, returning for it when you knew your King's need. Doubtless you would have delivered it into my hand had you not been prevented."

"Yes, Sire, it is a very fact, it is," replied Pym.

"And it has reached my ears that you have long desired a horse and wagon to take your wares from town to village on your route." At the tinker's puzzled expression, Quentin asked, "Is this not true?"

"Oh, yes, Yer Highness. More than ye know . . . but—"

"Yes? Was there something else?"

"The sharping stone, Yer Majesty, Sire. We'uns had in mind a sharping stone on a treadle-foot fer sharping knives and shears and such like."

"Of course, the sharpening stone! Such an oversight! Yes, you shall have the finest sharpening stone as can be found in all Mensandor. And Castle Askelon shall be your first stop whenever you pass this way."

Pym clapped his hands at his good fortune, and Tip barked her master's happiness. The two withdrew to the laughter and high acclaim of those gathered in the great hall.

"Lastly," said Quentin when silence again reclaimed the hall, "I would reward my old friends. Come forward, Toli, Theido, and Ronsard." He rose and descended from the dais to meet them at the foot of the throne. "No, do not kneel to me, brave sirs. Brothers do not kneel to one another, for your friendship has proven itself of highest mettle, stronger and more true than are the ties of birth and blood.

"How else can I reward your steadfastness and courage? What could I give you that you do not already have? Lands, position, title? And yet you stood ready to give of these things, and even life itself, for a friend—the more when that friend faltered. You did not abandon me, but acted for me with wisdom and courage, each one of you, in your actions, declaring yourself more noble than Kings.

"So I give you these tokens of my esteem and gratitude." Quentin beckoned to a page who came forward bearing a board covered with a runner of blue velvet on which rested three golden dragon broaches just like his own. The King took the first one from the board and fastened it at Theido's shoulder, saying, "Theido, whose counsel is ever wise and good. . . ." He took up the next, affixed it to Ronsard's cloak—"And Ronsard, whose dauntless courage is matched only by the strength of his arm. . . ." Quentin lifted the remaining broach and placed it on Toli's cloak—"And Toli, whose love and loyalty hold firm even unto death. From this day forth you are Princes of the realm." After a pause Quentin added, "Toli, you I would reward further by freeing you from your oath of service to me. Today and henceforth you are no longer servant."

Quentin turned to the assemblage and presented the three with a sweep of his arm. "Behold my royal friends," he said. "Let all men pay each one the courtesy and respect due a King."

At once the whole assembly made a deep bow and then affirmed the King's reward with loud shouts of acclamation that rang to the vault of the great hall and throughout the corridors and galleries of Askelon Castle.

Quentin mounted to his throne again and proclaimed, "This day will be a day of celebration throughout all Mensandor. Let there be feasting and music and entertainments for everyone!" The cheers which followed this address were drowned in the blare of the trumpets which sounded their clarion call throughout the castle and from the high battlements to the town and the countryside beyond. "The celebration has begun!" the trumpets said.

"Come and share in the rejoicing!"

And the people who heard that happy sound left their work, put on their finest clothes, and started for the castle to join in the high merriment and festivities.

IT WAS NEARING DUSK—THE RED-GOLD DISK OF THE SUN was lowering in the sky away westward over Gerfallon's broad back—before Quentin found an opportunity to slip away alone. Blazer was saddled and waiting for him and bore him quickly through the deserted streets of Askelon and out onto the plain.

Quentin found the shaded bower without any trouble; he had been there before with Durwin and remembered the bank overlooking the forest pool as a place where the hermit loved to come and idle away the hours on a summer's day. The grave mound was fresh and neatly overlaid with stones—a simple grave such as the hermit would have wanted—and already tender green shoots of new grass could be seen poking up between the rocks.

The King stood for a long time gazing reflectively at the grave, remembering the life he had known with the Holy Hermit of Pelgrin, as the simple folk called him still. That temporal life had now ended, but another had begun, and Quentin knew that he would see his friend again, that they would be together in a place without separation or the painful intrusion of death, and he was content to wait until that time.

The sound of hoofbeats signaled the end of his quiet reverie, and he turned to see two riders approaching. He waited while they dismounted and tied their horses to a poplar branch beside his. "So, I have been followed. I thought you two might have found a better way to occupy yourselves," said Quentin.

Toli grinned and took Esme's hand. "We wanted to talk to you in privacy," he explained. "I saw you leave the celebration, so we waited a little and came after you."

Quentin nodded, but said nothing, waiting for Toli to continue. Toli glanced sideways at the woman beside him and then back at the King, licked his lips, and announced, "We have made a decision. . . ."

"Oh?" teased Quentin. "Was there a decision to be made?"

Toli dropped his eyes. "Please, it was not an easy choice to make."

"I am sorry. Forgive me," said Quentin quickly. "Of course—it would not be easy for either of you. And it will not be easy for me. If I make light of it, it is only because I shall feel your absence most acutely."

"Absence?"

"You will be going away, I know. But I could not be happier for either of you. It is the best thing—" He stopped when he saw the look which passed between Toli and Esme.

ESME LAUGHED GENTLY AND REPLIED, "WE ARE NOT going away. At least not together. Not yet."

"No?"

"No," said Toli firmly.

"I have released you from service. You are free—you and Esme—to—"

"To do as we please. Yes, and we have chosen our course."

"I am going to Dekra," said Esme. "I felt something there that I must search out for myself. I felt the spirit of the God Most High move within me; I had a vision. He may be calling me to serve him in a special way. I want to go back and find out—I *must* find out. I want to learn all I can of the one I have pledged my life to before I make a life with another."

"I see," said Quentin nodding. "I know how you feel. I felt the same way, but it seems that Dekra was never chosen for me. My future lies on a different path." He turned to Toli. "And you?"

"I will remain by your side, Kenta. I told you once that for men of my race, no higher honor could come to them but that they serve a great master and help him achieve his greatness. You have released me from my oath, as you did once before, and I take it up again and renew it." Toli looked lovingly at Esme and clasped her hand more tightly. "It is true that we love each other, and perhaps someday we will join our lives. But for now—" He smiled, and the light kindled in his deep, dark eyes. "For now you are saddled with me once again, my friend."

"And forever more, so it would seem."

"Come, then," said Toli. "Let us return to the celebration together." He glanced at the grave, and then at his master. "If you are ready."

Quentin looked back at the simple mound and said, "Yes, I am ready. We have already said our good-byes. He came to me, you see. I did not realize it then; I was in no condition to know for certain.

"In those first black days when I was out searching for my son—insane with grief and exhausted beyond pain or sleep—I found myself on the Holy Island. Perhaps I had been led there. However it was, Durwin appeared to me; I know now that it was he. He said good-bye and told me we would be together again. He knew how much it meant to me to see him one last time, and he came back to tell me to trust in the Most High. Had I but listened, I would have borne this trial more easily and accounted myself more worthily."

Toli looked long at his master and said finally, "Yes, Kenta, you have changed. I saw it when you stood in the temple yard, and again in the great hall. You have come to terms with your frailties as a man, and this makes you more of a King than before—a true Priest King."

Quentin shrugged. "I only know that I no longer burn to inaugurate the new era. The Most High will accomplish that as he will, and in his own time."

The three rode back to Askelon across the plain, stopping at the site of the King's Temple ruins, where inexplicably scores of people moved among the toppled stones, clearing away the rubble. Quentin recognized his master mason among them and hailed him. "Bertram! What is happening here? What are you doing?"

"Sire," the man bowed, "we are preparing the site for building."

"Why? Who gave the orders?"

The old mason scratched his jaw and cocked his head to one side. "No one ordered it, my lord. It was the townspeople's idea; they insisted—said their new god ought to have a new temple. They aim to build one themselves. With your blessing, of course; we will follow the plans you have made." Bertram scuttled away then, returning over the heap of broken stone to supervise the work.

"Do you see this?" said Toli. "The new era has come in force. It is here around us. Do you wish to stay and help?"

Quentin raised his eyes to the sky where the first evening stars were already blazing like jewels in the clear high dome of heaven, though away to the west the horizon still held the rosy tint of the sun. "No," replied Quentin, lifting the reins and turning Blazer toward home. "Come. The Most High has chosen other hands to build his temple. That is as it should be."

BRIA MET THEM AT THE BALCONY OVERLOOKING THE garden. She wrapped her arms around her husband. "I wondered where the three of you had gone." She glanced at Toli and then back to the King. "Is all well?"

"It has never been better," replied Quentin, kissing her lightly on the cheek. Throughout the enormous garden below, lanterns were being lit among the trees to twinkle like stars in a firmament of leaves.

"Then come in to the table; the banquet is about to begin," said Bria, leading them across the balcony. The doors of the great hall had been thrown open wide to reveal long tables with food of every kind and description, and a host of eager guests waiting to be called to join in. Everywhere music played, and laughter drifted and mingled on the soft evening breeze, along with the sweet perfume of the garlanded flowers which bedecked the hall and garden.

"Yes, but the feast can wait a moment longer. First I want to see my children. Let me go and find them."

Toli, Esme, and Bria watched him hurry down the steps into the garden, darting among the merrymakers in search of the Prince and Princesses. "I remember a night like this—exactly like this—when King Eskevar returned," said Toli. "A celebration to rival this one, to be sure."

"No, not like this one," said Bria. Her voice held a trace of sadness. "My father even then did not care for his family as Quentin does." She smiled and nodded to where the King returned bearing one youngster on his back and two others in his arms, all of them laughing happily. "You see? He has changed."

Toli nodded slowly. "A new era is begun, my Lady."

"Indeed! Then let us hope it lasts a thousand years," said Bria.

"Ten thousand!" added Esme.

"Let us hope it lasts forever," said Toli.

"Come along," called Quentin, striding past them. "We must not be late for our own celebration!" He marched through the doors with his young ones, and Bria took her place at his side; Toli and Esme came on behind. They all reached the high table to find Ronsard and Theido, with Renny and his parents, Pym the tinker, with Tip at his feet, and all the other guests of honor already assembled and in their places.

Quentin seized his goblet and held it aloft, saying, "Welcome, fair friends one and all. Let the banquet begin!" And they all sat down to feast in the Hall of the Dragon King.